Praise for *Co___*

"Historical fiction at its finest. Powerful, poignant, and ___ ___,
Courage, My Love is a must-read."

—Chanel Cleeton, *New York Times*
bestselling author of *Next Year in Havana*,
Reese's Book Club pick

"A winning wartime tale set in the snake pit world of Mussolini's
Rome. Single mother Lucia and polio-crippled Francesca make ap-
pealing heroines, flowering slowly from reticent bystanders to fierce
resistance fighters as the Eternal City comes under German occupation. Kristin Beck's debut is a fresh, compelling read."

—Kate Quinn, *New York Times*
bestselling author of *The Huntress*

"A beautiful story of female friendship, and the unheralded but
hugely important resistance work the women of Rome undertook,
in the face of grave danger, during WWII. It's a fascinating, nu-
anced, and impeccably researched tale."

—Natasha Lester, *New York Times*
bestselling author of *The Riviera House*

"Portrays, with sensitivity and profound empathy, the many ways
in which ordinary people confronted evil with selflessness and true
valor. *Courage, My Love* is a beautiful and breathtaking book. It is
certainly one of the finest works of WWII historical fiction I have
ever read."

—Jennifer Robson, *USA Today*
bestselling author of *The Gown*

"Fans of Elena Ferrante and Kristin Hannah will relish this gritty tale of perseverance and resistance set in the Eternal City during WWII. I learned a great deal about the Italian front and the tangled web of friendship and romance kept me turning pages well into the night. A bold and gripping debut."

—Kerri Maher, author of *The Paris Bookseller*

"A profound anthem to the tremendous courage that transformed two ordinary Italian women into extraordinary heroes during the harrowing days of Mussolini and Hitler. A powerful story, powerfully told!"

—Stephanie Marie Thornton, *USA Today* bestselling author of *A Most Clever Girl*

"A powerful, moving story that so perfectly captures the turbulent and devastating times in Italy during WWII. Told with compassion and great skill, Kristin Beck draws a vivid portrait of two women, separated from the men they love, who join forces with the resistance. Beck is a strong, new voice in historical fiction."

—Renée Rosen, *USA Today* bestselling author of *The Social Graces*

"Kristin Beck transports us right into the heart of war-stricken Rome and creates a riveting story about brave women who will stop at nothing to protect the people they love. A tale of resistance, resilience, and friendship—this is exactly the type of historical fiction we need right now. Brava!"

—Elise Hooper, author of *Fast Girls*

"A stunning debut. . . . Each page is turned in suspense to find out if the Allies are indeed arriving to force the Germans out of Rome. Kristin Beck's characters are developed with equal amounts of childhood background, family strife, and political alignments. The secondary characters, Partisans, Nazi sympathizers, and German officers are written with such depth and personal detail that readers will find much to admire or despise, as appropriate."

—Historical Novel Reviews

"The tension never lets up in this gripping tale of WWII Italy. . . . Lucia and Francesca are unforgettable characters and stayed with me long after the final page."

—Janie Chang, author of *The Library of Legends*

"A moving story about how ordinary people can do extraordinary things when working together for good. Beck crafts a tale of both heart-pounding intensity and deep emotional resonance, with characters who will stay with the reader long after the pages are closed. Poignant and beautiful."

—Erika Robuck, national bestselling author of *The Invisible Woman*

"Powerful and immensely moving, Kristin Beck's debut novel plunges readers headlong into the dark days of WWII–era Rome. A beautifully written story of women at war, *Courage, My Love* will linger with you long after you turn the final page."

—Bryn Turnbull, author of *The Woman Before Wallis*

"Kristin Beck is an exciting new voice in women's historical fiction. . . . From the first page, Lucia and Francesca will grab you with their hearts and their fire. I haven't held my breath so much while reading a book in a while."

—Kaia Alderson, author of *Sisters in Arms*

"A riveting, realistic historical novel."   —*Booklist*

THE
WINTER ORPHANS

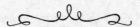

KRISTIN BECK

BERKLEY · NEW YORK

BERKLEY
An imprint of Penguin Random House LLC
penguinrandomhouse.com

Library of Congress Cataloging-in-Publication Data

Names: Beck, Kristin, 1979-author.
Title: The winter orphans / Kristin Beck.
Description: First edition. | New York: Berkley, 2022.
Identifiers: LCCN 2022016723 (print) | LCCN 2022016724 (ebook) |
ISBN 9780593101582 (trade paperback) | ISBN 9780593101599 (ebook)
Subjects: LCSH: World War, 1939–1945—France—Fiction. |
World War, 1939–1945—Evacuation of civilians—France—Fiction. |
World War, 1939–1945—Children—France—Fiction. |
LCGFT: Historical fiction. | Novels.
Classification: LCC PS3602.E2694 W56 2022 (print) |
LCC PS3602.E2694 (ebook) | DDC 813/.6—dc23/eng/20220408
LC record available at https://lccn.loc.gov/2022016723
LC ebook record available at https://lccn.loc.gov/2022016724

First Edition: September 2022

Printed in the United States of America
1 3 5 7 9 10 8 6 4 2

Map illustration by David Lindroth, Inc.
Book design by Elke Sigal

For my family,
Jeremey, Finnegan, and Lillian
with all my love

THE WINTER ORPHANS

PART ONE

✧

ONE

RÖSLI NÄF

CHÂTEAU DE LA HILLE, SOUTHERN FRANCE

AUGUST 1942

*R*ösli stood upright, a hammock of green beans weighting her apron, and filled her lungs with bright morning air. She'd been working in the garden since breakfast, but now she paused, stretching her lower back and assessing the tidy patch of vegetables painstakingly maintained in the château's shadow. Nearby, a handful of little girls and boys crouched in the speckled shade of trellises, snapping beans off vines and chatting as they filled baskets. Despite this rainless summer, the garden thrived. Rösli smiled. Nothing satisfied her more than watching the children wade among its loamy, leafy rows.

So much had changed in just one year.

She squinted in the sunlight, thinking of the day she'd arrived in France, newly appointed by the Swiss Red Cross to take over this colony of one hundred refugee children. That first afternoon, she'd faced a wary, wide-eyed crowd, fearing she wasn't up to the task. It was difficult, at first, to tell the boys from the girls: their heads were shorn, and from the general odor of kerosene, Rösli knew they'd suffered one lice infestation after another. They were thin as saplings, with open, weeping boils on their arms and legs. What had they been through? Could Rösli restore them to some level of well-being? Misgivings murmured, but she'd silenced them and gripped hands with the few adult caretakers, organizing a mental task list. She'd said she would manage this refugee colony, and so she would.

"Where is your garden?" she'd demanded following introductions, glancing at the building behind them. At the time, the group lived in an old granary barn. They'd left Germany and Austria after *Kristallnacht*, propelled into Belgium by their desperate parents, and had been fleeing invasions ever since. Eventually they'd washed up in France, sleeping on hay and eating cornmeal and rotten potatoes until one of the adults contacted the Red Cross for support. The colony came under Swiss care, and Rösli found herself standing before them.

"Our garden?" The adults had swapped glances, thrown off by her question.

"Yes," she'd said, frustration slipping into her voice. "Where is it?" She'd known, instantly, what was wrong with the children's skin: a diet lacking in green vegetables. When it became apparent that no garden existed, Rösli had cast about that desolate barnyard, seeking someone to reprimand, and then she'd sighed. She would have to change everything. The children had blinked up at their new *directrice* from the Swiss Red Cross, stunned, and she had merely turned and gone looking for a hoe.

Rösli shook away her memories of the previous summer, letting her gaze rise to the derelict castle they now called home. La Hille rested like an old gentleman in the sun, sand colored and guarded by medieval towers on each of its four corners. The Red Cross had rented it shortly after discovering the children struggling in their granary barn, and Rösli recruited the teenagers to make the neglected château habitable. They'd tilled the earth within the stone-walled courtyard, piling compost into muddy furrows and planting seeds. With hammers and donated wood, they'd built benches and tables, arranging them alongside the garden for summer meals, and moving them into a dining hall with parquet floors and a fireplace when the weather turned. Upstairs, each child slept in a real cot with bedding shipped over from Switzerland. They'd transformed La Hille in a single season, and within its ancient walls the children thrived.

Beyond the castle, rumpled green foothills rolled all the way south to the Pyrénées. Mist rose from their crevices, evaporating into a peerless blue sky. Somewhere in the forest, the voices of a dozen boys rebounded now and again as they tramped down to the river to bathe. Rösli pinched back a smile. Everyone called those boys *les Moyens*, the Middles, and they were as noisy and dirty as bear cubs no matter how often she sent them off to collect wood and swim.

The younger children, *les Petits*, flocked around Rösli in the courtyard. Most were still finishing morning chores, plucking weeds and filling baskets as they'd been asked to. A few played, and again Rösli suppressed a smile. The warm breeze loosened wisps of hair from her bun, tickling her face. She combed the blond strands back with her soil-stained fingers, watching the two youngest children race through tall grass just outside the garden walls. Little Hanni chased and Antoinette ran, passing the open gates. Seed heads whipped their knees as they darted back and forth, then Hanni caught Antoinette and they fell together, bare feet in the air, laughter rising toward the sun.

"*Du bist so langsam*," Hanni exclaimed, pushing up onto her elbows, her dark eyes lively as she teased her friend.

Rösli glanced toward the sun, already high overhead and growing hotter. It would soon be time for lunch. They had to finish the work.

"Children!" she called, waving a hand toward those who'd strayed from their chores. "Come and finish your jobs, please. Free time isn't until afternoon."

But Hanni and Antoinette continued to giggle in the grass, knees up, sun on their faces, and Rösli frowned. As much as she wanted to, she couldn't let them skip their chores. What would happen if other children followed suit, questioning their schedule, shirking responsibilities? If everyone didn't chip in, the community would fall apart, descending into disorder, like it obviously had in that foul granary barn.

She called out again, louder this time. "Hanni! Antoinette!" Clutching the green beans in her apron, she made her way through the courtyard gates, striding into the tall grass beyond. She sensed a pair of dark eyes, the same limitless brown as Hanni's, following her from a bench in the shadow of the château. She hadn't noticed Ella there earlier, patching faded clothes with a needle and thread, her ever-present sketchbook by her hip. But the girl was like that; she often drifted from the other teenagers, settling on the fringes with a solitary chore, her eyes on her sister.

"Hanni and Antoinette," Rösli said as her shadow fell over them. "If you don't come back to the garden, I'll have to double your chores tomorrow."

Antoinette scrambled to her feet, but Hanni gazed up from the grass, her eyes round and dark as chestnuts. She shook her head, chopped hair swinging. "No, Mademoiselle Näf. I want to finish our game."

No? Irritation pinched inside Rösli's chest, but she made an effort to remain patient. It wasn't her strong suit. "Don't be stubborn, Hanni. Now, go and finish in the garden."

"I don't want to," Hanni countered. Antoinette looked at the grass between her toes, taking a cautious step back, but Hanni held Rösli's stare. She was so tiny in her Red Cross dress, the cotton sleeves hanging like bells over her skinny, sunbrowned arms. But there was something fierce in her eyes.

Rösli puffed air from her lips, exasperated. "If you don't hustle into the garden, you'll scrub pots for Frau Schlesinger after lunch. And after dinner, too—"

"She's *seven*."

Rösli spun around to find Ella striding over, her narrow shoulders back, glaring. Rösli wanted to sigh, but she held it in. Showing frustration would get her nowhere with *les Grands*, the teenagers. She'd yet to figure out what *would* inspire their allegiance, however. There were over forty at the château, and most of them chafed at her, just as her peers had when she was an adolescent herself. It stung, but she'd never let them know it.

"Yes, Hanni's seven," Rösli repeated when Ella stepped into the space between her and the little girls. "And she needs to do her share. We all must do our part to keep our community strong."

Ella's jaw hardened. "Our *community*." She said the word with derision, as if community were a myth nobody believed in anymore. A breeze whipped up, blowing Ella's bobbed hair into her face. She swiped it away, maintaining her glare, and Rösli straightened in defense. With her freckle-dusted cheekbones and wide brown eyes, Ella looked so much like her younger sister—but their personalities couldn't be more different. Ella, pretty and slight for a seventeen-year-old, was normally quiet, even compliant, while Hanni seemed driven by spirit alone.

"All you care about is this garden, this place." Ella gestured toward the château. "It's all rules and chores—"

"How do you think food appears on your plate every day?"

"You should care about *us*," Ella persisted, color flushing her cheeks as her voice climbed. "Hanni and I haven't had a letter from our parents all summer. We don't even know what's happened to them, if they're still in Germany, or . . ." She glanced at her sister as if momentarily sorry, and Hanni's unblinking gaze dropped to the grass. But Ella went on, undeterred. "Let her play. The world's collapsing, Mademoiselle Näf. Germany will soon control all of Europe. I'm sure of it now. Where will we go? Nobody wants us. Not Germany, not France. We have nobody."

"You have me—"

"Don't you see that our hearts are breaking?" Ella's voice cracked and she looked Rösli right in the eyes, searchingly. "You know nothing about what kids actually need."

Rösli froze as if she'd been slapped. Doubt welled in her chest while she fought back a rise of questions. She wasn't good with feelings, it was true. But how could anyone tend invisible, broken hearts? That puzzle was beyond her. So she checked the long rows of beds each morning, ensuring they were made. She checked that the rooms were tidy, that the children had completed their tasks, that they met expectations. Was Ella right? Had Rösli gone about this all wrong? She'd drawn on her experience as a nurse, working in places more challenging even than wartime France. Rules had worked when she served a hospital in Africa, hadn't they? And they had worked here. The children were no longer malnourished. They were no longer listless. They had schedules, chores, lessons, and food from their own gardens at every meal. And yet, the teenagers despised her.

"That's enough," Rösli declared, squaring her shoulders. Doubt and anger would serve nobody. "If your sister or anyone else doesn't contribute, they will face consequences. That's the rule, and I don't want it questioned." She tried to erase the unease from her face. She didn't need to be liked here. In all her thirty-one years she'd never been liked much, anywhere. Respect was far more potent. "Do you understand me?"

Ella blinked the shine from her eyes, but she didn't move a muscle. Rösli stood her ground, too, still clutching the hammock of green beans in her apron. Despite the way she'd hardened her rhetoric, she felt momentarily awkward; too tall, all elbows and shoulders and flyaway hair. A familiar sensation washed over her—that she was missing something, that invisible something that hung in the air between people.

A noise echoed faintly over the trees, halting whatever Ella might have said. The girl's frown softened as she cocked her head, listening. The anger fell away from her eyes, replaced with a question.

Rösli held her breath, trying to make out the sound. Yes. It was an engine, still far away. She gripped the bundle of green beans with one hand and used the other to loosen the apron's knot at the small of her back. "Here," she said breathlessly, lifting the apron over her head and handing the bundle of beans to the girl. "Take these to Frau Schlesinger in the kitchen. I'll intercept whoever's coming." Rösli pivoted without waiting for a response, glancing at the rest of the children in the courtyard. They'd all stilled instinctively, listening to the sound of the distant engine. "Children," she called out, "go inside, please. Wash up and help Frau Schlesinger prepare for lunch."

She didn't have to say more. The children stood, dusting their knees and hoisting vegetables in their dresses and baskets. They clumped from the garden in their wooden clogs and bare feet, moving toward the heavy doors of the medieval building that had become their home. Rösli exhaled. They were used to following orders, mostly.

She set off for the narrow dirt road leading away from the château. She trotted briskly, stretching her long gait, until she was around a curve and could only see La Hille between gaps in the trees. The sound of the engine grew, ricocheting off distant hills and stone canyons and close banks of trees as it neared.

Rösli waited in the road at the hem of the property, branches whispering overhead, her heart accelerating. There wasn't anything to fear, really. What could anyone want with a derelict castle full of refugee children, after all? And it could be a friend in the car. Maurice Dubois, perhaps, who ran several children's homes like La Hille for the Swiss Red Cross. She warmed at the thought of him, a charismatic man who sometimes drove down from his office in Toulouse, visiting them in the wilds like a benevolent godfather.

But as the vehicle rounded a bend in the road, the knot in her stomach tightened. It was as she suspected. A police car bumped toward her, grinding to a stop where she blocked its way, hands on her hips, buffeted by a wave of dust as the engine died out.

Lieutenant Danielle stepped from the car, and Rösli remained planted where she was.

"Mademoiselle Näf, isn't that a strange place to stand—the middle of the road?"

"*Directrice* Näf, please. What's strange is that you continue to visit without an invitation," she countered, pursing her lips. She kept her hands on her hips as the gendarme approached. He was a head shorter than her, and he looked up with what she felt was an irredeemably unlikable face. He had big, pale eyes with dark pouches under them, as if instead of sleeping he drank every night away. A thin mustache crawled across his lip like a centipede.

"Police don't need invitations, mademoiselle. Why don't we go on up to La Hille to discuss the reason for my visit, *oui*? You might offer me something to drink. Some of that Swiss food and a little hospitality."

"Whatever food we have is for the children," Rösli said. "Not for well-fed gendarmes."

"Ah. While our own French children go hungry? I simply cannot understand why you Swiss would rather help foreign Jews than the many French children whose fathers—"

"We help plenty of French children, too, and you know it. The Swiss Red Cross—"

"The Swiss Red Cross is operating on our soil, mademoiselle. As I see it, that compels you to comply with our ordinances."

"I've complied with every ordinance."

"*Très bien!*" Without breaking eye contact, he smiled and un-tucked a pad of paper from under his armpit. "Then you won't mind providing an updated list. Once again, *s'il vous plaît*. Name all for-eign Jews over the age of sixteen residing in your residence, and I'll confirm the accuracy of my list, *oui*?" He smiled with false cheer, as if he were the teacher and she were his student.

Rösli's heart beat harder. Last winter, the Vichy government had demanded that all foreign Jews register with their regional pre-fects or face penalties. Rösli had lain awake for three nights trying to chart the best course for her colony. Why did the French govern-ment want to conduct such a census? And what were the penalties for evading it? Many foreign Jews were already living in internment centers in France. She'd thought of these forlorn camps and turned over in bed, chewing on her thumbnail until it bled. Surely they wouldn't target parentless children for internment? Surely children protected by the Swiss Red Cross were safe? Would the Swiss be allowed to remain in France, scooping up children in need, if they didn't follow the rules? In the end, she'd decided it was better to obey the law and avoid whatever punishment awaited those who escaped the census.

But now, with Lieutenant Danielle standing before her yet again, she feared that she'd erred. Ever since she'd registered the names of over one hundred foreign Jews, this despicable man had surprised them with visits and lists, demanding an accurate account-ing of the oldest children. And with the news from Paris, the sight of Lieutenant Danielle's simpering face made her all the more furi-ous. Men like him, gendarmes, had done the Germans' bidding in the occupied zone, even arresting Jews in Paris only a month ago.

Rösli and her staff had heard reports of deportations on the BBC, listening to their old, finicky radio tucked in one of La Hille's towers, utterly stunned.

"Nothing has changed," she said, staring down her nose at him. They were in *unoccupied* France, after all, not Paris. French law still existed here, and it still protected Jewish children until they turned eighteen. The gendarmes in the Vichy-controlled south might take roll for the Germans, but that was all they could do.

"None of the teenagers has had a birthday this summer? You've had no new arrivals this year?" He blinked his overlarge eyes. "I find that hard to believe. I heard talk in the village that a mother wandered through just last week, looking for a place to leave her teenage children. And it's rumored that your older boys are hiring out on farms. A Werner something or other? We can't have foreigners scattering around the countryside with no record of their whereabouts—"

"No," she interrupted, batting down a surge of anger. "There's not been a single change." She lied without flinching. "Now, Lieutenant Danielle, I need to go. We've had an outbreak of lice at the château, which is why I came down here to greet you. If you'd like to avoid catching it, I recommend turning around."

The short gendarme stared up for a weighted moment, studying her.

"I have it myself," she added, narrowing her eyes. "It's itchy as hell."

Lieutenant Danielle hesitated, then shook his head. Tucking the pad of paper back under his arm, he retreated to his car. "I'll be back soon," he called, stepping into the driver's seat without further comment.

Rösli stood in the road until he'd backed up and turned around. She stared at the silhouette of his capped head through the rear window as the gears caught and the car rumbled off in a cloud of dust. Just before he disappeared down the road, a hand lifted from the steering wheel to the nape of his neck, scratching furiously.

Rösli smirked. Then she turned back to Château de la Hille, and the children waiting for her within its thick stone walls, no doubt ready for lunch.

*T*wo nights later, Rösli lay awake, plagued by questions she couldn't answer. *Why* did the gendarmes want an accurate list of her teenagers? She thought of the appalling news from Paris, but shook her head on her pillow. Nothing like that could happen here, not in the free zone. She'd tried to say as much to *les Grands*, but their apprehension only grew as summer waned. All day they'd whispered among themselves, ceasing when she neared. She sensed their disdain, shimmering up like heat over the summer hills. If only she knew how to *speak* to them.

Rösli rolled over in bed, staring through the tall panes of glass separating her from the wilds of the Ariège. How could she reassure her teenagers, and guide them, when they barely tolerated her? Or did she misunderstand? Was she imagining that the girls swapped looks when she walked into a room? She sighed. It was all so familiar, this sense of not fitting in, of not knowing the customs of even her own people. It had always been that way, ever since she was a girl herself. It was as if Rösli were forever on the inside, gazing out.

A memory rose in the darkness. She saw a leaded-glass window from her own childhood, framed by blue Swiss mountains. She saw herself standing before it, her gangly frame clothed in a dress that hung a bit too short over her lengthening legs, exposing her knees. An apron bunched around her waist, soiled by the duster she'd placed on a shelf, silently, afraid someone might catch her sneaking up to this library in a house she cleaned with her mother. It had become her routine, a stolen hour she treasured week after week. The book in Rösli's hands was edged with gold leaf, and it told stories of jungles and faraway seas and scalded deserts. It sent her heart thumping against her breastbone while she ignored the room's dust, standing by the window, imagining a different life.

Then, one afternoon the family came home early. Rösli's mother was downstairs, finishing the heavy scrubbing on her hands and cracked, dry knees. Sometimes she asked what took so long upstairs, but she never pursued it beyond a flare of frustration. When Rösli glanced out the window and spotted the family coming down the garden path, she froze. The parents walked with their daughter between them, and the girl wore a dress the exact color of the sky. Her father bent to kiss her forehead. Rösli stared through the leaded panes, her breath shallowing. She recognized the girl. *Eva.* Just a week before at school, Rösli had tried to join a table of girls during lunch. Only, the moment she'd sat, the rest of them had stood, recoiling from Rösli and hurrying off to another table. Eva, in the same lovely blue dress, had glanced back and caught Rösli's welling gaze. And she'd *laughed*.

Rösli stared down at the book, noticing, for the first time, the dirtiness of her fingers on its white pages. Her shoulders suddenly seemed too wide, her bones too heavy, her elbows like knots hanging at her aproned waist. She couldn't be more unlike Eva, who never sat alone, watching everyone flow past her like water around a stone. She saw Eva's mother giggle and was certain that this was a woman who never shouted, never criticized her swan of a child, and never cried over her soup pot while her husband stayed out late.

Rösli had closed the book, its stories vanishing. Her cheeks burned. She slid it back onto the shelf and picked up her duster, leaving the library. Yearning burned in her soul like a lit coal. She couldn't be like the girls who avoided her, beautiful, adored, and at ease in the world. Her mother hollered up the stairs, and a decision found Rösli, sudden and potent.

Someday, she would escape this life.

She'd descended the stairs, thinking. Could she work in secret and save money, hiding it under her mattress? Yes, and when she had enough, she would go. She would find a way to be independent, and she'd seek out the places she'd read about in Eva's gilded books, places where she no longer had to be the cleaning woman's daughter.

And that's what she'd done.

Now, she stared at the stars through the château's window for another long moment, letting the memory fade. Rösli had escaped her upbringing, yes. Yet no matter where she went, no matter how hard she worked to change her circumstances, what she couldn't escape was herself. She closed her eyes and forced memories of her childhood, and the long road that brought her here, to evaporate.

When Rösli awoke, the room was still dark. She blinked at the cavernous ceiling, disoriented. What time was it? She pushed up onto her elbow, glancing toward the open window. The sky was the cobalt of dawn, but the moon still hung heavy over the foothills, not yet defeated. It must be earliest morning.

"Mademoiselle Näf!" someone whispered through her office door, which adjoined her small bedroom. Three sharp knocks sounded, chased with a voice that edged out of a whisper. "Please wake up!" Like a remembered dream, Rösli realized what had woken her: someone was calling her name.

"Just a moment," she whispered back, swinging her feet to the cool stone floor. Padding to the armoire, she swung a tattered robe over her shoulders and slipped into her office. She glanced at the letter on her desk, half-finished, asking charities in Switzerland to send warm clothing donations as soon as possible. Summer was waning. She opened the heavy door, her thoughts split between the day's looming tasks and concern for who was knocking so early, and why.

Hans, one of *les Grands*, stood in the hallway looking small. Even in the faint moonlight she sensed terror in his eyes.

"What in heaven's name are you doing awake?" she whispered, but he was already ducking past her, heading to the window in the bedroom.

"I got up to use the outhouse, but I heard a noise." Panic fractured his whisper as he sidled up to the tall window, careful to stay out of view, beckoning her to follow. "Mademoiselle Näf, look. The gendarmes are here."

Her heart stopped. She stepped behind him, peering out.

"*Mein Gott.*" Her pulse surged, flushing her limbs with skittering fear. Down below, figures drifted around the property like ghosts in the darkness. One detached from the pool of shadow under a tree, ambling across the lawn before settling in another shadow. Waiting. Others moved in sync, lining up, their approach as silent and synchronized as wolves stalking prey.

"*Mein Gott,*" she whispered again, breath shaking. What could she do? She glanced around the room, taking in the spill of moonlight, the rumpled bed, her tidy office, the long hallway beyond. Understanding took hold of her: there was nowhere to go. The police in this remote corner of Vichy France had surrounded her château full of sleeping children, and it was far too late to hide them.

"They can't do this," she sputtered. "They aren't allowed."

She pinned her eyes shut for a swaying second, seeing her own pen moving on paper, registering names. Nausea bloomed in her gut. They were here because she'd made a horrific, shameful mistake.

The gendarmes knew about this château full of refugees, thanks to her. And they could only have come for one purpose.

TWO

ELLA ROSENTHAL

CHÂTEAU DE LA HILLE, SOUTHERN FRANCE

AUGUST 1942

*E*lla had once been happy.

She blinked up at the dark ceiling, fingering the envelope she'd hidden under her pillow the previous day and currently held to her chest, unopened, her fingers running over it as though reading braille. She'd been happy so long ago that now, in the darkness of this dormitory, in this château nestled in the hills of southern France, so far from where she was meant to be—now, it was difficult to remember what happiness felt like.

She listened to the soft snoring of her roommates, their chests rising and falling while the cool breath of night swam through the open window. Ella swallowed a lump of pain. She would burn this letter as soon as there was a fire to stuff it in, so Hanni would never see it. She hadn't opened the envelope because it wasn't from their parents, or anyone else back home in Cologne. It was a letter she herself had written to Papa and Mutti, several weeks ago. She'd sketched a detailed picture of the château under the text, including Hanni in the foreground with a smile on her face. Ella had labored over the drawing, rubbing out mistakes and losing herself in the shading, until it was something she could be proud to seal and mail to her parents.

The envelope had returned during lunch with the rest of the mail. Her own handwriting, spelling out her old address, was obscured with a dreaded German stamp. She'd squeezed her eyes shut, the words repeating in her jumbled brain. *Gone without leaving a forwarding address.*

Ella hadn't been able to sleep, not with this news burning under her pillow in the form of creased, smudged paper. She tried to picture her mother, not as she was in the one photo Ella still had, but as she looked in real life, with her dark eyes, lively and warm, and hair curling against her long neck—but the image flitted away. That's how it was, lately. Like birds, memories of Mutti and Papa flickered from branch to branch, impossible to see before they vanished. Where were they now? Ella swallowed tears, closed her eyes, and sensed the faint tap of her own heart. It had actually started to hurt this summer. She'd always thought the word "heartache" was figurative, but now she knew it was not. With enough sorrow, enough loss, it was possible for the heart to ache like a wound.

A sound jarred her thoughts.

Her eyes snapped open, and she stopped breathing. Listened. Was it a voice? Who else was awake?

Another sound echoed from the hallway, knocking this time, and Ella shifted up, glancing at the beds surrounding her. The rest of the girls slept on, the black lumps of their bodies unmoving under their blankets. Who was out in the hall, knocking on doors in the middle of the night? Ella thought for a moment before swinging her feet to the floor. She may as well give up on sleep, anyway. She sidled between her cot and Dela's, careful not to bump her snoring neighbor, and slipped from the dormitory.

The next room was an adjoining dormitory, a much bigger space housing almost twenty of the littlest girls. Ella tiptoed across the cold stone, weaving between beds. She paused beside Hanni, the ache pounding in her heart. Hanni's dark lashes fluttered on her cheeks, and her little chest rose and fell in a slice of waning moonlight. She looked so peaceful, so small. How could Ella ever tell her sister that their parents were *gone*? She swallowed, struggling to summon the correct word. *Deported*.

Forcing herself onward, Ella slipped from the dormitory into the dark hallway. At its end, Rösli's door was open. Before Ella could take another step, Rösli herself bustled out, tailed by a wiry boy named Hans. Saying nothing, she strode past Ella, tightening the waist of her shabby robe as she went. Hans, hurrying in her wake, jolted as Ella stepped from the shadowed doorway into his path.

"What's happ—"

"*Les gendarmes*," Hans interrupted, raking a hand through his messy, slept-on hair, his eyes bright in the darkness. "Outside."

Ella shook her head, uncomprehending. Police? In the middle of the night? Before her splintered thoughts could make sense of what Hans was trying to say, he took her by the elbow and jerked her down the hall to Rösli's room, striding straight to the window where the moon dipped behind the hills, making way for day. Hans gestured toward the ground below. "Look."

She dropped her gaze, and there they were. A loose circle of French police hovered outside, dark and silent as bats. One raised his hand as Ella watched, flashing a signal, and they began to creep forward in unison.

"*Scheisse*," Hans swore, spittle bursting with the word. His eyes caught the last of the moonlight. "They're coming for us, you see? Like they did in Paris."

And with that, Ella understood. She stared out the window for another second, eyes smarting in the night air, the ache draining from her chest as fear bounded in. She pivoted and hurried from the room.

Only one thought rose in her mind as she dashed down the hall: *Hide Hanni.* Voices filtered up the staircase; the police were already inside. A man's baritone words were met with Rösli's crisp responses, no longer whispers but still impossible to make out. Ella reached the girls' dormitory just as the door opened and her friend Inge tiptoed out, questions widening her stare. But Ella stepped past her to the threshold of the dormitory, fear wedging in her throat as she looked for Hanni across the room, still fast asleep. Where could Hanni hide? Ella glanced between the many beds, paralyzed in the doorjamb, her mind racing. They needed to hide *all* of these little girls. Her hands tightened into fists. But where?

"*Psst.*"

Ella jolted and swiveled at the sound, but it was only Hans. He beckoned her from the room, a finger over his lips. Inge drifted down the hall to the staircase, her nightgown bright in the darkness. Ella cast her gaze again toward her sister, unsure, and retreated quietly.

"They're not coming for the littlest kids," Hans whispered, his voice hoarse. "They're coming for us."

"For us?" It was as if she were hearing him through water, trying to make sense of distant words.

"I eavesdropped, on the stairs. They're here for anyone age sixteen and up." He reached behind her and quietly closed the door. "Maybe the little ones can sleep a bit longer. They'll be so scared . . ." He scratched at his messy hair, agitated.

The near future came to Ella in a burst of clarity: *les Grands* were going to be taken from the château by the police flooding inside right now. Would the smallest children really be spared? Surely they would? She wavered where she stood, buffeted as though fear were a stiff wind trying to blow her down. She met Hans's dark stare, nodded once, and strode again down the hall after Inge, praying that Hanni would remain at La Hille. Safe.

Followed by Hans, she crept down the staircase to the first floor. With each step Ella took, Rösli's voice grew louder.

"You must leave at once!" she declared as Ella rounded the last bend and paused in a slab of shadow, next to Inge, watching. Rösli stood several steps farther down, at the foot of the staircase, illuminated by lamps burning on the first floor. She wore her blue bathrobe, and her blond hair swung on her strong back as she vigorously shook her head. "You're not allowed to enter the premises—"

"We have our orders, mademoiselle. It's out of your hands, and mine."

"It is absolutely *not* out of my hands!" She nearly shouted it. "These children are under the authority of the Swiss Red Cross, and I am their director. I *will not* let you up these stairs." Rösli straightened her tall frame, placing her hands on the terry cloth cloaking her hips. Though Ella stood at her back, she could imagine Rösli's stern, imperious stare, her small gray eyes narrowing in the same way that had irritated Ella so often. But now, despite her expanding fear, a gasp of pride gusted through her. This chief of the gendarmerie didn't know whom he was tangling with.

"You can't prevent this, mademoiselle. We have orders to arrest overage foreign Jews, and we will use force if necessary."

"*Overage*," Rösli scoffed. "You're talking about arresting children! How many are on your list?" She gestured to the folder in the man's hand.

"Forty. And four adults."

For just a second, Rösli seemed lost for words. Her hand flew to her lips and Ella caught her whispered echo. "*Forty-four.*" But she was only unmoored for a second.

"You intend to deliver forty children and four of my staff to the Germans? You should be ashamed of yourselves."

"Move aside. We don't have time for this."

Rösli held her ground, and the rest of the policemen below, perhaps a dozen, shifted expectantly. They wore blue uniforms and knee-high, polished boots. Each one had a revolver on his belt.

"If you don't move, mademoiselle . . . " The chief grimaced, glancing at the rest of the policemen in the room behind him. The silver brocade of his cap caught the light. "If you don't move, mademoiselle, I will move you. Physically."

Rösli widened her stance, and her bathrobe fanned out below her waist like a tent. "Then you'll have to pick me up because, by God, I'm not budging."

The chief sighed, pinching the bridge of his nose, and a slurry of murmurs swam behind him.

"Are we really arresting children?" one man whispered loudly, his gaze flicking up the staircase. His black eyes landed on Ella, and she shrank back in her nightdress.

"Mademoiselle." The chief stepped forward. "You leave me no choice."

Moving quickly, he wrapped his arms around Rösli and started to lift, but she shook him off, smacking his hands and speaking fast. Ella's heart plummeted. Rösli had lost. She couldn't hold back a dozen armed men, after all.

"At least allow me to go up and dress." Rösli freed herself, breathless, and took a step back. "And allow me to wake the children, so they aren't shocked by the sight of police at their bedsides. They should have breakfast—"

"Impossible," he said, beckoning his men. "We must maintain order and security, mademoiselle."

Inge patted Ella on the shoulder, gesturing upstairs. Together they scaled the steps, holding their nightdresses clear of their bare feet as the thump of boots started in their wake.

Back in the dormitory for teenage girls, Ella flipped on the light, and the last of her sleeping friends groaned and squinted up. Edith already sat on her cot, face white. Her hands trembled as she reached for a pair of glasses on her bedside table and slid them over her nose, blinking.

"The police," Inge murmured, as if there were no more to say. She tucked her hair behind her ears, also with shaking fingers. Ella swallowed, glancing at the rest of the girls as they rose from their beds, wavering, their nightgowns rumpled and their eyes wide.

"Can't we escape into the woods?" Ruth asked as male voices echoed in the hall.

Before Ella could say, "It's too late," the door flung open behind her.

Two gendarmes settled in the jamb, hands on their hips, eyes on the stunned teenage girls, saying nothing. Behind them, the little girls, shocked awake, drifted and shivered, many of them clutching blankets and crying. Rösli threaded between their cots, placing a hand on various heads and shoulders as she passed, her face flushed. She pushed between the gendarmes into the teenagers' room, blinking fast to stem an obvious urge to cry.

"The château is surrounded by police." Rösli's voice cracked. "Girls, we have no choice but to cooperate. Please get dressed quickly, and start to pack some things to take with you." She cleared her throat, swiping at her shining, startled eyes. "I'm so sorry. I have to go explain to the rest of the boys and girls, but please believe me when I tell you this: I will do everything in my power to help you."

When Rösli left, the girls looked questioningly at the gendarmes posted in the doorway. Inge, clutching her clothes, mustered her voice. "Please, could we dress alone?"

The younger gendarme simply grinned, shaking his head.

A flush of anger overcame Ella, and she straightened her spine. "Must you *watch* us?"

"*Oui,*" the other one said, smirking. He was older than Ella's father.

She glared at him until her flare of anger fizzled out, doused again by fear. With quivering hands, she turned from the police and rummaged through her things, finding the red dress supplied by the Swiss Red Cross for summer. Without speaking, all six girls started shimmying into their dresses, attempting to keep the pale parts of their bodies covered with nightgowns and sheets while their new guards stared.

Clothed, Ella inhaled, trying to steady her rabid heartbeat. She had to remain composed, for Hanni. She glanced at the doorway, where her little sister hovered beyond the threshold, framed by the leering gendarmes. Hanni stood with her hands clasped in front of her nightgown, her messy hair sticking to her wet cheeks as she blinked, her eyes still. She'd already lived through so much that she knew to stay calm, even amid catastrophe. Ella swallowed a surge of grief. They all did. She held Hanni's silent stare, giving her a weighted nod. *Be strong,* she wanted to say. *I'll be all right.*

She took inventory of her meager belongings. What should she pack? If only they knew where they were going. She picked up the framed picture of her family, taken before she'd left Germany for Belgium nearly four years ago. As she set it back on the shelf, changing her mind, it rattled under her unsteady hand. She turned to her clothing. Should she pack a sweater? Yes. And also the sketchbook her parents had given her, so long ago she'd filled the pages and now used the margins.

Before tucking it inside her bag, she opened the front cover, more from reflex than intention, and scanned the lines written there. In her mother's elegant handwriting was the Tefilat Haderech, the Traveler's Prayer, which Ella had read so many times now she knew not just the words, but the rise and fall of each letter formed by her mother's careful hand. She closed the sketchbook and added it to her bag with a nudge of worry. What would she do if someone took it from her? Should she risk bringing it?

A voice boomed from the doorjamb, interrupting her thoughts. "No scissors, knives, or razor blades allowed in your baggage. Your bags will be searched on arrival, so don't try anything." The girls looked up in unison, but the gendarme who'd made the announcement was already walking away.

"On arrival where?" Dela, slight and pale as a dove, held her folded nightdress to her chest and watched the gendarme disappear around a corner. Nobody answered her. They could guess, but saying it aloud would make it too real. Ella placed a comb in her suitcase and struggled to close it. Her arms felt weak.

"I suppose I'll take a book," Edith murmured. Tears spattered her glasses as she bent, placing a dog-eared novel on top of a small pile of clothes.

Minutes later, the guards hustled the girls from their dormitory. Hanni drifted on the edge of her room as they filed past, her cheeks shiny and her lips pursed in silent anguish, and Ella took a chance. She left the group, striding four steps to her little sister, and knelt.

"Come!" a police officer shouted from the door, already seeing the last girl out.

"Hanni," Ella said quickly, taming the tremor from her voice. "I will be fine. Can you be brave while I'm gone?"

"Where are they taking you?" Hanni's lower lip trembled while tears dripped from it.

"I don't know. Probably somewhere to work—"

Hanni melted into her arms, weeping silently, her little body shivering beneath her nightdress. "You can't go. You're my only family—they can't take you. Please Ella, please, please—"

"*Tu viens avec moi maintenant!*" the guard yelled from the door, and when Ella glanced up, she sensed the sharp edge of danger in his face. She pressed a palm to Hanni's wet cheek, pulled herself gently away, and looked one last time into her sister's brown eyes. "Stay up here, Hanni. Don't come downstairs until we are gone, please? Promise? Hanni, I love you."

Ella hurried away from her sister, who looked so tiny as she crumpled, sobbing, on her cot. "*Please don't follow me*," Ella whispered to herself, pleading in the dark hallway with nobody to hear. The policeman's boots clicked on the stone floor behind her. It would be better if Hanni didn't mingle with these gendarmes, didn't clutch at her in the courtyard, and didn't see her herded away like an animal. Ella swallowed, wiping at her own stinging eyes.

A half hour later, all forty teenagers, plus the four adult staff members who were also Jewish, stood in the courtyard, summoned by their names printed in the chief's folder. Shivering and quiet with shock, they listened to the rumble of approaching engines. Ella glanced at the boy who stood next to her, clutching a suitcase in his large hands, his black hair flopping over his forehead. "Isaak," she whispered, "where do you think they're taking us?"

Isaak looked down, his gray gaze hinging on her face, his brows low with worry. "Don't know." Without elaboration, he swung one of his hands from his suitcase to grip her free palm, and she held on, grateful. She didn't know Isaak especially well, and yet the weight of a hand in her own gave her strength. She held on to him, and he gripped her just as tightly as the faint blue light of morning brightened the château and the engines died somewhere down the road. As they began to file out under La Hille's watchtower, toward the road and its waiting buses, Ella and Isaak stayed together.

They walked along a dusty path toward the buses, and Ella spotted several figures standing in the shadows of the overarching

THE WINTER ORPHANS 27

trees beyond. There was a local farmer and his wife, whom she recognized well from trading their vegetables for his eggs. The sound
of engines, rare these days in the hills, must have beckoned them.
He held his hat in his hands, and his silver hair fluttered in the
morning breeze. His wife wept openly, palms pressed to her mouth.
There were three women Ella didn't recognize, whispering among
themselves, and next to them, the village schoolteacher and his
mother stood beside a bicycle, their expressions pained. "Don't take
the children!" the schoolteacher's mother shouted as they neared,
shaking a fist as the teenagers started boarding buses. "How could
you do such a thing?" The gendarmes didn't even glance at the old
woman.

Ella swallowed, grief coursing through her veins. The La Hille
children were liked in the village. Rösli had forged links between
them and their rural community, often boasting within earshot that
she was in charge of such a lovely, well-mannered group. Now Rösli
stood near the door of the first bus, her arms crossed over her blue
bathrobe, still arguing in her loud, breathless voice. The police chief,
clearly exasperated, shook his head at something she said while
more kids filed past, climbing aboard. As Ella approached, she
heard Rösli's tone change from demanding to pleading.

"Just tell me where you're taking my children. Please, I insist
that you tell me."

The chief merely shook his head, casting his eyes to the sky as
if his patience was running out. Ella slowed as she passed, caught
by the fury resurging in Rösli's stone-gray stare.

"Shame on you." Rösli pinned the officer with her glare, weighting each word. "*Shame*. I expected better of France."

Ella slowed further, letting go of Isaak's hand, transfixed. Was
Mademoiselle Näf going to spit on the chief? Rösli pursed her thin
lips as if she were preparing saliva, glaring as if she could burn him

with her eyes, and then Ella was jostled into climbing aboard the bus, her heart pounding, her small suitcase bumping her legs as she made her way to a seat.

Minutes later, the engines roared to life, shattering the morning air a second time. Ella pressed her face to the window's glass and watched birds explode from the trees, scattering into the sky.

As the bus slowly turned to lumber down the road, Ella craned her neck to look back at Château de la Hille, its stone shoulders rising over the surrounding trees, warming in the sun. Rösli still stood in the road. She was alone now in the dust of retreating buses, her blue bathrobe fluttering in the wind. As Ella watched, Rösli collapsed to her knees, burying her face in her hands, her broad shoulders shaking as sobs finally broke loose from their dam. Then the bus rumbled around a corner, and Rösli, and the château rising beyond her, disappeared.

❧

THREE

RÖSLI

*R*ösli fetched the bicycle where she'd leaned it against a stone wall of the post office in the tiny village of Montégut-Plantaurel. Her gut clenched painfully, as if she'd swallowed a wrench, and her eyes stung from weeping into the wind as she'd pedaled here, hard and fast, arriving just as the morning sun broke fully over the hills. She'd come for a telephone, which didn't exist at La Hille, and called the Toulouse office of the Secours Suisse aux Enfants of the Red Cross, just seventy-five kilometers north. Had there been raids in Toulouse, too? Her mind had hummed as the phone rang, on and on. She imagined Maurice Dubois walking to the office, perhaps whistling, still optimistic, still unaware of the catastrophe that had befallen her children.

"Where did they take them?" were his first words after she explained what had transpired, not an hour earlier.

"I don't know." She'd choked the words out. "They wouldn't tell me. Monsieur Dubois, can you find out? You must appeal to the highest authorities. Go to Vichy, I'm begging you. And can you send some help from Toulouse? Without the Schlesingers and the Franks and all of *les Grands*, we only have Herr Lyrer and our handyman, Señor Salvide, to care for the children."

He'd agreed to her requests and they'd hung up, but she didn't feel any better. Now she pivoted in Montégut's sleepy square, looking across the surrounding fields and hills as if she might be able to detect her children, somewhere out there. She wiped at her eyes and hardened her jaw. What could she do now? A sensible voice answered in her mind: she should go home and tend to the remaining children, who had lost both siblings and caretakers this morning. Yes, the sensible thing would be to go back to Château de la Hille and wait. But Rösli's heart stormed as she pictured the teenagers again, tearfully bumping away on those buses to an unknown destination. The near memory gripped her, as if by electricity.

She had to find out where they were.

She mounted the bicycle, pushing its loose pedals until the old tires wobbled into a rhythm, and pumped out of Montégut.

Over an hour later she pedaled into Foix, her legs burning after cycling as hard as she could through the increasingly steep hills pitching into town, which nestled into the greenery like a river into a canyon. Breathless, she leaned the rickety bicycle against the side of a building, glancing at it ruefully—let someone steal the blasted thing. She hurried to a door beyond it, striding into the office of the *préfecture*.

"Where did your gendarmes take the children of Château de la Hille?" she demanded moments later, seated across a gleaming mahogany desk from a tall man with round glasses and a balding head.

He seemed unconcerned by the urgency of her tone. "I'm unable to tell you that."

"Those are my children, do you understand? I'm their director—"

"That's of no importance to me, mademoiselle." He took his

glasses off and frowned, using an embroidered handkerchief to wipe out a smudge.

Rösli felt like she might explode. "You cannot arrest children protected by the Swiss Red Cross! You have no authority to do such a thing."

The man smirked, replacing his glasses. They flashed as he spoke, still in a measured, calm voice. "I assure you, my authority comes from further up the chain than you can possibly imagine. You have no business here. Get out of my office, mademoiselle. I have a busy day ahead."

Fuming, Rösli rose to her full height, pushing her shoulders back, ignoring the sweat circling her armpits and the state of her rumpled blue nurses' dress. "Shame on you." She said it for the second time that day, like a curse, nailing her gaze to him. He blinked placidly behind his clean glasses. Curse them all!

In the hallway, Rösli stopped everyone who looked anything like a government bureaucrat, imploring, "Do you know where they took the children of La Hille? Please, I beg you," but each person shrank away, avoiding her stare. She left the building defeated, yet she wouldn't give up.

From the *préfecture* she went to the police station, again interrogating anyone she saw. Her presence there was even less well received, and within minutes she was hustled to the door in the front office by a busty, frowning secretary clutching a heap of papers. "You need to leave," the woman said, as if this were the practical answer to Rösli's plea. For a moment, Rösli thought the woman was going to swat her out like a stray cat, and her heart dipped further. Did that disagreeable little secretary know where her children were? Why would nobody tell her?

She emerged on the stoop of the police station, squinting in the bright August light, suddenly weak. She hadn't eaten anything before leaving La Hille, an obvious mistake, but she'd been too distraught to think of it. And she wasn't used to riding bicycles, especially not this far. She limped from the station door on shaking legs and paused to lean against the stone of the building, next to the old bicycle, pressing both hands over her face.

What now? Did the children think she would abandon them? The idea smarted like a burn. Did they really believe there was nobody left who cared about their fate, like Ella had said the other day? Pain swelled in her chest. Because, for a start, *she* cared. She pictured them: the boys tromping through the woods, singing while they chopped wood, their faces brown in the sun. The way they'd burst into laughter at some private joke, buckling over like felled trees, deepening voices cracking. There was Walter, who played the old piano in the dining room so beautifully, surely the product of years of careful instruction. There was Dela, quick to laugh, and Edith, who loved to read, and Ella, who adored her sister beyond all measure, and Kurt, whose ready smile made everyone else smile more. And so many others, each of them with a story, each of them with a future that should be different from the one unspooling now.

Rösli had never cared about anything so much in her life.

"Mademoiselle?" A quiet voice startled her. She dropped her hands from her face and turned, cautious.

A small man in a suit coat stared at her from the nearby station door, papers tucked under one arm and his hat in his other hand. He took a few steps away from the building and glanced around, furtive as a crow, then met her stare again.

"*Le Vernet*," he whispered, looking around once more. "You'll find your children in Le Vernet, at the internment camp."

With that he hustled off, dropping his hat onto his gray head and vanishing around a corner.

Rösli's mouth hung open. Le Vernet. She turned to the bicycle, gripping the handlebars with trembling fingers, and swung her leg over the seat. Warring emotions mixed in her stomach, fueling her nausea. There was elation: she knew where her children were. And also dread, for her worst fears had come to fruition.

The next morning, Rösli again woke with the dawn. She slipped into her dress, picked up the bag she'd packed the night before, and forced down some breakfast before hurrying out into the courtyard. She wanted to leave before the little children woke, so they'd be less aware of her absence. When she'd returned from Foix yesterday afternoon, four adults had already arrived from the Toulouse office, and they'd agreed to take over until she could come back. Now she crept from the courtyard, found the bicycle outside the walls where she'd left it the day before, and was soon sailing down the dirt road leaving La Hille.

She was going to get her children.

The front bicycle tire wobbled as she pumped, pushing the feeble machine to its fastest speed, her muscles protesting. The sun, not yet detached from the eastern skyline, traced the hilltops in gold. Rösli began to sweat as she swung the bicycle onto a wider road. She'd fashioned straps for her bulky bag of clothing and medical supplies, and they dug into her dampening armpits as the luggage swayed on her back, shifting with each push of her thighs on the rusty pedals. The road spooled like a ribbon before her, winding through endless farmland, rolling hills, and stands of trees. From what she'd pieced together, Le Vernet was thirty-five kilometers away, which wasn't too bad. If she pushed hard, she could be there within two hours.

When the sun had fully risen, Rösli had already passed through the little town of Escosse, and her mood lifted. The thin road, surrounded by an endless patchwork of fields now, curved down for as far as she could see, giving her legs a needed break. She was sailing along beneath blue skies, sure she'd be there within the hour, when suddenly the handlebars jerked away from her grip. Before she understood what was happening, her front tire skidded out from under her and she was falling, heavy bag and all, into the gravelly dirt hemming the road. Her left elbow hit the hardest, grinding into the ground as the rest of her collapsed like a puppet cut from its strings. The bicycle clattered onto the pavement behind her, back tire still spinning.

Rösli struggled up, cupping her throbbing elbow with her right hand, fingering the bones through the skin for any sign of a break. Curses flew through her mind in two languages. *Scheisse. Merde!* She flexed her arm and exhaled through the ache. It was likely fine— nothing bandages and rest couldn't heal. She struggled up to stand, leaving the awkward bag in the dirt, and studied the bicycle. Its front tire had popped.

"*Scheisse!*" she cursed out loud, spinning in place on the desolate road. She shaded her eyes, squinting across the fields, sweat dripping beneath her hand and catching in her brows. Crickets sang in the golden field stretching west, cascading into a stand of trees. A farmhouse dotted the landscape, but there was no movement anywhere. She looked at the road ahead, snaking endlessly through these low, hot hills. After thinking hard for a long moment, her mind darting of its own accord, searching for solutions, Rösli sighed. She bent to pick up her bag, hoisted its awkward mass onto her sweaty back, and began to walk.

She'd trudged several kilometers when she heard an engine. Her heart leapt and fizzled all at once: who was coming? She envisioned a police car and felt momentarily sick, but then a truck lumbered over the rise of road and she squinted at it, recognizing its familiar shape. When it pulled up beside her, she heaved a sigh of gratitude. It was a milk truck, out making rounds.

A half hour later, the milk truck deposited Rösli in Pamiers, a decent-sized town, and she hunted down and hired a taxi with all the money she'd stuffed in her bag.

"The internment camp at Le Vernet?" the taxi driver repeated, eyebrows high in his thin face.

"*Oui.*" Rösli firmed her lips, passing him his fare. "I'm attending to official business."

He stared at her for another moment, pocketing the money and taking in her sweaty dress, dusty luggage, and bloodied elbow. He shrugged. "Bien sûr, mademoiselle. If you say so."

She stared out the window as they pulled out of town, blinking at the fields skipping by, her heart skipping along with them. What would she do when they arrived? She'd shelved the question until now, able to focus instead on simply getting there. But now that she'd managed it, she dared not tell the taxi driver the truth: she had no authorization to enter the camp.

She inhaled slowly, trying to calm her pounding pulse, and thought of other times she'd faced what seemed to be insurmountable problems. Of course, it was Africa that rose in her mind. She'd gone there in her twenties to work with the famous doctor Albert Schweitzer. She was fresh out of nursing school and eager to see the world, and within days she'd been completely overwhelmed. Everything was so different: the vegetation, the humidity, the long hours and new languages and new illnesses to tend. And the patients! There'd been so many every day, all of them from a different life than Rösli. She wasn't a woman who was gifted with people, and couldn't decode their nuances, despite having sought training in psychiatric nursing. She'd fumbled and cried and, eventually, found her way, taking over the hospital's gardening program. Over time, the original feelings of helplessness had hardened into competency, and the months bled on into three years before she came home.

What had she learned? Two things, she thought as the hills

flattened to farmland outside her taxi's window. First, one must keep going forward, no matter what. Second, when the way wasn't clear, it was wise to solve a single problem at a time. Whichever problem raised itself most directly in the path forward, that was the one to tackle.

Far ahead, something interrupted the fields, and Rösli stared into the sunlight, her heart hammering faster. There was the mushroom shape of a water tower, rising alongside the road, and beyond it? Yes—she made out a stretch of fence encasing rows of squat buildings. Many rows. The camp seemed to expand as they neared, and her breath caught in the thick air inside the taxi. The place was enormous.

They approached the giant, concrete water tower shading the road, and Rösli spotted the camp's gate just below it. The taxi slowed to a crawl as the driver, too, took in the stone pillars holding up an imposing sign hanging over the entrance. *Camp du Vernet.* Beyond the sign, a row of barracks marched in desolate uniformity. Two guards flanked the pillars, fully armed.

From the back seat, Rösli could see the driver's right eyebrow tip up as he slowed to an idle, still a hundred meters away. "Should I just drop you here?" He didn't turn to look at her as he asked. His eyes were on the guards who straightened, staring at the taxi.

"No. Get me closer to that gate," Rösli commanded.

The taxi driver turned fully around. "Are you crazy? Look at this place! They're not going to let you in."

"I'm on official business, I told you. Just drive up to those guards and I'll take care of it."

The driver hesitated for a moment before sighing. He muttered something to himself, then spoke over his shoulder. "If there's even a hint of trouble, you'll get out. *Comprenez-vous?*"

She clenched her jaw, nodding, and the taxi slowly approached the entrance. The guards detached from their posts and ambled over as it came to a stop, their tall boots crunching gravel. They stared out from under their helmets, expressionless. Before they could question the driver, Rösli unrolled her window and held out her Red Cross identity card.

"Swiss Red Cross!" she called out the window. The guards came closer, swapping glances, and Rösli breathed. They were very young. "I've been asked to come on official business," she said, still holding up her identification for inspection. She eyed the lane beyond the *Camp du Vernet* sign. It appeared to be long, lined with trees and wire fencing, with the water tower and a field beyond the left fence, and rows of barracks on the right. The headquarters of the place must be somewhere down the lane, off to the left past the field. That's where she needed to go.

"No entry without authorization." The guards shifted in their boots, their faces red from the sun.

The taxi driver glanced back at her. "We should go." He lowered his foot to the gas slightly, calling out from his unrolled window, "D'accord! Sorry to bother you."

Rösli blinked at the barracks as the taxi began a slow turn-around in the road, making the shape of a teardrop. She couldn't give up now, not with her kids locked in there. Without thought, she hooked her arm through the straps of her bag, opened the door, and tumbled out onto her feet. The taxi driver stopped, craning his neck out the window.

"Leave me here," Rösli called, straightening.

He shrugged, shook his head, and shifted gears, speeding away.

"Swiss Red Cross," she announced again to the stunned guards, and with every ounce of courage in her soul she adjusted her bag and walked under the imposing sign. *Camp du Vernet* passed over her head before either guard realized what was happening.

"*Mademoiselle!*" The shorter one barked, jogging to get in front of her. "You can't just come in here!"

"I'm from the Swiss Red Cross, here on official business." She kept walking and threw him her sternest glare. Beyond the fence on their right, people milled, glancing up to watch her advance. Their limbs were thin and their gazes tired, and Rösli moved forward on a surge of anger. Her children were somewhere in that sea of barracks and dust and hunger.

"Stop now! *Arrêtez-vous!*" the other guard shouted, striding alongside her, his face ever redder.

"You'll regret detaining me, so I'd advise you to get back to your post. Why would I be here if not for official business?" She glanced at the prisoners, who began to gather loosely along the fence line, silent. She didn't even need to get closer to see that these people were undernourished, like her children had once been.

The second guard hurried to her side, gripping his gun, his eyes wide as he traded glances with his partner. They were both shorter than her, and a good ten years younger.

"Stop walking now, mademoiselle. I order you to stop."

Keep walking, Rösli counseled herself. Would these French boys shoot a woman from the Swiss Red Cross? Swallowing, she trained her eyes on the path ahead. They wouldn't tail her much farther; surely they couldn't leave their post by the entrance. They would either shoot her or let her go. *Keep walking.*

Ten steps farther, her hunch proved correct. The two guards fell away, dashing back to their post, certainly radioing more guards to alert them of her presence. She walked faster, the bag digging into her armpits and sweat dripping down her back. She had only a moment of reprieve as a yard opened before her, dotted with more buildings, though these weren't fenced in. This must be the headquarters. She exhaled into the heat, just as four more guards hurried toward her across the flat expanse separating her from the buildings. *Keep walking and talking*, she ordered herself, repeating the mantra over her rebounding heart.

"Swiss Red Cross!" She called it out with a strong voice, belying the shake of every cell in her body. She moved purposefully across the yard as the guards closed in.

"Where is your authorization to enter the premises?" the tallest one barked, hands on his weapon.

"I have official business here," she said. "Please, let me through."

All four guards surrounded her, and Rösli fumbled for her Red Cross identity card, holding it high. "Swiss Red Cross!" she declared, as if that explained everything. The guards swapped glances, their faces open with confusion. For once, she felt that she could read minds: what were they supposed to do with this sweaty Swiss woman who seemed intent on breaking *into* the camp? Surely they were trained to keep people in, rather than out.

Just then, a man came around a building with squared shoulders and a deliberate stride. The line of his mouth was firm, and his eyes, shaded by the brim of his hat, were a cold gray.

"What are you doing here? You cannot just come in!" he shouted as he neared. He was older than most, with a lined face and frothy brows, and Rösli guessed by his air of authority that he was the camp commander. "Who let this woman through the gates?"

"I'm from the Swiss Red Cross," she said breathlessly, and he drew up close, pausing. His brows lifted slightly as he looked her up and down, taking in her wrinkled blue dress, darkened with sweat in various places, and her bloodied elbow and windblown hair. She straightened under his gaze, firming her jaw. "Forty children and four adults protected by the Swiss Red Cross were wrongly brought here," she said, her voice loud, her legs weak. "I've come to retrieve them."

The commander hesitated, his expression relaxing slightly. "Where are you from?" He squinted down in the dusty sunlight.

"Château de la Hille, about thirty-five kilom—"

"No," he interrupted, rubbing his jaw. "Before all this—where did you grow up?"

"Where did I grow up?" She stared up at him, knocked completely off-balance.

"You're from Switzerland, correct? Where, exactly?"

She caught it then. *His accent.* Everything in her heart gathered, a prism of hope. What were the chances?

"Ich bin in Glarus geboren."

The commander's face melted in recognition. *"Ich komme aus Riedern!"* he exclaimed. He switched back to French, with a clear Swiss German accent. "What are the chances! I've been to Glarus many times, before my family moved to France when I was still a boy. Such a beautiful place." He shook his head, chuckling a little, and Rösli stared up at him, bewildered. Was the man in his right mind? Or was he just so high ranking that he could allow nostalgia to take precedence over formality?

"You must miss it, living out here," she ventured, glancing around at the flat expanse of barbed wire and barracks.

"Ah, *oui, oui.*" He grinned and nodded, his eyes light with memory. "Especially lately. It's been so hot, and I find myself thinking of my childhood by the lakes, hiking through those glorious mountains. It's been a long time since I spoke with someone from home, mademoiselle. How funny to have a person from Glarus standing before me, here of all places!" He stared at her for a weighted second as if lost in some other world, and then his grin fell a little. The men surrounding them glanced among themselves, silent but clearly frustrated. One still had his hand on his gun.

"Why are you here?" the commander asked, his voice falling into seriousness.

Rösli inhaled to repeat her plea. "I'm from the Swiss Red Cross, sir. The French police erroneously took forty of the children in my care, and four of my adult staff, and detained them here yesterday. I've come to get them."

The commander was already shaking his head. "No, no, mademoiselle. That's not how it works at all. You won't be able to take them." He looked her up and down again, quizzical. "You came alone? On foot?"

"By taxi."

His frown sparked just a little, as if he wanted to grin. "And how would you take forty teenagers with you, mademoiselle, if it was even possible?"

Was he amused by all of this? Amused, when he had untold numbers of people detained behind all that barbed wire, damned to imminent deportation? Rösli forced her voice calm. "The Swiss Red Cross will send me transportation," she lied. They would *walk* home if they had to, by God. "I've sent representatives to Vichy to plead their case. They're under eighteen and therefore protected by the Swiss Red Cross."

"They're foreign Jews?"

She met his stare. "*Oui.*"

"Then nobody can protect them."

She held his gaze, her eyes latched to his, her spine straight. "I'm not leaving without my children."

He matched her stare for a long moment before sighing heavily and looking around at his guards. "I'll take care of this," he said loudly. "You're all dismissed back to your posts."

When they'd scattered, the commander crossed his arms over his uniformed chest, studying her as if she were an equation to solve. "Why do you call them *your* children?" he asked finally. "They're not yours at all."

She frowned, thrown off. "Well, they shouldn't be mine, should they? They all have families somewhere, and parents who loved them so dearly they tried to send them away to safety. They've been entrusted to me, and until they can be returned to their rightful homes, I *will not* let those parents down. I will protect them as my own." She held his stare. "I will not leave."

He hesitated, glancing about and running a hand over his sweaty neck. "Listen. I can't release these children. There is absolutely no way that can be done. But, in the past, we've had Red Cross officials stay here to support the detainees. Currently, the French Red Cross hut is empty. You can occupy it while the children are here, mademoiselle. That's the best I can offer you."

Rösli took a quick breath, her mind working fast. She'd discovered where the La Hille children were, she'd found her way here, and he wasn't going to make her leave.

Three problems solved. She nodded her agreement, hoisting the pack onto her back, feeling the burn where it had already chafed her armpits. She started toward the wire fencing, eager to get on the other side of it. As she followed the commander through a gate, the final, impossible problem loomed before her.

She needed to free her children before anyone could deport them.

≈≈≈≈

FOUR

ELLA

LE VERNET, FRANCE

LATE AUGUST 1942

*E*lla stood in the snaking line for supper, gripping her dented tin bowl with both hands, shuffling in the dust alongside the barracks. Her stomach roiled with hunger after only two days in Camp du Vernet. How much worse would it become?

Much worse, her mind whispered. She glanced around the desolate yard, at the line of women and children waiting for thin soup, at the endless barbed wire punctuated by watchtowers, and at the French guards who monitored them with cold eyes. Pain laced the hunger in her stomach. All of it, this entire orchestration, existed only to lock them away. But why? What threat were they to anyone? And what was next?

She'd heard the rumors that blew through the camp like wind, quiet and persistent. Already two new waves of people had poured in since the La Hille teenagers arrived, filling up the various blocks segregated by label and gender. *Spanish Partisans, Political Extremists, Jewish Men, Jewish Women and Children . . .* Rumor had it, when the camp filled up, the Jews would be deported, to make room for more.

Where would they be sent? *Poland*, the La Hille girls whispered, thinking of the fate that had befallen some of their own parents, a calamity communicated in notes sent through the Swiss Red Cross. Or worse: *camps in Germany.*

Ella trudged forward on weak legs, listening to the murmur of hungry people. The string around her neck, holding a cardboard number that everyone had to wear like an ugly necklace, itched. Ella's patch of cardboard read 368, as if this were her name. She wiped at her running nose. In the end, her parents had given her up for nothing. They'd sent her to Belgium after *Kristallnacht* for nothing; she had fled the German invasion in Belgium for nothing; she had survived in Vichy France *for nothing.* All of her trials, all of her heartbreak, all of her winding roads had led her right back to the Nazis. Ella closed her eyes to stave off tears, and Hanni rose in her mind, as if to remind her: Hanni, with her strong, impish spirit, might still survive. Was it fanciful to think so? If her sister made it through the war alive, Ella's journey would mean something, at least. She gripped her dented bowl, eyes closed, trying to picture Hanni safe at La Hille.

Instead, she saw her own hand, four years earlier, carrying another bowl, and she kept her eyes shut, trying to catch the memory. To hold it. The bowl landed on a plate with a clink, the tiny rosebuds painted along its rim glowing in the candlelight. The room smelled warm, of new potatoes and roast and simmering apples. In the parlor her father played the piano, his song dipping and rising through the flat like petals caught in a gust, falling and sailing. Hanni giggled somewhere. *Ella*, a voice called, and pain shot through her like an arrow. The scene shifted, dimming. She pinned her eyes tighter, trying to see the woman walking through the rooms of her memory. *Ella*, her mother's voice murmured again, *have you set the table?*

"Move up," a woman muttered behind her, elbowing her in the spine. Ella's eyes snapped open, and she stepped forward in line, wiping tears off her cheeks. Memories came like this lately, appearing in her thoughts and fading away like breath on a cold night.

A few minutes later she'd collected her soup, which really was just broth with a few sad chunks of cabbage and turnips floating in it, and walked toward her barracks to find her friends. The La Hille girls sat in a patch of shaded dirt, saying little, slurping soup hungrily and gazing at the civilian road flanking this part of the camp. If only they could float over all the barbed wire and land on that road, Ella thought. She glanced beyond the road to the train tracks, running parallel. Those tracks led nowhere she wanted to go.

Frau Schlesinger, La Hille's beloved, gentle cook, knelt alongside the other La Hille women, Elka Frank and her mother-in-law, Irene. The Franks whispered, their heads bent close, but Frau Schlesinger sat as if stunned. Her hair fell from its braid, and her eyes were red from weeping. She and her husband had both been arrested, but their little boy, Pauli, was still at the château. Ella folded her legs to sit by Frau Schlesinger. She placed a hand on the woman's shoulder, squeezing once, and Frau Schlesinger looked up with a weak smile.

"Be sure to eat something," Ella said, glancing at the woman's untouched soup.

Frau Schlesinger looked at the bowl in her lap. "I can't swallow, dear."

There was so much the older woman didn't need to say out loud for Ella to understand: she couldn't swallow because her throat was clamped tight with grief. Ella knew the feeling. And what point was there in swallowing if she would never see her little boy, Pauli, again? There was nothing Ella could say, so she simply leaned in and wrapped an arm around the woman's shoulders. The two of them tipped their foreheads together for a second before returning to their pitiful meal.

A young mother trudged by with a boy, perhaps five years old, clinging to her hand. Ella and Frau Schlesinger both stilled, watching the little boy keep up with his mother in his short pants and leather shoes, a cap shading his sunburned cheeks.

"At least Pauli isn't here with you," Ella whispered without thinking. She glanced at Frau Schlesinger, whose kind eyes widened in acknowledgment.

"Do you think we'll get better blankets wherever we're going?" Dela ventured, a frown darkening her pretty face. She, too, didn't need to elaborate. Here they'd been issued a single wool blanket, which was all the comfort available to soften their wooden bunks. Would it be the same in Poland or Germany, where it snowed heavily in the winter?

"Nobody's going to give us better blankets," Inge murmured. She tucked a chunk of short brown hair behind her ear, slurping her soup. "They don't care if we're cold."

Ella looked down, letting her mind drift while she swallowed the rest of the broth. She was tipping the bowl on end, seeking the very last drops, when she heard something. She lowered her bowl, holding perfectly still to listen. She looked around, but the girls surrounding her were talking quietly now. Frau Schlesinger had already gotten up to hide her dish in the barracks. There weren't enough bowls to go around.

Ella held her breath, listening again to the constant murmur of camp life. Had she imagined the voice? Was she losing her mind? She pushed herself up to stand, saying nothing lest everyone think she was addled. She cocked an ear while she walked, trying to filter through the many voices melding among the barracks.

There. She heard the voice again, or rather, a certain tone. Walking more quickly, she wove around a barrack until the words clarified in her listening ears.

". . . don't understand how you can call this a meal. There's no nutrition at all in those tureens! If you're serving this, I'd at least expect you to subsist on it, too."

It was Rösli. Could it really be Rösli? *No.* Here, at Camp du Vernet?

"And where exactly are my children? I've been here for nearly an hour and haven't seen even one of them . . ."

Ella rounded the barracks and there, striding through a gate in the wire fencing from the next block, was Rösli Näf. The Swiss Red Cross *directrice* stood alongside a guard, wearing her customary blue nursing dress with a high white collar, rumpled and dirty, minus the apron. Her cheeks were flushed red and her eyes wild as she entered the block, scanning the clusters of women and children. Her hair wisped in all directions, loosened from her bun and catching the light of the slanting sun like a messy halo.

Ella ran.

When she thumped into Rösli, hugging her as if she were a life raft in a deep sea, the *directrice*'s strong arms wrapped around her without hesitation. Sobs broke loose in Ella's clogged throat, and she was suddenly weak, overcome with shock and, though it was too faint yet to claim, hope.

"It's all right now," Rösli murmured in her ear, patting down Ella's hair as she calmed. "I'm here, and I'm not leaving. I'm not going anywhere."

That night, the La Hille girls lay awake on their hard bunks, whispering in groups of two and three. The barracks were more crowded every day. The buildings, hammered together with gapped boards and tar paper, had wooden bunks lining the walls that were meant to hold about sixty people. This one now housed close to eighty, based on Ella's count, which made her heart clench. The camp was clearly filling up. When would they empty it?

"Do you think Rösli will intervene before the next deportation?" Edith whispered, one bunk north of the one Ella and Dela shared.

"She said she'd try," Ella whispered back. "She promised she'd have more news tomorrow, and that she'd arrange a meeting for the La Hille kids to tell us what's happening."

"I hope the boys will be at the meeting, too," Inge said, shifting slightly next to Edith, surely thinking of Walter Strauss. Inge, with her dark curls and solemn expression, had taken up with a lighthearted, laughing boy. They'd walked the hills around La Hille all summer, hand in hand, and Ella had watched her friend and wondered what it was like to be in love. Would such a thing ever happen to her? She glanced at Inge's faraway expression in the dim light, answering her own question. No, of course she would never fall in love. It was too late for such things.

Ella shifted, stiff under her blanket, and Dela's breathing steadied beside her as she dropped off to sleep. At least she still had Dela by her side. Dela had a way of lightening even the darkest times, and it was a quality Ella had come to rely on. Like Ella, Dela loved to draw, and with some younger children they'd decorated the granary barn where they'd first lived in France, drawing pictures of cartoon animals directly on the walls. They'd been close ever since. Ella blinked at the single light bulb hanging in the center of the building, which remained on all night, faintly buzzing. Moths danced around it. That granary barn seemed so long ago now. In the bunk below theirs, a small child cried in his sleep and his mother murmured every so often, singing softly.

"Rösli will get us out of here," Edith whispered, clearly as far from sleep as Ella. Her glasses glinted in the thin light.

Ella nodded, looking back at the light bulb, her mouth dry.

Like a reflex, her mind organized what she saw into a composition, as though she could fossilize the moment. If this were a drawing, she'd use the moths, looping around the dusty light, as a focal point, with the bunks fading into darkness behind them. But she would also stray from reality, giving each person a visible face. *Include big and small shapes*, her old art teacher whispered in her mind. *Darkness and light, plain and busy, Ella . . .*

She closed her eyes, swallowing a sudden pulse of sorrow. She'd once been a girl who took art classes. Now she was one of countless souls trapped in this camp, trying to sleep in the glow of naked light bulbs, minds drifting to loved ones and dreams of home and wild notions of hope.

Was there reason to hope, now that Rösli had come for them? Rösli was only one person pushing back on this world of hate. She was a force in her own way, certainly. But what could just one person do?

*E*arly this morning, I was able to use a telephone here to call Monsieur Dubois," Rösli said the next day. She'd managed to collect all the La Hille teenagers, both girls and boys, into the camp's little Red Cross hut. Her hair was back in its tight bun, her elbow bandaged, her apron on. She looked like herself again. She glanced from person to person, as if assessing their condition, while she spoke. "Monsieur Dubois is currently in Vichy, meeting with officials to plead our case."

"Does he have a chance, Mademoiselle Näf?" Addi asked, pushing a shock of dark hair from his eyes. He'd asked the question on everyone's minds.

Rösli tightened her thin lips, clearly considering her words before speaking them. "I won't lie. He has a chance, but it's a slim one."

Isaak spoke from the back of the gathering, his voice deep in the small room. "Doesn't he have any leverage? As head of the Secours

Suisse in France, I mean?" His eyes bounced around the group, hinging on Ella for just a second longer than anyone else. She smothered a little jolt in her heart, scolding herself. This was no time to notice a boy.

Rösli hesitated, then gave an abbreviated nod. "Some, Isaak. The Swiss Red Cross shelters thousands of French children who either ended up in Switzerland through the course of the war, or are still in France, but under our care. Mind you, Monsieur Dubois doesn't have the authority to threaten those resources. There are several positions higher than his in Bern." Her pursed lips twitched, and she lowered her voice. "But when we spoke this morning, he promised to threaten them anyway. You all know Monsieur Dubois. He can be very convincing."

The group shifted a little, the faces around Ella tipping to the ground in the dim little hut, minds humming. Frau Schlesinger stood near the door, her weathered fingers pressed to her clamped lips. Her husband sat on a stool, his eyes focused on the slatted wall, lost in thought. There was so much unspoken subtext beneath Rösli's words: she and Monsieur Dubois would do everything in their power, clearly. But what power did they have?

As if she was thinking the same thing, Rösli sighed. She tipped forward and caught the various gazes that lifted to meet her stare. "The odds are against us. I think we all know that. But I promise . . ." She paused to clear her throat, inhaling. "I won't let them take you without a fight."

When they filed out of Rösli's hut a few minutes later, a line had formed outside. Ella's heart ached as she took in the many mothers with children strung in a loose queue outside Rösli's door. They bounced toddlers in dirty pajamas and whispered into the delicate ears of small girls and boys, gripping their hands tightly. They'd come for the medical supplies and minor services Rösli could provide with the bag she'd lugged here, but as Ella avoided the line, walking around the back side of the hut to head for her own barracks, she realized that they'd also queued for something else. A new voice filtered through the thin walls of the Red Cross hut.

"Please take my children, mademoiselle," a woman pleaded. "Can't they join your group? Please take them—"

"Madame," Rösli interrupted, and Ella paused, listening. "I would remove every single child from this wretched place if I could. But please understand—it's unlikely I can take anyone, even the children already under my authority." Quiet broke the exchange for a weighted moment, and Rösli cleared her throat on the other side of the slatted wall before continuing. "I'm so very sorry, madame. Now, I'll give your little girl something for that rash, *oui*? At least she'll feel better . . ."

Ella hurried away, stretching her stride until she was nearly running, her stomach curdling. She didn't want to hear more. She knew, suddenly, deep in her bones: Rösli couldn't prevent their deportation. And why had she let herself hope at all? Why had she let herself believe that a stubborn Swiss nurse could save anyone, when the whole world seemed to be against them? She shook her head as if she could shake the last of her hope away, letting it go like breath in the wind.

On their sixth morning at Camp du Vernet, the barracks door flung open at dawn, and a guard stood in its threshold, shouting.

"Pack your things," he hollered. "You're leaving today. Hurry, hurry! Tout de suite! Bread will be given out before you board the train."

By the time Ella's feet hit the barracks floor, the guard was gone. His announcement left eighty women and children stunned, thumping down from their bunks and milling about with tired, startled expressions. Ella wavered where she stood. Could this really be happening? They'd heard the rumors for six days now. They knew deportation was imminent, and still it was hard to believe.

Ella closed her eyes for a second. A memory appeared, a wisp of the dream she'd just awakened from. She saw a piano, with her fingers on the keys next to her father's, mirroring his strokes. *Good, Ella!* Her mother clapped in the background. Her silvery laugh wove into the duet, and Hanni, somewhere close, started to sing. Ella's fingers danced for another second, and then she opened her eyes and the dream evaporated. Her family was replaced with the dim room full of strangers, many clutching children, many weeping.

She exhaled, her breath shaky, staving off the urge to cry. Nothing in her childhood could have prepared her for this. She reached for her bag with trembling hands, shoving her few belongings inside, unable to say anything to her friends who did the same. It would only get worse. She knew it, somehow. This was just the beginning of the nightmare.

The barracks door opened again. Rösli hurried through it, her face strained and her hair in a messy bun. Ella lowered her bag and nudged Edith, whose glasses flashed as she glanced up. Without saying anything, Edith stared at Rösli threading through the crowd, and she began to silently weep at Ella's elbow. The news of Rösli's appearance spread instantly through whispers, and all the La Hille girls paused, clutching bags and nightgowns, staring toward the front of the crowd.

"She's coming to say goodbye," Frau Schlesinger guessed, a few bunks down. Her voice quavered. "I have to speak to her about Pauli."

Several girls fell into whispers, but Ella was unable to produce a single word. She watched Rösli pause her advance, offering her hand to an old woman who'd stumbled into a disheveled heap on the floor by her bunk. Rösli hoisted her up on her rickety legs. She straightened the woman's shirt where it had fallen open, fastening a row of buttons to cover the soft folds of a pale, wrinkled belly pinched by a waistband. For a moment they gripped hands, Rösli leaning close to say something in the woman's ear, and then she again made her way toward the La Hille girls. Rösli passed under the dim light bulb, a wildness in her face. Her eyes shone with unreleased tears.

"Girls," Rösli breathed when she arrived. She nodded to Frau Schlesinger and lowered her voice to a whisper. "You won't be going. Monsieur Dubois secured your release."

"Mine too?" Frau Schlesinger sputtered.

Rösli nodded. "Our whole group, including staff. Now, you must help the others."

Everything in Ella's soul froze. It was as if she were on the edge of a cliff, beginning to fall, and time suddenly stopped. She still hung in midair, heart beating violently, the cold expanse gripping her limbs.

"Are you sure?" Frau Schlesinger whispered back. "How can you be sure, Rösli?"

Several women paused near them, lowering their bags to eavesdrop, and Rösli glanced around and shook her head. "There's no time," she said. "I have to hurry across camp to speak with the boys." She detached from the La Hille huddle. "Help however you can, girls. Be brave," she whispered fiercely, then turned and hustled back through the milling crowd.

Shortly after Rösli disappeared, the door at the front of the barracks opened a third time. A stocky guard appeared, his face devoid of expression. "Everyone out into the yard for roll call!" he shouted. "*Maintenant!*"

It seemed that many of the women and children couldn't move. A young mother holding a small boy, no more than three, shrank back against a bunk near Ella, and Rösli's instructions reverberated in her mind. Ella forced her legs into motion.

"Can I carry your suitcase?" she said, and the mother's eyes swung to her, wide and blue. It seemed that Ella's words hadn't made their way through the young woman's shock, so she picked up the suitcase and wrapped her arm around the woman's narrow waist. "I'll walk out with you," she managed, and the mother met her stare again, nodding faintly, and they shuffled with the slow crowd funneling through the single door. Dela trudged ahead of Ella, her arm hooked through the thin elbow of the old woman who had fallen earlier. Under the light bulb, the tiny boy blinked at Ella from his mother's shoulder. He sucked on his thumb, gazing at her with startling blue eyes. Ella swallowed the lump of pain in her throat, inching forward. If only she could make this woman and her child disappear. She glanced over the gathered heads, jostling as they moved. If only they could all disappear, vanishing into some better world.

Outside, the three hundred people of their block lined up in formation, silent in the morning sun. Birds chirped from the branches of trees lining the entrance road, punctuating the quiet. Ella filed into her spot, her heart hammering, and glanced at the stricken faces surrounding her. Still, nobody made a sound. Somewhere in the distance, a dog barked.

The quiet didn't last. Soon a cluster of guards assembled at the front of the block, their caps moving beyond the gathered heads obscuring Ella's view. With no preamble, they began calling names over the loudspeakers. Women and children stepped forward, one by one, and walked through the gates of the section as the guards watched.

Time bled on. The sun rose overhead, the birds stopped singing to the morning, and the block emptied steadily around Ella. She stood ramrod straight, her pulse bounding. She barely dared to look left and right as people drifted away, causing gaps in the lines at first, and finally leaving no lines at all beyond those of the La Hille teenagers. Ella's stomach swam with nausea. Had Rösli really gained their freedom from this deportation? Or would their names be called any minute? She listened to names ring out over the loudspeakers. She watched people fill the entrance road, two long lines of women and men spilling out under the heavy *Camp du Vernet* sign, and her hands began to shake. She was desperate not to join them. *And yet.* Ella swallowed painfully. Was it right to watch these people leave? Was it right to be spared?

She didn't have time to think about it further. Down the road flanking her section, a sound grew. A low rumble, embroidered by groans and squeals of metal on metal, expanded in the morning air. Ella turned slightly to stare down the slice of road. A train was coming.

When the line of red cattle cars creaked to a stop across the street from the camp, the guards shouted at the people to move. As they obeyed the command, fanning out over the road toward the train cars, order fell apart. A man at the front broke away from his stream of men. He tried to run toward a woman with two children, their arms outstretched in the middle of the road. Within ten strides a guard caught the man. Ella gasped as a club raised over the crowd and fell on him, sparking screams from his wife and children.

But then they were obscured by more moving people, clutching their suitcases, many of them weeping. An old man collapsed by the fence, falling in a heap on the gravel. A teenager bent next to him for a moment, but a guard hurried over, kicking the teenager in the waist with the steel toe of his boot and shouting, gesturing toward the train. The teenager stumbled away, and the guard turned his boot on the elderly man. As the old prisoner struggled to stand, disoriented, the guard shoved him off in the direction of the train. Ella bent over, gasping, suppressing the urge to vomit.

The rest of the La Hille girls, all of whom still stood in the dirt outside the barracks, their baggage at their feet, watched with open mouths. Some turned away from the scene, burying faces in hands.

Others wept openly. Ella reached up to wipe her eyes before she realized that she was crying, too. Across the road, she spotted the young mother with the little boy. A sob raked through her soul as she watched the young woman turn, her hand on her child's back, staring around the moving crowd as if lost at sea. *Please keep walking.* Ella found the words in her mind. *Please don't let the guards see you. Keep walking.*

As she stared at the young mother pivoting, like a leaf in a current, a guard shouted, moving toward her, and Ella sensed someone else hustling from the periphery of the scene. Rösli strode out through the gates on her long legs, surpassing the guard, the skirt of her blue dress whipping in the breeze. She walked straight for the young mother, wrapping an arm around her back while the guard halted behind them. Rösli leaned close, speaking into the mother's ear as she walked her steadily to the waiting train and helped her step up. Then Rösli turned, her hands balled into fists, and hurried across the gravel to another elderly woman who'd stumbled to her knees. Ella stood as if rooted, unable to move over her wild heartbeat, and watched Rösli work amid the chaos, slowing the clubs of overeager guards.

Ella tried to swallow, and found that she couldn't. Because how could this be happening? And where were these people being sent? A camp like this one, only in a northern climate? Could the young mother and her boy, and all the elderly people and little children— could they survive at a camp like that until the war ended? Every filament of her soul burned. *Someone should do something.* The words pounded in her mind like a migraine. But what could anyone do? She watched as Rösli turned in the emptying street, her cheeks wet with tears.

When the doors of the cattle cars slammed shut, Rösli, alone with the guards now, reanimated. It was as if someone had shocked her into motion, for suddenly she hurried alongside the train, calling into the cars. After a few minutes of this, objects started to emerge through the slats. Hands gripping letters appeared, waiting for Rösli to hustle over and collect them. Ella imagined herself on the train, and she understood: if it were her, she'd yearn to send a letter to Hanni. Some people must have prepared for that. Hands shoved a few small packages through the slats, and they dropped to the gravel where Rösli could collect them. She went from car to car, fanning out the apron of her dress and filling it like a sack. The guards looked on. They seemed bemused watching Rösli, hands on their hips, their work done.

When her skirt was so full of letters and packages that her pale thighs showed below it, the train rumbled to life. Ella watched Rösli take several steps back, nearly to the road, as the wheels started to turn on the tracks.

"Long live Switzerland!" a man shouted from a cattle car, his voice booming over the groaning train. It was the last voice Ella heard from the deportees. Moments later the train slid away, hundreds of humans packed within, headed for an unknown fate.

Rösli swayed in the ensuing quiet. After a few seconds, she sank to the gravel, the packages and letters spilling out around her, and wept in the hot sun of waning summer.

Ella sank where she stood as well, falling into a heap of angles. She hugged her knees with her elbows and hid her face, sobs rising in her throat like vomit. She closed her eyes tight, trying to force darkness to obscure her thoughts, but the images she'd just witnessed remained. She'd never stop seeing them, she knew: the blue-eyed mother and her boy, the old man on the ground, the husband beaten for trying to embrace his family.

Ella would see them for the rest of her life.

꙳꙳

FIVE

RÖSLI

*R*ösli had to get her children out of France.

The thought gripped her as if it had her by the neck. She drummed her fingers on her knee, staring at flames popping in the hearth, half listening as her colleagues talked in a tight, firelit circle. It was many hours past bedtime, but none of them could sleep.

Twenty-four hours earlier, Rösli, her four staff members, and the exhausted teenagers had returned home from Camp du Vernet, traveling first by train and then several wagons volunteered by neighboring farms. They'd arrived at La Hille to the uproarious joy of the little children, who had made a sign and hung it over the gate to the courtyard that read *Bienvenue chez nous!* Some of *les Grands* had mustered smiles, hugging younger siblings and murmuring re- assurances as they trudged into the château's courtyard. Surrounded by ebullient *petits*, nobody spoke the truth: They had escaped depor- tation, yes, but nothing would ever be the same. This place, sur- rounded by its familiar, wild hills, would never feel safe again.

"What if we set up a camp in the forest?" Flora Schlesinger said now, her eyes darting between everyone's faces. For an hour, they'd been discussing what they could do if the police returned, but nobody had a real plan. Flora kept suggesting the forest, recycling the idea as if eventually it might solve their looming problem. First, she'd spoken of an escape route into the woods, stubbornly overlooking their previous experience of the encircled château at night. Now she'd progressed to the notion of moving into the forest entirely, and Rösli felt a headache starting in her temples.

Ernst shook his head yet again, his gaze on the parquet floor, hands knitted tightly between his knees. "Flora, darling. A camp could work for a month, I suppose, but what would we do during the winter? We can't live in the woods when it freezes. And don't you think a troupe of teenagers in the forest would be easily tracked down?"

"Perhaps not, if we went far enough—"

"I still don't know why you're all certain that the gendarmes will return," Herr Lyrer interrupted. He rubbed at the elbow of his tweed jacket absently, brows tipped in worry. Eugen Lyrer was La Hille's beloved Swiss teacher, a small man who spoke softly and led *les Grands* in endless reading and philosophical discussions. It was difficult to be angry with this gentle, absentminded teacher, but with his words Rösli's frustration sharpened. Like Flora, Eugen kept recycling the same talking points. It was as if they were all mice in a maze, bumping up against dead ends over and over, desperate for a false wall.

Eugen cleared his throat, fingering his mustache, forging on. "Didn't Maurice convince Vichy officials that Switzerland won't stand for it? That if they take our children and staff, we'll remove our services from the countless French children we're supporting—"

"Eugen." Rösli couldn't hear it again. "Maurice *bent the truth*, amid confusion, to persuade some Vichy official to release our group. The fact that it worked is nothing less than a miracle. Maurice can be convincing, but obviously he doesn't have the authority to threaten Vichy France with anything. Do you really think the Swiss Red Cross will remove services from thousands of French children just to save our colony?"

"Well, they should use it as a bargaining chip." Eugen frowned deeply, his idealism battling with reality. "Why wouldn't the Swiss Red Cross protect *every* child under their care? Would they really abandon our kids after all this time?"

Rösli felt her lips purse. "I hope not. But if the Germans pressure Vichy officials to round up Jews again, and they realize that we actually have no recourse against them, the gendarmes will come back. The Swiss Red Cross will then choose between protecting our Jewish refugee children, and offending German and Vichy officials. I can't be sure of the outcome." Nobody could be sure of anything anymore. Rösli tried to shave the edge off her voice. "As long as we're on French soil, our children are in danger. What we saw at that camp, Eugen . . . it didn't leave room for optimism."

Ernst and Flora Schlesinger nodded, expressions grave, and Eugen Lyrer sighed.

For a long time, nobody spoke, and the shadows seemed to deepen around them. Somewhere outside the dark window, an owl called. Defeated, Rösli began to contemplate her lonely bed, waiting upstairs.

Eugen broke the quiet. "What about a hiding place?"

They all looked to him, and Rösli's fatigue deepened. What hiding place could be good enough to outwit the police? Yet Eugen was shaking his head as though struck, his eyes flickering like sparks in the grate.

"I don't know why I didn't think of it before . . . There's an attic on the other side of my room. Have you seen it? I only looked inside once, and then promptly pushed a bureau over the door because it's full of mouse droppings, and frankly, it stinks. But it's quite a big space, and you'd never guess it exists from the outside." His knee began to bounce under his palm. "I think it could work. We could transform it into a hiding place—I'm sure of it."

Rösli frowned, but her thoughts gained pace. "It wouldn't be a long-term solution . . ."

"Yet better than no solution at all," Ernst supplied, his expression loosening for the first time all night. "I had no idea there was an attic up there. Near the chapel, perhaps? I can't even picture where it might be. You may be the only one that knows about it, Eugen, and that's something."

Rösli held her breath, thinking, and met Flora's gaze. How had she not known about a secret attic in La Hille? Well, she conceded, the building was enormous—it was impossible to know every inch of it. Flora shrugged, indicating that she knew nothing of it, either. Could a hiding place really outwit the police? Certainly, in a structure as large as this one, searching just the visible rooms would be an overwhelming task. Could a hiding place buy them time to create a long-term plan for the children?

"What about *les Petits*?" Rösli said after a moment, thinking out loud. "If we create a hiding place, and the little ones find out where it is, they could give it away inadvertently."

Eugen shook his head. "My room is on the other side of the building from their dormitories. They'll need to know there is a hiding spot, of course, but if they don't know where . . ."

Flora, frowning with contemplation, spoke quietly. "*Les Petits* don't trust anyone in a uniform. We'll teach them to say that the teenagers went into the woods, and they won't waver from it." She sighed. "I pray *les Petits* won't ever need a hiding spot themselves. How can we be sure the police won't come for children *under* age sixteen? We saw plenty of little ones deported from Vernet."

"You're right. We can't be sure of anything." Rösli met her stare, aware that Flora was thinking of her own little boy. "However,

Maurice said that anyone under age sixteen is not yet officially targeted. The children at Camp du Vernet were swept up with their parents, unfortunately. Had they been alone, they may have been overlooked during the sweep."

"So, for now, we'll hide *les Grands*." Ernst nodded and leaned forward, blinking through his exhaustion. "Let's sleep on it and have a look at the room in the morning, shall we?" He patted Eugen's tweed shoulder, then shuffled up to stand. "Well done, Eugen—a hiding place is a start, which is more than we had two weeks ago."

Two days later, Rösli climbed the stairs to visit the men and teenagers at work. She leaned in the doorjamb for a moment, watching them hammer and saw in Eugen Lyrer's little room. They worked as if their lives depended on it, which, really, they did. Yet the project was coming along well. Eugen's room had wood paneling on all sides, placed there by some former inhabitant, and the men and boys had stripped the panels from one wall. They maneuvered around the bed and bureau that had been shoved into the center of the room, using the mattress to lay out new panels, measuring twice and cutting once. The air smelled of sawdust and something sharper: onion. Eugen theorized that the attic had once been used to store onions, pulled from the fields by peasants and hung from the rafters over the winter. The odor was enough to convince Rösli; she'd guess that the space had housed onions for centuries.

Now, it would conceal something infinitely more precious.

"Looks like construction is going well?" she called from the doorjamb, and the saws and hammers paused. The Spanish carpenter, Señor Salvide, nodded at Rösli but kept measuring a length of the wall, muttering under his breath and making notes with a worn-down pencil. Like most Spanish refugees, Señor Salvide had faced internment himself in France, and was only safe now as an employee of the Swiss Red Cross. He worked with the intensity of someone who understood, too well, the stakes involved in getting this right.

Eugen, with his faded tweed suits and scholar's hands, had probably never before held a hammer. Rösli suppressed a chuckle as he grinned, cheerfully out of his element. "You'd never guess there used to be a door there, would you?" He glanced around, delighted by the transformation of his bedroom.

"Once we're done, it'll look just like a wall," Ernst Schlesinger chimed in. "Come and see, Rösli. We're concealing the door that leads into the attic with paneling identical to all the other walls. And here." He pointed to a gap in what otherwise looked like a solid wall. It was where the door to the attic had been, but now the opening was only two feet tall and wide—just big enough for a person to shimmy through. "Here's where our secret door will be. These panels will slide behind the wall, creating a tiny, hidden entrance. See how the panels slide back and forth? Then we'll push the bureau over it, for good measure."

Rösli got down on her hands and knees to gaze through this little door. Beyond it, the hidden attic room waited for its inhabitants, the light from its single, high window shining over the rafters to the floor. She stood, brushing sawdust from her knees while the teenagers and men stared at her expectantly.

"Excellent." She smiled at the boys. Isaak, Addi, and Walter Strauss leaned against the bed, their faces flushed from work and smudged in sawdust. "Boys, thank you for helping. What you've done here is simply ingenious. Far better than I could have hoped for."

"I've never built anything this complicated," Isaak ventured, clearly proud.

"Me neither," Addi said, and Walter flashed his ready grin as he lifted a plank of wood to his shoulder.

"I can't wait to show the others," Walter said under his plank. "It's good, *ja*? Except for the smell."

"Ah, just pretend Frau Schlesinger's cooking up some lovely onion stew." Eugen glanced up from his saw, hair in his eyes, grinning. "Shall we call it the onion room?"

Isaak cocked his head. "No—the *Zwiebelkeller*." He clapped the sawdust from his hands. "My grandparents had one when I was a kid."

Rösli nodded. *The onion cellar.* It was perfect—a name that would confuse anyone searching for it.

Addi frowned as if realizing something. He knelt, birdlike, and scratched out an equation in the sawdust while eyeing an unpatched section of paneling, dark eyes scrutinizing the gap. Rösli pinched back a smile. Addi, slender and serious, was a budding mathematician, and the accuracy of their work was likely his contribution.

The group resumed sawing and hammering, and something loosened in Rösli's chest. It was good to see the boys smiling again. Since their homecoming, La Hille's teenagers had been understandably despondent. They drifted around the château, performing the usual chores and reading their ever-present books, but they kept their ears cocked, listening. Boys and girls no longer paired off for walks in the hills. Instead, they sat in nooks around the building, talking quietly and freezing at noises. The ball games in the fields, the laughter, the singing—their youthful impulses had departed with those red cattle cars.

And it wasn't just *les Grands* who had changed; even *les Petits* were nervous now. Little Hanni had spent every day since her sister's return perched in a tree overlooking the road, watching for intruders. They couldn't compel her to descend even for school, which the youngest children attended in the village. In the evening they had to coax her down to eat and sleep, lest she nod off and fall from the tree like a sparrow from its nest. The child had given Rösli the idea to post lookouts, who could sound a warning. She'd chosen them from among *les Moyens*, the middle boys, and so now they watched for police instead of chopping wood. This hiding place would give everyone some relief, Rösli knew.

But it wasn't enough.

Addi stood from his math equation, and Rösli cleared her throat to speak over the hammering. She gestured to the men, sorry to interrupt them further. "Herr Lyrer, Señor Salvide, Herr Schlesinger—a word with you three?" It was time to shake herself from her thoughts and get moving. "Let's step outside for a moment."

When the men emerged in the hallway, leaving drifts of sawdust in their wake, Rösli closed the door behind them. The noise from within dimmed.

"I need to let you know that I'm leaving for a week or so," Rösli began. "I just told your wife, Ernst. Are you all comfortable managing the château while I'm gone?"

Eugen glanced at the other men before speaking. "Certainly," he said, but his brows tented in obvious worry. It worried Rösli, too. After what had happened, abandoning the château for even a few days felt risky. She understood, more than ever, how the colony depended on her. Of course, that was why she had to take this trip.

She glanced at the closed door. "I'd like all the kids over age fifteen to sleep in this room, the *Zwiebelkeller*, as soon as it's ready. Señor Salvide, do you think it will be finished tomorrow?"

The carpenter glanced up, as if calculating, and nodded once. "Yes. If we work all day."

"We will," Ernst Schlesinger agreed. "We'll make sure the kids are in there by tomorrow, Rösli. And I thought we'd organize a system of alarms and secret knocks in case we have to hide from police. There needs to be an all-clear knock, and something to signal quiet. I'll work on it with the kids tonight." Ernst rubbed at his scruffy jaw with calloused hands, pensive. "It must be an important errand, to pull you away."

She hesitated, reluctant to stoke even the adults' hope prematurely. "Well, first I'm going to Foix to speak with Madame Authié."

Eugen frowned. "The secretary at the *préfecture?*"

Rösli matched his frown. Madame Authié, a stern, humorless woman, worked among the very officials who tracked her children on lists. But Rösli had heard from a farmer that on the day of the raid, Madame Authié had wept on her walk home. The thought of that stern woman weeping had stuck with Rösli, like a pin. Perhaps she could be made into an ally. She was merely a secretary, but she had access to information at the *préfecture*, and information was something Rösli needed.

"Who knows if she'll soften to us, Herr Lyrer, but I'm going to try. If Madame Authié is unhappy about collaborating with the authorities, perhaps she'll also collaborate with me. Like a spy, I suppose."

"But what could she do?" Ernst asked, brows furrowed.

Rösli shrugged, unsure herself. "Maybe give us warning if something's afoot? Or, perhaps she'd let me see exactly who is on the lists as things change."

Downstairs someone started to play the old piano hunkered in the corner of the dining room. The song grew, echoing up the stairs, achingly beautiful. It could only be Walter Kamlet, their resident musician, at the keys.

"There's more," Rösli said after a moment, pulling herself from the lonely song wafting down the hall. "Don't tell the children, in case I'm turned down, but I'm also going to Bern. I intend to petition the Red Cross headquarters to move the entire colony to Switzerland."

"You think they'll consider it?" Eugen asked, his gaze flicking between Rösli, Ernst, and Señor Salvide. It wasn't hard to guess what they were thinking: it was the longest of long shots. Switzerland's record of accepting Jewish refugees wasn't good. Even before the war, they'd shut them out. Yet, Rösli had to try.

"I'll *insist* that they consider it, Eugen." Her whisper was fierce. Hope, absurd as it was, constricted in her chest. "If they're the humanitarians they claim to be, they will find a way to get our children out of France."

SIX

~~~~~~

ELLA

CHÂTEAU DE LA HILLE, SOUTHERN FRANCE
SEPTEMBER 1942

*H*anni was up in a tree again.

Ella stood with a dozen of *les Grands* in the tall grass outside of the courtyard, reciting the V'shamru under a canopy of yellowing leaves. Their voices joined like hands, lifting the prayers of their childhood up into the dappled sunlight. Ella mouthed the words, less sure of them than her more traditional friends; she'd belonged to a liberal congregation in Cologne, though her mother, raised Orthodox, had tried to teach her the Hebrew prayers of her own youth. Ella sought the peace that sometimes found her when they gathered this way, but today her mind strayed to her sister, down the road and high in the branches of a tree. She withheld a sigh, trying instead to focus on the rhythm of their words blending with the breeze.

> *V'shamru v'nei Yisrael*
> *et HaShabbat,*
> *laasot et HaShabbat l'dorotam*
> *b'rit olam . . .*

It was Ruth's idea to hold Shabbat services. Every week over the summer a handful of teenagers had gathered and prayed, remembering synagogues and temples where they'd once stood among their families and communities. In upcoming weeks, it would be Rosh Hashanah and Yom Kippur, and again Ella would pass them without her family, without her traditions, far from where she was meant to be. Regret sharpened in her chest as her lips moved, finishing the prayer. She wanted to open her eyes and find herself back where she belonged, in the temple of her childhood, standing alongside her mother. She hadn't realized then that she had everything.

And she hadn't realized that everything could be taken.

Isaak caught her eye across the circle as the makeshift Shabbat service ended. She nodded to him but turned away, heading down the road, quelling the pain gripping her heart. It had been there, like a tightening fist, since they'd returned from Camp du Vernet.

"Come on down," Ella called as she reached the tree, shading her eyes to see her sister against the bright September sky. Hanni looked so pretty up there, surrounded by leaves and fragments of blue, her little legs swinging in the bell of her dress. Her wooden clogs sat in the grass, and Ella picked them up. Hanni in a tree could inspire an impressionist painting, the bold color and sweeping brushstrokes conveying the freedom of childhood.

But this childhood wasn't free.

"I'm not coming down." Hanni gripped the trunk with one hand and scratched at her knee with the other. "I'm *watching*."

"You don't need to." Ella circled the trunk, gazing up at her sister from a different angle. "Remember? The boys are already watching from the tower. And it will be time to eat, soon."

"But the boys can't see this far down the road. It'll be too late if someone comes."

Ella sighed again. She swung the clogs, and they knocked gently together. Would she have ever imagined, in her old life, that she would one day wear wooden shoes? That her sister would spend her days in a tree, watching for police? "Hanni, I want you to come down." She tried to sharpen her tone. "And next week you're going back to school in the village."

"I hate school."

"Don't you realize how lucky you are to go to regular school?" Ella frowned up at her sister. She would give anything to walk down to the village school each day, yet only the youngest nineteen children were invited to go. The rest stayed behind at the château, where their beloved, sometimes befuddled Herr Lyrer plunged them into the world of literature and thought. She adored Herr Lyrer, who read to them each day in his resonant voice and distributed books he'd lugged in a suitcase from Switzerland. But she'd also love to switch places with Hanni, even for just a day, attending a regular school as if she were a regular kid, as if everything in the world were normal.

"How's our little lookout?"

Ella jumped at the voice. Hanni, too, swung her head around to look, narrowing her brown eyes as she spied Isaak sauntering toward them, his clogs kicking up dust. He walked with his hands in his pockets, shoulders slightly hunched, and a quizzical grin on his face.

"She won't come down," Ella offered, shrugging as he neared. Why had Isaak followed her? Ever since she'd taken his hand the day of the raid, gripping his fingers like a lifeline, he'd spoken with her more than before. And lately, when she spotted his head of black hair at mealtimes, taller than all the rest, or caught his gray eyes seeking her out, her heart skipped up like a breeze. But it was silly to entertain adolescent nudges when the world was crumbling. Ella wasn't a silly person.

Isaak joined her at the foot of the tree, gazing up as Hanni gazed down, scrunching her freckled nose like something smelled bad.

Please be polite, Ella found herself thinking, wishing she could telegraph the message right to her sister's mind. Hanni's spirit moved like the wind, unpredictable and sometimes wild. She'd always been that way, but her personality seemed a bit bigger every year, as if her little body couldn't contain the volume of her soul.

"Maybe she has the right idea," Isaak said, smiling up at the dirty feet hanging high over their heads.

"I do!" Hanni called down. "Those lookouts won't see someone coming quick enough. But I will. And I'll run up the hill to tell everyone next time the police try to catch you."

"I appreciate that."

Isaak squinted up, grinning with good nature, and Hanni cocked her head and scowled. All week, Ella and the adults had been trying to coax her out of trees; Hanni clearly didn't expect anyone to approve of her activities. She looked away, breaking a dead stick off a tree branch and dropping it without explanation. Isaak dodged it and Ella fought dual urges to giggle and to scold her sister.

"You're welcome!" Hanni called, voicing it like a decision. She tucked a chunk of messy hair behind her ear and peered down the access road.

Ella crossed her arms over her chest. "You shouldn't encourage her," she whispered, abruptly aware of her own cropped, messy hair.

Isaak cocked his head in reply, tipping his chin in the direction he started to walk. He slung his hands in his pockets, strolling under the scatter of trees where the field met forest, and Ella hesitated. She glanced up at Hanni, who was now using a stick to carve something in the tree bark, seemingly absorbed in her new task. So Ella hurried after Isaak, combing her fingers through her hair before falling in at his side.

"Why did you follow me down here?" she asked, breathless.

He shrugged, giving her a sidelong glance. "What if I just felt like talking to you?"

Heat seeped into Ella's cheeks, and she looked away. Was he really seeking her out, like some of the other girls and boys had done with each other over the past year? Her friends had whispered about boys every night, comparing their ever-evolving crushes and giggling long after the lights went out. Ella had participated half-heartedly since they came to La Hille, but such girlishness always felt out of place. Courtship and romance seemed like something for life before, when the world offered a future.

And now here she was, walking with a boy, her stomach hollow with nerves.

"Your sister's something else," Isaak ventured, glancing back toward the tree in their wake.

Ella smiled despite herself. "She's stubborn and strong, yes. Nothing like me."

"I beg to differ."

She looked up, meeting his gray eyes, surprised. "Really? Even my mother used to say that we were each other's opposite. Hanni has always been noisy and confident, even a little headstrong." *A lot headstrong*, she thought. "My parents used to say I was quiet and gentle, always. Even when I was little." She shrugged.

"That doesn't mean you're not strong." He gazed down at her as he walked, shortening his long stride to match hers. "I see you holding people up, Ella. Sometimes I look at you, thinking while everyone else is talking, and I wonder what you're thinking about."

He wondered what she was thinking about? She pursed her lips to smother a smile.

Isaak looked away and whistled a scrap of some song, reaching up to bat at the leaves of an overhanging tree. A cascade of yellow fluttered down around them. "I also came down to ask you a question," he said after the leaves had twirled to the ground. "When's your birthday? Winter sometime, right?"

She nodded, cocking her head. "Why do you want to know?"

"I turn eighteen in a few weeks." He sighed, his grin falling, and slung his hands in his pockets again. "The Red Cross can't protect us past eighteen, you know."

Ella's joy dissipated, replaced by ready nerves. "Past sixteen, if we're to learn from Camp du Vernet."

He nodded. "I think we need a plan."

"What kind of plan could we possibly come up with?" She tried to keep the bitterness from her voice, but it was there like salt in the sea. She'd heard kids whispering about grand escapes over guarded, mountainous borders. Such ideas seemed ludicrous. Most of them were city kids, raised far from glacial peaks and wilderness—how did they imagine they could cross the Pyrénées?

His hand fell to her elbow, tightening slightly as he turned her to face him. His expression was earnest, dark brows raised. "We have to leave the château, Ella. If we stay, it's only a matter of time before the police return for us, and nobody will be able to intervene next time. I've been talking with some of the boys. We could go live in the woods, where the police would never think to look—"

"In the winter?"

"We'd make a shelter. We could take turns visiting La Hille every week, to bring back food and supplies—"

"Don't be ridiculous." Ella cringed as he straightened, his brows falling over his eyes, but he held her gaze. She forced herself not to look away, even though grief and frustration welled in her chest, even though she wished she could fish back her harsh words. "It will be cold, Isaak. And wet, and it wouldn't take long for word to get around that a bunch of teenagers were living in the woods. Where would we hide if they came for us?"

He continued to hold her stare, his face hardening with thought.

"What other choice do we have?" he asked finally. He pivoted, crossing his arms over his broad chest and gazing up at the château, half-shaded now as the sun sank past a stand of trees. "What if they discover the *Zwiebelkeller*? I feel like we're trapped here, just waiting for them to come and get us . . ."

Ella slipped a hand into the crook of his elbow, subduing a wave of surprise at her own boldness. But the words that fell from her lips weren't those of a young girl talking to a boy anymore. She heard herself, and her heart dipped. She sounded so old already, so joyless.

"We are just waiting for them. And there's nothing we can do about it but hope there's time to hide when they come."

For a long moment, neither of them said anything. When Isaak found his voice, he chuckled sadly. "I keep thinking about what I imagined I'd be doing when I turned eighteen. You know? When I was a kid, your sister's age, I used to dream about growing up. Who I'd be, what I'd do. I definitely never imagined myself hiding in an old castle in France, fearing for my life."

Ella looked up, meeting his eyes. They were the color of an October storm. "What did you want to be?"

"A teacher." He grinned. "What about you?"

Ella gazed out at the spread of field before them, its long grasses silvering in the lowering sun, the birds diving and rising, the fall of shadow and light. She couldn't smile when she said the words.

"I wanted to be an artist."

For a moment neither of them spoke, and Ella blinked as tears beaded on her eyelashes. Darn it, she didn't want to cry. She reached up to wipe at her cheeks just as Isaak glanced down.

"Hey now." He turned her gently, using his thumb to clumsily wipe her tears away. "You're already an artist. Everyone talks about your drawings, how good they are—"

"Please don't," she interrupted, the words coming without thought. She looked into his eyes, shaking her head and trying to understand why she didn't want his reassurance. "I've lost my dreams, Isaak," was all she could think to say.

He held her stare, nodding as if he understood, his face grave. She could love this face, if given the chance. She could love the kindness in his eyes, the way a smile always threatened the corners of his lips, the way he seemed to notice small, unspoken things. But what was the point of falling in love? If she loved him, she'd certainly lose him, too.

"Nothing is as it should be," he said finally. His hands came up to grip her shoulders, as though he wanted to be sure he had her attention. "But we have to fight for some kind of life, Ella."

She nodded, hesitant. She would fight for Hanni. She'd decided that long ago, when her sister was four and they'd held hands on their very first escape, on a train away from their parents, both of them wide-eyed and Hanni, so tiny, stone silent with grief and terror. Ella had made a promise to her parents then, whispering it until her breath fogged the train's window, imagining her words seeping through the glass and sailing on the wind back to their bereft mother and father, moored in the station. She would protect Hanni as long as she could.

But hope for anything more was dangerous. Because the second hope swam in, the world's hatred crashed down like a wave and washed it all away.

𝓔lla and Isaak were walking back up to the château, their tears dry and stomachs rumbling, when Hanni started to scream.

"Run!" she shrieked, and Ella spun around to see her sister's tiny figure leaping from the lowest branch of the tree. "They're coming! They're coming!" she screamed, sprinting barefoot up the hill toward the château, unaware of Ella still down in the field.

Isaak grabbed Ella's hand and they ran, clogs thumping. The long grass whipped her bare legs as she stretched her stride, stretched her lungs, and the two raced toward the watchtower of the château like sprinters to a finish line. But when they reached the courtyard, they didn't stop. Isaak dropped Ella's hand and they hurried up the stairs, taking them two at a time, joining the stream of other teenagers flowing up to the *Zwiebelkeller* as the boys in the tower echoed Hanni's warning. They filed into Herr Lyrer's bedroom, and the teacher was already there, holding the sliding door open while kids dropped onto their stomachs and shimmied into the secret room. The Schlesingers and Franks were there, too, waiting their turn, wringing their hands while the youngest went first.

Ella watched Isaak shuffle through the tiny door, his broad shoulders and long legs disappearing quickly. Her heart beat so powerfully that it almost hurt as she dropped to her stomach, diving through like a person swimming underwater. She thought of Hanni as she emerged in the dim room, inhaling the tang of ancient onions. Hanni had been right. Ella shook her head a little as she rose, wrapping her arms around her chest as if she could squeeze out the shiver that overtook her body. Hanni had heard the engines first. Ella spun around, glancing at the milling teenagers, stunned quiet. Thanks to her sister, everyone seemed to be inside. The door slid shut behind the Schlesingers, and Ella walked on wavering legs to her blankets spread where she'd left them that morning. She dropped to the floor, listening hard. Nobody spoke, lest they be heard outside this room. Silence was safest.

The girls huddled on their bedding on one side of the room, and the boys spread across blankets on the other side. Several kids tried to distract themselves, reading or writing in the gray, dusty light, but their stares froze and they never turned the pages. Ella fingered her sketch pad, too shaky to draw. Were police in the château? Why had they come, so soon after *les Grands* had returned?

Were they searching rooms, right now? Or would they do as everyone hoped and assume *les Grands* had fled to the woods? There were no answers to her circling questions.

Dela reached from her blankets to squeeze Ella's cold fingers, and the girls nodded at each other as if they shared thoughts. Dela was folded on her blanket as tight as a package, knees to her chest and her thick-lashed eyes wide with fear. Ella squeezed her fingers back.

She'd first met Dela and the other girls in Belgium. They'd lived together in a home for refugees, their initial landing place after leaving their parents. Ella had been content there, just fourteen and still optimistic, but one morning they'd woken to the thunder of bombs shattering the sky beyond Brussels. When she'd joined the other girls at the window, Ella had seen parachutes drifting in the distance, like blossoms on the wind. Dela, tears on her cheeks, had been the first to speak. "The Germans have come. We'll have to run."

Hinges squeaked somewhere outside the *Zwiebelkeller*, chasing Ella's memories away. She stiffened, listening, and Dela's hand found hers again. Voices, indistinct, reverberated on the other side of the paneled wall. Boots creaked floorboards. Dela's fingers squeezed, but nothing else in the room moved—even the air seemed to still. Everyone sat, frozen, listening to gendarmes inspecting the next room. Shuffling, more voices. An indistinct thud. Ella became light-headed with fear. Would they find the tiny door? She tipped her head to her knees, still gripping Dela's hand, and tried to breathe.

Hinges squealed again, and the boots retreated. The voices faded, traveling down the hall, and still nobody moved. Every part of Ella's body seemed to shake minutely, like a leaf in the wind.

It wasn't until the light faded from the single high window that Ella could breathe again. Hours had passed, and still they waited, listening. Kids shifted gingerly, lying down on blankets spread across wide floorboards, staring at the rafters. Scurrying sounds started overhead, as they did every night. Mice, or rats. Or, could it be bats, trapped inside, unable to fly out into the darkening sky? Dela settled with her back to Ella, curled tight, and Edith stared straight up on Ella's other side, her eyes wide behind her glasses.

Isaak, across the room, caught Ella's eye in the fading light. He nodded once, as if to reassure her. *They're gone.* For an instant she imagined what it would be like to curl up in his strong arms, to sink against his rib cage and close her eyes while his chest rose and fell against her back. She pressed the thought away, holding her breath, for the hundredth time, to listen. Were police still in the building? Were they outside, waiting for someone to slip up and sneak out of hiding? Whatever the reason, the all-clear knock they hoped for didn't come.

When stars glittered beyond the window, Ella lay back as well. She stared through the glass, ignoring her cramping stomach, still waiting for the knock that would set them free. She closed her eyes, imagining stars over the château, constellations spreading as if some god had flung them there.

Some god. She rolled onto her side, chewing her fingernails. Why had she thought that? Wasn't it simply God who had flung the stars? The God she'd believed in for as long as she could remember? Her parents weren't strict in their faith, but Ella couldn't remember a time when God was far from her thoughts. She'd sought Him, just hours ago, during the makeshift Shabbat services in the grass. He'd always hovered over her life, as present as the stars.

But stars were distant. Ella swallowed the ache rising in her throat.

Her eyes were closing when the first knock came. A series of preplanned raps sounded on the wall, and the room exhaled collectively. *All clear.* Yet a second, double knock communicated another message: *Stay quiet.* Just in case, Ella knew. Their lookouts were probably worried that police hid in the dark forest, undetect-able, watching. They would wait until morning to make sure it was safe again. She rolled onto her back, staring at the wash of sky outside the high window.

The stars, winking through the glass, seemed cold as ice.

❧

SEVEN

RÖSLI

BERN, SWITZERLAND

SEPTEMBER 1942

"Out of the question."

Rösli stood before the leadership of the Red Cross in their Bern headquarters. She knit her hands against the waist of her dress, tightening her knuckles as if she could funnel all emotion into her fingers and thus keep her voice even, her words measured. Three men in suits stared up at her from their seats behind a large, gleaming table. These were top officials of the Swiss Red Cross, men who could make decisions for countless children in danger.

Rösli cleared her throat to find her voice. "I think you must not understand how perilous the situation has become for our children. The only way to assure their safety is to move them all to Switzerland."

"We understand the situation well," a short man interrupted, smoothing his necktie over his stomach. "And we've already been petitioned by Maurice and Eléonore Dubois to move the children. We said no to them, too, Mademoiselle Näf. The issue has been decided."

"But all the children over age sixteen are in serious danger, sir. And we can't be certain that the little ones will remain safe. We saw how quickly their status can change in France—"

"We succeeded in rescuing your children from Camp du Vernet, did we not?" An angular man wearing thick glasses spoke through tight lips. "How can you have lost faith in our ability to protect refugees on French soil?"

She pushed down a flare of frustration, for she had spoken to Maurice Dubois before traveling here. He'd told her again how he secured the release of the La Hille group, mostly through luck; it wasn't these men who had intervened in Vichy.

"I beg your pardon, but I have absolutely lost faith in your ability to protect my children." Rösli propelled her words with contained force. "You cannot protect anyone on French soil anymore. Just two weeks ago, I saw women, children, and elderly people loaded onto trains at the behest of the Germans. The horrifying behavior of the French gendarmes gave me no confidence concerning the fate of those they deported. Our children nearly disappeared on those trains as well. And many of them will be eighteen soon, at which point we have no authority to protect them. The Vichy government knows when their birthdays are, and they'll surely come—"

"We will not interfere with the Vichy government, mademoiselle."

The man who spoke was Colonel Remund, chief of the Secours Suisse branch of the Red Cross. He'd sauntered across the hall to this meeting with a bored glaze in his eyes, as if Rösli's presence was an aggravation. He sighed now, looking her up and down as he continued. "Swiss neutrality demands that we refrain from interference or protest, Mademoiselle Näf, and that pertains to every leadership position, including yours. If we depart from neutrality, can we expect the French and German authorities to allow us to care for all the *other* children under our stewardship?" He flicked cold eyes from Rösli to his colleagues. "Risking neutrality means risking our entire operation in France. Furthermore, you must understand that we cannot open our borders to a flood of refugees. We already have more displaced people living in Switzerland than we're equipped to handle. As Federal Councilor Eduard von Steiger says, the lifeboat is full, mademoiselle. It's why the borders are closed."

"Children are in peril, and you're telling me the lifeboat is full?" Rösli no longer managed to keep the anger from her voice. "Colonel, the Nazi regime has no regard for human life, especially if the human in question is Jewish. I've seen it with my own eyes. And the Vichy government has proven itself to be just as dangerous. They're hunting *people*. You haven't seen the police in the streets with *your* eyes, updating their infernal lists, seeking tips and bursting into homes, flushing out parks and forests as if refugees were criminals . . . I guarantee it's worse than you think. We're discussing the fate of *children*, sir."

"We're discussing far more than that," the angular man spat, narrowing his eyes at Rösli's tone. "We're discussing whether it's wise to offend the Nazi regime, Mademoiselle Näf. Is it wise to criticize the foreign nation on whose soil you currently live and work? The political situation is delicate. Do not minimize our commitment to neutrality, which has kept us out of this war. We will not actively oppose, criticize, or thwart the legal actions of sovereign nations."

"Legal actions?" Rösli shook her head, stunned.

"Yes. Legal actions." Colonel Remund raised his voice. "The French and Germans are acting in accordance with their own laws—"

"Laws that exist to persecute people? Colonel Remund, surely you must see that these laws run counter to obvious moral law."

Colonel Remund stood, his face brightening with a flush of anger. Clearly, he was unused to being questioned. "Mademoiselle Näf, if you cannot refrain from protesting the actions of French and German governments, then you shall no longer occupy your position as director of the children's colony at La Hille." He paused, drawing a stiff breath. "Refrain from protesting further, follow the law, and do not impede the authorities in whatever actions they take regarding refugees. If you fail to obey these directives, you will also fail to protect the Swiss policy of neutrality, and you will face consequences. Is that clear?"

Rösli inhaled. Her cheeks burned with rage, but she held Colonel Remund's stare.

"Yes, you've made yourself clear."

He continued to glare at her for a long, disapproving moment before waving his hand in dismissal.

Rösli turned from the men, who immediately withdrew into their own side discussions, chatting with each other quietly as if nothing important had just transpired. With shaking hands, she left the room, gripped the staircase railing, and made her way down to the front door, stepping out into the clean, cold air of impending autumn. She exhaled, trying to tame the flood of emotions coursing through her interior like a river bursting its banks. Her sensible shoes clicked the cobbles as she set off, unsure of what to do next. She had arranged to gather coats and winter clothes from a charity in St. Gallen before returning to France, but now she scowled at the thought of bringing mere coats to the children. What she'd yearned to bring them was freedom.

She glanced around the peaceful cobbled street, adorned with flower baskets heaped in burnished color. Her mind moved at the pace of the river folding and flowing through Bern's city center. Her brief visit with Madame Authié, at the *préfecture* in Foix, had gone much better than this meeting with self-important men. Madame Authié had frowned when Rösli spoke, lining up her pens on her desk while she listened, but then she raised her eyes and nodded once.

"I've been unable to sleep," she whispered. Her scowl deepened

84   KRISTIN BECK

and she lowered her voice. "I'm sick about that day. I'll warn you whenever possible."

Rösli slowed on the cobblestones. It was good to have Madame Authié as an ally, but it wasn't nearly enough. There *must* be some way for her most imperiled children, the oldest, to leave France. She pursed her lips in thought. It had taken her two days to travel from La Hille to the Swiss border. Was there any way for teenagers to travel that far through a country hostile to them? They would need money, false documents, and safe places to sleep. And once they arrived at the border, what then? There was no way to legally cross; as Colonel Remund had indicated, the border was closed to those without Swiss visas. Could they sneak across? She imagined the border, a squiggle on a map, cutting through mountains and forests soon to be buried in snow.

Her mind flitted to the much closer border to La Hille. *Spain.* Mountains rose in her thoughts, sharp and high and bright with ice. Could a teenager cross the Pyrénées to reach Spain? Could anyone? Rösli sighed, the questions stacking up in her mind, each with no apparent answer.

All she knew was that while the Red Cross officials had made their position clear, they hadn't noticed one crucial thing: she'd agreed that she understood them, yet she'd promised nothing. She lengthened her stride, forcing her thoughts to assemble in their customary order. She had to tackle this like she'd tackled the rest of her life. What were the first problems to solve, the first barriers to escape? Lack of travel papers, money, and safe harbors on the way to the border. Would the charity in St. Gallen raise money for her, like they had coats? And there were other Secours Suisse children's colonies in France, including two on the way to Switzerland. Rösli was planning to sleep at the colony near Lyon on her way south, in fact. Perhaps she would find kindred spirits there, who might provide safe beds for fleeing teenagers?

Rösli inhaled the crisp air, bolstered. She would try to find out if there was help along the route to Switzerland, and that was a first step. The rest would certainly appear as she pressed onward. She would create a way to save her children, because the only promise she'd made was to them.

Laws be damned, she wasn't going to let them down.

Two days later, Rösli walked up a long driveway in Montluel, a hamlet north of Lyon. Through the trees, she could see glimpses of a white château, and somewhere the voices of children filtered through the forest. Her heart ached at the sound of them, calling and laughing. How were her own children faring in the days since she'd left?

She was halfway up the long access road when an adult voice sailed through the trees.

"Bonjour!"

Rösli pivoted, looking for the source of the greeting, and spotted a young woman hurrying over from a swale of woods. Petite and wearing a rumpled, grass-stained dress, it looked as though she'd been playing right along with her charges. Small children galloped around her, and for a moment the woman was detained by a glossy-haired girl who bounced up and wrapped her in a hug around the waist. The woman knelt, cupping the child's cheek, speaking kindly.

"Rafaela, dear, will you be my helper? Go and gather all the children who were on our walk and lead them up to the house, so I can greet our visitor."

The child's black eyes sought Rösli out on the road. Then she nodded enthusiastically and was off, running on long legs, before her caretaker could utter, "*Merci!*"

"You must be the famous Rösli Näf!" the young woman called as she approached. "I heard you were expected today."

Rösli frowned, buffeted by her choice of words. "I am Mademoiselle Näf, yes."

"*Enchanté!*" The younger woman grinned as she shook Rösli's hand vigorously. "I'll walk you to the château, if you like."

"*Merci.*" Rösli hesitated, glancing over as her new escort fell into step alongside her. "And what shall I call you?"

"*Mon Dieu.*" The woman laughed, bumping her forehead with the heel of her hand. "Apologies! Anne-Marie Piguet. I'm one of the caretakers here."

"A pleasure to meet you." Rösli studied her for a beat. Anne-Marie had messy brown hair falling just above her shoulders, half of which was swept up. She smiled as if by reflex, her round face making her look younger than she probably was. Instantly likable, Rösli decided. But her own frown crept back in, and she hoisted her bag higher on her shoulder. "May I ask why you would call me famous?"

"Oh goodness." That swift smile again. "You must excuse me! My thoughts tend to slip out. I only meant that we heard what you did when your group was taken to Le Vernet, and I admire you so much for it. Perhaps you're a bit famous in my mind. You were so incredibly brave."

Ah. Rösli swung her gaze back to the château, rising through the trees, with its double staircase and white stone. "It wasn't bravery, mademoiselle," Rösli said. "It was simply what had to be done." Anne-Marie's disclosure was a good sign. Yes, this young woman had the potential of becoming a person Rösli could trust. "How long have you been working here?"

"Oh, I came in the spring. June, I suppose." Anne-Marie talked on as they closed the distance to the building, telling Rösli more than she would have thought to ask. Anne-Marie had been raised just over the Swiss border, in the Jura mountains, where her father worked as a forester. She adored reading and children and had thus studied to become a teacher, but how could she possibly teach school in Switzerland with so many French children in need?

"I thought they'd be French, anyway." Anne-Marie shrugged. "It turns out that not one of the children here is French. We have about forty Spanish refugees, and we keep getting new arrivals from the internment camps. The new arrivals are always foreign Jewish children."

Rösli glanced at her. They were in the shadow of the château now, but they paused before the stairs. "How exactly do you get Jewish children out of internment camps?"

The smile finally left Anne-Marie's face. "Just from one camp, actually. Rivesaltes. Last year, an alliance of international aid organizations persuaded the camp to release children. At first, it worked because the camp was overfull, and the organizations put pressure on the government to create a process for freeing children who needed it most. Apparently, Vichy used to care about foreign opinion, to an extent."

Rösli huffed. "If they really cared, there would be no camps at all."

"Exactly." Something flashed in Anne-Marie's eyes, but she continued explaining. "Liberating children is a laborious process, and it takes time—the government requires each child to have a documented place to stay, permission from the relevant *préfecture* to reside there, and proof of funds to support them. Friedel Reiter is the Secours Suisse social worker in Rivesaltes. Perhaps you've met her? She's the one who finds the children who most need to leave, persuades their parents to let them go, and then we start the paperwork."

Rösli nodded; she'd heard of Friedel. Indeed, she'd long wondered how Friedel managed to liberate children into Swiss care. "I'm surprised the authorities are still allowing it," Rösli said after a moment, her thoughts darting. "In light of the recent persecutions . . ."

"*Je sais*, it's all very precarious now. For a while after the raids, they didn't allow any children to leave Rivesaltes. Vichy officials insisted on deporting families together, so they even brought freed children back to the camps."

"That's what I saw at Camp du Vernet. Whole families, sent away."

Anne-Marie's brows gathered, and she nodded. "At Rivesaltes, too. Only now, camp officials have just started allowing liberation certificates again. Nobody knows why, but we're moving fast to take advantage of the confusion. Friedel is working on getting a group of young children certificates right now, in fact. The Germans seem preoccupied with the eldest kids, mostly, so I guess camp administration is overlooking her particular efforts."

"For now." Rösli looked Anne-Marie in the eye. "Get as many out as you can, before something changes. The Germans will put an end to it, I'm certain, if Vichy officials don't do it first. There's no empathy among them. Have you been to Rivesaltes yourself?"

"Not yet." Anne-Marie inhaled, worry in her eyes. "It's my turn to fetch the next group from Friedel, actually. We nearly have the paperwork completed."

Rösli frowned. "Steel yourself." It was all she could think to say. She glanced from Anne-Marie to a group of children trooping up from the grounds, and for a moment neither of them spoke. The supper bell clanged from some upstairs window, and a flock of birds burst from a nearby tree. A memory flashed in Rösli's mind. The birds, at Camp du Vernet, singing.

Anne-Marie reached for Rösli, linking elbows with her and breaking the spell. Together they went indoors.

After a supper of thin vegetable soup and bread, the Montluel colony director stood to make an announcement. "Children," she called, her voice loud, "you must all go outside to play, s'il vous plaît. The adults will be out shortly to watch you." She looked sternly over the rim of her glasses, picking out the half dozen adults in the room as the children stood. "Secours Suisse staff, please stay in the dining hall for an announcement."

Rösli remained seated beside Anne-Marie, though they both pivoted to face the standing *directrice*. The woman waited for the last child to scamper out, and then she leveled her stare on the handful of adults. "A message has come in from Bern, and I've been instructed to read it to the entire staff. This same memorandum is being read at every Swiss Red Cross facility in France tonight."

Rösli cocked her head, her nerves involuntarily gathering. If it was a message from Bern, it couldn't be good. She studied the director, who adjusted her glasses to better read the paper in her hands, but Rösli couldn't sense what kind of a woman she was. She glanced to Anne-Marie, who shrugged.

"This comes from the Executive Committee of the Swiss Red Cross in Bern," the director clarified. She cleared her throat to read.

"*The laws and decrees of the government of France must be executed exactly, and you do not have to consider whether or not they are opposed to your own beliefs. The French government trusted us for our mission to help children. The execution of this work can only be done if we do not undermine this trust and if we do not undermine it through reckless action. If the situation develops in the future in such a way that you feel that it is impossible for you to take up your task, we will ask you to resign rather than continue your work and jeopardize the prestige of the Red Cross, Switzerland, and our country.*"

Rösli felt as if there were no air in the room. She stood, turning from the group, and moved toward a window. Voices murmured behind her, drifting toward the dining room door, but Rösli couldn't discern what they said over her own speeding thoughts. They were ordered to set aside their beliefs? She could barely breathe. To execute French decrees without question? The message echoed everything Colonel Remund and his colleagues had impressed upon her, days ago, as she stood before them pleading for the safety of her children. Had they written it in response to her visit?

Anne-Marie appeared at her shoulder. Rösli met her stare, and recognized fury there. Gone was her constant smile. "They're forbidding us to intercede," Anne-Marie whispered, glancing around the empty dining hall.

"I know." Rösli shook her head, unmoored. "But I *must*."

"Intercede?"

"How can I not?" Rösli placed a hand on the windowpane to steady herself. Had she said too much? She barely knew Anne-Marie, but somehow she already trusted her. Outside, small figures ran around the grounds of Montluel, playing in the twilight. These children were far beneath the crucial age of sixteen, thank goodness. Would they, and Rösli's *petits*, continue to be safe? There was no way to be sure. She inhaled. Yet, she *was* certain that nearly half of her own group was not safe, and the Swiss Red Cross couldn't be counted on to save them again.

"I need to get them out of France," she said, looking Anne-Marie in the eye. "My eldest children."

Anne-Marie nodded, crossing her arms over her chest as though suddenly cold. "Have you thought of a way to do it?"

"Maybe the Spanish border? Or I was hoping they might sneak into Switzerland, but they'd need places to sleep along the way. I'd imagined Montluel could be a possibility, but now I'm not sure. In light of that memorandum . . ."

Anne-Marie puffed air through her lips, thinking. "Our *directrice* is a good woman, truly, but she tends to follow the rules set before her. Anyway, we're too far from Switzerland here to be of much help. Have you contacted the Secours Suisse colony in Saint-Cergues? That house sits right along the border."

"They're next on my list, actually." Rösli raised her brows. "You've thought about this, then. Escape routes to Switzerland."

"Ever since the raids, *oui*. I can't help worrying about what we might do if they come for our little ones. I don't have a clear plan, but it haunts me."

"It should." Rösli looked again to the children playing, mere shapes now in the quickly falling night. "Keep thinking about ways to save them, Anne-Marie." A bird sailed across the darkening sky, and Rösli's heart ached.

"Nothing in the world makes sense anymore," Anne-Marie whispered.

"No, it doesn't." Rösli thought for a long moment. "But I can see that you are a person of conscience."

She looked at Anne-Marie, who held her stare.

"Follow your conscience and forget the rules." Rösli sighed. "In France, your conscience may require much of you, but it's the only guide you can trust."

PART TWO

~≈≈≈⁀

EIGHT

ANNE-MARIE PIGUET

In France, your conscience may require much of you.

Anne-Marie stared out the train window while Rösli's words rattled around in her mind, giving her strength. Today, strength was something she needed desperately. She felt young, sitting alone on the train, her hands clamped tightly over the bag on her knees, the precious paperwork tucked inside. She felt naive, as though she were merely pretending that she could do whatever lay in the path ahead. Like a child, she thought ruefully, playing at being a grown-up. Yet anger, flickering somewhere under her nerves, propelled Anne-Marie forward. Ever since that infernal message from Swiss Red Cross headquarters, something deep inside of her had burned like wildfire.

Until recently, she hadn't thought of herself as naive, or even, at twenty-six years old, particularly young. She watched hills and farmland slide past the window, burnished under the rising autumn sun, her thoughts turning. She'd finished university, after all, and was a credentialed teacher, something her own mother could only have dreamed about. And now she was living in a different country, all on her own. The train rounded a bend, and Anne-Marie's thoughts curved to her father, who always had confidence in her. Memory rose of the last long hike she'd taken with him, before coming here. It was when she'd told him of her plans.

"I'm considering volunteering in France," she'd confided that day, over a year ago, her elbows propped on her knees before a warm fire in the woods. Her father's blue eyes had flipped up to meet her matching set, and something bent in her stomach. Her parents had long given her the freedom to forge her own path. And yet, she yearned for their blessing if she was to step out into a dangerous world. Would they give it?

He picked up a stick to stir the fire, turning his thick hand as he expertly stoked the flames. A flurry of sparks burst into the air, rising. "What kind of volunteering?" His laugh lines creased as he glanced up.

"With the Swiss Red Cross. So many children have been up-rooted in France, and there aren't resources to feed them, and house them—"

"Indeed." He nodded. "It all goes to the Germans. If they keep the people weak enough, hungry enough, and scared enough, *alors*. Makes it difficult to fight back."

Anne-Marie sensed his belief under those words: the people should fight back anyway. Her father, with his philosopher's soul, often spoke of religion and politics around the campfire, his skepticism for both deepening over time, congruent with the shadow of war seeping over Europe. Charles de Gaulle, exiled in London, had become their family hero since the fall of France. De Gaulle spoke of resistance over the airwaves, stirring something in the Piguet family's wild mountain hearts.

Somewhere in the trees, an owl called. Anne-Marie met her father's swift glance. "Pygmy owl," she said, and he nodded. It was a hobby they shared, spotting and naming birds. The owl called again, and her chest smarted. She would miss her father. She would miss these woods.

"What about your career, Anne-Marie?" His gaze met hers again, catching the firelight. "You've worked so hard to become a teacher."

She shrugged, belying the restless stirring of her soul. France had fallen to the Germans with shocking speed, and ever since, it both weighed on her heart and tugged her, incomprehensibly, forward. She couldn't just stay in her peaceful village, ringed by serene lakes and mountains. Not now.

"It feels wrong to go on with my life as if nothing's happening beyond our borders. I want to do something."

"*Oui, je comprends.*" Her father had stared into the fire, nodding slowly, the light flickering in his eyes. "And so, you shall."

When Anne-Marie stepped off the train, the sun had risen fully. She clutched her bag and wove her way along the platform toward the station, sick with nerves. But why? She had all the necessary paperwork, and others from Montluel had completed this same journey, many times now. Still, she glanced at the gendarmes guarding the station, their dull eyes on the departing crowd, and doubt flickered. What if someone stopped her? What if they'd decided to change the rules, as Rösli seemed so sure they would? Her anxiety buzzed as she looked for the car that was arranged to pick her up.

An hour later, she emerged from that car, facing Rivesaltes.

From the moment Anne-Marie stood at its gates, all nervous thoughts scattered from her mind. There was no room left for them amid the shock. Rivesaltes, set on a barren, gusty plateau, was vast. So much bigger than she'd imagined. Anne-Marie waited near its entrance with an unsmiling guard, wind whipping at her skirt and spitting sand against her calves and face. A French flag rose over the entrance gates, flapping. She stared out at whitewashed cement buildings with red roofs sprawling under the autumn sun as far as the eye could see.

"Anne-Marie Piguet?" a soft voice called, and she jolted from her thoughts to see a young woman in a nurse's uniform hustling toward her. She forced a smile as the small, dark-haired woman approached. She wore a white apron, and a matching white kerchief secured her hair from the wind, though several strands whipped her face as she stopped in front of Anne-Marie. When she smiled, her dark brows lifted over her eyes, like brushstrokes.

"You must be Friedel?" Anne-Marie asked, reaching to grip the woman's hand.

"*Oui*, Friedel Reiter. Now come along—the children are already waiting."

Anne-Marie followed the Swiss nurse as they started off through the never-ending camp, passing guards with impassive expressions standing at intervals along barbed wire. Even in the cold wind, the smell of sewage and decay grew with every step, and within minutes Anne-Marie spotted three fat rats scuttling along barracks walls. People with thin, weary faces gazed out from beyond the fencing, sometimes raising a hand to Friedel, who hurried along in her worn boots. How did she manage to keep going out here, amid all this desolation? Friedel had been working in Rivesaltes for well over a year on behalf of the Secours Suisse, trying to provide relief to the children imprisoned here. She fed them food donated from Switzerland, tended to medical needs, and loved them through all the sorrow. The strength that required was suddenly, achingly clear.

"Do you have any advice?" Anne-Marie ventured. "Concerning the children on our trip north? I've been worried about their heartbreak, in leaving their parents."

Friedel glanced over. "Just be kind and calm for them. They've already endured so much. They will endure this, too." Grief flashed in Friedel's dark eyes. "Separating children from parents is devastating, but getting them out has never been more urgent. It was bad enough when we only had to worry about their health. Now, if they don't escape Rivesaltes, they'll be deported alongside their parents."

Anne-Marie couldn't withhold the question that had been burning in her heart, and was much discussed at Montluel since the summer deportations began. For some reason, she whispered it. "Where do they take them?"

Friedel slowed, glancing around and lowering her voice to a hush as well. "It's not to work, as they claim, I can tell you that much. They deport everyone—the old, the infirm, the very young. The Germans say they want people for labor, but I don't believe that." She held Anne-Marie's stare. "I believe the very worst."

Anne-Marie nodded, caught by her words.

Friedel sighed and picked up her pace abruptly, as if she'd just remembered what else she had to convey. "*Alors*, the children you'll take today: three of them are five years old—two girls and a boy. The other two are siblings, ages nine and thirteen, a girl and a boy. All of them understand what's happening, and why. Their parents' names weren't on the lists for earlier deportations, so they've seen people loaded onto the trains . . . they understand why they have to go."

Anne-Marie's own parents rose in her mind as she listened; her father shaded by the grandeur of the forest, her mother's laughter as she cooked. Could they have given her up when she was little, if they'd had to? The thought stung like a bite. Anne-Marie glanced at the lines of barracks, and the ghost of her parents vanished. She shifted her bag full of paperwork. Documentation freeing five children seemed like far too little.

"If only there was a way to get more out," she said. "A faster way to do the paperwork, or a way to bend the rules—"

"Don't be afraid to *break* the rules when opportunity arises,"

Friedel whispered, flashing her dark eyes again at Anne-Marie. Friedel clamped her lips, as if surprised she'd spoken the words out loud. For a second, they held each other's stare, and a question passed through Anne-Marie like a current. What rules had Friedel broken to save children's lives? It struck her how much this little Swiss nurse sounded like Rösli Näf.

They passed through a guarded gate, and a trio of children rushed over to hug Friedel around the waist, all of them speaking at once. They were dirty, clothed in rags, and each clutched a rusty tin can. Friedel bent to look them in the eyes, her face transforming with warmth. "Are you off to find something to drink?" she asked, smiling at each child. They nodded, shivering in the wind, and Friedel cupped a little girl around the shoulders and touched a boy's forehead as if to measure his temperature. She sent them off a moment later, with a smile and a kiss, and led the way through yet more barracks.

When they finally stepped into Friedel's office, Anne-Marie looked around, taking in the humble room with its bed and desk. Someone, perhaps Friedel, had painted cheerful pictures, mostly of mountains, along the walls. Anne-Marie clasped her hands at her waist, trying to smother her dread. The time to take five children from their mothers was fast approaching. How could she help them through such heartbreak? She moved on her shaky legs to sit on the bed, but Friedel called out, "Don't sit!" and Anne-Marie paused mid-step.

Friedel smiled apologetically. "Everything's full of bedbugs, is all. I don't want to give you the plague if I can help it. I'll be right back with the children, d'accord?"

Anne-Marie nodded, glancing dubiously at the neatly made bed. Seconds later, the door opened and five small children crept in, their eyes downcast. Three mothers walked at their sides.

The mothers already wept. One woman hugged a shawl around her thin shoulders and stroked her tiny daughter's blond hair over and over, as if smoothing it for school. She looked to Anne-Marie with shining blue eyes. "You'll take care of my Sabine?" she asked with a Belgian accent, her voice shaking.

Anne-Marie's nervousness sharpened into anguish. Why should these mothers have to give up their children to save them? What had any of them done to warrant such cruelty?

"I will take care of Sabine," she answered. She took the woman's hands in a firm squeeze. Then she looked at the other two women, trying to memorize their faces.

"I'll do everything I can for your children," Anne-Marie said. "I promise you, with all my heart."

The women bent before the three smallest children. The little blond girl wept in her mother's arms, and the other girl, her hair brown as coffee, stared at the floor. Her mother cupped her face, kissing her sunburned forehead. A pretty woman with glittering, dark eyes knelt before her little son, speaking to him in swift Polish. She touched his cheek, nodding continually, and he nodded back. He blinked eyes identical to hers, and tears spilled from them to his dusty shoes.

Behind them, Friedel had a pair of slightly older children wrapped in each arm. The boy's sandy hair fell in his eyes, and he stood as stiff as the floorboards under their feet. His younger sister wiped at her nose while Friedel whispered assurances into her ear. Anne-Marie swallowed a wedge of pain. These two must have already lost their parents.

A guard appeared at the open door of Friedel's office, interrupting the tearful goodbyes with a hard stare. He didn't have to shout anything to convey his message.

"I'm so sorry, everyone." Friedel squeezed the children's shoulders and met the mothers' eyes. "It's time."

As Anne-Marie left the little room, a child clinging to each hand, the sound of weeping filled her ears. The children sobbed as they walked with her, dutiful but broken by the weight of the big world. And the mothers wept in their wake, crowded around the door of the Swiss nurse's office, hands over their anguished mouths, surely suppressing the urge to call their children back.

Anne-Marie aimed for the camp gates, gripping hot little hands in her own, blinking back her own constant tears. She already knew: those mothers were the bravest people she would ever meet.

Anne-Marie wouldn't let them down.

The night train leaving Narbonne was packed with travelers. Anne-Marie ushered her little group down the dark corridor of an overloaded car, where people sat on suitcases and slept in the aisle. They stepped over a snoring man and gazed into a full compartment. The little girls at the front of the group swayed on their feet as Anne-Marie scanned the hallway for space. The children needed to sleep. Where could she put them? If only a few people in the hall would scoot down, perhaps the littlest could sit on the laps of the bigger children. Though none of them were very big—the largest of the five, the thirteen-year-old boy, was as slender as ryegrass.

"I can make room," a voice called, and Anne-Marie glanced back into the compartment. An older woman struggled to her feet, forcing a smile onto her grandmotherly face. "Are you tired, little ones?" she asked the girls. Sabine, the blond girl, nodded solemnly.

Anne-Marie nudged past the children into the compartment. The other passengers stared at their books or out the window, refusing to make eye contact, but the older woman and a man who must be her husband already stood. "We can make room," the woman said, "bien sûr. What if we empty these luggage racks so the littlest can sleep up there? Like bunks, oui? Or is that too crazy?"

Anne-Marie found a smile. "That's a lovely idea, madame. No, monsieur, let me lift them . . ."

Not three minutes later, they'd emptied the luggage racks and hoisted all three of the smallest children up in place of the suit-cases. Sabine giggled, despite her grief and fatigue, as she stared down at Anne-Marie. The other passengers said nothing as Anne-Marie laid their suitcases flat on the floor and told the siblings to spread out on them as if they were a lumpy mattress. The train began to creak out of the station just as all five children settled, and Anne-Marie exhaled. She found a wedge of space to sit on the floor, knees to her chest, next to the door. She allowed her head to tip back against the seat of the rocking train.

Despite her exhaustion, Anne-Marie knew she wouldn't sleep. Grief plagued her, and she wanted to remain alert in case papers were checked somewhere along the way. Her heart skipped up at the thought. To reassure herself, she patted the documents she'd tucked into an inside pocket of her jacket. Also, each child now wore a square badge, with the Swiss Red Cross symbol, pinned to their shirtfronts. Still, she wouldn't feel safe until they were on the grounds of the château of Montluel.

As the train rocked out of Narbonne, the car dimmed and the compartment quieted. The children slept, and adults closed their eyes for the long trip north. As it often did, Anne-Marie's mind drifted to Switzerland, with its snow-strung mountains and sparkling lakes. Her heart swelled, memories of home soothing her burning sorrow. She imagined the hush of the vast Risoud forest, the playground of her childhood. She closed her eyes and she could see the sun filtering through branches, its light falling over the forest floor.

A voice murmured in her mind, mingling with the rustling memory of trees. *I need to get them out of France.* There was Rösli's frown, her worried eyes. *My eldest children.*

Was Rösli working on an escape route now? Anne-Marie opened her eyes, staring at dark shapes slipping past the train windows, tight-ening her arms where they wrapped around her knees. Had Rösli contacted the colony of Saint-Cergues? Ever since the raids, her mind had returned to the Swiss border over and over, to the forests that she knew so well. It was what had made her think of Saint-Cergues, located so perfectly along the border near Geneva. It wasn't an area she knew well, not like the Risoud forest, but it seemed the most likely crossing point.

Would the colony director of Saint-Cergues allow threatened children to hide there, preparing for an illicit border crossing? If not, what could be done?

The Risoud. The forest rose in her mind again, insistent, like an answer to her question. But it wasn't actually an answer, for it only raised more questions. Anne-Marie didn't know anyone on the French side of the border, yet escapees would need the help of people who lived there, farmers and foresters, if they were to hike across. Was such a thing possible? She'd also heard from her father that the forest was now heavily patrolled by police. Could it even be crossed safely?

She couldn't answer any of these questions.

Yet she had promised three mothers, just hours ago, that she would look after their children, and *all* the mothers whose children were sheltered by the Secours Suisse deserved the same promise. Anne-Marie didn't know Rösli's teenagers, but somewhere they had parents who'd saved them, just like the mothers she'd met today. The grief hardened in her chest, and without planning it, she made a decision.

If necessary, Anne-Marie would find a way out of France for children in danger.

*D*id I ever tell you all about the time I got lost in the snowy wilderness?"

Several weeks had passed since Anne-Marie's trip to Rivesaltes, and she now stood in the dining room surrounded by children, telling them a story. The children, gathered in a loose circle, shook their heads. Anne-Marie grinned, looking between a dozen expectant gazes. Stories were one of her tricks to get them to sit still, at least long enough to comb and fix their hair. They'd eaten their meager dinner, and a fire danced in the grate, warming the room and casting flickering shadows over their gathered faces.

"It happened in the heart of winter, when the wind blew so cold we'd forgotten what the sun looked like hanging in the summer sky. We couldn't remember what it felt like to be warm, and to see flowers dance in the light and bees land on them, little legs full of pollen . . ."

Anne-Marie kept speaking, her voice a singsong, as she squinted down at Rafaela's long, beautiful hair. She should have started the lice check earlier, when she could have sat them by a window's light. The latest new arrivals from Rivesaltes often brought the cursed bugs with them, and so Anne-Marie and the Swiss nurse Yseult checked everyone daily to try to get ahead of the scourge. But, like most scourges, lice were persistent.

Rafaela's head passed inspection. Anne-Marie wove her hair into a long, glossy braid, looking up as she worked to meet the gazes of her little audience.

"On this deep winter day, I went out into the woods, and walked much farther than I should have, even though I knew better. Why? Ramona, Sabine." She met the eyes of the named girls, who had started to squirm in their chairs, and Rafaela reached up like a reflex to squeeze Anne-Marie's hand as she moved to the next child. She squeezed back, giving the little girl with gleaming black eyes a wink. "Children, I was searching for a violin tree."

"One with no branches," Sabine offered, and Anne-Marie nodded.

"All trees have branches, but yes. The best violins come from strong trees with smooth trunks, spruce trees that have grown slowly for a long, long time. And you all know where the best violin trees grow—"

"The Risoud," Joseph interrupted, and all the children nodded. They'd been fascinated when Anne-Marie described how the wood for violins came from her childhood forests, that certain trees were more resonant than others, that the potential for music was hidden within their ancient, wooden hearts.

"I wandered into the snow, quite enjoying the crunch of it beneath my boots, and the way it laced every branch and trunk in white. I looked up at all the trees as I passed, searching for the kind my father had taught me to look for, like it was a game. I didn't notice that it was growing dark. I didn't notice that I'd lost my way."

Anne-Marie paused while combing her fingers through little David's sparse hair. He'd come from Rivesaltes in the last week, and he sat on his stool as loose as a doll, as if no skeleton held him up. David had arrived with three other children, two with dysentery and all of them badly malnourished. Conditions were deteriorating in the camp, clearly. His eyes rolled in their sockets, and Yseult had whispered that there was damage to his optic nerve due to starvation. Anne-Marie swept her fingers through his hair, exhaling with gratitude that the sweet child had no lice. One less battle for David.

"As I walked along in the snow, the light faded from the sky, children, and suddenly I became aware of a sound. Can anyone guess what it was?"

"Bears!" Jacinta yelled, bouncing on her seat bones.

"A storm," Joseph offered, blinking his long eyelashes as if this were the only logical answer.

"Wolves!"

Anne-Marie paused her story for a brief second, letting the suspension build as she bent to give David a kiss on the cheek. He cocked his head in response, smiling slightly, and she held his gaze and thought, *You are loved*, hard, as if she could print this message in his soul. She told all the children this, often, and she would whis-

per it to David later as he fell asleep. She patted his knob of a shoulder, moving on.

Sabine's lovely blond curls were hopelessly tangled from an afternoon running in the wind. Sabine smiled up, and Anne-Marie
cupped her cheek, warmed by the fire, before tackling her golden
mess.

"Joseph, you're right. It was a storm. A thunderclap made me
jump in my boots," she said, glancing around the circle. The children now sat still, their attention caught. In the next room a radio
buzzed to life, crackling before low voices swam through the door.
The other adults rarely missed an evening broadcast, but Anne-Marie
usually spent her evenings with the children.

"The wind began to howl, shaking snow from the branches onto
my head, and I grew cold. I shivered, and thunder rolled through the
clouds. I realized what a terrible mistake I'd made, traveling far into
the forest on the darkest day of winter, all alone. You see, one must
always pay attention in the wilderness. I turned around in a little
snowy clearing, looking for my footsteps, but can you guess what
had happened, children?" Twelve heads shook. "It had started to snow,
big heavy flakes, and my footprints were gone. I didn't know which
way to go."

"You could look for dents in the snow," Joseph suggested rea-
sonably, scratching his curly head.

She pursed her lips, amused. "No, I couldn't see them. I was
alone in a snowy forest, with a growing storm, and I was too terrified to think as clearly as you, Joseph. All paths looked the same to
me. But just as I was about to lose hope, something happened. A
little bird dove down from the trees, buffeted by the wind, and do
you know what color it was?" A dozen heads shook once more. Joseph reached up to scratch his head again—she would have to check
him thoroughly. "The bird was yellow, children. A little speck of
yellow flitting through white and green trees, fighting the wind—"

"Did you follow it?" Sabine piped up under Anne-Marie's plaiting fingers, unable to stay quiet. She'd turned into a precocious child, full of ideas, but she sobbed herself to sleep most nights whispering for her mother.

"I did, Sabine. I followed as it swooped from branch to branch. And this was the surprising part, the part I will never forget: that little yellow bird led me down through the wild forest. In fact, it led me all the way home—"

The door to the next room flung open, halting the finale of Anne-Marie's story. Yseult strode in. Her cheeks were so red that her eyes, by contrast, seemed a vibrant blue.

"Anne-Marie, come quick and listen." She beckoned toward the radio. "The Americans and British have invaded North Africa. They've landed on French-controlled coastlines. Casablanca, Oran, Algiers—"

"Americans? In French North Africa?" Anne-Marie nearly dropped the comb. "*C'est merveilleux!*"

Yseult didn't smile. Her blue eyes flicked to the children and she lowered her voice. "It's wonderful, yes. But Anne-Marie, what will happen *in France*? Francisco thinks the Germans will react badly if Vichy forces lose the coastline." Francisco, a Spanish refugee who had found safe haven as the colony's gardener, had a quick mind for politics, having lived through more war than anyone else.

Dueling feelings rose in Anne-Marie's heart as she dismissed the children and followed Yseult to the radio. Hope bloomed at the thought of this new Allied invasion. Yet, beneath that hope, a dark fear grew. She fought it back as she quieted before the broadcast, holding her breath to listen, hoping Francisco's dire predictions wouldn't come true.

~~~~~

NINE

RÖSLI

CHÂTEAU DE LA HILLE, SOUTHERN FRANCE
NOVEMBER 1942

A few days after the Allied invasion of North Africa, Rösli set out, as she did most mornings following breakfast, for the village of Montégut. It took a bit more than a half hour to walk to the village if she moved at a good clip, and once there, she'd collect both news and mail at the little post office. Today, she would also use their telephone to call Germaine Hommel, the *directrice* of the colony of Saint-Cergues, and arrange a visit. For several weeks, Rösli had worked tirelessly, setting up every other link in her escape chain: she'd collaborated with Maurice, quietly, to source forged documents; she'd studied maps and train schedules; and she'd raised money through Swiss charities, claiming it was for provisions. The final step in her plan required a safe harbor along the border, and she'd lain awake nights, hoping Germaine Hommel would provide it. What she knew of the other *directrice* gave her confidence, but she had to meet her. This was a conversation she couldn't conduct from a distance.

The morning sky was dark and windless, with heavy clouds

sinking down among the highest hilltops. Rösli veered off La Hille's driveway to take a shortcut to the village, following a farmer's footpath through fields and forests. Every now and again, she heard a strange, distant thunder as she walked. A storm, she thought absently, gathering on the horizon. Yet, as she closed the distance to the village, the sound expanded, shifting into something she didn't quite recognize. Rösli paused, stilling under a skeletal tree, listening to the rumbling distance. The branches overhanging the path were motionless—no wind shook them. No rain fell. *Was* it thunder? Her heart accelerated, and she matched it with a quickening stride. "*Scheisse*," she whispered involuntarily, skipping up into a run.

Something was happening.

When Rösli finally neared Montégut, the very air seemed to shake. She turned a corner, her heart vibrating with the sound all around her, and she saw it. Along the road skirting the tiny village, tanks lumbered by, one after another.

Germans.

Rösli wandered, as though lost, all the way to the edge of the rural thoroughfare. Whatever segment of the German army this was seemed to go on and on, a terrifying parade, rattling the breath in her lungs. Following the tanks came a line of trucks, their canopied beds carrying uniformed soldiers who gazed out at the bucolic countryside. Rösli studied their passing faces, feeling as though someone gripped her by the throat. She couldn't move, could barely blink. The men were young. One, unthinkably handsome, flicked his eyes in her direction and she shrank back.

Rösli inhaled, shaky, her thoughts jumping. *Germans are invading southern France.* All at once, the notion of a free zone toppled. If they were here, in the sleepy Ariège, they were most certainly everywhere.

No part of France would be free anymore.

At last, the rumble of vehicles left the narrow road, streaming in the direction of Foix, and Rösli hurried through the vacated space. She needed to get to the post office, quick, and its telephone. First, she would call Maurice Dubois, who was always well-connected, to get all the news. Then she would call Germaine Hommel at Saint-Cergues and tell her that she was coming for a meeting. Immediately.

There was no time to dither, because the Germans who hunted her children were here now, swarming through southern France, so close she'd seen the whites of their eyes.

Two days and seven hundred kilometers later, Rösli approached a big, pale house perched on a hillside in the hamlet of Saint-Cergues. Unlike La Hille and Montluel, this Swiss Red Cross colony served mostly French children displaced by war. The building's many windows overlooked a valley rolling into yet more hills and, glittering in the distant sunshine, a sliver of Lake Geneva. She paused before starting up the walkway, staring through the naked treetops below the house, her breath hanging in the frigid air. Distant mountains rolled beyond the lake like a restless sea, snowcaps reflecting light. Her legs ached from sitting on the train, and her mind blurred after watching so much of France slip past her window on the endless trip here. She frowned, studying the shifting blues and greens cantering to the horizon. Where did the French landscape become Swiss? Where exactly was that imaginary, crucial line? She turned in to the frosty shade of the house and knocked.

The door creaked open and a woman, perhaps fifty years old, blinked out. She was small and buxom, with hair in a loose bun and intelligent, raven eyes. The woman flicked her gaze from Rösli to the surrounding trees and descending road, scanning. Satisfied, she waved Rösli in without a word, bolting the door.

"Looks quiet out there, but you never know. Patrols are *everywhere*," the woman whispered, beckoning Rösli down a long hall.

The chatter of children filtered through the house, but the woman stepped through another door before they saw anyone, murmuring, "We'll talk in my office."

It wasn't until they sat down in the cozy room, already inhabited by a younger woman and warmed by a crackling fire, that the house director exhaled. "My goodness, I didn't even introduce myself, did I? Germaine Hommel, *directrice* of the colony. It's so nice to finally meet you in person, Mademoiselle Näf."

Rösli returned the smile. "Call me Rösli." They'd corresponded enough that first names seemed in order. But Rösli studied Germaine's answering smile, trying to sense her thoughts. If only she were good at reading people! She hesitated, unsure how to proceed. Was her hunch about this woman correct? How far might she go for refugee children? Would Germaine Hommel disobey the orders of the Swiss Red Cross? Would she break the law? Her colony perched on its hillside in the Haute-Savoie as if a bolt of luck had set it there, just for them. Rösli's hope gathered.

Would Germaine Hommel help the La Hille teenagers escape France?

"This is my assistant," Germaine said, interrupting Rösli's thoughts. "Renée Farny." The younger woman flashed a nervous smile that transformed her face from pensive to lovely.

"A pleasure." Rösli sat back in her chair. She had the sense that the two women were studying her as well, equally unsure of their next words. She cleared her throat. There was no use in small talk; the only way to proceed was forward. "Before knocking I studied the view. Where exactly is the border, from here? Is it possible to walk there?"

Germaine folded her hands over her soft belly and grinned, her eyes taking on the glint of mischief. "So, I was right." She glanced at Renée, who visibly relaxed, pursing the lips of her wide mouth to subdue a smile.

Rösli let go of breath she didn't realize she'd been holding. She lifted her hand to her hairline, tucking back some blond wisps, and saw that her fingers shook as they passed her gaze. She'd forced herself to ignore the great risk of sharing her intentions with these women, and the greater risk of asking for their help. They could report her to the Swiss Red Cross, if so inclined. Or worse, they could call the police. She'd known that all along, of course, but hadn't let herself dwell on it.

Germaine, perceptive, scooted her chair closer to Rösli and reached for her sweaty palm, gripping it firmly. She spoke fast and low. "It's quite all right. You're among friends. We heard what you did when your kids were taken to Camp du Vernet, and we admire you for it. Renée and I are disgusted by what's taking place in France. Most of our children here aren't in any danger, being French, but one of our girls was arrested—"

"One of yours, actually," Renée interrupted, earnest, and Rösli nodded. It was what had given her confidence in Germaine: one of La Hille's oldest girls, aged nineteen, had traveled here for employment, taking care of the colony's young children over the summer. She'd been arrested like everyone else on August 26, but Maurice had managed to free her and send her back to La Hille with the rest of the teenagers. The girl had spoken admiringly of Germaine Hommel, describing her outrage when the police forced their way in that summer day.

Germaine squeezed Rösli's hand. "We're appalled at the persecutions, and we've prayed for the opportunity to do more."

Rösli found her voice. "You'd help them across the border, then? The teenagers?"

Renée nodded, nervously smoothing her skirt. "I've already been scouting routes." Her voice was light and swift, and she punctuated her words with reflexive smiles. "The border runs through the valley below us, perhaps three kilometers from here. We often walk down there with little ones so they can run and play in the fields and forests. Everyone around here knows our children, and we've always taken them on long walks, so it doesn't seem suspicious. We can get quite close to the border in places. There's a barbed wire fence and regular patrols, but if a person was careful—"

Germaine nodded decisively. "We could show them the way."

"How good are their chances of crossing safely?" Rösli bit her lip in the wake of her question, watching the other women exchange glances.

"Hard to say," Germaine said. "Patrols walk the fence—both German soldiers and French gendarmes. But it's a long stretch of fence through the valley. They can't possibly watch every part of it all the time. The children could behave as if they were simply out for a walk, and they could sneak through when there was nobody watching. We know a farmer who lives in the valley who will help— I'm sure of it."

"And the barbed wire," Rösli interrupted, "It's passable?"

Renée answered, tipping forward, elbows on knees. "It might be. In places." She spoke with breathless earnestness. "I've studied it whenever we walk close enough, and I think, with some effort, our farmer friend could loosen a section, discreetly. Perhaps where it crosses brush."

Germaine inhaled audibly, her generous chest rising and fall-ing. "Let's not pretend that this will be easy." She stared directly at Rösli, her dark eyes reflecting the firelight. "It's exceedingly dan-gerous, what we're proposing. People are caught trying to cross all the time. We hear rumors in the village, and there are hearings in Annemasse and Annecy for the lucky ones."

"The lucky ones?"

"Those caught by the French. The Germans don't conduct hear-ings, you see." Germaine held Rösli's stare while her meaning sank in. "And yet, if these children remain in France, what will happen to them? Will they be arrested if they stay? Hunted down? And if the Germans win the war, what then? It's a matter of weighing risk."

Rösli nodded, all too familiar with weighing risk. An image of the cattle cars at Camp du Vernet flashed in her mind. She heard the sobbing women within, clutching their children. She saw the elderly people buckling to the gravel. She heard the police shouting, threatening. The clang of doors. Locking.

Rösli looked between the women. "I'll leave it up to the children themselves to decide whether they want to go." She cleared the emotion from her throat, returning to the task at hand. "If they decide to escape, I'd send them to you in small groups, spaced apart by several days, to avoid attracting attention. Could they sleep here before crossing? It's an eighteen-hour trip from La Hille, and every hour will be dangerous. They'll need to be fed and rested before hiking across."

"Of course." Germaine glanced between Rösli and Renée, who nodded vigorously. "We'll have to be discreet about it, mind you. Perhaps they can blend with the children we already care for—what are you thinking for papers?"

Rösli withdrew her hand from Germaine's, knitting her knuckles together and tightening, subduing her nerves. She wouldn't tell them that she'd asked Maurice Dubois for help securing false identity papers. She had no doubt that he could do such a thing, and he promised he would, but she had to make sure nobody found out. "I'm arranging for false documents, so they can travel to Annemasse on trains. I'm also working on securing people they can contact, once they reach Switzerland, for assistance. A significant challenge is that the teenagers will have to pretend that they're under age sixteen, and French." She looked between Renée's warm gaze and Germaine's shrewd stare. It was actually a monumental challenge: most of her children spoke French with heavy accents. She'd counsel them to stay silent if caught. Just as bad, some of the teenagers were very tall. Who would ever believe that Isaak Goldberg was fifteen?

She shook the worries from her mind. "My teenagers will come with money to travel, false papers claiming they are younger French children, and instructions on how to get here. When they arrive here in Saint-Cergues, can I count on you to help them cross over the border? Do I have your word?"

Both women nodded, in sync. "Our solemn promise," Germaine said.

Rösli exhaled, releasing the last of her hesitation. She glanced around the small, firelit room. Before she knew it, a smile pricked her lips.

Germaine reached for her hand again, and Renée flashed her dazzling grin, as if something inside of her was unleashed. Rösli understood. It felt so good to speak plainly of the plans she'd been concocting, of her intention to break the law. It felt good to be among women who also believed the lives of young people were worth any risk.

Renée levered forward again, conspiratorial. "The Germans may be winning the war," she whispered, glancing around as if someone might be listening through the walls. "But that doesn't mean we can't fight back."

TEN

~~~~~

ELLA

CHÂTEAU DE LA HILLE, SOUTHERN FRANCE
DECEMBER 1942

*E*lla glanced around, uneasy. Rösli waited for all *les Grands* to be seated on their blankets, her small gray eyes flicking around the group. They'd shimmied into the *Zwiebelkeller* for this meeting, which struck Ella as strange. Why not meet in one of the regular dormitories? She knelt on her bedding, looking from Dela, at her right, to Isaak across the shadowy room. A beam of filtered sunshine fell over him from the high window, dusting his dark hair and shoulders with light. He shrugged slightly, as if he, too, wasn't sure what to expect.

"Before I explain," Rösli began, her lips a thin line of tension, "you all must promise not to breathe a word of this conversation outside of this room. You cannot even tell the younger children what I've said, in case they're ever questioned. We will only speak of this in here, where nobody can overhear. Do you all understand?"

She glanced between the teenagers, waiting while each nodded their agreement. Then Rösli cleared her throat, delivering her next words like a declaration. "Every one of you must consider leaving France. I can no longer guarantee your safety here."

For a moment nobody spoke, and her words seeped like rain into winter soil. Of course, they knew they weren't safe. They hadn't felt safe since they'd returned from Camp du Vernet, and even less so when the German army snaked down the country roads surrounding La Hille, occupying all the little towns they used to frequent. They were surrounded by Nazis, and there was nothing but Rösli and the château's ancient walls protecting them from deportation.

"But is it even possible to leave France now?" Edith ventured, and Ella glanced over to see the glint of her glasses and the worry in her eyes behind them.

Rösli turned, unblinking. "Yes, I think so. But before I say more, I need to be clear about the danger. I want you to weigh this decision carefully, knowing full well that you'd be risking your life by leaving."

"We're risking our lives by staying," Isaak interrupted, his voice low. His elbows rested on his propped-up knees, and he clasped his hands so tight his knuckles whitened, but his face was calm and open. Several boys nodded around him. He flicked his gaze to Ella again, as though asking a question.

Rösli nodded slightly. "Exactly. Now, let me explain what I've been up to. Earlier this fall I went to Switzerland and lobbied the Red Cross leadership to bring all of you into the country legally."

Heads turned in a chain reaction as kids exchanged glances, enlivened by her words, but Rösli held up a palm to stop them. She swallowed, lowering her hand into her lap and weaving her strong, calloused fingers together.

"It didn't go well in Bern. There's no way to get you out of France legally. So, we are left with only illegal options. And you must know that I'm acting without the knowledge or the approval of the Swiss Red Cross. There's nothing official about this—it's just me now."

For a moment, everyone held their breath. Ella watched Rösli shift where she sat on the floor, ringed by pensive teenagers, inhaling to bolster herself.

"Days after the Germans overtook the free zone, I went on to Saint-Cergues, near a French town called Annemasse, where another Secours Suisse home is located," Rösli continued. "It's only three kilometers from the Swiss border, and Geneva isn't far beyond. The *directrice* and her assistant are willing to help us." A hint of something, more vindication than smile, played on Rösli's thin lips. "If you choose to go, I'll furnish you with the safest routes, false identity cards, money, and contacts. Once you get to Saint-Cergues, the women of that house will walk you to the border. I've also organized a handful of women in Switzerland to house and vouch for you until arrangements can be made there."

Warmth flared in Ella's chest, like a struck match, as Rösli paused. The idea that strangers were willing to break international laws for them? That people cared about their fate? She no longer expected such goodwill.

"Is it possible to go to Spain as well?" Norbert asked, tottering a little where he crouched on his bedding.

"Yes." Rösli hesitated. "Obviously it's much closer, but the mountains are higher, Norbert. I'd only recommend it for those of you who have experience with such things. And I only have helpers on the way to Switzerland, but I'll try to support you either way."

Isaak cleared his throat. "When can we go?" His voice tugged Ella's gaze to him, but he stared at Rösli, transfixed. His eyes were wide, his jaw squared as if he was biting down, hard. The match died out in Ella's heart, instantly cooling. Isaak had already decided to leave, then. She pictured the silver promise of Switzerland, and it felt like a sail unfurled in her soul, billowing forward. She realized, suddenly, that she, too, would go without deliberation if she could. But an anchor held her back.

Rösli nodded in response to Isaak's question, anticipating it. "I think it would be best to go soon. Surely the border patrols will be a bit looser around Christmastime, especially as snow and storms roll through. The weather will be both a friend and an enemy—it can hide you, but your journey will be cold and treacherous." She looked between the many faces, clearly intent on her message. "You'll be in great danger the entire way. Please weigh that before making any decisions. The Germans have been known to shoot on sight near the border. If you're caught . . ." She looked down at her hands again, suddenly unable to finish her sentence. Once more, there wasn't a sound in the room. Rösli's meaning was clear enough.

"Think it over," Rösli said eventually. "For those of you who decide to escape, we'll have another meeting tomorrow night to discuss specific plans. I'll choose who will leave, and when, and none of you will know who's next until they're gone."

Edith looked uncertainly around the group, pushing her glasses up the bridge of her nose. "Does this mean we won't get to say goodbye to each other?"

"Say your goodbyes now." Rösli met their surprised stares. "I realize it's hard not to know who's leaving, but we'll need to minimize chatter and rumors, especially among the youngest children so they don't accidentally spill our secrets at the village school. It's best if people simply disappear quietly in twos and threes. Now go and think hard. Weigh this decision carefully."

Everyone stood, shaking out legs that had fallen asleep, whispering in small groups or staring at nothing with faraway eyes.

Ella was one of the first to leave the *Zwiebelkeller*. She didn't speak to anyone before shimmying out. Her friends were immersed in whispered conversations, excitement and fear written clearly in their faces. Ella emerged in Herr Lyrer's familiar room, blinking in the brighter light, a flood of conflicting emotions surging in her chest.

She couldn't leave France. She hurried downstairs, trying to dam the currents running through her. Isaak would go, clearly. Perhaps all of her other friends would go, too. But she wouldn't, because she had Hanni to think of. And she would never leave Hanni again.

*O*utside, the day was cold and bright. Ella walked as if charged by lightning, her sketch pad under her arm, the December air aching in her lungs. Thoughts buzzed in her mind, zipping around before she could catch a single one and sort it out. Why was she upset? She looked at the slope rising before her, each blade of dead grass silver and distinct in the winter sunlight, the ground still frozen in patches of shade. Shouldn't she be happy that her friends had the chance to escape? She shook her head as if to knock away the question, before realizing: She was. The idea of Inge or Dela or Edith crunching through the clean snow of Switzerland sent a zing of joy through her heart. She would lose them, yes, but Ella was accustomed to loss. What was it, then? Was she worried about them? She strode uphill, thighs burning, and her imagination took over, conjuring Isaak near barbed wire, his hands up and snow falling all around in big flakes. His chest jolted and blossomed red, his gray eyes widening, his long, strong body collapsing—

She stumbled on a rock, catching herself, and the horrific image jostled from her mind. Ella straightened and turned, breathing hard, looking down the hill spreading in her wake. She stared at the stone shoulders of the château, basking in the winter sun like it had for hundreds of years. She looked at the sky, ice blue, clear and cold. Ella breathed in, calming her pounding pulse. The forest interrupted the grassy slope nearby, so she walked to a wide boulder and sat down. She wanted to be in the sun. She wanted to be alone, rooted by her seat bones to this frigid rock, away from everyone so she could sift through her warring interior. She opened the sketchbook on her lap, pausing on the first page to run a gentle finger over her mother's familiar handwriting, her eyes catching on a bit of the prayer.

May it be Your will, Lord, our God and the God of our ancestors, that You lead us toward peace, guide our footsteps toward peace, and make us reach our desired destination for life, gladness, and peace . . .

Had her mother sensed, when she wrote the words of the Traveler's Prayer in Ella's sketchbook, just how long this journey would be? Ella closed her eyes, remembering how her mother had knelt before her daughters as they waited for the train to Belgium, pressing the sketchbook into Ella's hands.

"A little gift, from me and Papa." She'd smiled through her tears, her dark eyes glittering, and opened the sketchbook. "I wrote the Tefilat Haderech on the first page, you see? We say it at the beginning of a journey. Hanni, Ella can read it to you, all right?" Worry flashed in her eyes. "Quietly, of course. Remember how we love you, my darlings."

Ella wiped at her cheek and flipped through the pages, finding a patch of paper with room for a drawing, and swept her pencil up in a clear line.

She'd meant to draw the château, rising below her on this glorious day, in this beautiful niche of France, visually unchanging even as everything changed within and around it. But she arced her pencil in a curve over that line, and only as it moved did she realize that she was drawing something else. The lines led her in, as they always did, inviting her to become lost in their curves and shadows, their simplicity and complexity, their quiet. Drawings had a way of folding Ella into their silent world, smoothing out the jagged parts of her soul so she could think.

The first line became a neck, long and graceful. The second formed a head, arching up to a hairline, and without thinking about it, Ella knew what she was drawing. A minute later her mother's right eye took shape, and then the left, and they were perfect. Ella paused, looking into her mother's eyes staring out at her from the paper, and something broke inside. A single sob bubbled from her lips, but she wiped her cheeks with her wrist and kept drawing.

"Mutti," she whispered, unthinking. "I wish I could talk to you again. Just once. I'm so alone here, so scared all the time." Her pencil flicked as eyebrows appeared, curving across her mother's faintly lined forehead. "Well actually, I'm not alone at all," she whispered, sketching her mother's long hair. "I have Hanni, of course. She's doing well, Mutti. If only you could see her—she's as bold and wild as ever." Ella smiled briefly. "There's also a boy . . ." She drew the slope of her mother's thin nose, just like her own. "It's silly to mention him. There's nothing between us, really, except that he seeks me out to talk. And I like talking with him. There's something about him. He's a bit like Papa—reassuring and strong, with a big laugh. He wants to be a teacher." Ella made the lines of her mother's mouth, and her heart warmed as she recognized the smile expanding on her paper. Her mother had a big laugh, too. "I didn't tell him that Papa was a teacher. But doesn't it seem like a sign? I miss Papa so much. But I *need* you. I don't know what to do, how to live—I wish I could just talk to you, Mutti . . ."

Ella's pencil stopped. She stared down at the picture of her mother that had evolved, the mischievous smile like Hanni's, the bright eyes like both Ella's and Hanni's, the nose and cheekbones that matched her own. It was her mother, there, staring out in graphite, and her heart split open. She bit her lower lip, forcing back the sobs that threatened to pour forth. She'd been talking to a drawing. Ella looked up at the sky, blinking away her impossible emotions. She wanted to be as cold, and as strong, as the rock beneath her. She wanted to stop wanting. To stop feeling. To stop risking her beaten heart.

But, mostly, she wanted her mother back.

*E*lla?"

An hour had passed on the hillside, and the sun was already dipping behind the trees, casting winter shadows below. Ella turned to see Isaak coming up the rocky path. His long legs swallowed the ground as he loped up, hands plunged in his pockets, cheeks red in the chilling air.

"Ella," he said again as he neared. "I've been looking all over for you. Have you been out here since the meeting?"

She nodded up at him, steeling her heart but scooting over a little on her boulder so he could sit down.

"I just needed to be alone for a bit."

He glanced at her, his face pensive. "Should I leave you—"

"No." She held his stare, looking into his eyes long enough to pick out the flecks of deeper gray. What could have been between them, if they'd had a chance at a regular life? In a week or two, she might never see him again. She cleared her throat. "No, I'm glad to have some company now."

He nodded, leaning forward to prop the knobs of his elbows on his knees. His dark hair fell in his eyes as he gazed out. "So, what did you think about everything Rösli said?"

"Isaak. I can't go."

His head swung around. His brows came down as he studied her. "You've already decided?"

Ella sighed. "There was nothing for me to decide. I could never leave Hanni alone in France and sneak off to Switzerland. Never."

He nodded again, turning to stare down at the château, his handsome face solemn. "When I couldn't find you earlier, I thought you might be worrying about Hanni. Couldn't you just take her, Ella? I'm sure Rösli would let her go."

"No, I'm sure she wouldn't. She's too sensible for that. And she'd be right. Hanni's safe here."

"For now."

Worry slid over her heart like a shadow, but she shook her head and looked him in the eyes. "She's safer here than walking through the snowy wilderness, dodging soldiers who've been told to shoot on sight—you see that, don't you? Also, if I leave her, Isaak, she's alone in the world. Our parents . . ." She hesitated, her unspoken words crystallizing in her heart like frost. His gaze held hers, unwavering, and she inhaled. Saying it out loud wouldn't make it more true. "Our parents were deported, and I just can't sense them anymore, out there. You might think I'm crazy, but I don't care—I used to be able to feel them. I knew, somehow, that they were in the world. And now, it's just . . . quiet."

His hand slid over hers, gripping hard. "No. I don't think that's crazy." He sighed heavily. "I know what you mean. I don't have any sort of sixth sense, but my father has been gone for so long now, with no word at all. It's hard not knowing . . ."

Neither of them spoke for a moment. Ella glanced at their joined hands before asking the question that lingered in her mind. "And your mother?" He'd never mentioned her.

He stared at the château while he spoke, his voice low and even. "My mother was Polish. I wonder about her family sometimes— we'd visit them near Krakow when I was little. She died before I left Germany. She was sick, for a long time. But after *Kristallnacht* she made my father promise to get me out of the country. That's why he sent me to Belgium."

"I'm sorry," she whispered.

He shrugged, but pain crept into his expression. "She died believing I was safe." He cleared his throat, his stoicism unconvincing. "It's why I want to get over the border, Ella. I want to live, obviously. I want to have a career, and a family with lots of kids. A wife." A shadow of a smile died out quickly. "But also, I want to honor what my parents did for me. Does that make sense?"

She nodded, tightening her hand in his. He did the same, and they sat for a long moment, gripping each other, while the sun slid slowly behind a tree, casting its wandering light.

"We have to live for our families," she said eventually. "It's a far greater responsibility than I would have thought. Before."

"What was life like for you, before?"

She tried to smile. "Easy."

He laughed a little, but the sound was hollow.

"Our house in Cologne was lovely." The smile became real, remembering. "It wasn't big, but we lived on a nice street and had everything we needed. My father played the piano, and my mother loved anything artistic. She could cook, and draw, and write poetry that made dinner guests laugh and cry. There was a lot of life in our house."

Isaak glanced at her, the solemnity falling from his face. "So that's where you get it." He motioned to the sketchbook, closed now, then looked out at the fading day and smiled a little. "That's the kind of house I want someday. Lots of life."

Ella shrugged, following his gaze to the château below. It rose from slanting shadows and incoming fog, the silent mist drifting and eddying over the cold earth. Did Isaak really think he could still have a future like her past? The simple things she gripped so hard in her memory—home, family, music, and laughter—those simple things were impossible dreams now. Her birthright, stolen.

"Did you realize that it's Hanukkah?" Ella said after a moment, glancing at Isaak.

He nodded, looking out over the hills. Ever since the Swiss Red

Cross took over their colony, they'd been made to celebrate Christmas instead of their own holidays. It had stung. But this year, Ella realized, she hadn't even thought of Hanukkah until Ruth said something at breakfast.

"My father used to love lighting the candles." She smiled a bit at the memory.

"What was your father like?" Isaak asked, turning. His stare was earnest, as if he really wanted to learn about her life, to hear her voice, to imagine her past.

"Kind and easygoing." She tried to picture her father's face, but what came instead was his hand, broad and strong, holding her smaller palm as they strolled. "He used to take me on long walks, no matter the season, and buy me sweets along the way. He'd whistle and swing my hand and point out anything interesting. He had a way of making everything feel safe and predictable. Even when it wasn't."

"What did he do for work?"

She half smiled. "He was a teacher."

"Ah. I see." Isaak chuckled. "Have you heard that girls seek men like their fathers?"

Ella laughed, surprised at his boldness. She pulled her hand from his, swatting lightly at his shoulder. "Do you think I'm seeking you, Isaak Goldberg?"

He held her stare, his gray eyes laughing now, and shrugged. "Maybe not. But I'm definitely seeking you, Ella Rosenthal."

Before she could think about his words, his head dipped forward in the dying sunlight, and she felt pulled toward him, like the wind pulls clouds, and their lips found each other. They kissed for two beats of her heart, and each pulse was a jolt of joy, spinning through her veins, before he fell away.

For a strange moment, they simply stared at each other, mutually stunned.

"Isaak." She found his hands again, warm, and swallowed the words that nearly escaped. *I don't want you to go.*

A few mornings later, Ella came down for breakfast, and something in the dining hall felt immediately different. She glanced around the room, taking in the clink and clatter of spoons. Chatter leapt from the younger children, who were always wide awake in the morning. Ella picked out Hanni, nestled next to her friend Antoinette on one side, and Rösli on the other. The rest of the tables weren't yet filled, though that wasn't unusual; the older kids had a notoriously harder time waking up, while the youngest bounced around their dormitories before the sun rose. Ella glanced at her sister, who grinned up with a mouthful of porridge, giggling while Ella made a face. Rösli followed Hanni's gaze, and her spoon froze in midair for a second, her eyes snagging on Ella's. Understanding zipped between them, invisible but palpable. It was not a normal morning. Ella's heart stuttered.

She filled a bowl with porridge and slipped into a seat next to Edith, across from Inge Joseph. They exchanged glances, and again Ella looked around the dining hall. There were several empty seats. She guessed, from Rösli's silent stare, that the first kids had slipped away in the night, trekking across the hills under frosty starlight, headed for the train station with their forged documents.

The escapes had begun.

Inge studied her bowl, her expression wooden. Ella lifted her spoon to her mouth, her heart pounding, trying to figure out who had gone and who was still trickling down from their beds. What she'd noticed the second she entered the room, before she'd understood, was that Isaak wasn't at any of the tables. She stared at her spoon, unable to finish the task of lifting it to her lips and swallowing. Would he have left without saying goodbye? Yes, of course he would have, she scolded herself. He wouldn't have known he was going until Rösli woke him in the dead of night.

Edith leaned close, her breath hot in Ella's ear. "It's started, right?"

Inge looked up sharply, shaking her head to shush them, her short brown curls bobbing. They couldn't speak of it now. It was best to pretend things were normal so the littlest children didn't start whispers that might leak into the village, compromising the escapees. Ella swallowed her first bite of food, subduing her nerves, and glanced around again. Was Isaak really gone? Had he been in the *Zwiebelkeller* when she woke up? She tried to remember the rows of rumpled bedding, dotted with still-sleeping kids, but nothing had seemed unusual; they always trickled downstairs. Who else was absent? *Lucien. Norbert.* She pivoted to scan the room, running names through her mind. *Walter Strauss.* Ella met Inge's grave gaze, understanding all at once. Inge and Walter had been inseparable for months now, walking in the hills, talking over books, holding hands, and swapping secret looks. Had he really left without her?

Ella turned back to her porridge, her chest tightening with grief and frustration. There was no such thing as romance, not for them. She'd been a fool to develop feelings for Isaak. What feelings could she possibly have? Her affection was borne of loneliness, and in a normal life it would mean little. The problem was that this was not a normal life. Her heart was fractured, like ice that had been hit too many times and verged on giving way. Imagining that Isaak could mean something was like inviting another hit of the mallet, another crack, another risk.

Ella pinned her eyes on her bowl, forcing her spinning thoughts into submission. She spooned porridge, willing her throat to swallow, and tried to shut off the rest of the world as it continued on around her. She was nearly finished eating when voices filtered in from the courtyard. She sat up a little, meeting Inge's widening eyes. Footsteps scuffed outside the heavy door. Ella gripped her spoon as if she could bend its metal, listening. The door swung open, the creak of hinges punctuated by a loud, familiar laugh, and the new pain in Ella's chest eased.

Isaak sauntered in, still chuckling with Walter Strauss, both of them messy haired from the courtyard and late to breakfast. He sought her gaze across the tables full of younger children, nodding over his swift grin.

Inge buried her face in her hands, overcome. Ella nodded back, trying to make sense of her own reckless, rebounding emotions. The ice inside her heart thawed. But how was that different from shattering? She still sensed the water moving beneath her soul, deep and cold.

She pulled her gaze from Isaak's and set the spoon in her bowl. She hadn't lost him after all, she told herself, subduing the flood of feeling under her placid surface.

Not yet.

≈≈≈≈⟩

ELEVEN

ANNE-MARIE

MONTLUEL, FRANCE

DECEMBER 1942

Anne-Marie walked with Yseult through the cold, blustery forest. Ahead, children ran and played, their voices high as the wind. It had been raining all morning, and Francisco, the gardener, seemed sure that snow was coming soon, but for the moment it was dry. The youngest children had been bouncing around the big house like popcorn kernels in a pot, so Anne-Marie and Yseult hurried them out for a walk while they could.

"Run, run!" Anne-Marie called ahead, urging the children down the path. "Tout le monde! We want all of you to sleep well tonight!"

Rafaela, holding hands with Sabine, glanced over her shoulder, black eyes glittering. "Watch us, Señora Piguet! We can gallop like horses!"

The two little girls took off, Rafaela leading on her long legs, and a trio of boys burst after them. A handful of others trickled out of the woods, skipping to catch up, crunching over dead leaves.

Anne-Marie and Yseult watched for a moment, waiting for all

the children to move safely ahead. Then Yseult dropped her voice to continue a conversation that had been interrupted by the presence of young ears all day.

"Antonio says it's getting worse in Lyon," she murmured, and Anne-Marie frowned, her nerves gathering.

Yseult had become fond of Antonio, a Spanish man who, for a time, had found safety working at Montluel. Yet he'd begun to fear that the Swiss Red Cross wouldn't prevent his internment if the police came for him, so he was now in Lyon. Yseult couldn't say much, but Anne-Marie understood that he was hiding and finding ways to fight back. He'd also become a conduit of information about the atmosphere in the city.

"Worse how?" she asked quietly.

"The Germans are tightening restrictions." Her gaze flipped to Anne-Marie. "They're intensifying searches for Jews and resistance members."

Fear chilled Anne-Marie. "What if they come for our children?" She watched Sabine and Joseph crouch up ahead under a beech tree, scratching at the dirt with a stick. A bird passed over the naked branches, and the children looked up to follow its flight. *Eurasian kestrel*, Anne-Marie thought, like a reflex.

Yseult shook her head. "For now, I think our *directrice* is correct. They won't bother with the little ones, especially those in Swiss custody. The Germans want those they consider to be adults—"

"But what about all the reports of deported children?" Anne-Marie interrupted, struggling with rising anxiety. "They took whole families, Yseult. I saw children in Rivesaltes who were bound for trains."

Yseult frowned, thinking. "We can't be sure what will happen," she relented. "But Monsieur Dubois explained that the official policy is to take only people of age, unless they're part of a family— they take whole families. He thinks small children with Swiss caretakers will be left alone, because the French need the Swiss Red Cross to feed French children, too. They'd be in a bind without us."

Anne-Marie felt sick. What kind of world made this discussion necessary? "I think we need an escape route, Yseult. Just in case."

Yseult shook her head again. "Don't go digging around the border right now. I asked Antonio what he thought about all of this, and he believes that we'll endanger our colony if we attract attention to it. You mustn't go making escape plans yet, *chérie*."

Anne-Marie nodded, her anxiety deepening, and watched as Joseph and Sabine stood in the path, the wind lifting Sabine's curls as she ran ahead. Joseph turned, his heavily lashed, brown eyes catching Anne-Marie's gaze, and he smiled shyly. Then he was off with the breeze, his little leather shoes pounding the forest path.

She would do anything to keep them safe. But what *should* she do?

The first snowflakes began to fall, and Yseult walked ahead to gather the children who had scattered farther into the forest. Anne-Marie paused on the path, looking up through a gap in the trees. Snow eddied and spun on the wind, dancing down to earth. She closed her eyes, thinking of other walks in the woods, with her father. She yearned to speak with him. All her life, she'd shared her worries and questions with him as they hiked through the Risoud, and he'd listened. What would he say to her now?

"Do you believe in God?" Anne-Marie had once asked her father. It was early spring, she was barely a teenager, and they were out in the mountains together, which was her favorite place to be. She hiked in his wake, climbing a steep incline. For a long moment he said nothing, and she watched his broad back as he bent to grip a root, hoisting himself over a shelf of limestone. She did the same, hopping up like a mountain goat, and they continued toward a break in the trees. She understood her father's silence; he liked to consider his words before he voiced them.

"I suppose I do," he said eventually, and they walked out from under the embrace of trees onto a steep slope of scree. The trail cut straight across the rock field, exposing them to the wind and final glow of the lowering sun. "Not in the traditional sense," he said, moving steadily across the scree. Before Anne-Marie could ask her next question, she stumbled a little, sending a stream of rocks skittering downhill. Her father turned, alarm in his eyes. He saw she was still on her feet, and the alarm shifted to a look of warning. "Careful, now. Choose your steps."

She nodded, focusing on the trail until they reached the next bank of trees. There they paused, looking out over the view, catching their breath. The first stars winked in the sky.

"Only a bit farther to our campsite," her father murmured, squinting out at the tumble of hills spreading from their vantage point. He shifted the pack on his shoulders and watched a bird dive across the scree. "An Alpine swift," he said absently.

"What did you mean, Papa?" Anne-Marie persisted. Her mind was still on God. Their conversations were often like this, interrupted by stretches of forest and trailing thoughts, but she was used to her father. She knew that when he gave her an answer, it would be well considered, and he wouldn't make her feel silly for asking. Her brother and sister often teased her, affectionately, for being so earnest. *There goes Anne-Marie again*, her sister would say, *philosophizing about the meaning of life*.

She looked at her father now as he pulled a canteen from his pack and offered it to her. She took it, speaking between swigs. "Grand-mère always tells me that when I have questions, I should pray. But I have *so* many questions, and I pray all the time, and the questions don't go anywhere."

He smiled slightly, amused. "I've had questions all my life, and mine don't go away, either. The God I believe in doesn't give me answers. Not really."

She frowned, and he read the confusion on her face. The need for more.

"The God I pray to, Anne-Marie, is out here." He gestured to the view, and she looked. A sea of treetops spread from this notch in the mountain, tossing in the wind. Hills multiplied as far as she could see, the sky purpling over them. Her father glanced up at the scatter of brightening stars. "I don't find answers to my questions out here, Anne-Marie. The mountains and forests, they can't tell me why things happen or how to live my life." He caught her gaze, fingering his mustache. "But here, I find something more important than answers."

"What?"

"Peace. The world has a rhythm, Anne-Marie. The sun rises every morning, the soil connects the trees, strengthening their roots, the seasons come and go. I don't believe anyone can give you the answers you seek, but sometimes, if you come out here and you listen, you'll find your purpose. We fit into the order of things, you see."

She thought about that, and he smiled in the darkening evening. "If you're ever lost, come to the forest. Stand among the wind and stars and listen, my love. You'll find your way."

Anne-Marie opened her eyes, and the memory evaporated. She stood in a different forest, far from home, her questions and worries so much larger than anything her thirteen-year-old mind could have fathomed. Was her father right?

If she listened hard enough, would she find her way through a world gone mad?

𐓶

RÖSLI

CHÂTEAU DE LA HILLE, SOUTHERN FRANCE

DECEMBER 1942

*R*ösli glanced out the darkened window as she crept into Herr Lyrer's room. The glass sparkled with frost and starlight, and everything beneath it was black. She exhaled, but her breath caught on nerves. She leaned closer, trying to scrutinize what she could make out of the grounds below, searching for movement, the glint of metal, the wave of an arm, or anything else that shouldn't be there. Seeing nothing, she straightened, scolding herself because she'd just stared through her own window not five minutes ago. Ever since that terrible August night, when the gendarmes had come for the children, she couldn't shake the need to check, over and over again, for danger. Fear nipped at her like a wolf on her heels.

"Rösli," a voice whispered, and she jolted a little. Herr Lyrer lifted himself to his elbows, but she could see only the rumpled shape of him in the darkness. "How many tonight?"

She cleared her tight throat to let a whisper through. "Four." She hoisted the sack on her arm, packed with everything needed for a journey: money; a map with detailed, coded notes; bread and cheese; and, most precious, false identity cards for four teenagers. "I'm going to walk them partway to the train station, so I'll be gone for a couple of hours. Will you manage breakfast if I'm late returning?"

Herr Lyrer nodded in the darkness.

Rösli dropped to her knees and slid the door to the *Zwiebelkeller* open. Eugen Lyrer could be counted on; he'd keep watch until she returned, maintaining the château's routine while the second group of teenagers slipped away, northbound.

Norbert and Lucien had been first to go, though they'd made a last-minute change to Rösli's plan. The boys, fit and confident, wanted to try for the closer, yet more treacherous border into Spain. "I grew up hiking in the Alps," Norbert had explained, earnest. Rösli had glanced between them, weighing their options and wringing her hands so tightly they hurt. They had to leave La Hille. On her last visit to Foix, Madame Authié had told Rösli that anyone over eighteen was in immediate danger, and these two would hit that milestone soon. Which was safer for boys who knew mountains: the seven-hundred-kilometer journey to Switzerland through occupied France, or the towering Pyrénées in the dead of winter? They'd pressed her, having already decided themselves, and with a heavy heart Rösli had given them her blessing. The weight of their fate hadn't left her since they'd gone.

Rösli shook away her worries, shimmying into the secret room. The tang of onions, mixed with the breath of dozens of slumbering teenagers, hit her. It was cold, and so dark she had to feel her way through the blanketed figures on the floor, careful not to bump anyone. She found Regina first, a slight girl asleep in a fetal curl. Rösli didn't even have to touch her; Regina, apparently sensing the monumental moment approaching, pushed herself upright, glancing around to get her bearings, her eyes glinting in the darkness. Without a word, she picked up the packed rucksack she'd used as a pillow. The departing teenagers didn't know it was their turn, but they were ready nonetheless. Everyone went to sleep dressed, wearing whatever they could assemble for a long walk in the cold. Their heads rested on rucksacks containing only items a fifteen-year-old French child might carry to visit relatives. Regina drifted away, and Rösli crept toward the next girl. *Margot.*

When the girls waited by the door, silent as ghosts, Rösli made her way to the line of boys. She'd assembled groups carefully, pairing those who spoke poor French with proficient speakers, and those who were less savvy with kids who knew how to be inconspicuous. Still, her heart pounded. Could they pass as French children all the way to Annemasse? Would their documents pass inspection? And could they find the house in Saint-Cergues safely? She'd made them study maps and repeat routes back to her. She'd lain awake at night, trying to plan for every eventuality they might encounter. She paused now, scanning their sleeping forms, her breath tight. Was it right to encourage Jewish teenagers to cross occupied France and hike over a patrolled, snow-covered border? The journey would win them their freedom, but it could also cost them their lives.

And yet, at La Hille their lives were in danger every single day.

Rösli found the two boys she'd chosen for the group. Peter and Jacques woke as if they, too, had been waiting in their sleep, ready, their compasses already pointed north.

Minutes later they all crawled out through the *Zwiebelkeller* door, silently shook Herr Lyrer's outstretched hand, and gathered in the dark hallway. Without a word, Rösli led them downstairs and through the château's main door, taking care to close it without a sound.

The sky was a wash of winter stars. The boys swung into loping gaits alongside Rösli, and the girls linked arms and walked as a pair. Without a word, they crunched out past the shadowy garden, under the watchtower that guarded La Hille, and up into the frosted, dark hills.

The first leg of the journey was a hike to the village of Saint-Jean-de-Verges, where the children were less likely to be recognized boarding a train. Rösli's legs burned on the incline, yet she was grateful for physical exertion as a distraction from her racing mind. Her gaze swung to the stars, cold and silver, and every gust of breath hung in their light. She could walk only partway to Saint-Jean-de-Verges if she was to be back at La Hille by breakfast, eating with the younger children as if nothing had changed.

Regina came up beside Rösli, panting in the darkness, and reached for her hand. Rösli squeezed her cold fingers, glancing at the girl's slender form as she climbed. Doubt pricked Rösli's heart. Regina was one of the youngest of *les Grands*, not quite sixteen, but she was determined to leave. Rösli had wanted to sway her, if only because she seemed so young. Yet she'd also seen children Regina's age deported. She had to let her go.

"Is it a long walk, Mademoiselle Näf?" Regina's eyes caught the starlight. Margot strode along on her other side, tall in a dress she'd outgrown and surely must be uncomfortable wearing, her gaze on the boys pacing ahead.

"Three hours, if you walk fast," Rösli whispered.

The girls nodded, and Regina tightened her grip on Rösli. Regina must have once held her mother's hand, years ago, on happier walks than this one.

Please, Rösli thought, looking again to the swath of stars. *Please let them make it.*

Several days later, after a Christmas that passed with little acknowledgment at La Hille, Rösli again strode through crisp winter air. This time it was daylight, and she was headed not over the hills, but to a doctor's office in the village of Montégut.

She squinted her tired eyes as she walked. Rösli had barely slept all week. In the nights leading up to Christmas, she'd taken three more teenagers midway to Saint-Jean-de-Verges. She'd heard nothing of them since.

Compounding her worry, *les Petits* were scheduled to return to school shortly after New Year's. The tables where *les Grands* usually sat steadily thinned, and the littlest children glanced at it with wide eyes, sometimes whispering to one another while they spooned their breakfast. Rösli planned to send five or six more teenagers north before school resumed; would the small children mention to their teacher that *les Grands* were disappearing? If questioned in the village, what would they say? Rösli had spent a sleepless night imagining possibilities, and just before dawn, she'd thought of a potential solution.

Now she strode into the doctor's office, settling before an older man who looked as though he were built of angles hemmed together under his faded suit. Nerves fluttered in her stomach as Dr. Martineau peered at her quizzically from a chair behind his desk. How could she broach the question? He could turn her in to the police, if so inclined.

She stared right into his eyes, the brown of winter leaves under bushy white eyebrows. "I'm sorry to call you in, Dr. Martineau. Have you had a nice holiday with your family?"

"It's just the two of us now, mademoiselle. One day's like any other." He waved a hand as if to bat away the notion of holidays altogether. Wrinkles boxed his mouth as he frowned, clearly impatient to get on with things. "What do you need, Mademoiselle Näf? Do you have need of a doctor at La Hille?"

She hesitated, unconsciously pursing her lips while gathering the words. There was nothing to do but say them.

"In fact, I'm here because the situation at La Hille is grave, Dr. Martineau. I'm afraid we need a quarantine."

He blinked at her, puzzled, reflexively eyeing his traveling case. "A quarantine? How many of the children are ill?"

"There's no illness."

The doctor hesitated, his age-spotted hand still drifting to his traveling case while his thoughts caught up. He huffed. "Well, if there's no illness, why in heaven's name would you want a quarantine?"

Heat flushed Rösli's face, but she maintained her deliberate stare. "I need a way to prevent anyone from visiting the château, Dr. Martineau." Would he understand what she meant? Would he be sympathetic, or outraged at her desire to skirt the authorities?

The doctor gazed at her, confusion slowly fading from his expression, though he continued to frown. Eventually he cleared his throat laboriously, as though his own plumbing no longer functioned. He reached for a pad of paper across his desk with a slightly shaking hand, and Rösli's heart hammered. What was he thinking? Would he report her to the police?

"I was horrified when the gendarmes raided your château last August, Mademoiselle Näf," he said quietly, reaching for a pen. "Think of it—arresting children. It would have helped to have a quarantine then, I suppose." He looked up, holding her stare.

Rösli hardly dared to breathe. She nodded slightly.

The doctor straightened, newly decisive. "I'll just jot down the symptoms you're reporting. What I hear is that your children became suddenly ill . . . severe vomiting and diarrhea. Next came red, irritated rashes, beginning on chests and spreading throughout the body, accompanied by fatigue . . ." His words drifted off, and the scratch of his pen filled the silence. Rösli knew the symptoms he described, and the vise around her heart loosened.

"*C'est bien*," Dr. Martineau said momentarily, again clearing his clogged throat. "I'll announce to the village that La Hille is under quarantine due to an outbreak of scarlet fever. No children should leave the property for any reason, and nobody may enter the premises for several weeks. I'll let the school and the police know, Mademoiselle Näf."

She blinked back threatening tears. "I don't know how to thank you, Dr. Martineau."

His gaze was troubled, but again he waved his hand as though to bat her words away. "Never mind that. Go on and take care of those children now."

Rösli stepped out of the doctor's office, her heart lighter for the first time in ages. She forced herself not to smile as she walked to the post office. There were still good people in the world. People who wanted to do the right thing. There were the women of Saint-Cergues, willing to help refugees cross the border, and now Dr. Martineau, who understood what she needed and granted it without question.

Rösli walked into the quiet post office, pausing in a square of sunshine segmenting the floor. The postal worker glanced up.

"Ah, Mademoiselle Näf," he said, adjusting his glasses and shuffling paperwork behind his desk. "Got some mail for you here, and a telegram came in just an hour ago. Lucky you stopped by."

A telegram? Rösli froze in her square of sunshine, her breath shallow. Would it be about her escapees? She'd been waiting to hear something, desperate for news, but suddenly the existence of a telegram felt like too much. What if it conveyed bad news?

The postal worker, unaware of her distress, simply shuffled through the mail and handed her a bundle, stretching to pass it to Rösli where she stood, still frozen. She glanced down at the sender: *Germaine Hommel*. "Thank you," she managed, pivoting to stride out the door, forcing herself not to read anything until she was well away from the eyes of the village. She hurried down the narrow street, past a spatter of buildings, and into the fragmented shade of roadside trees. When she'd gone far enough to feel safely alone, she paused, lifting the telegram, split between terror and hope.

Hope cascaded into joy. Rösli pressed her free hand to her forehead as if to contain herself. She looked out at the winter sunlight, and for the first time in a long time, it seemed that things might be all right.

Because her teenagers had made it. She glanced again at the telegram from Germaine.

Your packages were received and sent on with success.

Rösli found herself nearly laughing, alone in the road. Were children from La Hille really in Switzerland, safe and sound? She blinked back tears, tucked the mail into her bag, and kicked up a swift walk.

She couldn't wait to share the news with the rest of *les Grands*, eagerly waiting in the *Zwiebelkeller* for their own chance at freedom.

꧁꧂

THIRTEEN

ELLA

*E*lla turned eighteen.

The morning of her birthday she walked down to breakfast, the date hanging in her heart like an omen. She was officially an adult. Fully grown, without her parents to witness the end of her childhood. Now, she was also legally beyond the protection of the Swiss Red Cross. Ella walked into the dining hall, glancing around as if danger might already be coming for her, but there was only the usual talking and bobbing of heads as children bent to eat, blocks of light falling over tables and the clink of silverware against bowls.

Hanni bounded over and wrapped Ella around the waist, more excited for her birthday than anyone. Ella listened to her chatter and scanned the room, looking for new empty seats indicating fresh escapes, but there were none. Isaak, talking with Walter Strauss, held up a palm when he spotted her, shifting to stand. But before he could rise, Dela sprang up from her seat, her pretty face breaking into a smile. Hanni skipped off, and Dela hurried over, a piece of paper clasped in her slender fingers, and wrapped Ella in a hug. Some of the ice coating Ella's spirit cracked while her friend pulled away, blinking her dark-lashed eyes.

"Happy birthday, Ella. Here." Dela shrugged like an excited child, offering the paper. "I made you a card."

Ella unfolded it and found several dried flowers, plucked last summer, tucked inside. On the paper itself, Dela had sketched a picture of the two of them, arms around each other's waists, on one of the hillsides that could have borne the flowers. *Use big and small shapes*, a voice whispered in Ella's thoughts as she ran a finger over the drawing. *Darkness and light . . .* Her art teacher would have been pleased with this simple drawing, sketched by a refugee girl, that captured so much nuance. Dela's looping scrawl underlined the picture. *Happy birthday, my dear friend. I'm grateful you've been beside me on this long journey.*

Ella looked into Dela's pretty eyes. "Thank you—it's beautiful."

"You think so? I've been practicing."

Ella nodded, and they held each other's gaze for a weighted moment, leaving the rest unspoken. Dela had asked to leave La Hille, so their journey together would soon end. Every night Dela laid her head on her packed rucksack, ready to go. Every morning Ella woke knowing that her best friends could be gone. She looked down at the card, smiling a little. It was a gift that this morning, on her birthday, they were still here. It was a gift that when Dela did vanish some morning, Ella would have a bit of her friend's heart on this paper.

Ella sat down and Isaak discarded his breakfast bowl, sauntering over with an eagerness in his step. "How about a walk this morning, just the two of us?"

"Is it safe to leave the grounds?" She glanced around as if looking for someone to grant them permission.

He nodded. "I asked Rösli. She said it should be fine as long as we stay close. She doesn't expect visitors because we're all so sick with scarlet fever." He chuckled. "We don't have to go far—let's just stretch our legs a bit."

Minutes later they passed under the tower guarding La Hille's courtyard, filling their lungs with cold air, feeling the weak winter sun spill over their cheeks, and Ella continued to sense that the day was a gift. A reprieve, unexpected. As soon as they were out of eye-sight, Isaak reached down, gripping her hand, and warmth expanded in her chest. She stretched her legs to match his stride, happiness in her soul, and decided: She wouldn't fight today. She wouldn't push back on hope. She wouldn't bar joy from her heart. She wouldn't think about Isaak leaving, about losing her friends, about her parents, about the sorrow that covered her like permafrost.

On her eighteenth birthday, Ella would allow herself to be happy.

They strode up a hill, the wind in their hair. A stand of trees neared, the sunlight fingering their naked branches and casting a patchwork of shadow. Isaak pulled Ella into the fragmented light, gathered her in his arms, and kissed her. She rose to him, surprising herself, wrapping her hand around his neck and pulling her body and soul as close to his as possible. And the world stopped. The pulse of war faded, the sobs of children at night scattered on the wind, the fear melted against a fire growing in Ella's heart.

When Isaak moved away, just slightly, he looked down at her with his ocean eyes. He half smiled, his hands tightening on her waist. "Happy birthday. I wish I was able to get you a gift."

She shrugged. "You're all I want." The words surfaced without thought, and she smiled. They were true. She could feel his heart beating against her own chest.

Isaak ran his hands to hers and tugged her toward a patch of light. He sat down and she followed, nestling into the nook of his chest and heavy arm.

"I've been thinking about my decision," he said, tracing her fingers where they'd landed on his knee. "And I'm not going to go."

Her stomach dropped, her happiness suspended like a note held, long and wavering, in the air. She pulled back a little to look him in the eyes. "To Switzerland? Isaak, you have to go. So many kids have already made it—"

He shook his head, solemn. "I don't want to go without you."

Ella stared at him for a long moment, her mouth hanging open. He would stay? For her? Did she mean that much to him? With a pulse of her heart, she realized he meant that much to her. Despite her vow to abandon grief, a bubble rose in her throat.

"Isaak, I can't let you do that for me. You'd be risking your life. Passing up your chance at freedom. What if the border tightens even more in the coming months? What if it becomes impossible to leave?"

He pivoted a little, his knees bumping hers, and took both of her hands. His stare was so deep she felt she could fall into his eyes and swim in their sea. "Ella." He squeezed her hands. "I know we haven't been close for long. But I feel something about you, and it's more than a whim. It's more than infatuation. Don't you feel it? It's like . . ." He glanced around the hills, vibrant in the morning light, searching for words. "It's like our hearts match." His gaze swung back to hers, latching on. "I've lost everyone. I don't have anyone to find in Switzerland. How could I go off, alone, when the only person I could love is here?"

She held his hands, tightening her grip as her heart beat with something like fear. *The only person I could love.* Before she realized it, tears spilled onto her cheeks. She could love him. She'd known it, somehow, from the start.

"But what if they catch us?" She leaned into him, grounding herself on the solid weight of his shoulder. She thought of Hanni, with her fierce affection and wild heart. Was there a way to take Hanni over the border? Could she propel both Isaak and Hanni toward a safer world? An image flashed in her mind: Hanni in her winter dress, snow up to her little knees alongside a barbed wire fence, the beam of a searchlight falling on her. She saw her mother and father, years ago, waving from the train station, hope and fear straining their fading smiles.

"I don't know what to do," she whispered.

Isaak's arm tightened around her shoulder. "How about this." He glanced down at her, using his thumb to wipe a tear from her cheek. "Today, we will sit here and talk of other things. It's your birthday. We don't need to make any decisions. Except that we will stay together, no matter what. How does that sound?"

She found a smile. Nodded.

"All right, then. Let's talk about something more fun. What kind of house do you want, someday? I don't care about houses much, myself. All I know is that I'm going to plant five apple trees in our future yard."

She giggled, despite the roar in her heart, and the roar quieted. "Five? Are you planning to run a cider mill?"

He shrugged, laughter in his face. "After a long day of teaching, I might want some cider, sure. And pie."

She giggled again. Her mind moved from the snowy border to a future she never dreamed about anymore. What would she want in a house?

"I'll have an art room," she ventured. "With lots of windows."

He grinned, and his arm tightened around her shoulders again. "I'll build you an easel. After the *Zwiebelkeller*, I think I can build anything."

Ella stared out at the morning sunshine, imagining a room with windows and light, an easel, apple trees outside, and, most of all, Isaak.

Late in the afternoon, Ella and Isaak walked hand in hand back down to the château. When they wandered into the dining room, Dela sprang up, her face brimming with something.

"Did you hear?" she asked as they neared. She'd been talking with Inge Joseph, who looked up with her serious gaze and smiled. "Norbert and Lucien," Inge said, picking up where Dela left off. "They made it to Spain. Rösli heard from their guides this afternoon."

"Hurrah!" Isaak exclaimed, and when Ella glanced at him, she saw a spark of triumph in his smile. Her own smile faded a little. Isaak was big and strong. If it weren't for her, maybe he would have gone with them. He reached for her hand and squeezed as if he could sense her sudden misgivings.

"I bet we're next," Inge whispered.

Dela nodded, adding, "Just think. We'll be in Switzerland for spring!"

When Ella woke, it was very dark. She didn't move, but listened to the rustle and whispers around her for several minutes. Someone was shifting at her side, smoothing blankets, and Ella watched as Dela stepped delicately past her.

Her heart swelled. She sat up a little, turning to find Dela kneeling nearby, reaching for her hand. Inge Joseph and Inge Helft hovered behind her, and the figures of two boys waited by the door. Five seats would be empty in the morning, and there would be corresponding holes in Ella's heart.

She grasped Dela's slender fingers, squeezing, and her friend bent a little and kissed her on the forehead.

"Good luck," Ella managed, whispering the words into Dela's ear like a prayer.

Dela nodded, and both Inges held up their hands in the darkness to say goodbye. Then the girls crept out to meet the waiting boys, and the door to the *Zwiebelkeller* slid closed.

~~~~~

FOURTEEN

ANNE-MARIE

MONTLUEL, FRANCE

JANUARY 1943

*A*nne-Marie stood at the dining room window, watching a couple walk up the twilit driveway. Snow fell around them, complicating the darkening sky, and the man paused to brush a scrim of white from his wife's shoulders. A smile passed between them, and they moved toward the château's exterior stairs. Moments later the front door creaked open, and Anne-Marie turned to see Maurice and Eléonore Dubois step inside.

Montluel's *directrice* came forward to pump their hands in greeting, and several other staff members drifted close, eager to say hello to the couple who managed all the Swiss Red Cross children's colonies in France. They visited from Toulouse occasionally, bringing news, small gifts for the children, and general cheer. Anne-Marie had yet to meet them, however. Their last trip to Montluel had overlapped with her mission to Rivesaltes, so she'd merely heard about the beloved leaders of the Secours Suisse.

Anne-Marie hung back from the cluster by the door, studying Maurice and Eléonore. She'd long been curious about them, especially after hearing of Maurice's intervention in Vichy on behalf of Rösli's captured teenagers. Lately, some staff members whispered that Maurice was helping Rösli with some illicit scheme. Many didn't believe it was true, in light of the risks involved, but Anne-Marie did. She remembered the fervor in Rösli's voice when she'd spoken of her vulnerable teenagers; Rösli would certainly break not only Swiss Red Cross rules but also the law to save them. Were Maurice and Eléonore Dubois really her accomplices? She studied them, wondering.

Maurice was how he'd been described by several female colleagues at Montluel. His dimples showed as he smiled, greeting each person as though they were old friends. *Tall and blond, like an American film star* was the usual observation. Yes, Anne-Marie thought, Maurice was dashing, with his easy warmth and swift grin. In contrast, Eléonore seemed quite serious. She was petite, with dark hair and strong features. Eléonore glanced over, catching Anne-Marie's eye, and abruptly left her husband's circle.

"You must be Mademoiselle Piguet," she said with an American accent, reaching for Anne-Marie's hand. Rumor had it that Eléonore had once gone by the name Ellen, when she was growing up in America, before she'd met and fallen in love with Maurice Dubois.

"*Enchanté*," Anne-Marie managed, just as Maurice crossed the room in his wife's wake.

"Mademoiselle Piguet, at last. We missed meeting you last time." He took her hand and pressed it, leaning close to whisper. "But the children gave me an earful about Miss Anne-Marie, their clear favorite, so I feel like I know you."

"Merci beaucoup, Monsieur Dubois," Anne-Marie said, a bit flustered. She had much to say to these two, but not here, among listening ears. "I know our *directrice* has a whole evening planned for your visit, but I hope we might find a moment to chat in private while you're here?"

"Bien sûr," Maurice said gallantly, and Eléonore glanced from her to him, adding, "may we ask what about?"

Anne-Marie looked toward the *directrice*, who remained by the front door. "Just some ideas regarding the La Hille colony," she said quietly, and both Maurice and Eléonore nodded, glancing around, immediately understanding the need for discretion. Indeed, Anne-Marie would need complete privacy to make the offer she'd rehearsed: she wanted them to know that she could help people escape, if necessary. That she was willing to cross borders and break laws.

"Later," Maurice said with a smile, "after the children go to sleep."

Unease gripped Anne-Marie as the Dubois couple walked away, melting back into the mingling staff. What if she'd gotten it wrong? What if they weren't, in fact, supporting Rösli's endeavors? What if the Swiss Red Cross memorandum, forbidding such actions, had convinced them to stay within the law? Maurice could fire her. She frowned, nervous. If she'd miscalculated, she'd be in a world of trouble.

Just then, the sound of thumping feet grew in the hall. Sabine and David burst into the room, only to shrink back at the sight of so many adults.

"Exactly who I wanted to see," Maurice declared, dropping to a crouch and looking them in the eyes. He smiled, and Sabine smiled back, displaying her missing front teeth.

Anne-Marie exhaled. *Talk to him*, she told herself. Surely, he could be trusted.

*L*ater that evening, Anne-Marie moved about the dining room, clearing the remains of supper and listening to the sound of carols filtering down the hall. A handful of the littlest children sat at a table nearby, their heads bent as they drew pictures instead of singing with everyone else.

Sabine looked up, her eyes flicking from the shuttered window to Anne-Marie. It was snowing outside, in the darkness, and Anne-Marie knew that Sabine yearned to ask about it, or, even better, to go outside and see it herself. Anne-Marie went to her and dropped close, offering the child a chance to whisper.

"It's snowing still?" Sabine asked, overloud.

Anne-Marie nodded, pressing a finger to her own lips. "Whisper, *chérie.*" These were the wiggly children of Montluel, those who could not pipe down or stand still, so Anne-Marie had offered them respite from the solemn performance happening across the château. Though Christmas had passed, the *directrice* had organized a long list of French carols to entertain Maurice and Eléonore. The Duboises likely wouldn't mind if some of the children giggled or danced or announced their need to use a toilet during a carol, but the *directrice* would.

Sabine's voice dropped into a theatrical whisper. "Do you like my drawing?" A few of the other children glanced at it.

Anne-Marie looked at the scrap of paper under Sabine's pencil. Three figures, mostly comprised of circles and sticks, held hands. Over their heads, arcs linked in the air to make birds.

"That's you." Sabine's finger tapped the tallest figure. "And me and Joseph."

Anne-Marie smiled despite the sudden ache in her heart. Memory flashed: this same little girl, months ago, nodding as her mother stroked her golden curls.

"Do you like it?" Sabine repeated, no longer whispering. Anne-Marie bent to kiss the top of her head, answering right in her ear. "I like it very much. It's lovely, *chérie.*"

Down the hall, the chorus rose.

Les anges dans nos campagnes / Ont entonné l'hymne des cieux . . .

How strange it must be for the Jewish children, Anne-Marie thought with a pang, to sing Christmas carols.

Sabine couldn't withhold the urge to talk. "Mademoiselle Piguet," she whispered, "did you feel bad when a violin tree was cut down?"

David's expectant gaze flicked up to her, his frail hand stilling over his paper. They often asked her about the ancient, resonant spruce trees, fascinated with the idea that a skilled forester could sense a violin within a trunk. Anne-Marie had explained how they waited for just the right time to fell a violin tree, when the moon was far from the earth, pulling the sap the same way it pulls waves in the ocean, leaving the wood dry.

"Shush," she whispered now, and Sabine's eyes dropped. Anne-Marie relented, settling into a chair and keeping her voice low. "I did feel sad when we felled a violin tree, *oui*. But I knew that it would go on living, in a different form, and that helps."

"It wouldn't live if you cut it down," Rafaela ventured, glancing up.

"Wood never really dies." Anne-Marie smiled. "It just becomes something different. Violin trees transform into something beautiful, almost as beautiful as a tree."

A phone rang, cutting through her words and startling the little group at the table. Anne-Marie rose, hurrying from the dining hall in an effort to stop the ringing before it interrupted the performance. When she picked up the receiver, the voice on the other end made her freeze.

"This is Germaine Hommel from the colony at Saint-Cergues," a woman said, speaking fast. "I've been trying to track down Monsieur Dubois regarding an urgent matter. I was told that he's currently visiting your colony?"

"Bien sûr," Anne-Marie answered, her mind racing, "I'll go and fetch him for you."

She set down the receiver, moving through a swell of dread as she hurried along the hall toward the singing voices. What would Germaine Hommel be calling about? She was the director of Saint-

Cergues, and possibly working with Rösli. Anne-Marie felt suddenly sick as she approached the room full of singing children, their voices expanding before her.

Glo-ooo-ooo-o-ooo-oria, the children sang. *In excelsis Deo* . . .

She beckoned Maurice from the performance, and the chorus sputtered to a stop as he stood.

"Keep singing," he called with a smile, finding his way through the seated adults. "I'll be back in just a moment, children. Sing for Madame Dubois in the meantime."

When he picked up the telephone, Anne-Marie retreated to the dining hall, but she settled just behind the doorjamb, listening. Sabine looked over, ready to call out, and Anne-Marie held up a finger to still her.

"*Mon Dieu*," Maurice said after a moment, his voice low. "Who else knows about this? Have you telephoned the Toulouse office? Does Rösli know?"

Anne-Marie leaned into the jamb, chewing on her thumbnail, listening hard now.

"I see. I'll send someone to La Hille to tell her, right away. Merde."

More silence.

Maurice's voice dropped further when he spoke again, and there was a shake in it. "*Oui*, we need to know where they're detaining them, at the very least. Find out what you can about the interrogations, will you?" There was another long moment of quiet, which Maurice punctuated with a final instruction. "Thank you. *Bon courage*, Madame Hommel."

A moment later, he hung up the telephone, and a second pair of footsteps sounded in the hallway. "Maurice?" Eléonore's voice gained urgency. "Why, you look ill! What's happened?"

He cleared his throat, answering quietly, but not so quietly that Anne-Marie couldn't hear. "That was Germaine, from Saint-Cergues.

Five of Rösli's teenagers were apprehended at the border. Eléonore, what will we do?"

"*No.* Oh, God above." Eléonore paused. "*Five* children?"

"Yes. One got away during interrogations—Inge Joseph," he whispered. "But they caught her again, so all five are in custody."

"German or French custody?"

"It's complicated. Walter Strauss was caught by the French, but the others somehow ended up with German border patrol. They'd actually made it into Switzerland, but got lost and crossed back into France. And Inge Joseph managed to escape through a window in the jail. She tried again for Switzerland, but the Swiss patrol arrested her on the outskirts of Geneva and they handed her to the French police. Apparently refugees now have to get twelve full kilometers inside Switzerland or they'll be returned to France. She was close."

"Unbelievable," Eléonore whispered, her voice full of disgust. "Swiss police forced a Jewish girl to return to France? What's the world coming to? There must be a way to intervene, Maurice."

For a moment, they were silent, likely lost in thought. Anne-Marie barely breathed, her own mind moving furiously. Five La Hille teenagers had been apprehended at the border? What would happen to them?

"I'll make calls," Maurice said eventually. Again, the hallway was silent while its occupants thought.

"Maurice." Eléonore's whisper sharpened. "If the children were interrogated, we'll all be implicated. Especially Rösli."

Maurice cleared his throat again. "I know. Merde," he swore under his breath. "We should leave in the morning for Vichy. I'll speak with Ambassador Stucki to see if there's anything we can do. It's . . ." He seemed to seek his words. "It's a catastrophe, Eléonore. We very well may lose those children this time."

Anne-Marie stood frozen against her doorjamb as the couple

retreated down the hallway, still whispering. After a moment, she wandered back over to the table full of little children, feeling dazed as half a dozen eyes flipped up to study her. Sabine smiled, hesitant, and Anne-Marie glanced down at her drawing. She looked absently at the stick legs, the circle bodies, the big, uneven eyes and smiles. *Five teenagers had been apprehended at the border.*

She closed her eyes, wavering where she stood, and saw the familiar forests draping Switzerland's border. She could easily imagine the kids, tromping through the frigid night, trying to find their way and getting lost. It was confusing in the forest at night, especially in heavy snowfall. She imagined the beam of flashlights, German shouts, and her anguish grew. If three of the teenagers were in German hands, their fates were sealed. She knew it in the very pit of her soul. There was nothing Maurice Dubois could do to save them.

They'd been without a guide. Her own forest rose in her mind, as it always did, clear and persistent. Deep in the Risoud, the border wove through a break in the trees. She'd seen it many times, before the war. There, the border was no more than a stacked stone wall, waist high and easily climbed. And what about the other side? If refugees had to travel twelve kilometers into Switzerland to avoid being sent back, they needed someone to walk them not just to the border, but all the way to safety.

She could do it. In the Risoud. She knew every path, every forest hut, every cliff and crevice.

Anne-Marie glanced down the hallway, where the singing had quieted. She had to help get these children to bed so she could speak to Maurice and Eléonore Dubois.

*L*ate that night, she settled with the Dubois couple before a crackling fireplace.

"I overheard your telephone call," she confessed as soon as they were seated, her words tumbling forth. "I apologize, truly. I know

I shouldn't have eavesdropped. But I suspected that Mademoiselle Näf would try to help her teenagers cross the border, and I've been thinking about it ever since—"

"You know about the escapes?" Maurice whispered, his worried gaze darting to his wife's face.

"Only because of a conversation I had with Rösli. I'd like to help, monsieur."

Maurice leveled his stare on her. "You know it's against the law, and that the Swiss Red Cross has forbidden us to intervene."

"I do understand, but to me there is no higher law than moral law. I cannot sit by and watch the persecution of young people when I might do something to stop it."

"What could you do to stop it?" Eléonore asked, assessing her sharply.

Anne-Marie inhaled. "I grew up in the Risoud forest. My parents' home is fifteen kilometers over the border, on the Swiss side. My entire childhood was spent in those woods, and I know every trail and hiding place. I could lead people to safety."

For a long moment, nobody spoke. Both Maurice and Eléonore stared at her, taking her offer in.

"It's not so easy," Maurice said eventually, and something softened in his blue eyes. "Perhaps you could lead them through the woods, *oui*, which is obviously very dangerous. But the trouble Rösli faced was with stopping points on the French side, and now the entire border you speak of, through the Risoud, is known as the Forbidden Zone. It's heavily patrolled. Impenetrable, and three kilometers deep. Trust me. I've looked into it." He sighed. "Escapees would have to get within that Forbidden Zone, and then they would need the help of people who live there, farmers and foresters on the French side. And before all of that, they would need to travel seven hundred kilometers *to* the Forbidden Zone. Where would they sleep?"

"Perhaps here," Eléonore said, and Anne-Marie glanced at her in surprise. "I think I could talk the staff into offering Montluel as a place to rest en route."

Maurice nodded slowly, rubbing his chin. "But it's not nearly close enough to the border." He stared off into the distance, and Anne-Marie's thoughts darted like fish looking for hideouts. Could she find a way through this Forbidden Zone he spoke of? Was such a thing possible?

"Listen," Maurice said, leveling his gaze on her again. "I want you to keep thinking about this, but tell nobody of your ideas, and don't do anything—not yet. We're headed to Vichy tomorrow to see if we can save the teenagers who were caught—" His voice cracked, and Eléonore reached for his hand. He cleared his throat. "We will try to avert this crisis, and see what consequences it brings."

"But, Mademoiselle Piguet," Eléonore whispered. "Keep thinking. I suspect a time will come when your offer is needed."

Anne-Marie nodded in the firelight.

She would wait, and she would be ready.

~~~~~

FIFTEEN

RÖSLI

ANNEMASSE, FRANCE

JANUARY 1943

*N*ever had Switzerland's border seemed so far away.

Rösli stared out the window of the train compartment where she'd been sitting for almost eighteen hours. She watched the snowy landscape slide steadily past, her spine stiff against the train's gentle movement. Beside her, a pair of German soldiers laughed and talked, sharing a flask pulled from one of their breast pockets. Rösli couldn't even look at them. She tried to block out their banter, mostly about cards and women, seething.

She shifted in her seat. She would be there soon. The anger stiffening her limbs and pounding along with the train's rhythm lessened a little, transforming into dread. Because what could she even do once she arrived in Annemasse? After Maurice had delivered the terrible news of her five escaped teenagers, she'd caught the next train north. She hadn't deliberated. She'd simply packed a change of clothes, a warm coat for the frigid weather along the border, and headed to the nearest train station as if she were compelled to find her teenagers by magnetic force.

But would she even be able to see them once she arrived? *No.* The answer to her own question reverberated in her mind. She turned to the memory of Camp du Vernet; it had seemed hopeless then, too, but she had kept going, tackling one problem at a time, and all forty of her teenagers had come home with her.

Yet, this was different. She stared out at the swirling snow, blinking fast. This time, the Germans had her kids. There was hope for the two in French custody, but Maurice could do nothing to sway German authorities. Rösli wiped at her stinging eyes. If the Germans really had three of her teenagers, they probably weren't even in Annemasse anymore.

The train slowed, rocking into the station, and snowflakes thickened outside the fogged window. Rösli watched them tumble, each tiny flake adding to these frozen borderlands with silent inevitability. The German soldiers stood in the compartment, stretching in her peripheral vision, and she forcibly avoided looking at them. Did these young men know the terror they provoked? She gathered her bag, lips clamped in a determined scowl, and forced her way past them and toward the opening doors.

The train station was small but busy. Rösli stepped out onto a platform, the engine still hissing while people seeped from train cars and others waited, shoulders and hat brims crystallizing with snow. She wove her way through a door and into the crouched building, inhaling a blend of exhaust and wet wool. It was busier inside than expected, with a line at the ticket counter and French police milling on the periphery, scanning travelers with weary eyes. Rösli headed for the front door, holding her bag close so it bumped against her thighs, and then her name was called.

"Mademoiselle Näf!" She pivoted, searching the thinning crowd. Germaine Hommel clutched a handbag in one arm and waved with the other, trying to flag Rösli down from across the building. "Mademoiselle Näf! Over here!"

A sprout of joy poked through Rösli's dread. She'd telephoned to say she was coming, but wasn't sure if Germaine had received the message. She lifted a hand in acknowledgment, making her way toward Germaine, when another voice caught her from the ticketing counter.

"Mademoiselle Näf? Rösli!"

She pivoted, the teenage voice yanking her like a harness, while her mind sped to catch up. Could it be one of her children? How? She searched the line of people for a second, and there was Walter Strauss, jostling to look at her while a pair of gendarmes held him by the elbows. His wrists were handcuffed at his waist.

Rösli nearly ran. Germaine huffed up beside her as they reached Walter, whose guards relaxed a little at his sides when the women neared.

"They're taking me to a jail in Annecy," Walter sputtered, his eyes wild and his shoulders hunched to accommodate the handcuffs. "They said there'd be a trial. How are you here? You heard?"

"We heard, Walter. I'm so sorry." Rösli studied the feverish flush in his cheeks, and her worry grew. His ill-fitting clothes were damp and dirty; he needed warmth and good food. A clean bed. Safety. "We will fight for you."

"Officers," Germaine said, pinning them with her dark, intelligent stare. "Surely you can give us just a moment? We need to speak with this young man before he boards his train." She reached a proprietary hand to grip Walter's arm while giving the gendarmes her most motherly smile.

The men, silent until now, glanced at each other. "We have orders to catch the train to Annecy, madame. I'm afraid we can't—"

"He's lived with me in a Swiss Red Cross home for almost two years," Rösli interrupted. "I'm responsible for him, you see. I promise we'll just have a quick chat." She looked from man to man, finding only impassive expressions. "Please," she added.

One shifted uncomfortably and rubbed at a scaly patch on his weather-burned cheek. "Five minutes," he murmured, looking to his partner for objection. Walter's head hung on his neck, his eyes on the ground between all of them, and he sniffed.

Rösli reached for him, wrapping her arm around his waist while Germaine led him by the elbow, and the two women nearly carried the boy over to a bench before the gendarmes could change their minds. Walter sniffed again, unable to wipe his own nose with his cuffed hands, and tears slid silently from his eyes. Rösli rummaged in her pocket for a handkerchief, which she used to dab at Walter's dripping nose and cheeks. If only there were a way to hide him. To make him invisible. To get him out of this wretched place. Fury burned in her chest as he wept quietly, gulping air to calm himself.

"I heard they got my friends," he managed after a minute. He lifted his head to look at Rösli, and his dark hair, wet from melted snow, hung limp in his eyes. She reached up to clear it from his forehead. Walter was an unfailingly cheerful boy, so generous of heart that he was loved by everyone at La Hille. In all the time they'd spent at the château, living through terror and grief, she'd never seen him cry.

"Did you know that your Inge is close by, Walter?" Germaine said. "She's in a jail in Annecy, where they're taking you."

His eyes widened for a moment while that sank in. "She's not with the others?"

Rösli shook her head, pressing his handcuffed hands between her own, willing warmth into his cold fingers. She glanced at the gendarmes, who leaned against a wall chatting, their voices lost in the cacophonous station. They most certainly overheard nothing. Still, she spoke quietly. "She escaped the Germans, only to be caught by the French. Monsieur Dubois will find a way to free you both—he still has leverage with French authorities. You and Inge can come back to La Hille. I'm sure we can get you through this trial."

"I'll be there," Germaine said quickly. "At the courthouse in Annecy. As luck would have it, I know the judge. It can only help us."

Rösli opened her mouth to say that she would come to Annecy as well, but Germaine sensed her intent and shot her a sharp glance, dark eyes flashing, and shook her head. "I'll take care of the trial." She paused, choosing her words. "Anyway, it's better for everyone if you wait for Walter and Inge back at La Hille, Rösli."

Rösli hesitated. Germaine must believe her presence wouldn't help at the trial, possibly because she was already compromised.

Walter looked between them. "What will happen to the others? To Manfred, Dela, and Inge Helft?"

Rösli squeezed his cold hands again. "We will do everything—"

"I'm sorry," he blurted, anguish returning to his face as he chastened his voice to a whisper. "It's my fault we were caught out there. We were lost in the snow, and then we saw a light through the forest. I was sure we were in Switzerland and that it was a farmhouse, and we were freezing. So I went to scout it out to make sure it was safe, and I left the others waiting in the woods. But it was a border station. Somehow we'd crossed back to France. If I hadn't separated from my friends, if I hadn't tried to be the hero—"

"Walter," Rösli interrupted, her heart aching. "I know you well enough to know, with certainty, that you were incredibly selfless and brave out there. That you did your very best in an impossible situation—one you shouldn't have been forced into at all. Nothing is your fault."

"But the Germans have them now. Dela and Manfred and Inge Helft—"

"Walter." Germaine interrupted him this time, her voice stern. "Blame the Germans and their blasted French collaborators, for heaven's sake, but don't blame yourself. You're faultless."

Walter nodded weakly, snot dripping from his nose again and his eyes bright and unsure. "Inge will go back to La Hille?"

"She'll be in court with you," Rösli explained once more, studying the confusion in the boy's face. Again, she worried about his fever. "She tried to cross a second time and was caught on the Swiss side, so she's being detained just like you."

"Monsieur Dubois will ask the authorities to send you and Inge back to La Hille." Germaine said this as if she were sure of the outcome. But nothing was sure anymore.

"We'll do everything we can to free you," Rösli said again, wrapping her arm around his shoulders, willing warmth into his stooped frame. How strange to have said those words so many times now, and always to young, innocent people. *We will do everything we can to free you, though you've done nothing wrong.*

The pair of gendarmes shifted where they leaned against a wall, glancing over. Walter was nothing more than an assignment to them, just another person to manage before they could return home to their own warm beds. Rösli despised them for it. She forced conviction into her voice, belying her anguish. "Have courage, Walter. I'll see you soon, back at La Hille."

The gendarmes detached from the wall, striding over, their patience apparently up. Rösli and Germaine walked as far as they could with Walter before the gendarmes lost what remained of their tolerance. Then they stood, helplessly, on the snowy platform and watched him board the train, tottering on the steps with his hands bound, flanked by police officers and so very young.

"You should go back to La Hille," Germaine whispered to Rösli when they reentered the building, surrounded by strangers. "Your children need you, and your presence here only implicates you further."

Rösli shrugged, fighting the heartbreak overtaking her interior. "I'm already implicated, Germaine. There's nothing to be done about it." The question arose: What would happen to Rösli? Would the Germans arrest her, too? The thought should terrify her, but it didn't. Instead, it filled her with regret. If she were removed from La Hille, would her successor keep the children safe? The children, after all, lived in fear of arrest every day.

"No, Rösli—Walter lied when questioned." Germaine glanced around, taking Rösli by the arm and leading her to an empty corner of the station, far from the police who shifted from foot to foot, eyes vacant. "I poked around with local authorities, and he told them that he'd stolen the money and identity papers. He didn't say you'd helped."

"But the others were also interrogated, and the Germans are unlikely to leave any stone unturned. Anyway, I'm not worried about myself right now." Rösli watched travelers bustle by, their clothes worn and faces distracted, unaware of the catastrophe facing her château full of children. Twenty-four young people were now safe in Spain and Switzerland, yes. But a third of the teenagers still waited at La Hille, in danger, their escape route compromised. And the three who were caught by Germans? It was unthinkable. The question she needed to ask, that she was terrified to ask, gnawed at her.

She cleared her throat. "Did you find out anything more about Inge Helft, Manfred Vos, and Dela? Germaine, where did the Germans take them?"

"Rösli, I'm so very sorry." Germaine blinked her dark eyes, hesitating. "They're headed to Drancy."

For a moment, Rösli couldn't breathe. *Drancy.* Everyone knew that Drancy was merely a stop on the route east, to camps in Germany or Poland. She had to bend over, breathing quickly while the blood rushed from her head. *She had lost them.* This time, she had really lost them.

"Rösli," Germaine whispered, maneuvering her back to the bench. "Breathe now, that's it. Hope is not lost. Maurice will intervene . . ."

But Rösli ceased listening. Instead, she concentrated on the sickness rising in her stomach, the pounding in her skull, and forced herself not to throw up all over the train station's dingy floor. Because she knew, already, that there was nothing Maurice Dubois could do for those three teenagers. If they were on their way to Drancy, they were gone. Dela, with her pretty eyes and ready laugh. Manfred Vos, a quiet boy who looked out for his little brother. And Inge Helft, who loved to write poetry and talk about the meaning of life.

They were gone.

*B*ack at La Hille, it didn't take long for the summons to come, though it wasn't what Rösli had expected. She walked to the post office in Montégut every day, using the telephone there to call Germaine in Saint-Cergues and Maurice in Toulouse. Some mornings, the news was good. Germaine kept her promise to Walter, accompanying him and Inge Joseph when they went to court after a few nights in jail. They had good luck with the French judge who knew Germaine. He apparently delivered a long lecture about law and order, but freed them nonetheless because the Swiss Red Cross promised to take responsibility for them once again. Both Walter and Inge were still seventeen, if barely, which worked in their favor.

But then one day Rösli telephoned Toulouse to find out which train Walter and Inge would be on, and Maurice lowered his voice into the receiver.

"You're going to be called to testify before the Swiss Red Cross, Rösli."

"Before the Swiss Red Cross?" She frowned, confused, and dropped her voice to a whisper. "Not the French or the Germans?"

"No, fortunately. None of the captured teenagers implicated you during interrogations. I've nosed around enough to feel certain that neither the Germans nor French know you, Germaine, or Renée aided them—so you're all safe there."

Rösli's thoughts raced, and she met the questioning glance of the postal worker behind the desk. As though to give her privacy, he nodded and ambled over to the front door, stepping out for air.

What did this mean? She would not be arrested. She should feel relief, but couldn't in the shadow of grief: her captured teenagers had lied, and lied well, to protect not only her but all of their peers still trapped at La Hille. Their nobility, in the face of unimaginable pressure, broke her heart.

She gathered her questions. "Are you saying that the Red Cross is putting me on trial?" The very thought stunned her. A humanitarian organization was *trying* its staff for endeavoring to save young people?

"Yes, unfortunately. There is going to be a hearing in Bern—they want to dismiss you from service. Colonel Remund is going after both you and Germaine. So far, we've managed to keep Renée Farny out of this. I'll fight it, of course."

Rösli glanced around the village post office. Winter sunlight streamed through the windows. A clock ticked on the wall. Would they really dismiss her? "But, Maurice, without pressure from France or Germany, why would they do this?"

"They think you're a troublemaker." He cleared his throat. "And they don't want illicit escapes to resume. Ultimately, they care more about staying in the good graces of the Germans than saving our kids."

Rösli squeezed her eyes shut. "Maurice," she said finally, "whatever we do, we have to make sure nobody learns that you also supported our efforts. The Secours Suisse needs you in France."

"I know it does. And it needs you, too." He sighed heavily. "Listen. I've been summoned to a meeting with officials near the Swiss border, so I'll contact you next week to let you know what's happening. With the border being closed, Colonel Remund is talking about having you questioned in Vichy."

"Not at the hearing in Bern?"

"No, he's very keen to handle this internally, and bringing you over the border would raise questions. The rules have just changed again, Rösli. Even people with Swiss visas need special permission from the Germans to leave France right now, and seeking such authorization could spark unwanted attention. I'll let you know what's decided, all right?"

Rösli nodded, partly to herself, fighting dread. What would this mean for the children of La Hille? "Thank you, Maurice."

"Of course. And, Rösli, listen." He inhaled audibly over the telephone line. "I'm sorry this is happening. Please hear me when I say you've made me proud to work alongside you. I'll fight to keep you working alongside me until our job is done."

✦

SIXTEEN

ELLA

CHÂTEAU DE LA HILLE, SOUTHERN FRANCE

LATE FEBRUARY 1943

*R*ösli was mysteriously gone again, which sharpened Ella's anxiety. Why did Rösli keep traveling north, with no explanations for everyone still at La Hille? What pulled her away in these waning winter days?

At least Inge Joseph and Walter Strauss were back. They had returned after being released by a court in Annecy, and Ella and the rest of the remaining teenagers hung onto their stories for days. They had been agonizingly close to freedom, and now here they were again, listening for approaching engines and sleeping in the *Zwiebelkeller*.

But even worse, three of their friends were now gone. Rösli didn't try to hide the truth when they first huddled around her, before even Walter and Inge returned, digesting the terrible news.

"Can't we get them out of Drancy?" Isaak had pressed, frowning. "There has to be a way."

Rösli had looked close to tears, kneeling in the dim *Zwiebelkeller*, ringed by the remaining *Grands*. Ella had sat off to the side, glancing from Rösli to her cold feet in their wooden shoes, tears streaming down her face.

"With the Germans involved, there's little we can do. We'll try, but I can promise nothing."

"Should we still try to escape?" Bertrand asked while everyone else stayed silent, too stunned to speak.

"I don't know." Rösli's voice wavered. "The route that gave us so much success is compromised. They know we received help from the women at Saint-Cergues, and I'm quite certain they know where the escapees slipped through the wire. It's far riskier now."

Ella had risen, unable to listen further. Wiping her tears, she'd inhaled in an effort to stem them. She couldn't think about how she would never see Dela and Inge Helft again. The pain of losing her friends, who had stood beside her when parachutes fell in Belgium, and when they lived in a granary barn in Seyre, and when they were interned and freed from Camp du Vernet—that pain would swallow her whole. And Manfred Vos's little brother, Henri, was near Hanni's age and still at La Hille, suffering a loss so great that Ella had tried to prevent her own tears when she left the secret room that night, pressing them deep into the crevices of her heart.

And now, weeks later, Ella still tried to suppress her anguish. She shook the pain of that meeting away as she wandered the château, listless. It was February and the day was wet and dark, matching her mood as she glanced through the windows in the long corridor overlooking the courtyard. Noticing something, she paused, stepping closer to the glass. Down below, huddled against the weather, she spotted her sister kneeling in the dirt.

Ella quickened, moving down the stairs and outside to check on Hanni. What was she doing? When Ella emerged in the bracing air, she found her sister poking around in the vegetable garden, unfazed by the light, misting rain soaking her through. Hanni's face was wet, drips gathering and coursing through her freckles, and the mist beaded her bobbed hair like a spatter of jewels. She glanced up when Ella approached, showing her gap-toothed smile for a hesitant second before bending back to her work. One of her front teeth had fallen out the week before, and the second hung by a thread.

"What are you doing out here, Hanni?" Ella trudged across the strip of packed gravel, perching on a wooden bench that sat alongside a garden bed lined in rocks. It was empty of course, its rows nothing more than clods of mud for months now. The winter had been a cold one.

"Mademoiselle Näf said it'll be time to plant potatoes soon. And peas." Hanni went back to poking at the mud with a stick, her little hands white in the cold. "I'm digging the holes. Couldn't find a shovel."

Ella smiled, despite the ache in her heart. "We probably won't plant potatoes for another month, sweetheart. And peas are after that, I think. Are you sad? Is that why you're out here alone?"

Hanni glanced up, wiping a clump of wet hair from her cheek and leaving a streak of mud. She shrugged her bony shoulders. "Don't know." She looked back at the ground and kept on scraping out a shallow hole with her stick. "Everyone's sad. Henri cried at breakfast." She glanced sidelong at Ella. "You're sad, too."

Ella blinked her eyes, but there was no sense in denying it. "I don't want you to worry, Hanni. Listen, why don't we go inside and get cleaned up? I'll read you a story."

"No."

Hanni tossed the stick and dropped to her knees, using both hands to scoop dirt from her shallow hole, and Ella cringed. She must be freezing. An image of Hanni in the trees, months ago, rose in her mind. This was the same, somehow. When her sister was upset, she found something to do.

"There," Hanni declared, sitting back on her haunches. "One

hole done. I'll dig them all today and Mademoiselle Näf will be pleased when she returns. So will Frau Schlesinger. She'll have lots of potatoes to cook next winter."

She shuffled a few feet down the garden row, plunging her hands back into the frigid mud to start another hole.

"This is silly. Hanni, please. It's raining."

Hanni didn't acknowledge that Ella had spoken. She kept digging with her bare hands, the line of her jaw sharp.

"*Stop*." Ella said it so sternly her little sister froze. She sat back, and a look of confused grief flashed in her eyes before she lowered them.

"Come on—this is no good. You'll make yourself sick out here. If something's worrying you, just tell me."

Hanni knelt for a long time, eyes lowered, examining her muddy fingers where they hung in her lap. When she looked up again, tears streamed through the streak of mud on her cheek. "I don't want them to catch you, Ella." The words emerged in a quiet wail. "I'm afraid."

Ella reached for her sister, pulling her up onto the bench and into her lap, mud and all, and smoothed her wet hair. "They won't catch me. Shhh . . ."

"But they caught Mutti and Papa, didn't they?" She shuddered as she spoke, sobs hitching her words. "I don't remember Mutti and Papa anymore. If they catch you, maybe I'll forget you, too."

Ella pulled her close, rocking slightly as if Hanni were still the five-year-old she'd fled Belgium with. Her sister wept big, hot tears that she'd probably been holding inside for far too long. Ella wanted to tell her not to be silly, that all was well, that she would never, ever vanish from her life like their parents had.

But, as the misty rain beaded on her shirt and joined her tears, she couldn't say anything around the lump in her throat. Because she wouldn't make a promise that she didn't have the power to keep.

*R*ösli was gone as February neared March, and the weather warmed. For weeks, police had stayed away from the château, ostensibly because of the scarlet fever quarantine. But, even if the La Hille children had actually endured scarlet fever, the threat of infection had long since passed. Ella began to listen for engines again, staying within the building's thick walls.

On a bright morning that hinted at spring, several of the older boys pulled on their winter coats, procured through Rösli's letters to a Swiss charity, and prepared to tromp out to gather wood. Ella was in the courtyard, enjoying the cold sunlight while Hanni played with Antoinette, when Isaak and Bertrand and Walter Strauss emerged from indoors. The door swung wide behind them, and piano music wafted from the dining room as Walter Kamlet plucked out song after song, his own restlessness quickening even the mildest melodies.

The door swung shut, quieting the piano within, and Isaak clomped over in his wooden shoes.

Ella stood, nerves tightening. "You're not leaving the courtyard again, are you?"

Isaak shrugged, but guilt crept over his face. "We're low on wood, and they could use my help, Ella."

"So let the younger boys go." She glanced at Hanni, lowering her voice to a hiss. "Isaak." She flicked her eyes to the other boys, hovering nearby. "Walter. Bertrand. What if they come while you're out there? You could run right into them. And you can bet you'll be on their lists."

Isaak sighed, and the boys exchanged glances. Bertrand drifted toward the exit tower as if she hadn't spoken, clearly itching to stretch his legs. They'd been venturing out for wood, like they used to before the raids, off and on for a few weeks. Every time, Ella tried to stop them.

"I'm going crazy in here, Ella," Isaak said as Walter joined Bertrand, sheepish. "I just want to move around a bit, get some air. Nobody will find us in the woods."

"They certainly *could*." She glanced around the courtyard, trying to decide if she was being overcautious. It was true that the police hadn't surprised La Hille for a long time, and the boys were always back by lunch. She took in their tall figures and ropy muscles, and she could almost feel the pent-up energy coursing through them, the desperation. She understood—she felt like she would burst, too, most days. It was hard to stay in such a small space all the time, trapped and afraid.

"Don't be long," she whispered, her tone harsh. She watched them saunter out under the tower, a mix of dread and frustration welling in her gut. Who was she now? An old housewife? She picked up her sketchbook, looking for a clean corner to draw in, stewing. She didn't want to nag Isaak. Why couldn't they have a normal life, a normal courtship, free from uncertainty and fear?

She'd sketched Hanni's and Antoinette's heads, bent together in the sunlight as they played a game with small stones, when she heard it. She nearly dropped the nub of her pencil. Hanni's head shot up, and her eyes found Ella, wide and shining. *Engines*.

Ella waited two heartbeats, listening as a motor ground into a lower gear, turning onto the road snaking up to La Hille. Then she shot up as if electrified and ran, clutching her sketchbook, to the tower. She looked out, not at the service road, where the sound of an engine grew, but up toward the forest. Hanni started to scream behind her.

"Run! Ella, run upstairs!" Seconds later little hands landed on her waist, and Hanni pushed her toward the château with all the force in her limbs. "Go, Ella. Please," she sobbed as Ella stood unmoving, staring at the woods, her heart thrashing in her chest.

"They're going to get him," she heard herself saying. Her voice was a croak and came on its own, as if it were some other part of her. Hanni kept pushing at her waist, sobbing, and Ella's mind moved with the slow rhythm of the truck gears grinding uphill. *I need to hide.* The words formed in her mind at the moment Hanni reached up to slap at her cheeks, stinging her back into consciousness.

Ella nodded, unsticking her feet as if some force held her there, looking for Isaak, and her mind caught up.

"Run!" Hanni screamed as a truck came into view down the hill, flashing through the trees, and Ella turned and obeyed. She sprinted across the courtyard, hurried inside, and joined the scramble of teenagers snaking upstairs. Frau Schlesinger shouted from the hall, her voice high and shrill, alerting anyone who had ears. Ella ran into Herr Lyrer's room, dropping to her stomach in one fluid movement and sliding into the *Zwiebelkeller*, followed by Frau Schlesinger, moments before the door shut. She glanced around at the silent stares of the other teenagers. Their faces were white, drained of blood. They sat frozen on their bedding, cocking ears to listen.

Ella gulped shaky breaths, forcing herself to stay quiet, forcing hope into her mind. Edith scooted over to sit next to Ella, pushing her glasses onto the bridge of her nose and blinking fast behind their glare. They were the same age, but there was something matronly about Edith, as if she'd lived many lives already. Ella leaned her head on Edith's shoulder, focused on regulating her breath, and shivered.

Perhaps Walter Strauss, Bertrand, and Isaak would be all right. Who else was with them? Had Ernst Schlesinger gone out to chop wood as well? She scoured her recent memory, thinking back to breakfast. Hadn't he stood and said something about the wood supply to Frau Schlesinger as she ladled breakfast into bowls? Was that today, or yesterday? She glanced at Flora Schlesinger, whose gentle eyes barely blinked as she stared at the floor between her feet. Ella didn't dare whisper her question.

It must have been today. Because he wasn't here, sitting beside his wild-eyed wife. Ella's gaze skipped between the shadowy faces surrounding her. They were also missing Manfred Kamlet and Henri Brunel, who must have gone out early with Ernst. She closed her eyes, willing her thoughts to travel through the stone walls surrounding her and over the sunlit hills into the forest, where Isaak and the rest worked, unaware of danger. *Stay there*, she thought, hard, as though the words could reach him. If they stayed away, there was a good chance the gendarmes wouldn't find them. Ella stifled the urge to weep. She had to remain silent, in case the police crept into the room adjacent to this one, looking for clues, looking for a hidden door. Her mind scurried. Isaak couldn't stay in the woods forever. How long would the gendarmes wait? How hard would they search?

Time crawled. Ella lay down, a dull pain growing in her skull. She tried to force her mind blank to stave off the weeping and panic that threatened to overtake her. She was attempting to picture nothing, nothing at all, when she heard a faint rumble somewhere outside. An engine. Cautiously, she sat up and exchanged looks with Edith and Frau Schlesinger. Was it coming or going? Could the police be leaving, or was it a trick?

A few minutes later, the secret knock sounded on the *Zwiebelkeller* door. They slid it open, cautiously, and Herr Lyrer's solemn face peered inside. One at a time, they crept into the teacher's bedroom, still afraid to make a noise.

Even Herr Lyrer whispered, his expression grave. "They're gone." His voice was thick. "But they took some of our people."

"How many?" Frau Schlesinger asked, her soft face drawn, clearly afraid to voice the question hammering at her. The same question hammered Ella: *Who?* Inge stood as if petrified, barely breathing.

"Five." Herr Lyrer looked among the silent group, and Ella's heart pounded. She wanted to scream. *No!* She wanted to crumble. *Not Isaak.*

"Who?" Frau Schlesinger managed, her eyes shining, her voice like a plea.

Herr Lyrer sighed, and his breath caught on the gravel in his throat. "I'm so sorry, Flora. They took Ernst. Also Walter Strauss, Bertrand, Henri, and Manfred Kamlet. Inge—"

Before he could finish, Inge darted off, hands pressed over her mouth, and Frau Schlesinger crumpled to the floor in a heap, gasping. Ella bent to wrap her in an embrace, and Herr Lyrer's eyes found hers. He whispered over the older woman's sobs.

"They didn't get Isaak. For some reason, he didn't come down from the woods with the others. I'm going out to look for him now."

*S*oon after, Isaak walked in with Herr Lyrer, his face drawn with a mixture of fear and fury. He lowered, shaking, onto a bench in the dining room, looking between Ella and their teacher.

"I wasn't quite finished with my stack of wood," he said without preamble, his voice low and pained. "They all wanted lunch, but it felt so good to be out there that I said I'd stay and keep working. I just . . ." He shook his head, staring at the floor, unmoored for a long moment. "I was caught up in the work, enjoying the sun, but eventually I did get hungry and I realized that they should have come back. So I crept to the edge of the forest, and I saw the truck." He swallowed, his Adam's apple bobbing with the effort. "I saw them force my friends into that truck. And I just sat there, at the edge of the woods."

"Isaak, listen to me. There's nothing you could have done." Herr Lyrer bent in front of Isaak, forcing him to look him in the eye. His face was stern and lined, his eyes unblinking. "If you'd shown yourself, they would have taken you, too. Your name was on the list."

"I should have done something," Isaak said quickly. He looked searchingly between Ella and Herr Lyrer. "To just sit there and watch? Powerless?"

Herr Lyrer nodded, still holding Isaak's gaze. "I know. It's the worst feeling in the world."

Ella stood by, barely breathing, unable to digest the fact that Isaak was still here, beside her, when others had been taken. Guilt mired her own good fortune, because upstairs gentle Frau Schlesinger sobbed over her lost husband, and their son, Pauli, wept in her arms. And Inge had disappeared in the château, pleading to be left alone to grieve for Walter Strauss. How could Ella feel glad that she didn't lose Isaak, while so many mourned around her?

Somebody tugged at her hand, knocking her from her thoughts. She glanced down to find Hanni, who wrapped her little arms around Ella, melting into her waist.

"I don't want them to get you, too," she sobbed. Ella picked her sister up, still so light at age seven, and scooted onto the bench beside Isaak. Herr Lyrer drifted off into the periphery with worried eyes.

"You should go," Hanni whispered, sniffing and looking between Ella and Isaak. "Run away."

Ella swallowed the pain in her throat, combing Hanni's hair from her wet cheeks and tucking loose strands behind her little ears. "I don't want to leave you, Hanni. I can hide upstairs if they come again—"

"They *will* come again," Hanni said forcefully. Her wide eyes took on the heat of determination, the fire of her impish spirit rising. "They asked us questions. They wanted to know where you were. I lied. But you have to run away now. Please."

Ella looked from her sister to Isaak, whose gaze was lost in thought. "We could go to Spain," he whispered. "Switzerland's border isn't safe anymore. But we could hike the Pyrénées into Spain. From there, we could go to Portugal, and then England."

Ella couldn't answer for a long moment. He spoke as if the Pyrénées were safe compared to Switzerland, but she'd seen their icy peaks, towering over the gentler foothills. There was no way her sister could come on such a trip. She held Hanni's light weight on her lap and looked toward a window, trying to think, sinking in a quicksand of sorrow. Did Hanni really want her to go? Did she understand that she wouldn't see Ella again for a long time? Maybe never?

It was as if Hanni read her mind. She reached her hand up, mimicking Ella's own movements and smoothing the hair from Ella's wet cheeks, tucking it behind her ears with deft fingers. "If you go to Spain, I will know where you are," she said quietly, brown eyes fervent. "But if Germans take you, I'll never know, like Mutti and Papa. I'll have to miss you forever."

She needs me to stay alive. It was what her little sister couldn't find the words for, but it hung between them, suddenly clear. Hanni needed to have a sister somewhere, safe, even if they couldn't be together. And if the war ever ended, Hanni needed to have a family member, somewhere in the world, who had survived it.

Ella found herself nodding slowly while Isaak studied her with his storm cloud eyes, unblinking.

꧁

SEVENTEEN

RÖSLI

*R*ösli pinned her eyes shut for one aggravated second after sitting down in a hard chair. The situation felt so familiar: here she was, seated across a gleaming table from a pair of men who ranked higher than she did. But one of those men was Maurice Dubois, who held her stare when she opened her eyes, nodding slightly. She returned the abbreviated nod. Someone in this situation, at least, was on her side. She glanced at a slender, silent woman seated in the corner, eyes down, her fingers poised over a typewriter.

"Yesterday we questioned your collaborator, Madame Hommel," her interrogator began, and the typewriter keys began to click. The man was Walter Stucki, Swiss ambassador to France, who had been asked by Colonel Remund to conduct questioning. He was older than she expected, with a stern, sharp-featured face, broad shoulders unbent by his years, and a shining, bald head. When his eyes flicked up to meet hers, they were not unkind. Nevertheless, his words sliced her open.

"Because you are the last person we need to question before the meetings in Bern, we already have a clear picture of what transpired at the border near Saint-Cergues. Please note that there's no need to obscure the facts, Mademoiselle Näf."

"I have no intention of obscuring the facts," she lied. For Renée Farny had not yet been summoned, and Rösli wouldn't give her away. She glanced at Maurice, who seemed to study his laced fingers on the tabletop. He wouldn't mention Renée, either.

"Then we're agreed," Ambassador Stucki said, straightening to look at a page of notes. "We've established that you, Rösli Näf, *directrice* of the children's colony at Château de la Hille, personally supported approximately twenty-four teenagers in escaping from the colony. Do you have anything to add to this fact?"

Rösli cleared her throat. Her mouth dried as she tried to form her response. "The leadership of the Swiss Red Cross was unwilling to move the colony to Switzerland when I inquired this fall," she began. Her thoughts skimmed under her words: how ironic that she, lifelong champion of rules, was in trouble for breaking them. She noticed the shake in her hands and tucked them under the table where they could shiver on her lap, unseen. "Everyone knows that the French arrested forty of my teenagers and four of my staff last summer, Ambassador. After the occupation began in the free zone, I believed that I had to prevent them from being arrested and deported."

He studied her for a long moment, a series of wrinkles forming on his brow, while the typing died out in the corner. "Yet three of your children *were* arrested and deported, having been sent by you to illegally cross the border."

Rösli glanced at the impassive typist, committing all of this to paper, and a surge of anger flooded through her. She nodded.

"Out loud, please."

"Yes." She cleared her throat. An image of Dela flashed in her mind, younger and laughing in La Hille's garden. Inge Helft and

Manfred Vos strolled through her thoughts, shimmering like ghosts. Grief matched her anger. "That's correct."

"Did anyone assist you in concocting these escape plans?"

"No. Nobody else knew about them."

"Not the staff at Château de la Hille?"

"Especially not them. Nobody else was involved."

Ambassador Stucki glanced between Rösli and Maurice.

"Did Maurice Dubois, or anyone in the Toulouse office, assist you?"

"Certainly not."

"And Germaine Hommel?"

Rösli hesitated. Germaine was already implicated. It would be safest to admit that they had collaborated, so her lies concerning the rest would appear true. "Madame Hommel and I did work together. You must already know this."

Ambassador Stucki sighed, as though exhausted by all of this. "Our reports show that the château hasn't been subjected to a search by local authorities for quite some time. Is that correct?"

Rösli couldn't tell him that the searches had tapered off because she'd put the château under false quarantine. "That is correct. But we have no way to predict the timing of searches. We cannot assume they won't happen again."

"We also cannot assume that they will. Mademoiselle Näf, has it occurred to you that if you hadn't sent those children away, encouraging them to cross an international border illegally, that they would still be alive and well at La Hille?"

Rösli's gaze clouded with the heat flushing her eyes, but she would not cry in front of this man. "It certainly has occurred to me, Ambassador Stucki. It has also occurred to me that if I *hadn't* sent twenty-four other teenagers across borders illegally, they *all* could have ended up in camps."

Maurice continued to stare at his hands, his eyebrows tipped together; he could only listen, for now. The ambassador sighed. "I've been asked to convey to you, Mademoiselle Näf, that you had neither the authority nor the judgment to make the decisions you did. That you are not capable of evaluating the full political environment, nor the dangers facing the children in your care. Colonel Remund has emphasized the incomprehensibility of sending young people over a treacherous border, and the political foolishness of disregarding the clear instructions of the Swiss Red Cross. You've ignored our tenuous position as humanitarian guests in an occupied country. As such, Colonel Remund will recommend to the leadership in Bern that the organization distance itself from you, starting with your dismissal."

The clicking of typewriter keys filled the ensuing silence. Rösli's thoughts ricocheted, as they had since she'd lost Dela, Manfred, and Inge. He'd managed to prod her deepest bruise, her whispering doubt: *Had* she done the right thing? Perhaps not, since her actions had resulted in the loss of three beloved youths. But how could she have forced imperiled teenagers to remain at La Hille? What other options were there? Could she have misunderstood the climate in France? Was Ambassador Stucki correct to imply that if she'd *not* acted, the three lost teenagers might still be safe in her care? Her mind rebounded back again, and she straightened. No, of course they wouldn't be safe. They would have been deported long ago from Camp du Vernet if she'd followed Swiss Red Cross orders all along, doing nothing to intervene.

She would not allow this ambassador to manipulate her sorrow.

Rösli raised her gaze to the men across the table. Maurice fixed his stare on her, pained, but she looked from him to Ambassador Stucki. She would lose her position, whether or not she'd been morally correct; yet if the Germans had come for her, she would have lost much more than that. Now, the Swiss Red Cross would use her as a scapegoat with the Germans, erasing her in order to stay on their good side, playing a game of politics that secured safety for the Swiss position while abandoning the foreign Jews they'd pledged to protect.

Ambassador Stucki would take the secretary's notes to Bern, where Colonel Remund, apparently determined to appease the Germans, would make his recommendation official. Yet Rösli's punishment was inconsequential compared to the losses her children grieved every day. It barely mattered, except for the problem it raised: Who would take her place when she was forced to leave? Who would protect the children of La Hille now?

"It's clear that my fate has been decided," she said finally, forcing out the words. "I don't believe anything I say will change anyone's mind, so if you're quite finished, Ambassador Stucki, I'd like to leave." Again, she forced herself not to shed her threatening tears.

The ambassador sighed. "Yes, I believe we're done here," he said, and Maurice appeared to be in some kind of pain. She knew Maurice would fight for her at whatever meetings remained. But what could he do at this point? Rösli knew her days in France were numbered.

The typewriter in the corner clicked out the last of their words, making them final. She scooted back in her chair, cheeks burning, and left the room.

*L*ater that evening, Rösli was jarred from the daze that had overtaken her the moment she walked into her hotel room. She'd lain on the bed, something she never did during daylight, her mind racing. *Dela, Manfred, and Inge.* Their faces rose in her thoughts, over and over, complicating her fury at the Swiss Red Cross. The ambassador's words reverberated in her mind, shaking loose a cyclone of questions.

Has it occurred to you that if you hadn't sent those children away, encouraging them to cross an international border illegally, that they would still be alive and well at La Hille?

She rolled over on the lumpy mattress, paralyzed. Was there any truth to it? If she'd made different decisions, if she'd been more discerning, could she have saved them all? What if she'd continued to hide them in the *Zwiebelkeller*? Or, what if she'd waited until spring to send them over the border, when there was no snow to obscure their path? She shook her head, trying to revive her confidence. Danger was everywhere for her teenagers. She knew, to her core, that the best solution was to get them out of France, far from the grasp of their hunters, as soon as possible. That if she hadn't acted on her instincts, every one of them would have been deported months ago.

And yet. Saving most of the children didn't diminish the grief of losing three. It couldn't assuage the guilt she felt, misplaced or not, for failing Dela, Inge, and Manfred. And now she would be forced to fail those who still remained at La Hille, hiding in the *Zwiebelkeller*, hoping for a chance to live.

She had to find someone to take her place.

It was a knock on the door that jarred her. Rösli blinked, stiffening, and listened. Had she imagined it? Another knock sounded, sharp and officious, and it pulled her upright like a lever. She smoothed her disheveled hair and wiped the tearstains from her cheeks. It must be Maurice. She swung her bare feet to the floor and padded across the room. What could he want? Perhaps he was headed back to Toulouse already. He'd certainly ask her to meet him there, where they could debrief and decide when she would officially depart for Switzerland.

When the door swung open, Rösli's mouth opened with it, freezing in a tiny, stunned circle. Maurice was nowhere in sight, and instead she was met by the slender woman who had typed notes during her questioning.

"Mademoiselle Näf, I'm sorry to surprise you like this," the woman said, glancing up and down the hall, her purse hitched tightly up under her arm. "Ambassador Stucki sent me to get you. He'd like you to come back to his office immediately."

Rösli shut her mouth, thinking fast. What could Ambassador Stucki possibly want with her now? To castigate her further? To tell her not to return to La Hille at all? "I assume his office is closed at this hour," she managed. "Perhaps he'd rather see me before I catch my train in the morning."

"No, he specifically said for you to come right now." The woman blinked her brown eyes. "I really do have to go. My children are home waiting for dinner. Will you promise to visit the ambassador tonight? Otherwise, I might face a reprimand for not walking you back there myself."

Rösli sighed faintly, fighting both irritation and nerves. "It's all right. Go home to your children. I'll just fetch my handbag and walk there now."

Soon after, she strode down a hall flanked with darkened offices, past the secretary's empty desk, and knocked on Ambassador Stucki's door. She stood, wooden, her cheeks flushed, waiting for him to answer.

"Mademoiselle Näf, thank you for coming," he said when he appeared behind the opening door. He stepped back and gestured gallantly to one of the seats at his desk.

"It's a bit unconventional to summon me so late." She gave him a wide berth as she entered.

"I know it is." Ambassador Stucki's broad shoulders hunched a little as he sat, and he firmed his jaw as if pondering his next words. Rösli layered her hands in her lap, her spine rigid, bracing herself for whatever was coming.

"I'm afraid I'm leaving for Switzerland shortly, but I wanted to speak with you alone, Mademoiselle Näf. I'm not sure I'll ever get another chance."

She stared at him, expressionless.

He cleared his throat, pinning her with his solemn gaze. "I just wanted to tell you, off the record, that I'm proud of you."

Rösli stiffened. Only her brows moved, burrowing over her eyes as she fought confusion. "Proud?" Was this some kind of trick?

Ambassador Stucki nodded, the wrinkles multiplying on his forehead. He tipped forward, and his suit coat fell open a little as he clasped his hands on the desk between them.

"I only wish more of us possessed your courage."

Rösli looked down at her own hands, her confusion expanding. Why was he telling her this?

"But this morning you insisted that if I hadn't sent those children to cross the border illegally, they would still be at La Hille. That I had made a profound mistake—"

"No."

She glanced up to meet his stare. "I don't understand."

"The Swiss Red Cross lost its ability to protect foreign Jews when the Germans invaded the free zone in November, whether or not they'll admit it. I believe that the La Hille teenagers will continue to be hunted by the Germans and the French police, and if nobody intervenes, they will eventually be caught. Mademoiselle Näf, by helping those twenty-four children escape, you played a critical role in saving their lives."

She hesitated, unable to grasp the change in this man, the difference in what he was willing to say on and off the record. "I don't require your praise," she said, finally. "Any decent human being would have intervened."

"No. We've all seen that most people value their safety over decency. You risked your life for them, Mademoiselle Näf."

"The lives of my children are in danger *every day*," she snapped. "And why? Simply because they exist in this dreadful world? My risk was nothing compared to what they will continue to face, now without me alongside them to do what I can. And all I know is that it wasn't enough." She studied him. "But why did you punish me this morning, Ambassador Stucki, if you believe I did the right thing?"

"The political landscape is dangerous, more so every day." He sighed, the lines creasing around his eyes. "This morning, I had an unfortunate role to play, and so I did what was expected of me on the official record. It's like I said before." Sorrow crept over his face. "Mademoiselle Näf, I wish more of us possessed your courage."

The following evening, Rösli sat with Maurice Dubois in the empty Toulouse office, where they'd planned to debrief. Instead, she cradled her head in her hands, overwhelmed by the news he'd just delivered. She sensed Maurice studying her as she stared at the floor, clenching her jaw, trying to recover her bearings. He'd just explained that while she was away, five more people had been snatched from La Hille.

"Damn them all, Maurice." She wiped at her eyes, and five more names joined her internal vigil for Inge, Dela, and Manfred. *Five more people lost.* She inhaled, trying to tame the urge to sob. "Colonel Remund forced me away from the château for that infernal hearing, and this is what happened in my absence? *God damn him.* How can he make me leave La Hille? How can he ignore what's really happening in France?"

"Colonel Remund thinks the Germans are going to win the war." Maurice shook his head, grim. "He'd rather appease them than break rules to save our kids. That's the stark truth, Rösli."

"Do you think they'll really dismiss me? The ambassador claimed that if I'd kept everyone at La Hille, they would be safe, but it's demonstrably untrue."

"I'll fight it. Especially in light of these new arrests. They can hardly say you were overreacting now, can they?" He sighed. "I have some more bad news. Ambassador Stucki let it slip that Renée Farny is indeed suspected of helping you. I don't know how they found out about her involvement, but there it is. They want to dismiss her, too."

"*Scheisse*," Rösli whispered. She'd been hoping that Renée would be spared so she might continue their shared mission somehow. "Who will be left to take our place? Someone *must* step in, Maurice. If the Red Cross dismisses me, someone has to find a new way out of France." She hadn't known that it was possible for her anxiety to grow, but now it filled her so full it felt like she'd burst. What would happen to her teenagers still in France? What would happen if the Germans ever turned on the younger children of La Hille? Someone had to shield them all.

He nodded. "I know. I have an idea."

She looked into his troubled eyes, and he lowered his voice. "Anne-Marie Piguet."

An image of the young woman dropped into Rösli's mind. She nodded slowly, thinking. Anne-Marie had said all the right things the day they met, it was true. She'd thought Anne-Marie might be an ally who could be enlisted as needed, not someone who could replace Rösli. She was passionate, yes, but she seemed quite young— could she take on so much responsibility? So much danger?

"Anne-Marie has already been thinking of escape strategies," Maurice continued, catching Rösli with his blue stare. He reached out to grip her hand, squeezing as though he sensed her rising doubt. "She confided that she'd spoken to you about it as well, so evidently she's wanted to assist escapes for quite a while. I instructed her to wait until we needed her. She seems capable, Rösli. I think she can do it."

Rösli couldn't be sure. Still, she cleared her throat. "Call on her," she said, forcing confidence into her voice. "But wait a few weeks for things to die down, to avoid arousing any suspicion around her. She'll need to seem like nothing more than a young counselor, completely unrelated to the current catastrophe, when she's transferred to La Hille."

"My plan exactly," Maurice agreed. "We'll let the storm pass, and then we'll bring her to the château this spring, whether or not you're still there."

Rösli subdued a surge of sorrow. It was impossible to accept that she might not be there. "Well," she managed, "it appears that Anne-Marie's time has come."

❦

EIGHTEEN

ANNE-MARIE

MONTLUEL, FRANCE

LATE APRIL 1943

A letter came for Anne-Marie.

She read it breathlessly, lowered it to think, and then read it again.

> *Dear Mademoiselle Piguet,*
>
> *You've been selected to transfer from the children's colony at Montluel to the children's colony at Château de la Hille, where you will serve as counselor and caretaker. Staffing changes are underway, with similar transfers among counselors, teachers, and directors in several colonies. It is probable that a new director will join you as you begin your tenure at Château de la Hille. Please proceed south at the end of this month, with a stop at the Toulouse office to confirm relevant paperwork.*
>
> *Once you've settled at Château de la Hille, you will take your allocated, unused holiday time. You currently have*

three weeks available. Please plan to return to Château de la Hille before end of June.

You may ask any necessary questions in person at the Toulouse office.

Sincerely,
Maurice Dubois

Her hand shook slightly as she took in the layers of meaning in this letter. On the surface, the message was simple. If it had been intercepted, it would seem like routine administrative correspondence.

Only, Anne-Marie knew it was not.

Once you've settled at Château de la Hille, you will take your allocated, unused holiday time. She read it again, her mind racing. Maurice Dubois was taking her up on her offer. Three weeks would give her time to scout an escape route from France to Switzerland. With Rösli in trouble and her route compromised, someone needed to create a new option.

It seemed the person Maurice had in mind was Anne-Marie.

And what about Rösli? Anne-Marie looked back at the letter. *It is probable that a new director will join you as you begin your tenure at Château de la Hille.* Did this mean that Rösli was being transferred as well, as a punishment? She pinned her lips, thinking. Well, she would find out soon, when she arrived in Toulouse.

She folded the letter, ruminating, and bent to pull her suitcase from under the bed. A thought rose, insistent: How on earth could she leave her beloved children?

The next morning, Anne-Marie walked down the long staircase, wiping the tears she tried so hard to will away. She didn't want the children to see her crying. When she turned into the great room of the château, the reason for her tears sprang up to encircle her. Small hands gripped her around the waist, multiplying by the second as children ran to embrace her. Over a dozen of them patted her bottom and hips, wiping their own bright eyes, stunned by the sudden news of her transfer.

"How can you leave us?" Sabine asked haltingly. A pearl of mucous dripped from her nose as she blinked up from the throng. Anne-Marie set down her suitcase, rubbed several small backs, and ran her fingers through Sabine's golden curls. She was unable to answer for a long moment. How *could* she leave tiny Sabine, when only a season ago she'd escorted her away from Rivesaltes, promising her mother that she'd look after her child? And little David sat outside the throng, his thin legs crossed on his chair, his head buried in his hands. How could she leave him when he'd already lost so much?

She inhaled shakily, reminding herself that these children were still safe in France. She'd come for them if that changed. But, for now, she was needed elsewhere.

Anne-Marie squatted before the children, squeezing Sabine's cold fingers and touching Joseph's cheek as he blinked solemnly, his long lashes beading. "David," she called through the huddle of little bodies. She looked over Sabine's head while David detached himself from the chair slowly, as if he were sleepwalking, and threaded his way to Anne-Marie. She balanced on the balls of her feet, squatting, but David crawled right into her lap like a toddler, folding his limbs up into a tight package. She rocked back, sitting down with her arms around the little boy, and the rest of the children lowered around her. It was as if they were waiting for a story, like they had on so many cold nights, their eyes catching the lamplight.

Anne-Marie fought for words. She cleared her throat, taking her hand from David's shoulders to wipe her own cheeks. He weighed almost nothing on her lap. Her heart ached. She had wanted so badly to see him grow.

"Children, do you remember when I told you about the yellow bird? The one that helped me find my way out of the snowy woods when I was lost?"

Heads bobbed all around.

"Well, I've been thinking about that bird. It knew I needed help, did it not? It must have been flying over the forest, looking among all the frozen trees and hills and limestone cliffs for a warm place to rest. Then it saw me, because it could see everything. And it saw my home, far away."

"How could it know?" Joseph asked. He pursed his generous lips, skeptical. "It was just a bird."

Anne-Marie held his serious stare. "Joseph. Do you believe in magic?"

He shook his head, but Rafaela called from the back of the group, waving her hand. "I do. I do!"

A murmur rolled through the children while they considered their belief in magic, and Anne-Marie forced a smile. "Now, I'm not talking about magic *tricks*, about magicians onstage making things appear or disappear. I'm talking about the little things, the little good things, that sometimes happen just when you need them to. The way help sometimes comes, just when you need it to."

"Like you came," Sabine whispered, blue eyes wide. A memory of Sabine in the hut at Rivesaltes flashed in Anne-Marie's mind, the way her mother had hugged her goodbye, smoothing blond curls behind her seashell ear and cupping her cheek. Anne-Marie couldn't talk. She took a salty breath, mustering her strength. The children needed to see her strong this last time.

"Yes, Sabine," she managed. "Maybe the magic was with me that day. Now, I've been wondering about the birds. Children, if you start to look—to really look when you're out in the forest—you'll notice that birds are everywhere."

"Not in winter," David supplied, his voice muffled in her lap.

"No, not as often in winter. But if you search, you will see them, even when it's very cold. And this is what I think about the magic of birds: I think that they look down on us with the eyes of all the people who have loved us, and all the people we've loved." She could barely say it, her throat was so tight. "I think that love is always with us, flying overhead, watching, and even helping us sometimes. So, when you miss me, or when you miss your parents, go outside and look up at the sky. Find the birds in the trees—they're all around you, children. Even in winter, there will be one. And feel the love of your friends and families looking down on you."

David shuddered on her lap, and she combed through his patchy hair. He sobbed, his little shoulders heaving, but he was also nodding. Anne-Marie held him tight, thinking the words as hard as she could, the words she would say in the final minutes before she left.

Remember, you are loved.

NINETEEN

RÖSLI

CHÂTEAU DE LA HILLE, SOUTHERN FRANCE

LATE APRIL 1943

*R*ösli walked through the woods, the air brisk in her lungs, a towel and dress tucked under her arm. It was early, and the sky was pale and as fresh as the buds fattening on branches, poised to burst into spring. She brushed away a spray of twigs, ducking a bit as the stream appeared before her, and her heart smarted at the sight of its glittering, rippling water. Behind her, up the hill, she felt as if she could sense the château full of children still sleeping, the rhythm of their collective breath as familiar now as her own pulse.

How many more mornings would she step into this bracing stream, snaking through a cleft in the hills, as she had for nearly two years now? How many more times would she return to the château, cold skinned and clean and wide awake, to join her children at the noisy wooden tables for breakfast? How many more times would she see the gap-toothed smiles of *les Petits* eating porridge, or hear the unharnessed laughter of *les Moyens*, or talk with the newly serious *Grands*, who carried the weight of the world on their young shoulders? Her superiors would surely make her leave soon, yet she couldn't imagine being anywhere else.

She sighed, letting her tattered, blue bathrobe drop from her shoulders, and the morning air hit her skin. She tottered barefoot toward the water, thinking of her latest talk with Maurice. The meetings in Bern hadn't gone well, and it stung to imagine Colonel Remund, red-faced and furious, condemning Rösli, Germaine, and Renée. Maurice had omitted the details, but every day since, Rösli had walked to Montégut, her heart in her throat, expecting a letter of dismissal. So far, she'd been spared.

Shivering, she made her way out over the rocky stream bank, her long feet finding ground as the water started to flow over them, prodding gooseflesh to sprout on her pale body. Her stomach tightened in familiar anticipation as she found the place where the bank dropped off, the water eddying in a deep pool, and Rösli sank in. The freezing water embraced her, washing away any remnants of sleep, sweat, and dirt. *Mademoiselle Näf!* A voice squealed in her memory as the water rushed over her head. *How can you stand it? I could never be so brave!*

She surfaced, inhaling morning air. The voice was Dela's, two summers ago, when the children had first arrived at La Hille and Rösli herself was new. She closed her eyes, let water run through her fingers, and saw Dela as she'd been that morning, hugging her slender arms on the stream bank, unable to muster the courage to plunge in and bathe.

Dive in headfirst, Rösli had called out. *You're braver than you think.*

She scrambled for the bank, slipping on the rocks under her feet. Dela had been braver than she'd thought, indeed. They all had. And yet, now Dela was gone.

Rösli toweled off, pulled on her dress, and was tying her apron when a figure emerged from the trees, silhouetted by the rising sun.

Her heart jumped, and she listened hard for engines, a reflex now, but all she heard was waking birds. She shaded her eyes; it was Ella, picking her way down the path, her expression solemn.

"Sorry to interrupt your bath," Ella called as she skidded down a steep stretch of crumbling bank. "I just need to speak with you alone."

Rösli mustered a smile, as she always did now, though it had never occurred to her in the beginning. Smiling for no reason wasn't natural to her, but the children needed the reassurance. "You can find me whenever you need me." She gestured toward a log, inviting the girl to sit. The sun crested over the hills, and the air suddenly yellowed as they settled, hip to hip, and stared out at the moving water. For a moment Ella said nothing, and Rösli glanced sidelong at her pensive face. Her brown eyes moved slightly, as if following the flowing water, and she hunched with her arms folded across her belly.

Fear surged in Rösli's own belly. Was Ella in trouble? She'd been meaning to speak with the girl about her growing attachment to Isaak. For a year now she'd pulled girls aside in groups of two or three, choosing those who'd been spending time with boys, and explained the frank facts of life. But with all the upheaval, she hadn't gotten to Ella yet. Heaven help them if she was pregnant.

"We're going to leave," Ella said, interrupting Rösli's tumbling thoughts. She turned to look Rösli in the eyes, scrunching her freckled nose a bit as if she'd said something unpalatable.

Rösli exhaled, replacing one fear with another. "You and Isaak?"

Ella nodded. Her deep eyes started to shine like the stream, filling with tears.

"It's all right," Rösli murmured, wrapping her arm around Ella's narrow shoulders. "I trust you've thought through every angle. Which border are you hoping to cross?"

"Isaak's looking into *passeurs* who can take us to Spain. We wanted to talk to you about it earlier, but you've been gone quite a lot. And, honestly, I've wondered if you're in some kind of trouble, because of what happened in Saint-Cergues."

"It's not for you to worry about." The words escaped before Rösli realized that they were too clipped, too harsh, too characteristically her. But Ella, unoffended, leaned a bit closer, staring out at the moving water and responding quietly.

"Of course I'm worried. We all love you, Mademoiselle Näf."

Rösli's gaze blurred, and she tightened her arm around Ella's shoulders. The children at La Hille understood her, finally. She finally fit somewhere. She watched the water, sparkling and folding in the rising sun, wishing for the millionth time that everyone could just stay at the château, safe. That they could work in the garden, and chop wood, and read, and learn, and fall in love, and grow up.

"I'm worried about *passeurs* into Spain, Ella," she said, still watching the stream. "I wish I had something safer in place. A guide we could trust. Who has Isaak spoken with about this?"

"The old woodcutter. The one we worked with last winter."

Rösli nodded, her thoughts skipping. She could picture the man, but didn't know him well. They'd bought wood from him here and there, so many of the boys had met him and sometimes worked alongside him, but she couldn't even think of his name. Was he trustworthy? More importantly, could he find a trustworthy guide?

"Maybe I should try to arrange it," she ventured. "It could take some time to develop contacts, but—"

"No," Ella interrupted, turning. "Rösli, I know you're in trouble with the Red Cross." She spoke with authority, like an adult. Technically Ella *had* come of age, but it still knocked Rösli back. In her mind, she saw Ella as she'd been two years ago, skinny, shorn, and wide-eyed, too shy to speak up unless it concerned her sister. Now here she sat, her shoulders back and her gaze both clear and immeasurably sad, as if in two years she'd lived a long, long time.

"Inge saw some mail on your desk," Ella said apologetically. "It mentioned your potential dismissal. She only told me, so nobody else knows. But Isaak trusts the woodcutter, and if you're in trouble, you shouldn't be out trying to find new guides for another border. Maybe, if you avoid attention for a while, they'll let you stay."

"Well, they haven't dismissed me yet. I can still be of use to you—"

"Stay quiet for a bit, Rösli," Ella interrupted. "La Hille needs you."

Rösli sighed, letting her facade slip. "All right. But don't tell anyone about my difficulties, please. I don't want to worry the children. Also, if I'm honest, it's embarrassing to be under such scrutiny."

Ella reached for her hand, gripping it. "You did it for us." She spoke fervently. "We all know it. Everything you've done has been for us."

For a long moment, Rösli was unable to speak. The birds filled the air with song, and she listened as the sun lifted beyond the trees.

"I'll find you some proper shoes," she said eventually, glancing at Ella's worn, wooden clogs. "You'll need trousers and a good wool sweater. And I can help with money, if you need to pay the *passeur*. Have you told your sister?"

Ella nodded. "Hanni started it, actually. She asked me to leave after the last raid." Worry floated into Ella's beautiful eyes. "We can't take her over the Pyrénées, obviously, so she'll have to stay at La Hille. Do you think she'll be safe, Rösli?"

"The Germans haven't put any pressure on our youngest children so far."

"But what if they do? I don't know what my parents would say if they knew I was planning to abandon her." Ella's voice broke. "They trusted me to take care of Hanni. I love her so much."

"And she loves you, which is why you must leave." Rösli turned to face Ella, who watched her carefully, still gripping her hand. "I will do everything in my power to keep your sister safe. If I'm dismissed, I'll leave her in good hands. But, Ella, your mother and father would want you to survive, too. They sent you away to save you. You deserve a future." She forced a smile. "When the war ends, you'll be alive and able to send for Hanni. And the two of you may be able to find your parents."

Ella blinked, her eyes catching the sunlight. "Do you think I'll make it? Over the mountains?"

Rösli's heart accelerated as she contemplated the question. The Pyrénées bit into the sky like teeth, white capped and forbidding. Germans and French Militia patrolled every road to the border. They'd been ordered to arrest refugees and resisters and, if necessary, shoot them on sight. She wouldn't lie.

"After what happened in Saint-Cergues, we both know you're facing real danger. But you're strong, Ella, and you're smart and watchful. Listen to your instincts and take care of Isaak. If something goes wrong, you'd be the one to notice, not him." She inhaled, thinking of the latest raid on the château, when they'd lost five people. Maurice was still fighting for the two under age eighteen, but the other three were lost. They'd been shipped straight to Poland.

Ella was eighteen. So was Isaak.

"Yes," Rösli added finally, giving Ella's hand a squeeze. "I think you have a very good chance. A better chance than if you stay in France."

*T*he next day, the letter came. Rösli read it in her office, standing in the slanting light of the tall window through which she'd first glimpsed impending danger. She looked from the letter to the grounds below, and a memory of that fateful night flashed in her mind: the trees, moonlit, haunted by dark silhouettes. They'd approached like phantoms, sliding from shadow to shadow. It was the night everything changed.

And now, months later, she held the ripple effect of that first raid in her calloused, soil-stained fingers. A crucial sentence leapt out from the sparse text.

Fräulein Näf is hereby dismissed from her tenure at Château de la Hille, and ordered to return to Switzerland.

She sighed, folding the letter with shaking fingers. So that was it. She had to leave this château, which had become her home, and all the children filling its ancient walls with noise. With a tight throat and weak legs, she drifted to her desk, opened the top drawer, and slid the letter inside. But then she paused, the drawer still open, staring at the neatly folded paper. Where would she go? Would they make her leave right away?

An image rose in her mind again, and she closed her eyes. She saw Ella and Isaak ascending. They trudged up a granite, glacial peak, their booted feet kicking out ladders in the snow. Ella's freckled cheeks burned in the sun, and a rucksack hung from her narrow shoulders. Isaak pointed at something, his lively gaze looking back. *Spain*, Rösli thought, her heart jumping a little as if this were more than a daydream. She opened her eyes and straightened her spine, making a decision without any thought. She wouldn't leave until Ella and Isaak were on their way. Until then, she'd refuse, hold her ground, help them prepare, and see them off.

They would be her final escapees. Her final act of resistance.

Strengthened, she slammed the desk drawer shut.

Rösli strode from her office toward the stairs. She would help the children plant a long row of snap peas, and then she would walk to Montégut and call Maurice from the post office. She'd ask him when Anne-Marie was expected to arrive at La Hille. Had he already arranged the transfer? If possible, she would like to speak with the young woman before returning to Switzerland.

Would Anne-Marie really help children escape France? She'd seemed full of conviction the day they met, ready to rebel on behalf of people in danger, but so much had changed. The stakes had climbed, dramatically, since their brief conversation. Rösli stepped out into the courtyard, squinting in the spring sunlight. Several children flocked to her, and she smiled, but her mind hummed even as she strode toward the garden, surrounded by little people.

She knelt next to the furrows, her knees smarting, and turned the soil. Certainly, she approved of the sentiments Anne-Marie had expressed in that strange, suspended moment in the dining room of Montluel. Rösli sat up, nodding as little Antoinette knelt beside her and plunged her hands into the cool, clean earth. Hanni skipped up a moment later, singing under her breath, her hair whipping in a gust of spring wind. It couldn't hurt to bring Anne-Marie to La Hille. If nothing else, the sweet-faced young woman would love the children when Rösli was gone.

That alone granted her a measure of solace.

~~~~~

TWENTY

ELLA

CHÂTEAU DE LA HILLE, SOUTHERN FRANCE

EARLY MAY 1943

*D*id you pack a change of underwear?"

Ella glanced at Rösli, who stood between her and Isaak, and paired an eye roll with a smile. "Really, Mademoiselle Näf?"

Rösli shrugged, but her lips twitched with a relenting grin. "You wouldn't believe how many of the boys didn't this winter. After a few dozen kilometers of walking, I'm sure they were glad enough that they had something fresh to change into. Now, you have the good socks on? You both have plenty of bread and cheese in your bags . . ." Rösli spun around, glancing at their neatly folded blankets on the *Zwiebelkeller* floor as if searching for something she'd forgotten. Isaak met Ella's gaze, amused.

But Ella inhaled, glancing toward the high, darkening window, and any amusement she'd felt evaporated. The first stars blinked in the deepening blue sky. Grief and fear joined hands over Ella's heart. "It must nearly be time to go," she murmured, still staring at the window. Downstairs, the rest of La Hille's children were finishing a late dinner in the courtyard as the spring evening faded toward darkness. Hanni would be among them, busily chatting with Antoinette over her dish of snap peas and cornmeal, yet unaware that tonight was the night Ella and Isaak were leaving.

"It's time indeed." Rösli was breathless. "Now remember: you'll walk along the paths marked on the map to Saint-Girons. The map makes sense to you? Isaak, please reassure me that you remember the shortcut from woodcutting—"

"I remember." Isaak nodded, his face falling to seriousness. Rösli's worries were legitimate now; they couldn't afford to get lost on the eight-hour hike to their first resting point. Or caught.

"When you're walking along roads, stay well off to the side. Be prepared to disappear into the trees—always have an escape route in mind, every step of the way. And you're sure you can find the barn in Saint-Girons? I just wish I'd been able to scout it out for you." Rösli pressed her fingers over her thin lips, snagged in thought.

"We'll find it," Ella said, infusing more conviction into her voice than she felt.

"Don't let your guard down. Not even for a second. If you hear anything—engines, voices, anything—hide. If you feel compromised at all, turn around and come home."

Home. The word rang in Ella's mind. What did it mean anymore? Was home here, in this familiar château, or back at her empty childhood house in Cologne, or was it somewhere in the future, yet unknown? For a second she felt hollow, as though her heart beat in a cavern, but she shook the feeling away and nodded at Rösli. "We'll return if anything goes wrong. I promise."

For a long moment, Rösli held Ella's stare with her small, intense eyes. She reached for Ella's and Isaak's hands, squeezing them, and blinked the shine from her gaze. "All right, then," Rösli said quietly. "You'll need the entire night to walk, so it's time to say goodbye."

Isaak cleared his throat, but his voice still hitched. "We can't thank you enough, Mademoiselle Näf. For everything."

"I just wish I could do more." Rösli firmed her thin lips. "Now, go. The children should be finishing up in the courtyard, so you can slip past them when I ring the bell to come in. They won't notice amid the commotion. Ella, I'll bring Hanni to you in a moment. Wait outside the courtyard, at the edge of the forest, and we'll find you."

As they filed downstairs, Ella's legs trembled with every step. Was it really the last time she'd pass through these rooms and halls? They walked into the courtyard, where the children and remaining teenagers played and milled as stars pricked the sky, and the questions became more painful. She caught the solemn gaze of Inge Joseph from where she sat at a wooden table with Edith. Some of the boys stopped laughing where they huddled on the other side of the garden, their stares finding Isaak as he sauntered past, his face anxious though he flashed a smile. They wouldn't say much to their friends; leaving quietly was an undiscussed custom now. Nonetheless, Edith and Inge stood as they neared the tower, ambling over as if to chat while Rösli rang the bedtime bell. They paused in a loose circle, hidden in the tower's shadow.

"Good luck," Inge whispered. Her eyes sparkled in the half-light. "Keep your wits about you, all right?"

Ella nodded, and Edith reached for her hand. "Stay safe," she said simply, her gaze earnest behind her glasses.

Ella was unable to speak around the lump in her throat. She and Isaak detached from their friends, their château, and everything they'd known for the past two years. They strode out under the watchful tower, hand in hand, into the unknown.

Rösli found them at the hem of the forest, leading wide-eyed Hanni.

Ella bent to her knees and held out her arms, and Hanni dropped into them. Her little arms encircled Ella's neck, elbows tightening, and she sobbed, wetting Ella's shoulder.

"You'll send for me?" Hanni's voice was high and halting when she could finally speak. "When the war ends?"

Ella squeezed her tighter, and it was as if she squeezed her own heart. "The second it ends, I'll come for you." How could she do this? Hanni needed her. Ella couldn't possibly go through with this. She should abandon this plan, go back inside and unpack and hide for as long as she needed to, close to her sister. Her breath came in tight gasps as she fought her warring interior. Surely, if she walked away from this little girl, the pain would split her in half.

Hanni pulled back a little, scrubbing the tears from her freckled cheeks, still standing solemnly in Ella's arms. "I'll say the Tefilat Haderech for you," Hanni said, staring at Ella with her lovely, glittering eyes.

For a second, Ella couldn't breathe. Memory came like a burst of light: Hanni on the train, only four years old, and Ella fourteen. Their car rocking in a steady rhythm, snaking away from their parents and everything they'd ever known, and Hanni's little bow of a mouth moving as they whispered together, practicing the words their mother had written for them. *May it be Your will, Lord, our God and the God of our ancestors, that You lead us toward peace, guide our footsteps toward peace, and make us reach our desired destination for life, gladness, and peace.*

It seemed like another lifetime now, before they knew how long they'd be gone, and before they knew how peace would evade them. And yet, a remnant of that night rose now in Hanni's fervent gaze. She placed both of her small hands on Ella's wet cheeks as if to hold her still.

"I love you."

"I'll love you always." Ella was breaking. She reached into her bag and retrieved her sketchbook, holding it out to Hanni. "I want you to have this."

Hanni gasped. "But, Ella, you'll need it—"

"I need *you* to keep it safe for me." She forced a smile, but her voice cracked. "Please. And if you feel lonely, you can read Mutti's prayer. There are drawings of Mutti and Papa in there, too, and of all the places we've been together. Please, Hanni, take it."

Hanni hesitated, and then she nodded vigorously.

From the corner of her eye, Ella saw Rösli gesture, and she knew the goodbye was over. It was time to go. Now or never.

"Love you always," she repeated, standing as Hanni's bottom lip began to shake.

And then Ella turned to leave, her soul tearing in two, and Rösli led Hanni away. Ella pivoted over and over as she walked, peering through the darkening trees, trying to get one last glimpse of her tiny, wise, wild-hearted sister drifting back to the château, a mere silhouette hanging on Rösli's arm.

Her mother's face appeared in her mind, clearer than she'd remembered it in years. Mutti blinked her brown eyes, a worried smile flitting over her mouth. She faded slowly, like she had that night they left her on the station platform, her face vanishing beyond the fogged window as the train rocked away.

That night, her parents must have felt something like Ella did now. Like they were separating from their own beating hearts. Ella turned for one last look at Hanni but could no longer see anything through the trees. Her mind continued the prayer.

May You rescue us from the hand of every foe, ambush along the way, and from all manner of punishments that assemble to come to earth . . .

Isaak reached for her hand, pulling her close until her stride fell in with his.

By the time it was fully dark, a new, unbidden sensation nudged around Ella's heartache and fear. They crested a hill, striding along a path that broke through the trees and into a bald clearing, lit by moonlight, and the feeling grew. Ella crossed the meadow, steps behind Isaak, and tried to name it. Was it a different kind of fear? Why was she jittery, her heart skipping every so often as they climbed?

It came to her, like the moonlight clearing their path: she was *excited*. Despite her grief, a future was opening for her, for them, different than ever before.

"Isaak," she whispered, stretching to walk alongside him. He glanced at her, cautious. It was best if they didn't talk, but she suddenly felt as if the words bounded in her chest, tiny and leaping. "Isaak, do you think we'll really make it? To Spain? And beyond?"

The moonlight illuminated his lopsided grin. "I'm certainly planning to."

"It's just that I haven't let myself imagine it. Until now." An image of a sunlit road, untraveled by Nazis, flashed in her mind. "I haven't let myself feel excited. But I can't help it, suddenly."

Isaak's grin expanded, evening out as he glanced at her again and reached through the shadows for her hand. He gripped it as they neared the edge of the bald patch, melting into another dark forest.

For now, they walked a shortcut Isaak had traveled often on La Hille business, cutting the distance to farms and villages where he'd worked and procured supplies over the past two years. Rösli had explained that this wooded leg, up and down hills, would be the safest part of their trek. Eventually, the path would spill out onto a country road leading to Saint-Girons, which they'd carefully bypass, reaching a farm well south of the town. There, they would meet their *passeur*, the guide Isaak had arranged through an old woodcutter. After resting the day away in the barn south of Saint-Girons, they would continue hiking the following night, and three more after that, scaling the formidable Pyrénées.

They began a steep descent, and the path, clear until now, became overgrown. Soon Ella could barely see Isaak, only a step ahead of her, in the leafy darkness. She held a hand before her face, deflecting branches and brambles that seemed to reach out from the depths, scraping her skin as she walked. The path pitched yet steeper. Ella strained to see the ground through the overgrowth.

"Careful here," Isaak whispered over his shoulder.

He'd barely finished the words when her foot slipped, skidding down a bank of rocks, and she scrambled to find purchase. Her hand grasped at a thorny bush, and for a second it was as if she were in space, her sense of gravity and direction pitching, when Isaak reached for her. His hand encircled her waist and hoisted, and she was on her feet again, standing against him. For a moment they froze, their hearts beating fast against their joined chests, their breath loud in the forest's deep quiet.

"You all right?"

She considered the question, sensing the sting in her scraped hands and a dull ache starting in her ankle. *Scheisse.* She'd twisted it. *Merde!*

"I'm okay," she answered, her lips close to his bent head. She would have to be.

"We're almost to the road." Isaak's breath was hot in her ear. She inhaled his smell, savoring his warmth, and commanded her heartbeat to slow. The road would be easier going, yet far more dangerous. What if they met someone along the way? Did Germans patrol these byways in the dead of night? Did the French Militia?

Despite her fear, Ella was relieved when the path spilled out onto a country road, lit again by the moon. Isaak slowed for her, and she fell in beside him, limping.

He paused, concerned. "You hurt yourself?"

"Barely."

He glanced up and down the curving road, his expression hard to read in the moonlight. "Should we turn back?"

"No." The word came out a little too loud. She reached for his hand, tugging him onward, and after a second he relented. They walked together, stretching their strides to make time, keeping to the deepest shadows of the dark, glittering night.

Hours passed. Ella's sore ankle ached, then throbbed like a second pulse with every step. Blisters sprouted and burst on her heels and toes, leaving her feet raw in the leather shoes Rösli had hunted down for her. Still, she and Isaak didn't slacken their pace. The moon arced over the sky as they passed through long stretches of hills and fields. When they crossed forests, the moon disappeared behind the net of overhanging trees, casting fragments of pale light. Several times Isaak paused, unfolding the map and squinting at it, muttering to himself.

"You know where we are?" Ella asked tentatively, every time, and he'd look up at the countryside and pause, searchingly.

"Yes," he always responded. "And I'll recognize the outskirts of Saint-Girons, I'm sure."

Would he? Ella frowned as they trudged on, worrying. How many times had he been there? And how recently? She couldn't bear to ask the questions out loud, as if the answers alone would taint their luck. What if they were walking entirely in the wrong direction? What if Rösli's careful counsel, and Isaak's long study of the maps and trails, weren't enough to get them there?

Finally, when the moon dipped behind a lump of dark hills, Isaak refolded the map and nodded as if he was sure.

"We should be there in an hour. Maybe two."

"What time is it, do you think?" Ella whispered. The moon was gone, and they'd been walking so long every muscle in her body ached. Her mind was numb, the night never-ending. Yet, it would end, and probably soon. They had to skirt the town of Saint-Girons and find the barn before daylight.

"We'd better hustle," Isaak replied, and Ella winced as they set off again, moving quickly.

When dark shapes of buildings appeared on the horizon, Isaak and Ella swung south off the road, ducking into the forest edging a freshly plowed field. The sky was still black, but the faintest breath of light lit the eastern horizon, and Ella's heart clenched tighter. Did those houses really belong to the outskirts of Saint-Girons, or was this another town entirely? What if a farmer was up early, checking his field? What if a dog barked?

Not a half hour later they spilled out onto an empty road following the curves of a black, swift river, and Isaak exhaled. She could sense his smile more than see it in the darkness.

"The Salat," Isaak whispered, his voice barely discernible over the sweep of her own breath. He spun, releasing a half chuckle as he scanned the ribbon of water. "We really found it! It should be just ten or fifteen minutes more." His voice dropped even quieter as he took her hand, moving again. "We're looking for a farm with a wagon wheel out front."

"A wagon wheel?"

"In a flower bed by the road, like a decoration. It'll be south, alongside the river."

Ella nodded but said nothing. She wouldn't let relief flood in, not until they were concealed behind a barn's heavy door. Several bends later, the road narrowed and she stared, her pulse accelerating. The way forward was hemmed on one side by the river, and on the other by a stone wall retaining the weight of an abrupt hill. It was like walking into a chute, with no way out on either side. Wasn't there another route? Isaak glanced at her, and even in the darkness she sensed the worry in his face. But what else could they do, if the farm was on the other side of this trap? Rösli's voice whispered in her mind. *Be prepared to disappear into the trees—always have an escape route in mind, every step of the way.* There was no escape route here except for the river itself. She glanced at the water, glittering in the faintest dawn.

Ella bit the inside of her cheek, her nerves clenching, and followed Isaak. She listened hard as they hurried, decoding every sound over the scuff of their shoes, the burble of the swollen river, the rustle of new leaves as they passed into an overhang of trees. She glanced backward, again and again, but the quiet of the road was unbroken. It stretched behind them in the darkness, curving with the river, disappearing into the waning night. She glanced at the thin line of trees separating the road from the brushy riverbank, calculating. Should they try to scramble down the steep bank, which was more like a drop, and walk alongside the river? Was there even a bank to walk on? She couldn't tell. But, not far ahead, the hillside eased, offering escape if they needed it. Ella walked even faster, her blisters stinging and ankle firing with every stride.

And then she heard it. She slowed for a step, cocking an ear to listen over the rushing water, and her heart throttled forward. "Isaak!" she whispered, her voice harsh and desperate, but he was already tugging her hand. He'd heard it, too. A pair of lights swung into the darkness behind them just as they scrambled into the trees hemming the river. The lights were dimmed for the blackout, but nausea burst in Ella's stomach because she felt as if their beams had caught her, only for a second. The sound of the engine grew, ricocheting against walls of hills and trees, and Ella slid down the steep, brambly embankment behind Isaak, feetfirst, enveloped by darkness. Had they been spotted? Brush shook over their heads as they wormed their way down, their backs and arms scraping rock and dirt and brambles as they slid, stones dropping into the water's edge below. The sound of the engine grew overhead, rumbling through the quiet dawn, and then it cut out sharply. Isaak hit the bottom of the bank and froze. Ella stopped her slide abruptly, grabbing at the base of a bush and holding on tight. Above them, not twenty feet away, boots thumped earth.

"Just here." The voice was confident, clipped, and German. "I knew I saw something. See those footprints?"

A deeper voice answered. "Quiet. They're close."

Boots paced again, scuffing the ground, and flashlights lit the raw, spring leaves right over Ella's head. "Broken branches," the first voice murmured. The flashlight lowered, scanning the tunnel Ella and Isaak had broken through the bushes as they slid. She felt it hit the crown of her head. Her heart thrashed in her chest. Did they see her? Isaak didn't move below her. Should they run? Would they shoot her now? Every cell in Ella's body went cold, as if she were already dead.

"Come out. We've caught you," the voice said calmly, and suddenly Isaak reanimated. His hand gripped Ella's sore ankle and pulled, hard, and she slid the rest of the way down the bank like a marble in a chute. Then his hand found hers in the darkness, and they sloshed into the water, slipping over rocks while shouts erupted behind them.

"Halt!"

In the second it took the German patrol to unholster their guns, Isaak and Ella plunged into the current. Ella didn't think. She moved as if mechanized, skidding her heels on the river floor toward deeper water, her hand tight on Isaak's, her pulse bounding between her ears when the first shot rang out, shattering the darkness. Isaak's hand slipped from hers as the river took him, his head a bobbing, black silhouette, and another shot fired as Ella spun into an eddy and lost her footing.

Water rushed over her head, shockingly cold, as she plunged down and surfaced, spinning like a cork. She gasped, sputtering, her mind flooding like the snowmelt-swollen river gripping her limbs. Had either of them been hit? She blinked, disoriented, gasping and swallowing as she swiveled and paddled, trying to touch ground in the inky torrent. Another bang resounded, and something skipped over the chop close to her head. She turned and paddled, gaining speed, and saw the beam of a flashlight in their wake. Shouts volleyed, muffled by the water sloshing in her ears, and another gunshot split the air. She managed to turn, raising her arms to swim after Isaak's dark shape, zipping ahead of her like a leaf in a hurricane.

The flashlight faded behind the trees, and then the river turned a corner and the German patrol vanished. Ella cupped her hands and tried to swim, thrashing against the whipping water, and then she spotted Isaak ahead, scrambling up the opposite riverbank. *Alive*. She gasped in relief. He spun, searching, as she struggled toward him, sucking air and trying to gain purchase on the riverbed skidding under her feet. Isaak stumbled back out into the water, bracing his long body as she neared and holding his arms out like a net. She swept into them and they stumbled, but he kept his footing. Together, they fumbled up onto the bank. Ella leaned over, gasping. She wanted to collapse, to sob, but Isaak pulled her along.

"They'll search the river," he whispered. "We didn't get far."

He didn't need to say more. They'd only reached the margin of brambles when dimmed headlights appeared again across the river, moving slowly, and the beam of a flashlight bounced over the water. Ella and Isaak ducked into the bushes, curling up into tight balls, barely hidden by an umbrella of leaves. The flashlight bobbed between the currents and the bank, scanning, and Ella shivered and held her breath. Her heart pounded so hard she could barely think. Isaak's arm wrapped tight around her shoulder, and she focused on the feel of his skin, clammy but solid under wet clothes. The headlights continued to move slowly across the river, the flashlight dividing the trees and bushes into shadows, and the car moved on.

Ella exhaled. Then, without thought, she leaned over and emptied the contents of her stomach between her sloshy, freezing shoes.

$\mathscr{D}$awn whispered when they finally crossed the river again, having backtracked south along its brushy bank after the German patrol vanished. They found a place where the river thinned and widened over its rocky floor, allowing them to wade across, slipping and sliding as the current tugged on their legs. Ella could barely breathe as she slipped over the rocks, every cell in her body shivering, again exposed to anyone who might be searching the waning darkness for movement. But then she reached the bank, a step behind Isaak, and they climbed it and stared up and down the road.

"We'll run," Isaak whispered, crouching under a bush. "As fast as you can, okay?"

She nodded, her pulse in her throat. He took her hand, squeezing, and then they were up on their feet. They pounded across the road, and with every step she expected the bang of a gun, the jolt of a bullet. Then they were on the other side, threading into a stretch of trees, and not a sound broke the silence behind them. A hundred feet in they stopped, panting, bending over as the adrenaline drained from their sodden limbs.

"It can't be far," Isaak whispered, glancing up. With their rucksacks lost to the river, they no longer had a map, but Isaak was decisive. "We'll just stick to the forest until we see the farm."

She nodded, declining to say the obvious: there was no way to see the wagon wheel landmark from the forest. They wove through the trees until a bundle of farm buildings appeared across a narrow field, strung along the road like loose beads on a string. Ella stopped beside Isaak, staring through the lightening trees at a small stone house and the hulking barn beside it. Fear bounded back in. Could there be a flower bed with an old wagon wheel here, out by the road? The place looked swept and utilitarian, as if whoever lived here had no time or use for flower beds.

"This must be it," she breathed, feeling far less certain than she sounded. But daylight threatened, and their chance to find shelter waned. They'd have to take a risk and hide in that barn, certain or not.

He nodded, his expression equally unsure. "Run for it?"

She nodded back. His hand squeezed once for luck, and again they ran out into the open, sprinting for the wooden barn door.

The hinges squeaked as they swung it open, and a dog began to bark somewhere. Ella's heart beat so fast she thought it might explode. What if this was the wrong barn? She stepped inside, suddenly certain they'd made a mistake. Perhaps they should have hidden in the woods somehow, backtracking uphill, taking their chances outdoors. Because whoever lived here might find them and turn them in. She followed Isaak into the darkness, barely breathing as the dog's bark grew more frantic, approaching, and then a voice cut through the shadows.

"You're from Château de la Hille, *oui*?"

A man, gruff and grizzled, materialized as the door swung shut behind them. Ella exhaled, sucking in the smell of manure and mildewed hay, realizing she'd been holding her breath.

"*Oui*," Isaak managed, his voice shaking under the word. He looked around the shadows, speaking to nobody in particular. "I can't believe we made it."

"I was afraid they'd caught you. Expected you hours ago." The man came closer, looking them over, squinting in the darkness and rubbing the scruff on his chin. "You look like drowned puppies."

"We had to run from a patrol." Isaak subdued the shake in his voice. "A German patrol. We swam across the river to escape."

For a moment, the old man said nothing, but his bushy brows gathered in thought. "Where?" he whispered after a moment. "Close to here?"

Isaak nodded.

"Merde. You'd better get up into the hayloft." New urgency animated his weathered face. "If a patrol saw you, they won't quit looking. Quick." He gestured over his shoulder, striding across the shadowy barn. "Get up that ladder. See it? And don't make a sound. I'll send my wife out with blankets and something to eat, and she'll figure out how to dry your clothes." He shooed them up the ladder, his final words rising with Ella as she started to climb.

"Not a sound, you hear? Get into the hay, deep as you can—" A wet cough interrupted his warning. "They might search house to house."

TWENTY-ONE

RÖSLI

TOULOUSE, FRANCE

EARLY MAY 1943

*R*ösli walked down Rue du Taur, heading toward the Secours Suisse office in Toulouse, a slender bag on her arm and her heart heavy.

She cleared the anguish from her throat, reaching the correct door on the cobbled road and hoping most staff would be away for lunch. She had no interest in seeing anyone other than the person she'd come to talk to: Anne-Marie Piguet. She'd called the Toulouse office a day before, learning that Anne-Marie had just arrived there, and would travel on to La Hille in a day or two. The timing was perfect, really. Maurice was scheduled to be away this afternoon, so Rösli could make her visit to the office brief. She'd catch Anne-Marie and hopefully avoid everyone else, even Maurice—she couldn't abide their pity. Today, the feelings of other people were simply too much to bear, because today Rösli had left Château de la Hille for good.

She'd stretched her tenure for as long as possible, staying on to see Ella and Isaak leave for Spain, but she could no longer stave off the inevitable. The administration in Bern was breathing down her neck, ready to force her out, and she wouldn't give them the satisfaction. Anne-Marie's arrival at La Hille was as good a time as any to disappear. If the children missed Rösli, at least they would be distracted by the arrival of their new caretaker.

She sighed now, thinking of her children as she climbed the steps to the upstairs offices. Early that morning, she'd gazed over the dining room, its tables full of *les Petits*, *les Moyens*, and the remaining *Grands*, who risked life at La Hille because they had nowhere else to go. It pained her, physically, that she'd been unable to propel every one of them over foreign borders. Would the teenagers survive the war? Would the new colony director, whoever that might be, protect them? Would the *Zwiebelkeller* continue to keep them safe from police raids? She sighed. There were no answers to her questions.

It had been heartrending to leave La Hille, though the children were unconcerned as she tramped out, as she did every morning, toward Montégut. Rösli hadn't told them the truth. When she left, her heart in her throat, only *she* knew she'd never return. Her reason for going quietly, without fanfare, felt obvious: the children had lived through enough goodbyes. She wouldn't make them endure another. But now unease crept in, sudden and familiar. Was departing without a farewell the right thing to do? Or was it her final mistake as *directrice* of Château de la Hille?

Rösli shook her questions away and entered the main office. There, crouching over a suitcase, was Anne-Marie. Nobody else seemed to be around, thank goodness. They would be able to speak in private before parting ways.

Anne-Marie rose from her battered suitcase, into which she'd been carefully tucking a pile of children's drawings. "Mademoiselle Näf," she said brightly. "I've been expecting you. A secretary told me to wait for you this afternoon, before catching my next train.

I'm afraid the rest have gone to lunch, but if you want to see them—"

"I don't," Rösli interrupted, batting the suggestion away. "I only wanted to see you."

Anne-Marie blinked. "Oh! Well, I've been eager to speak with you, too. I imagine we'll catch the train back to the château together, and chat on the way?"

Rösli sighed. "Actually, I've arranged for one of the younger boys to meet your train this afternoon, so you won't get lost trying to find La Hille on your own. I won't be traveling back with you, unfortunately. I'm headed to Switzerland this evening."

Anne-Marie frowned. "Maurice told me you'd be leaving, but I didn't realize it would be so soon."

"It's not nearly soon enough, at least in the eyes of the Swiss Red Cross." Rösli grimaced. "They sent my notice weeks ago, but I had a few things to finish up. Maurice won't be surprised to hear that I've finally left."

"Won't he want to say goodbye?"

Rösli shrugged, shifting the strap of her bag. "I'd rather nobody make a fuss."

Anne-Marie's expression darkened, and it took her a moment to gather her words. "I can't believe they've punished you this way. It infuriates me, Mademoiselle Näf. How can they dismiss you for saving lives?"

"Well." Rösli shook her head a little. "I didn't manage to save them all, did I? In fact, that's why I requested *your* transfer, to La Hille. Monsieur Dubois and I agree that you're the person needed there now. There will be another director hired as well, and I have no idea if he or she will support whatever efforts you undertake. You may have to act alone, Anne-Marie, if you decide to act at all."

The younger woman nodded, holding Rösli's stare. "I've been given three weeks off, after I settle at La Hille—"

"To arrange a new escape route to Switzerland," Rösli said, completing the thought. "Did Maurice say as much when you arrived here?"

Anne-Marie nodded, lowering her voice despite the empty office. "But he seemed deeply skeptical of my chances. Apparently, the border is tighter than ever."

Rösli formed the question she had to ask, the question she was afraid to voice in case the answer let her down. "Have you decided to do it anyway, despite the risk? To take on the burden of helping young people escape?"

"*Oui.* Of course." Anne-Marie didn't hesitate. "I've thought of nothing else for weeks."

Relief came in a flood. It was powerful enough to weaken Rösli, and she reached for the wall to steady herself. "I . . ." She couldn't find the words. An image of Ella, sitting on the stream bank in early spring, shot through her mind. Thank God she was on her way to safety. Edith's face rose next, her glasses catching the light. Then she pictured Walter Kamlet, bent over the piano, La Hille's frail genius who had nowhere to go. They all had a chance again, with Anne-Marie stepping in. Rösli swiped at her eyes, blinking. "I'm grateful to you."

Anne-Marie reached for Rösli's calloused hands. "I *will* find a way out of France, Mademoiselle Näf." Her voice was quiet and steady. "I promise. I'm only sorry you can't stay to continue this work yourself."

Rösli nodded, glancing out the window, trying to forestall unbearable pain. "I wish I could stay." It was almost too much to fathom: she would never see her children again. She pressed Anne-Marie's hands in farewell. "Bonne chance, Anne-Marie. I will think of you and the children every day."

With that, Rösli pivoted, and left the office, sensing the younger woman's gaze following her until she disappeared down the stairs.

Soon, Anne-Marie would head south, arriving at La Hille in time for supper. It comforted Rösli. For reasons she couldn't pin down, she suddenly believed in Anne-Marie Piguet. She never sensed much about other people, yet Rösli did sense that Anne-Marie would do what she said, and that she just might pull it off. She was grateful for this shot of uncharacteristic intuition. It would help her now.

She stepped out into the sunlight.

It would help her to go.

TWENTY-TWO

ELLA

*E*lla stopped shivering as the morning lengthened. She lay in Isaak's arms, wrapped in a scratchy blanket and burrowed deep alongside the loft's far wall into even scratchier hay, struggling to keep her eyes open. The farmer's wife had appeared soon after they arrived, a short, strapping woman with flyaway gray hair and kind eyes. Wasting no time on pleasantries, she'd set down a plate of bread and cheese, ordering them to remove their wet clothes and wrap themselves in blankets. Despite her fatigue and fear, Ella had hesitated. She'd met Isaak's similarly questioning expression, and the woman flicked an impatient hand, gesturing for them to hurry so she could get back inside the house before anyone came knocking. Pragmatism overtook modesty, and Ella stripped down to her underwear in front of the woman and Isaak, glancing only once at his pale rib cage as he wrapped himself in the wool blanket. How strange her life had become, she thought as the woman disappeared with their wet bundles and Ella slumped down into the hay, scooting backward into its musty smell and Isaak's arms. She was practically naked with a boy in a stranger's hayloft, and all she wanted was to sleep or weep from nerves.

Sleep won. The loft warmed as the sun rose, gilding the hay layered over their heads, and exhaustion fell over them both like a shroud.

When Ella finally reopened her eyes, she was disoriented. Isaak's bare skin warmed her back, rising and falling with his breath, and the light drained slowly from their little cave in the hay.

"*Psst*," someone whispered from outside the pile, and she realized that a voice had woken her. She blinked, her mind scrambling as her pulse bounded back up to pace. But the voice came again, halting her panic. "Wake up—it's only us."

Isaak shifted behind her, and Ella unwrapped herself from his arms and crawled out, clutching the blanket around her bare shoulders and puffing hay from her lips. Her muscles were sore, her throat dry with dust, and her eyes itched, but she felt revived. Her head was clear. Even her twisted ankle only ached now, instead of throbbing.

The farmer and his wife stood in the loft, blinking in the shadows of evening. As Ella emerged, the elderly man turned to face the wall. "I won't look," he muttered. "Get dressed."

Isaak crawled from the hay, and again Ella hesitated, glancing between the grandfatherly man's back and her boyfriend's tall frame. The woman pressed the clothes forward, whispering. "Hurry now. No time for modesty, child."

Ella dropped the blanket and felt her cheeks flush as Isaak pulled on his dry pants beside her. The sensation of him revived in her mind: his chest, bare and warm, on her back only minutes before. She shook her head and dressed, tackling her thoughts into submission as the woman whispered.

"We have a problem. The Germans didn't come knocking today,

thank God, but my husband walked into town to connect with others in our network and find out what's going on."

Others in their network? Ella pulled her sweater over her head and studied the woman. She appeared to be an aging farmwife, solid and weathered, and yet she had a clandestine network? She was part of the resistance? Admiration sparked in her chest, and the farmer turned around and picked up where his wife left off.

"The *passeur* who was to take you no longer wants to make the trip. He believes there will be added scrutiny. Too many patrols. The Germans know escapees are around."

Because of us, Ella thought, finishing his sentiment. She met Isaak's startled stare as he sputtered, still adjusting his shirt.

"But he *has* to take us. We barely made it this far without a guide—"

The farmer held up his palm, commanding quiet. "He won't. But I found another *passeur* who was already planning to make the trek tomorrow night. He's taking an older couple. I don't know him, but he's willing to accept the money you would've paid the original *passeur*."

"Good." Isaak nodded, breathing quickly, already certain.

But Ella glanced between Isaak and the farmer's wife, who seemed worried. The woman tucked several sprigs of loose, gray hair under her kerchief, mustering words.

"Please understand that we don't know this new guide," she said, her hands falling from her kerchief and crossing tightly over her chest. "The other one was vetted—we've known him since he was a boy. But this one? I'm concerned that he's willing to go even with increased German surveillance. And I'm concerned that we don't know him."

"Bernard seems to trust him," the farmer murmured, catching his wife's eye. He shrugged, as if to emphasize that he couldn't be certain, either. "The two of you will have to decide," he added, looking between Isaak and Ella. "If you want to go, I'll lead you to the new *passeur* tomorrow night. Otherwise, I'll help you through the woods until you're on a safe path back to where you came from."

Ella barely breathed as the farmer's wife set out a humble meal, offering a distracted smile but wasting no more words. Isaak glanced at Ella, holding her stare. Should they take a risk on a *passeur* nobody knew? Or should they stay in France, hiding at La Hille, and possibly never get another chance to escape again?

"You can tell us in the morning," the old farmer grumbled eventually, trudging toward the ladder. His wife paused, reaching out to grip Ella's hands with her papery palms.

"I'm sorry," she said, squeezing. "For everything. We raised four daughters on this farm. I remember when they were your age, so beautiful and young . . ." She paused, as if trying to connect the memory of her daughters with Ella and Isaak, standing here before her. Her eyes glittered under soft, hooded lids as she sought words. "You both deserve better than the world's giving you."

Ella managed a nod, and the elderly woman turned for the ladder. Her kerchiefed head disappeared, rung by rung, and the words hung in Ella's mind like bitter berries. *You deserve better.*

Isaak's arms encircled her waist from behind, and she leaned into him as the barn door creaked shut below. Frustration welled in her chest. They *did* deserve better. They deserved a normal life, the life their parents had raised them for, with school and faith and laughter and a real home. They deserved their families, and a future that wasn't constantly in peril. She turned to face Isaak, looking up into his gray eyes while the last of the sunlight seeped through cracks in the barn walls.

"I think we should go with the new *passeur*," he whispered, studying her face, and she nodded once even though she wasn't at all sure. She didn't want to talk about it now. She lifted her hand to

THE WINTER ORPHANS   229

his neck, pulling him down, and kissed him as if there were nothing else in the world beyond them, alone in this hayloft, adrift in France. Together.

Isaak responded, kissing her back, gaining momentum as she tugged him down onto the blankets thrown across the hay. She sensed his breath quickening, blending with hers. She felt his strong arms encasing her as he folded onto the wool beside her. Her thoughts were barely present now, yet still they whispered as Isaak's mouth found hers again.

Be careful. She tugged his shirt where he'd tucked it into his waistband, finding the bare skin underneath with her fingers, newly bold. Judgment whispered in her mind, prodding her. *Careful!*

But as Isaak's hands found her skin beneath her sweater, rebellion flared in her heart, drowning the prudent voices she'd learned to heed. *Why* be careful? Yesterday they'd been shot at by a German patrol. Tomorrow they could be caught, killed, or separated on a train snaking to Poland. Nothing in the world felt as safe as Isaak. Nothing felt as true. And they might only have this night.

Isaak pulled gently away from her, leaning back on the blanket, his elbow propped in the hay while he took her in, his other hand moving from her waist to her cheek.

"Ella. We should stop."

She shook her head, and her heart cracked fully open. The voices of prudence and rebellion fell away from her mind, and all that was left were his eyes, the gray of spring rain. The tufts of his hair, always a little wild, the curve of his lips as he subdued his constant smile. Sunlight pierced a crack in the wall, falling golden over their humble bed in the hay, and Ella reached for Isaak. She kissed his questioning smile, climbed into his arms, and let her soul take fully over as the day faded into night.

Later, they lay curled together, a wool blanket draping their skin as the night air chilled the quiet loft. Isaak stared at the ceiling as if stunned, his arm wrapped tightly around Ella's bare shoulder. She turned a little, resting her chin on his chest, and savored his answering smile.

"Do you think we'll make it to Spain?" she whispered, the question surfacing again, insistent. "Should we go with the new *passeur*?"

He turned a little, looking her in the eye, and smoothed her hair behind her neck with his rough fingers. "I think we should." He bent to kiss her forehead, her temple, and the soft skin under her ear, whispering, "I want to start a life with you. A real life somewhere, with no more hiding."

No more hiding. The idea was like a silver sail, tugging her forward.

"We can do this," he whispered, his voice gaining conviction.

What would it be like, to be free? Despite the hope unfurling in her soul, she couldn't smother her doubt. "What if we can't?"

But Isaak shook his head. "We can." His fervent stare pulled her in. "We'll make it over the Pyrénées."

The next night, Ella and Isaak followed the farmer through another moonlit forest. She was shaky as she walked, flinching with each step on her bad ankle and every rub of old blisters, reopening. But she'd slept another day in Isaak's strong arms, and she felt as sure as she ever would.

So she mirrored his footsteps and the farmer's surprisingly swift pace until they found three other people in a clearing somewhere above Saint-Girons, waiting in the moonlight. Ella and Isaak hung off to the side while the farmer whispered with another man, his head dark under a beret and his thick mustache moving as he murmured back and counted money, still a bit damp, with quick fingers. Ella swallowed. It was money gathered by Rösli, pressed into their hands only a few nights ago, and kept safe in Isaak's pocket even from the river's snatching currents. What would Rösli say if she knew how the plan had changed? Would she advise them to go, or stay? Suddenly Ella wished, with a deep fervor, that she could talk to Rösli Näf. That she could see her deliberate stare and seek her careful counsel.

The farmer intercepted her thoughts, shuffling over to stand before them, his voice low and gravelly. "I think this *passeur* is capable, but I didn't like how intent he was on payment. I don't know what advice to give you, honestly." He glanced between the older couple huddled off to the side, and the mustached *passeur* who seemed eager to set off. The farmer sighed. "I'd take you myself if I was ten years younger."

"We'll keep our wits about us," Isaak whispered, placing his palm on the farmer's shoulder. The old man nodded, reaching up to pat Isaak's hand.

"Bonne chance, son." He tipped his head to Ella. "Mademoiselle. May God go with you."

Ella's throat tightened, and she nodded at this stranger who had hidden them, fed and warmed them, and seemed to care about them, no matter the danger. "Thank you, monsieur. For everything."

They turned away from each other, walking opposite directions, and when Ella glanced back, the farmer had already vanished into the depths of the dark trees. She looked forward to their guide, already pacing ahead, and inhaled.

They'd made their decision. Now all they had to do was walk.

Nobody spoke for several hours. They simply hiked in a loose line, huffing up the ridges of steep hills, into the shadows of forests, and through meadows, following what appeared to be little more than a goat trail. Ella stared at the dark ground disappearing under her aching feet as the moon traveled its arc over the sky. The older couple, who panted in her wake, had tried talking with each other once on the trail, but the *passeur* had pivoted abruptly, striding back to them and whispering harshly, thick finger shaking for emphasis. Ella couldn't hear his words, but she glanced toward Isaak, who nodded slightly. The message was clear: *Be quiet.*

They struggled up a steep incline for what felt like half the night. Ella's legs went from aching to screaming with every step, her muscles loose with exhaustion. Yet on she climbed behind Isaak, mimicking the certain movements of their guide, who still strode several paces ahead, as limber and comfortable as the mountain goats that must lurk in these increasingly open, rocky hills. Eventually most of the trees faded into the scenery below, and as the eastern horizon glowed they emerged on the spine of a foothill. The *passeur* paused, his breathing steady as he turned to gaze at the view spreading in every direction. The older couple collapsed to sit alongside the trail, their heads hanging between their knees as they sucked breath. Ella stared at the outlines of mountains, dim under a sky still twinkling with the last stars. The moon, reluctant in retreat, hung opposite the whisper of a waking sun.

Ella pulled thin mountain air into her lungs. The breeze smelled earthy and fresh, like spring. The Pyrénées, clear for the first time, spread from where they stood, glowing like whitecaps pitching over the dark edge of the world. She pivoted again, stunned by the majesty of the view.

The older woman's voice broke the silence. "Can we speak now?" Her accent was heavy. "Surely there are no German patrols way up here."

The *passeur* simply looked over his shoulder, his gaze emotionless over his heavy mustache. He studied the couple where they sat in new grass, their faces shadowed by the remnants of night, and nodded once. "Talk if you like. We'll rest for ten minutes, and then we'll push on to the village to arrive by morning. We have two hours left, at most." He took off his hat, scrubbing at his thick, dark hair.

"Where are you from?" The woman asked, her gaze hinging on Isaak.

"Germany," he answered simply.

"Ah. We're from Poland, but we lived in France before all this. The war." The woman puffed air through pursed lips, her dark eyes traveling the horizon. "You're Jews, too, I suppose?"

Isaak nodded, and the woman's gaze moved from him to Ella.

"We're on our way to see our daughter." The woman smiled faintly. "The last time I saw her, she was about your age. She has pretty eyes, like yours."

Ella let her expression soften. Again, she'd reminded a mother of her own child. She imagined Mutti, noticing girls in the world who might be the age of her own daughters, and pain needled her heart.

"Where is she now? Your daughter?"

The woman looked out at the fading stars. "America. We should have moved to be with her long ago, before it became so difficult, but who could have known?" She waved a hand, as if to ask, *What can you do about such things? Such regrets?* "We're trying to go to her now. Through Spain and Portugal."

Her husband looked up, exhaustion saturating his face, and the woman reached to link her arm in his. Her words switched from French to Polish. They murmured with each other, the wife nudging her husband and smiling here and there, prodding life back into his slumping body.

Isaak found Ella's hand and he squeezed, luring her away from the group. She followed him up the trail a bit as the *passeur* lay back in the grass, staring at the lightening sky.

"Can you believe it?" Isaak said, stopping and pulling Ella's back to his chest, his heavy arms falling around her waist. "We'll be in Spain in just a few days." His chin rested against her temple as she snuggled into his embrace, and they stared out at the galloping mountains together.

"We have a long way to go yet," Ella murmured, her eyes on the mountains. But excitement lit her heart. Here she stood, safe on a high plateau watching the rising sun, with a young man she loved wrapping her in his arms. They'd grown up, found a way out, and the future awaited as surely as the sunrise.

"Ella," Isaak whispered. He raised his hands to her shoulders, spinning her gently against him so their faces nearly touched. "I should have asked you already." His expression tightened. "Before last night."

She felt her heart kick up against his, tapping at his chest. She stared into his hopeful, intent gaze and sensed his nervousness, his excitement, like a shift in the wind.

"When we get somewhere safe—Spain, or maybe Portugal—" His face was serious and eager at the same time, and he inhaled, seemingly building the courage to finish his question. "Will you marry me?"

Everything in Ella rose, like a funnel of wind lifted her soul over the wild hills. She found herself laughing and blinking back tears all at once while joy, sudden and strong, spun in her heart. She stood on her tiptoes to kiss his lips, their breath joining for a long, suspended moment. When she fell away, she managed to say the words that would certainly change her life.

"Yes." She laughed. "Yes, I will marry you."

The next two hours passed in a blur. Ella and Isaak walked with their hands joined whenever the trail widened enough to allow it, and she was barely bothered by the ache in her limbs and the sting of blisters on her feet. Everything hurt equally, so she no longer limped. Pain couldn't weigh her down, not now. As the morning brightened, she and Isaak glanced at each other frequently, grinning like children with a secret.

Ella still couldn't picture the future. She didn't know what to expect of Spain, and Portugal if they ever reached it. She couldn't imagine the boat they might take to safer shores. But she could see a future with Isaak. She imagined that with every step she took, he would now be by her side. And someday, when the world allowed it, they would send for Hanni. She would have a family, once again.

The waves of joy were enough to propel her the rest of the way to the tiny mountain village, where the *passeur* said they'd find lodging and rest. It was fully morning when he held up a hand, looking over his shoulder and whispering.

"We're close. Not a word."

They continued on through a stand of thick trees, and Ella breathed the scent of pine and savored the weight of Isaak's hand in hers. Soon they could collapse in someone's barn, resting their swollen feet and aching muscles. She could shift into her love's arms and sleep.

The older couple trudged behind them with shuffling, dragging gaits. A clearing opened through the trees, and their guide again raised his hand, signaling everyone to stop.

"This is it," he whispered, his dark gaze skipping between each person.

"We rest here?" the older woman asked. She glanced around, incredulous.

"No." The *passeur's* tone was impatient. "You'll rest here for a bit—fifteen minutes, at most—while I go ahead to check with our contacts. When I've confirmed that the route to the edge of the village is safe, I'll come back for you." He looked between them again, clearly eager to press on. "*Comprenez-vous?* Wait here."

With that he pivoted and strode off, leaving the four of them hesitating on the edge of the clearing as he vanished into the opposite stand of trees.

"I suppose we can sit," the husband ventured after a minute. He shuffled forward, eyeing a patch of soft grass under the trees. His wife followed, her face pained with each step, and they collapsed in the shade of the clearing.

Isaak moved to follow, but Ella tugged him back. Something formed in her stomach, like the weight of a stone, but she couldn't place her feelings. What made her hesitate? She looked from Isaak's questioning face to the couple, spread on the grass, and her sense of dread grew.

Something wasn't right.

It was as if an external force blew through her, reanimating her wasted limbs. She strode forward, pulling Isaak along, and bent next to the older couple.

"We can't stay here." Her words were breathless, anxious, but she still couldn't say why. Was she being paranoid?

"What are you talking about?" The man propped himself up on an elbow, blinking lidded eyes. "He said to wait here."

"Something's wrong." She looked between the pale, worn faces staring at her, grasping for the right words. "I don't know why, but I'm just sure something isn't right. Why would he leave us here?"

"To check with his contacts," the man said, slumping back to the earth. He lay flat on his back, as if in bed, and closed his eyes to the brightening sky. "You're being hysterical."

His wife's expression darkened, but she didn't move. "That's not very nice," she said, conciliatory. "*Ma chérie*, you're just tired. There's nothing to worry about."

Isaak, still gripping Ella's hand, opened his mouth to speak but couldn't seem to find words.

"Please," she tried again. "Let's just wait deeper in the woods. When we see him return, we'll come out."

"And if he thinks we've gone?" the woman asked, opening her eyes with the question. "I won't be able to stay awake, and I doubt you will, either. We'll miss him."

"I'm not moving another step," the man burbled, already on the edge of sleep.

Ella stood and turned to Isaak. She shook her head, trying to find words to explain her tumultuous, panicked heart. *Was* she being hysterical? Had exhaustion addled her good sense?

Isaak shrugged. "There's no reason we can't wait in the trees." He glanced around the clearing. "We'll just stay quiet, so we hear him coming. And we'll have to stay awake."

They backtracked, hand in hand, and when Isaak wanted to stop, Ella tugged him farther, veering off the trail they'd come up. "See that outcropping? Above the clearing?" she asked, gesturing to a clump of boulders rising above the trees, halfway up a small hill.

He nodded, catching her meaning. They could see the clearing from there, but if they wedged into the crevices atop the granite, nobody would notice them from below. They could wait and watch until they knew it was safe.

Ella's muscles screamed and her blisters seared as she scaled the incline to the boulders, and Isaak dropped her hand with the effort. When they reached the outcropping, they shimmied onto a ledge together, staying just out of view, and Ella was finally able to exhale. She nestled close to Isaak, her chin resting on her arm, and watched the clearing below. The older couple was asleep in the grass. A shard of sun broke over the trees and lit the meadow, slicing at their feet. Isaak closed his eyes, his breath evening out, as unable to ward off sleep as their fellow refugees down below.

But Ella stayed awake. She watched the sun creep over the clearing, her heart beating against the boulder underneath her chest, and her dread expanded with each passing minute. Where was the *passeur*? He'd said that he wouldn't be gone long. *Wait for fifteen minutes,* he'd said, and he'd return. Had something happened? Where was the village from here? What if someone else stumbled upon them first?

Isaak's breath lengthened further, and she fought the same overwhelming fatigue, staring at the clearing, forcing her eyes to stay open. What would they do if the *passeur* didn't return? Trudge on alone?

Her questions multiplied, buzzing around her weary mind, and then she heard it. *Footsteps.* She lifted herself slightly, listening to the scuff of boots in the woods. More than one person was coming, but that wasn't what made her breath catch. She elbowed Isaak, hard, and when his eyes opened, she pressed a hand over his mouth before he could say a word. She shook her head slowly and cocked her ear to listen to the approach of boots.

There was something in their rhythm. She glanced at Isaak, equally frozen beside her. Then several men burst into the clearing below.

"Wake up!" The *passeur* shouted, striding over to the sleeping couple. He swung his booted leg back and kicked the husband in the gut before he could shake himself from sleep. Three Germans strode in the *passeur*'s wake. Their coats flapped in the morning breeze as they swiveled in the meadow, hands on their guns.

"You said you had four," one of them said in accented French. "We paid you for four Jews."

"I did have four!" the *passeur* exclaimed, spinning and rubbing at his mustache. He stared into the trees, his eyes narrowing, and Ella didn't dare breathe.

"They must be close." Their guide studied the woods, scanning, while the German patrol did the same.

"Go on down the trail," he said after a minute. He glanced around, and then his gaze rose to the outcropping.

Ella's heart exploded in her chest. Isaak's hand found hers and he tugged her, hard, shimmying backward. She did the same, as silently as she could, but the *passeur* was already shouting below.

"*Ils sont là-haut!* Come! They can't outrun us."

But Ella and Isaak were already on their feet. *Running.* They sprinted from the outcropping along the crest of the hill, just above a line of trees. Suddenly Ella didn't feel the pain in her legs, in her twisted ankle, in her raw heels. All she felt was fear.

Like hunted deer, they raced frantically, propelled by only the faintest sense of direction. *Away* was all Ella could think as she ran, stretching her legs as far as she could, pounding alongside Isaak. Her mind seemed to fly ahead, picking out each footfall, each turn, zipping through the trees to make her a path. It was as if her thoughts and fear separated, and one propelled her forward while the other carved the way.

Shots fired behind them. Ella didn't flinch, and Isaak didn't slow. Instead, they ran as if caught in the wind, and more gunshots split the air at their backs.

Neither of them fell. They just ran, long and hard, into the wild mountains. The forest embraced over their heads as they sprinted on, ducking and scrambling, putting distance between themselves and everything they'd hoped for.

The promise of sleep in a village vanished. The dream of crossing over glacial peaks evaporated. Spain became farther away with every frantic step.

And the Polish couple. A sob broke through one of Ella's desperate breaths. They would never find their daughter now.

They must have run a kilometer before they stopped, gasping, deep in a forest without a trail. Isaak's head hung, and his hands rested on his knees as he sucked air, his cheeks ruddy in the mountain breeze.

"You think we lost them?" he whispered, glancing up at Ella.

She listened, hard, but the only sound was of birds in the trees. She tried to breathe, tried to soothe her rapid heartbeat, and nodded.

"How will we find our way back? To La Hille?" she said finally, putting words to the inevitable end of their adventure. To the best end they could hope for now.

Isaak held her stare, still breathing hard. He stood, took her hand, and they started to walk. When he spoke, his voice hollowed with defeat.

"We'll drop down off this ridge," he muttered. "I studied the map every night for a month. All of the valleys lead back to Saint-Girons. If we find a valley, we can follow it north and go back to the farmer's house to rest before hiking to La Hille." He sighed, his breath gaining rhythm, and scowled. "That double-crossing *bastard*."

Ella sniffed bitterly, staving off tears, forcing them to harden in her throat. She'd wept enough. She would give this world full of double-crossing bastards no more tears.

PART THREE

TWENTY-THREE

ANNE-MARIE

THE FORBIDDEN ZONE, FRANCE

JUNE 1943

*A*nne-Marie wasn't sure how she should feel.

She sat in the crowded train compartment, wrapped tight as a package. Was she nervous? Excited? She glanced at the countryside spilling from the window, trying to inhale a full breath. Really, she should be terrified. Fields rolled by, interrupted by forests and closer stands of trees. Sunlight skipped through leafy branches as the train nodded past. The blend of green outside the window was both familiar and tantalizing. Anne-Marie breathed in, imagining the air of the Risoud that would soon fill her lungs, the oxygen quickening her blood as she walked under towering spruce. She closed her eyes, trying to believe it: she was going *home*.

That is, if she made it.

I'll be fine, Anne-Marie thought, her mantra for the many hours she'd been seated on this train. Would she, though? Tomorrow morning, she planned to walk over an international border, no exit visa in hand, through heavily patrolled forests and mountains, breaking who knew how many laws. *Alors*. She puffed air through her lips. She didn't have much patience for the law these days, anyway.

Her thoughts moved to the teenagers at La Hille, some of them not much younger than her, and all with their own hopes and dreams. They retreated into their secret room every evening, terrified that this would be the night the gendarmes found them. *Oui*, somebody had to go to the border to see if an illegal route could be forged. It was that simple, and it might as well be Anne-Marie.

The train slowed at the tiny station in rural Foncine-le-Bas, the final stop before Anne-Marie would start off on foot over the hills rising in the east. She wore hiking shoes under her skirt and carried a backpack. This area was still a popular hiking spot among locals, so Anne-Marie hoped she could blend in, claiming to be out for fresh air and exercise. Was that ridiculous? Perhaps, but it was the best cover available. The train groaned to a halt, and she stood to disembark. As she climbed from the carriage, she smiled at a gendarme posted nearby, as if she really were going on an adventure instead of risking her life.

In tiny Foncine-le-Bas, Anne-Marie found a hotel room, without incident, in which to sleep off the long train journey. She stared at the ceiling for much of the night, unable to rest, and finally rose at dawn. She crept down the stairs and out the unwatched front door, adjusting her backpack and pointing her stride east.

According to her map, it was about five kilometers to Chapelle-des-Bois, the last town before the Forbidden Zone. Anne-Marie set off along a thin dirt track, snaking away from the sleeping village and into the dark woods.

Finally, she could breathe. She walked as the morning brightened, noticing everything: the vibrant green of new beech leaves, a rabbit trail in the undergrowth, a wood lark flitting between branches. She saw no recent signs of people. Here and there, mud had dried in the shape of a footprint, but such prints were old. Light scattered through the branches overhead, and Anne-Marie pulled fresh air into her lungs. The forest gave her confidence. She walked on, entertaining herself by listening to birdsong and naming each call. *Skylark, garden warbler, nuthatch, common swift . . .*

Two hours later, she made her way through the seam in a long hayfield, squinting into the sunlight at a village across the waving grasses. This was the village she'd studied on her map, snugged up against the Swiss border. It was called Chapelle-des-Bois, Chapel of the Woods. Such a pretty name, Anne-Marie thought. In the distance beyond the village, more fields rolled to an abrupt cliff face separating France from emerald Swiss hills.

A church spire rose in the center of Chapelle-des-Bois, and a spatter of buildings and houses populated the road dividing the village. Even from the field, Anne-Marie could see the barbed wire lining that road, skirting the buildings like a net. The cliffs and hills beyond the net were where she needed to go, and suddenly the very idea seemed absurd.

"Onward," Anne-Marie whispered to herself, and she didn't break stride as she swung onto the main road. She glanced at the barbed wire without turning her head, in case anyone was watching. This village, at the edge of the Forbidden Zone, was most certainly full of Germans. What if they scrutinized her presence here, with her hiking boots and backpack and map? *Mon Dieu*, she thought frantically. Were her intentions as obvious as they suddenly seemed? She'd planned to explain that she was visiting the area on holiday to hike the French woods, but now, with the wire glinting in her peripheral vision, the danger surrounding her rose, sharp as metal.

Forcing expression from her face, Anne-Marie strode calmly into town, looking up at the church presiding over the main street, the sun warm on her face. An old woman who had been pinching dead geraniums from a pot paused, squinting, a broom poised in her other hand. She watched Anne-Marie pass with rheumy gray eyes, looking as if she held her breath. As Anne-Marie neared the church, a German soldier stiffened where he guarded the empty street. Like the old woman, he studied her approach, inscrutable, his blue eyes narrowed against the white morning light. Anne-Marie's heart pounded in her chest as she nodded to him, feigning confidence, her hands gripping the straps of her pack as if it tethered her to safety.

"*Arrêtez-vous!*" The soldier called instead of nodding back. He strode toward her, his gaze scrolling up and down, speaking competent French. "Papers, s'il vous plaît."

She rustled through her bag, glancing at him, then trying to tame the shake in her hands as she held out her papers. The guard frowned as he looked over the documents, and Anne-Marie forced her voice steady. "I live near Toulouse at present, though I'm a Swiss citizen—"

"What are you doing here?"

She forced a smile. "I work for the Swiss Red Cross in the south, but I'm on holiday for a few weeks. With the border closed, I couldn't go home without a load of paperwork." She shrugged, assessing this guard and taming the pound of her heart. He appeared to be near her age, with his boyish, well-fed face. "I'm a bit homesick, sir. I thought these forests might help with that."

He didn't return her smile, and his blue eyes didn't seem to blink as he bent over her documents again, examining them.

"Isn't it beautiful here?" she ventured, glancing around the sunlit, empty street. "Last night I stayed in Foncine-le-Bas, at a little hotel. Alas, I only have a night or two here, and then I'll go back to my job in Toulouse."

He studied her, expressionless, as she chattered nervously, and she maintained a lighthearted smile while her stomach soured in fear. She'd once heard that lies were most believable if they hugged close to the truth. But was it foolish to admit that she was so near home? Yet, if he dragged her in somewhere for questioning, everything in her story would appear to be true. She was Swiss, and she'd been given a holiday. So far, she was indeed only hiking through the forests, looking at birds. She'd gambled on him understanding homesickness, but his gaze remained blank, his face grave, and her legs weakened.

"D'accord," the soldier finally said, handing her papers back. "But you're far too close to the Forbidden Zone here—this is no place for a hike. Where will you stay tonight?"

"Chaux-Neuve." Anne-Marie held her breath, standing still as a pine. "I'm sorry. I didn't realize I was so close to the border, sir," she added, rushing her words.

He hesitated. After a long moment, he looked from her to the street, straightening. "You may go."

She didn't give him a second to reconsider. Anne-Marie walked through the rest of the village, trying not to obviously hurry, calming her overactive pulse. She could have been arrested. God above.

Yet, she hadn't. She closed her eyes for a moment, quieting her thoughts, and entered a field split by the road and the menacing fence. Her plan reassembled in her mind. She would walk until the fence passed through the forest, somewhere up ahead, offering her cover. Then she'd sneak under the wire and sprint into the woods. Her terror was mitigated only by the fact that these were *her* woods. An international border crossed them, yes, but these trees still belonged to the Risoud. They would shelter her. Anne-Marie lengthened her gait. The sooner she disappeared from the village outskirts, the better.

It wasn't long before a thick tongue of forest lapped over the road, shading the wire from the glaring sun. Anne-Marie walked until branches crossed above her head, and then she stopped, listening, looking up and down the fence line for movement. The only sound was the gust of her own breath, and birdsong in the trees.

Shadows fluttered down, mingling with patches of light. Anne-Marie studied the road's curve, brightening as it left the forest. She searched for the shapes of men, hidden. Waiting.

Nothing.

She walked a bit farther, studying the ground for tracks. She looked for footprints, broken ferns, scuffs on the forest floor—anything that might indicate that she wasn't alone in this swath of trees. Still, nothing. She retraced her steps, examining the fence, searching for the right spot.

Anne-Marie breathed deeply, marshaling her nerve. *Now*, she thought. With that she bent, lifted a patch of wire toward the bottom of the fence, pulling up as hard as she could so a gap formed over the ground. She placed her backpack in the gap so the wire would stay tented, dropped to her stomach, and shimmied under the fence. It took only seconds. She unsnagged her backpack, spruce needles falling from her hair, and ran.

Ferns whipped her knees as she wove into the brush, driven by a surge of fear. *Nobody saw me*, she thought, hard. How much noise was she making? She slowed a bit, considering her footfalls, compelling herself to remain careful. She thought of the German soldier's blank gaze, and the gun fastened to his belt. She glanced back toward the road, catching sight of the fence strung through the trees, and then she dipped into a shallow gully and swung to an abrupt stop, crouching in the shadow of an ancient spruce.

She leaned against its bark, pinning her eyes shut and forcing her breathing to quiet. A kestrel's call echoed over the treetops. Anne-Marie listened, filling her lungs, releasing slowly. Would patrols notice the inevitable scuffs she'd made sliding under the fence? Ferns she'd bent in her headlong rush? No, that was unlikely, unless they were trained to look. She held her breath, listening again. Wind rustled branches. Somewhere nearby, a squirrel skittered up a trunk. There were no human sounds.

Mon Dieu. She opened her eyes to the forest, still cool with morning shadows. She'd made it inside the Forbidden Zone. It was dangerous, concealing patrols on both sides of the border, but it was also *her* forest. She placed her palm on the bark at her back, crusted with lichen. The odor of spruce and soil filled her senses. She rose to her feet. She knew these trees; they'd risen over her all of her life.

It was approximately three kilometers to the border, mostly up-hill. *Easy.* Anne-Marie moved forward, quietly now, placing each footstep carefully. She'd leave no trail. She threaded through close trunks, slipping into their shadows, scanning for movement. Her heart felt tugged forward, as if pulled by a magnet toward the hills. The ground steepened under her boots, and a splash of sun warmed her face as she passed through it. A familiar burn started in her thighs as she climbed, and she all but smiled. Still, she listened. The forest could give her a false sense of peace, she knew. German patrols and French Militia scoured these woods, searching for smugglers and resistance fighters and fleeing refugees. She'd made herself an outlaw when she crossed that fence, and patrols were known to shoot on sight.

She ascended steadily, scaling the forest floor as it rose like a long, steep wave, jagged with rocks. Once, she stumbled over the roots of a tree, a branch snapping under her heel. She froze and held her breath. Something moved downhill, and her fear returned in a gallop. She stared into the leafy undergrowth, searching in panic, but then she saw the immobile gaze of a deer. Her held breath released in a gust. The doe dipped her head, studying Anne-Marie. She nodded as if to an old friend, and turned back uphill.

If she brought refugees on this route, could they be silent? Even she hadn't achieved it. Still, the forest offered no human sounds. At a crest in the hill Anne-Marie paused, calming the sweep of her breath and gazing down at the tree trunks multiplying below. It felt as though the entire forest had eyes.

Eventually, the ground leveled. Panting, Anne-Marie swung into a swift pace. She could sense Switzerland now. This stretch of forest felt even more familiar, cousin to the paths she'd walked her entire life. It was as though she could sense her parents' hearts beating, not too far off now. *Home.* What would they say when she appeared at their doorstep? She continued to scan the silent underbrush, certain that the stone wall separating two countries would appear soon.

And then, to Anne-Marie's wonder, it did. Ahead she spotted stone, sewn through a seam of silver-trunked beech trees, and her heart pounded. In mere minutes she reached it, and as she placed her palms on its spine, a triumphant smile spread on her face, unbidden. She'd done it. With renewed energy, she hopped the border wall, her boots landing on Swiss soil.

She was home.

*B*ut what if you were just lucky?"

Anne-Marie's father peered at her over the well-used kitchen table, his face a battle of joy and worry. Her mother set down a steaming bowl of soup. They'd both been stunned when she arrived on their doorstep an hour ago, exhausted and elated.

"Well, obviously I was lucky—"

"You could have been killed," her mother interrupted. "They've shot people on the French side of the Risoud—I hope you realize that? And others have been arrested and taken away to their camps in Poland."

"I know." Anne-Marie looked into her mother's kind face, a mirror of her own, and then lowered her eyes to meet her father's blue gaze. "But you know who else is being hunted and sent to their camps in Poland, right? *Kids.* The kids I work with now."

"And you're *our* child, Anne-Marie," her mother persisted, wringing a clean washcloth in her weathered hands.

"Maman, you'd feel differently if you knew them. Listen. There's a girl—Inge. She's quiet and smart and she fell in love with a boy named Walter. They tried to escape to Switzerland, but were caught and sent back. The three kids they'd traveled with were deported. Then, just weeks later, Walter was caught and deported while Inge hid upstairs in a secret room in the château. And the colony's cook? She's a bit younger than you, Maman. A gentle woman who all the teenage girls flock to with their questions. Her husband was taken alongside Walter. They have a son named Pauli. What if they catch his mother, too? There are so many stories like this—I could go on and on. And do you know how they get to the camps? In livestock cars, as if they were animals. The children at La Hille have seen it with their own eyes. They fear deportation to Germany and Poland more than anything else."

Her mother lowered into a chair beside her father, pressing her hands over cheeks flushed from the kitchen. Her hair, messy in a loose bun, wisped into her pained stare. "We've heard the stories," she conceded, as Anne-Marie had known she would. "We've wanted to do something."

"Well, this is it." Anne-Marie looked between her parents. "You can be the final stop on the escape route. You can provide food and beds. Safety." They sat very still across the table, clearly hinging somewhere between their own convictions and concern for their daughter. Anne-Marie looked down, breathing in the steam rising from her soup. "Over the next two weeks, I'm going to try to set up a route out of France," she continued, dipping her bread in the broth, suddenly ravenous. "I won't be able to bring kids over the border the way I came. They'll need a safe place to sleep, close to the Forbidden Zone, but obviously a hotel risks too much exposure. I need to learn more about where the German patrols travel, and when. There was a German sentry on the main street of Chapelle-des-Bois and I still can't believe he didn't prevent me—"

"I know who you can talk to," her father interjected, his words tumbling forth as if he was afraid he might not say them if he waited another second. "Anne-Marie, our valley's full of people who've been trying to do their part. French children have been brought through the Risoud to shelter with families here, and there's a regular passage of goods crossing the border. I know some of these smugglers gather at a house in Campe." He paused, and her mother gestured for him to continue, though her brow knit tighter. He cleared his throat. "The smugglers I know of are good people. Not profiteers. They work for a cause."

Anne-Marie nodded, his words falling into place in her mind and a fire kindling in her heart. Of course her wild-willed father knew who crossed his woods, hopping the border illegally. Of course he knew who had a good heart, who could be trusted. A smile found her lips, and her mother fought back a smile of her own, batting a hand as if she disapproved altogether.

"Oh, Anne-Marie. I suppose if anyone can do this, it's you," she relented, huffing as she stood to bustle around the table. "And I'm glad to have you home."

A few days later, Anne-Marie walked into town to join a meeting. She hung her coat beside the door, listening to a mix of voices speaking all at once, but when she turned in to the parlor, the room fell quiet. A handful of people stared up at her, and her chest unclenched.

"Anne-Marie! Welcome home."

She laughed, stepping into an eclectic circle of people she'd mostly known all her life. The Risoud forest spilled out along a valley, hugging the sparkling water of Lac de Joux, and the majority of people strung along its shores knew one another. A young woman named Georgette stood, smiling under sunburned cheeks, and her brother Jean-François tipped his head in greeting before resuming a conversation with an older man.

"Your father stopped in the other day to let us know you'd come through the Risoud from France," Georgette said as the rest of the group resumed chatting. She grinned again, her pretty face mischievous. "We've been crossing the forest, too, so he told us about your children in France. Come, meet Victoria. I think she'll be a great help."

Georgette tugged Anne-Marie across a room bubbling with conversations, stopping before another young woman who was seated at the edge of the group. About Anne-Marie's age, the woman was tall and slim and sat with her trousered legs crossed, her hair upswept around a long face and shoulders back, and a glass of water perched on one knee. She smiled pleasantly when Anne-Marie settled in a chair across from her, and a ruddy young man flagged Georgette back across the room.

"Victoria Cordier," the woman said without preamble. "I understand you're Anne-Marie Piguet?"

"*Oui*. Pleased to meet you." Anne-Marie matched her smile. "And how do you fit into this group?"

Victoria leaned forward slightly, balancing the glass of water in the palm of one hand, and studied Anne-Marie with quick, intelligent eyes. She spoke swiftly, never breaking cadence. "I met Georgette and her brother some time ago, when they crossed the border and landed nearly on my mother's doorstep. My mother lives outside of Chapelle-des-Bois, in the Forbidden Zone, you see, so her house has become something of a hub."

"A hub for what?"

Victoria's eyes glittered. "The resistance. And I understand you've been caring for Jewish children in the South of France?"

Clearly, Victoria was way ahead of her. "Foreign Jewish children, yes. Some are German, some Austrian. So, you understand they're in grave danger—especially the older ones."

"And you want to smuggle them into Switzerland."

Anne-Marie held Victoria's gaze, and a grin grew on both of their faces. It was a strange sensation, Anne-Marie thought, to meet a person so closely aligned with one's own heart. She could feel it in the air between them, an invisible connection like electricity, as if they understood each other immediately and only needed words to confirm what they already sensed.

Victoria leaned a bit closer. "I've taken lots of folks across the border already. There's a cliff directly behind my mother's home—"

"I saw it," Anne-Marie interrupted. "Is it the cliff face beyond Chapelle-des-Bois? You can see it from the road, right?"

"*Oui*, that's the one. I grew up at the foot of it, and my mother lives there still. My sisters and I have figured out a way to scale it between patrols, and my mother plays her role perfectly with the Germans. You know—simple farm widow. I make lots of trips up it and over the border."

"If I brought my teenagers to you . . ."

"I'd take them. Bien sûr." She batted a hand as if to signify that this wasn't a question that required asking. "They can sleep at my mother's house before the trek. We already have a system worked out, in fact. But we need somewhere they can land on the Swiss side. You know that the Swiss patrols will kick them out if they're caught within twelve kilometers of the border?"

Anne-Marie nodded, her smile falling. "*Oui*—a few La Hille kids were caught that way. Listen. My parents live at the edge of the forest. If you can help me get the kids to the border wall, I can take them the rest of the way to my mother and father. They'll hide there, and then go on."

Victoria nodded, set down her glass, and fished a map out of a rucksack at her feet. "Let's have a look," she murmured, unfolding the map and meeting Anne-Marie's stare. For a second they held each other's gaze, and it was as if the plans formed in the air between them. Never had Anne-Marie understood someone so effortlessly.

"How did you join the resistance?" she asked as they bent together over the map.

"After France fell, I considered what God required of me," Victoria said simply. "Once I'd aimed my heart in the right direction, unseen hands guided me along." She smiled. "As they do."

~~~~~~

TWENTY-FOUR

ELLA

CHÂTEAU DE LA HILLE, SOUTHERN FRANCE

JUNE 1943

*T*here was no justice in the world.

Ella glanced out of an upstairs window of La Hille, eyeing a haystack across the field from the château. Gendarmes had been hiding behind it off and on for days, hoping to catch the teenagers by surprise if they ventured outside. Fury boiled in Ella as her eyes moved from the haystack, absent of motion, to a stand of trees lining the road. She realized now how lucky she and Isaak had been to sneak back into the château, weeks ago. Back then, they didn't know about the dangers of haystacks; they were simply fortunate that nobody had been watching La Hille the evening they returned. She frowned. It felt as if every shadow, every hidden corner, every curve in the path were hostile.

And they were. Bitterness burned in her chest. The whole world was hostile.

A hand landed on the small of her back, and she jolted a little, turning to catch her breath while her mind caught up with her extended nerves.

"Didn't mean to scare you," Isaak murmured, stepping closer and placing both hands on her waist. His head came down until his forehead met hers, resting there. "Watching the haystack?"

"I haven't seen anyone yet today, but those damn gendarmes think they're so clever."

"Not clever enough to find the *Zwiebelkeller*." Isaak turned to stare at the haystack, one hundred meters from the château walls. "But they might not be there today. Did you know Anne-Marie paid them off before she left on holiday?"

"Paid them off?"

"She bought their goodwill with a sack of potatoes. Almost as good as gold these days. She said she hoped it would keep them from searching the château until she gets back."

Ella frowned. She wasn't disposed to feel generous toward the new faces at La Hille. There was Anne-Marie, a young woman who effused warmth but had the audacity to take nearly a month's holiday mere weeks after her arrival. The idea of a holiday, with all that was happening in France, soured in Ella's stomach like unripe fruit. And then there was Margrit Tännler, the new *directrice*. Again, she seemed nice enough, but she wasn't Rösli.

Isaak studied her scowling face for a long moment, and she realized that he was holding on to something. Hesitating. She turned, looking him fully in the eyes.

"What is it?"

His hand raised to her face, moving some hair from her cheek and smoothing her frown away at the same time. Her heart cracked like brittle clay. Every day since they'd returned from their attempt at Spain, she'd battled growing fury. It flooded her interior like a tide, ever rising. She couldn't stop thinking about how things might have been. How they might have been in Spain right now, feeling the sun on their faces instead of hiding inside a dusty French château, avoiding the outdoors and those who waited there, stalking them. She thought about Isaak's mountaintop proposal, which seemed fanciful now that their future was again imperiled, everything they'd dreamed of imploding like a mined bridge. There'd been only one glimmer of joy in her return to La Hille, and that was Hanni. Her sister had wrapped her in a ferocious hug the moment Ella limped into the dining hall behind Isaak, muddy and exhausted and terrorized.

"You came back," was all Hanni could say, over and over again. And despite the crush of Ella's disappointment, a tiny part of her was relieved. At least she had her sister again.

Isaak cleared his throat. "Some of the boys are making plans to go to Spain," he began, and her heart stopped.

"You're not planning to join them?"

He shook his head quickly. "No. I would never leave without you."

"What is it, then? Are you worried for them?"

He sighed, resting his forehead against hers once more. "Beyond worried. They're hiring a *passeur*, and after what happened to us—"

"Lots of people have made it, Isaak," she interrupted. "We shouldn't assume they won't. Who's going?"

"Fritz, Kurt, Werner, Edgar, Charles, and Addi."

Ella gasped faintly. That many of the older boys were leaving? It was no wonder Isaak was unmoored. He must feel more alone than ever, marooned inside La Hille while his peers scattered and fled. She'd sensed energy building in him, like it would in a strong horse locked in a small stall, muscles coiling tighter with every passing day. Ella understood. She drifted in her own sea of fury.

"Do you wish you could join them?" she ventured, terrified of what he might say.

He held her gaze, his eyes close and unblinking. "No. But I'm thinking of doing something else. I can't just sit here, Ella. Waiting for them to catch us. I want to fight back."

"Fight back?"

"There are boys in the woods. Resistance groups, hiding outside of Foix. They call themselves the Maquis." He watched her as she stood very still, barely breathing. "I heard about them from the farmer who brought milk last week. I might go and see if I can fight with them."

"You trust him? The farmer?" She thought of the woodcutter who had led them astray on their journey to Spain, and everything within her tightened.

Isaak nodded. "I know what you're thinking, but he's trustworthy. We've bartered with him ever since Rösli took over the colony. She trusted him, too—she once told me what a good man he was. And his son is also hiding out with the Maquis." He hesitated, and the enthusiasm clear in his expression shifted, softening into something like regret. "I wouldn't be far, Ella. Just near Foix."

She didn't know what to say. Her thoughts scrambled as she searched for a response. Fight back? But Foix was so heavily guarded by Germans—was such a thing possible? There was something compelling about the idea. She had only the faintest notion of what the Maquis did in these sunbaked hills, except that they, too, were hunted. It was hard to imagine what fighting back might look like. But the word "fight" hung in her mind like breath.

"Ella?"

She turned from Isaak's embrace to see Hanni wandering into the room, her eyes very brown in her tanned, freckled face. She folded her skinny arms, looking between Ella and Isaak, and tipped her head to one side as if chiding them.

"I hope you're not kissing in here."

Ella laughed. "Just talking. What are you up to, Hanni?"

"I was practicing reading with Herr Lyrer and the rest of *les Petits*. Want to come out to the garden? Maybe you can stand by the gate and watch me climb a tree outside the courtyard. There's one pretty close and I can go really high."

Ella glanced over her shoulder, again scanning the unmoving haystack down below. She imagined doing what Hanni proposed: standing in the shade of the courtyard, staring out while her sister scaled a tree beyond the walls. She saw herself, hovering in the shadows, trapped.

Powerless.

Ella thought again about the boys hiding in the woods outside of Foix.

The June days lengthened, and Isaak's friends assembled at La Hille, some of them coming from farms where they'd hidden in exchange for labor. Then, in the depths of a warm night, they vanished into the hills. Ella spent the next day imagining their journey as well as she could while she moved around the château, listless. She pictured Saint-Girons, with the river running through it, the mountains lapping at the town's feet, and the old farmer and his wife who had sheltered them there. With a zing she recalled the hayloft. She saw the sunlight piercing through its walls, the smell of dried grass, and Isaak there with her, their bodies and the path of their lives intertwining. She held that memory as if it were cupped in her palms, as beautiful and fragile as a sparrow's egg. It was difficult now to imagine how that night would ever grow wings, allowing the two of them to lift off together.

A day or two later, Ella sat on a bench in the courtyard, letting the sun cook the inertia from her limbs, when two figures appeared in the field beyond the tower, hurrying through the long grass. She sat up straighter, heart pounding, and watched as Addi and Edgar jogged in from the forest, looking every direction as they rushed, their faces tight with fear. They skidded into the courtyard without being seen, and Ella rose from her bench, peering at the landscape behind them for pursuers. There was no movement. Perhaps the gendarmes had tired of watching the château from behind haystacks and trees, and weren't out today. Or, perhaps they, too, had been lulled by the sun and didn't notice the flight of two teenagers running in from the woods.

"What happened?" Ella asked, pivoting while Isaak and Herr Lyrer spilled out of the château. Addi tried to catch his breath. He was a lithe boy, quiet and smart. Herr Lyrer put his palm on Addi's shoulder, patting as if to reassure him, but the teacher couldn't tame the alarm in his own face.

Edgar, panting, managed to speak first. "We went to Aurignac, where we were supposed to meet the rest of the group. We'd traveled in pairs, so as not to attract attention—"

"But Kurt and Fritz never arrived," Addi sputtered, straightening his slender frame. His intelligent eyes skipped between the growing huddle in the courtyard. Walter Kamlet had arrived with Edith, who linked her arm through Ella's elbow.

"Never arrived?" Herr Lyrer repeated. He fingered his mustache unconsciously, eyes skating back and forth, as he always did when he was thinking.

Addi's voice cracked. "We don't know what happened to them. They didn't make it through Saint-Girons, but we don't know if they were caught or just turned back."

Herr Lyrer's voice hitched. "We haven't seen them here."

Ella's heart hollowed. An image of flashlights, bobbing through the murky dawn, thudded into her mind. "Halt," a word flung like a bullet, echoed in her memory.

Edith tightened her grip on Ella's arm. "And the others?" she asked, her glasses reflecting sunlight.

"Charles and Werner went ahead of us, so I guess they're on their way to Spain," Edgar said, wiping at his eyes with the heel of his dirty hand. "We were supposed to leave thirty minutes after them, but Addi and I thought it seemed suspicious. Nothing felt right." He glanced from Isaak to Ella. "We thought about what happened to you, and we turned back."

Herr Lyrer continued to finger his mustache for a long moment while the other teenagers stood in an immobile circle around Addi and Edgar, frozen with worry. Then Herr Lyrer swung his arm around Addi's shoulders and patted Edgar on the back with his other hand to get him moving inside. "Come, boys. Come eat and rest. We can't do anything now regarding your friends, so we'll wait to see if they manage to send us news."

*I*t didn't take long for news to hit La Hille. June hadn't yet folded into July when a postcard arrived at the château, apparently thrown from a train. Written in a cattle car by Charles, it recounted how he and Werner had been arrested on their way to the Spanish border, and once again it was due to a double-dealing guide. Even worse, Charles explained that Kurt and Fritz were also on the train. They'd been caught by Germans in Saint-Girons, just as Addi had feared. Ella heard the news in the dining hall, where Walter Kamlet read the postcard out loud from his piano bench, and she had to run out into the courtyard to vomit into the bushes.

She gasped over a feeble boxwood, spittle trailing from her bottom lip, the sun hot on her neck. Werner and Charles had been betrayed by their guide? Could it be the same double-crossing bastard who'd betrayed her and Isaak? For some reason, the question pushed nausea back up her throat and she gasped again, choking. How many of them would be betrayed? She sank into a crouch over the dirt, sitting on her heels and sobbing in the heat.

Four boys. Gone. Ella pressed her hand over her sour mouth, picturing their youthful smiles, their uproarious laughter, the sun on their faces as they sang and chopped wood at La Hille, or tramped off to swim, or chuckled at their table in the dining hall while Rösli chided them, ever trying to maintain decorum in this once-crowded château.

Loss rose up inside Ella like water, mixing with the tide of rage already there.

When Isaak came out to find her, Ella had already wiped the tears from her eyes. He crunched over to the sun-scalded bushes, glancing at where she'd gotten sick, and she rose to him on slim, strong legs.

"I want to help in Foix," she said.

"In Foix?" He ran a hand through his messy hair, his eyes focusing while he caught up with her meaning.

She cleared the sting from her throat, straightening, her chest against his. "Isaak. Let's fight back."

~~~~~

TWENTY-FIVE

RÖSLI

*R*ösli was relieved to have work once again, and she knew she should feel fortunate. She walked up an alley between a long line of numbered beds on one side and improvised sleeping mats on another, packed as tightly as the generous room would allow. The morning was young and the light thin as she bent down, over and over, gently rousing slumbering children. They blinked up at her under the white sleeping caps wrapped over their heads, squinting as if they couldn't quite remember who she was, or even where they were. And it was true—in this room, everyone was new. Even Rösli.

An image came to her mind, unbidden, as if to remind her of how she'd come to be here, back in Switzerland, working as a simple nurse and caretaker. In a rush, she saw her own soil-stained fingers, mere months ago, unfolding a letter in her private office in a château where she'd directed every aspect of her own children's colony. *It is recommended that the Swiss Red Cross distance itself from Mademoiselle Näf completely.* The memory still stung, like a slap. So she hadn't asked questions when they'd employed her here, at the Henry

Dunant Center, also run by the Swiss Red Cross. She'd been grateful to be reinstated in a position that allowed her to help struggling children, and she'd been thirsty for work. Work had always been her salvation. Her way out. She needed work now more than ever.

Yet, she thought, bending to pat the shoulder of a preteen girl reluctant to wake, despite a slab of sunlight illuminating her face—could anything really be distraction enough? She sighed. *No.* There was nothing in this country, or any other, that would remove the faces of *her* children from her mind. Her Inges and Walters. Her Edith, Addi, Dela, Isaak, Ella, and Hanni—and so many more. Nothing could dull the pain of never seeing them again.

Nothing eased her fear for them.

She straightened, some scrap of her mind wandering to the next task of the day, which involved ladling breakfast into bowls. She tried to shake away her difficult feelings as she walked toward the improvised cafeteria. She'd been asked by an acquaintance recently if she was proud of helping her teenagers escape. The question had startled her. Proud? "Of course not," she'd snapped, overly harsh. "I did what had to be done. In the end, it wasn't enough. They're still in France, and I'm here."

Rösli took up her position in the cafeteria, nodding wordlessly at another nurse in her white veil and dress, her pretty face flushed over a vat of steaming porridge. Rösli picked up a ladle, aware that her mouth was a tight line instead of a smile, her gaze a grim stare. The sum of it all was that she'd tried with everything she possessed—mind, body, and soul. Now here she was, wishing with everything in her heart that she could have done more.

She blinked firmly, forcing herself to smile as the murmur of French children grew around her and bowls were raised as they waited politely for breakfast. Her spoon clinked bowls amid murmurs of "s'il vous plaît" and "merci beaucoup." These French children were safe in Geneva, protected by Swiss goodwill, and that begged the question that nagged her daily, refusing to leave her alone as she served meals. *Why* couldn't the La Hille children have had a similar fate? Was there anything she could have done to secure it?

"Did you sleep well, Mademoiselle Näf?"

The question jolted her from her thoughts. Rösli turned to the young Swiss nurse at her side, who handed out bowls to a dwindling line of children. The tables had filled in the cafeteria, and the room echoed with talk and clattering spoons.

"No." Rösli knew her tone was too harsh, but she didn't muster the effort to moderate it.

"Me neither. Can't quiet my runaway mind, if you know what I mean," the woman said, causing Rösli to pause and look at her closer. The nurse smiled, adding, "I'm Emilie. Do you mind if I call you Rösli?"

"I suppose I don't."

Soft brown hair framed Emilie's veiled head, and her face was pretty, flushed, and pensive. "Sorry if I've surprised you. It's just that I heard you came back from France not long ago, and I've wanted a chance to speak with you, but you know how the days slip by. So much to do."

A tentative voice interrupted them, piping up, "S'il vous plaît, mademoiselle," in an accent. Rösli turned to a little girl with bright brown eyes, handed her a bowl of porridge, and watched her totter off through the thinning crowd of children. She turned fully to the young nurse at her side, appraising her. "And you've been here all along, Emilie?"

The woman shook her head. "No, that's just it. I returned only a few weeks ago, which was why I wanted to get to know you." She hesitated, glancing around the cavernous room. "Even with all these refugees here, and the sick wing and the long days . . . I don't know. I feel sometimes as though nobody in Geneva understands what's really going on out there. What it's really like."

Now Emilie had Rösli's full attention. She, too, yearned for someone who understood. Someone she might talk to about the past two years, and her aching heart. "Where did you come from?" she managed.

"From France, like you." Emilie's voice was quiet. "I served the last year in Gurs."

The internment camp. Rösli felt her eyes widen in recognition. Gurs was likely where her *Grands* would be sent and held if they were caught, temporarily—all French camps were transit camps now. Having been in Camp du Vernet for a week, she could well imagine what this young nurse had witnessed and all that she'd fought against.

"After morning chores are finished, would you meet me for tea in the courtyard?" Rösli managed.

"Bien sûr," Emilie said, nodding once, her dark eyes detaching to travel the crowded room. "It would be nice to talk with someone who understands."

"The grief," Rösli said, without meaning to.

The young nurse nodded again, solemn, and her gaze returned to Rösli's. "*Exactement.*"

TWENTY-SIX

~~~~~~

ELLA

THE FOREST AROUND FOIX, FRANCE

JULY 1943

Ella followed Isaak into the forest. The air smelled of pine and sun-warmed earth, and her lower back slickened with sweat as they walked. She reached for his hand, seeking its weight in her palm, squeezing for reassurance. His gray eyes swung to hers as they started up an incline. He smiled nervously. They couldn't speak to each other, not out here on this well-traveled trail. They had to listen as they went, decoding the gentle sounds of the forest—birdsong in the trees, the whisper of leaves, and the thump of their own boots, gifted to them by Rösli before their first, doomed foray into the wilds. They had to listen, because enemies could be anywhere, waiting.

The hike stretched on for a handful of hours. They skirted several small hamlets and farms until, based on the time elapsed and the familiar pitch of the hills, they knew they must be approaching Foix. Isaak's expression sharpened, and his eyes combed the forest as they walked, looking for the subtle landmarks he'd been given by the farmer to guide their way.

"He said his son would come out to meet us on the trail to Saint-

Jean-de-Verges," Isaak murmured, turning to study the path in their wake. They'd walked this way many times before the German occupation had swept into the south and forced everyone to remain close to La Hille. Foix was crowned by an old castle, and back when afternoons were free and terror was far away, that castle had been the end point for long hikes designed to tire them all out. Ella had sat in the shade of its ramparts many times, eating bread and apples and laughing with Dela, Inge Joseph, and Edith.

But this hike, on this familiar trail, would end very differently.

Movement caught her eye up ahead. A young man with shaggy hair rose from the shadow of an oak tree, taking shape where he stood on the dappled trail, his movements furtive.

"Bonjour," he called as they approached, slinging his hands uneasily in his trouser pockets. "Have you come to discuss labor?"

The farmer had said that his son would use this phrase. Isaak nodded and grinned, his smile as natural as if this were an old friend and danger was nowhere near. "*Oui*, labor in the hayfields."

Their young liaison nodded, visibly relaxing, and waved them forward. "We should hurry off this main path," he murmured, striding ahead without further deliberation. "It's too well traveled. Follow me, and stay quiet."

Minutes later they ducked off the path, mimicking his movements to crouch through a thick stand of bushes. They elbowed their way through heady summer leaves, twigs scratching exposed skin, and spilled out onto a narrow trail that looked to be no more than a deer track. They straightened but remained silent, simply moving up the winding trail, brushed by alternating shade and sunlight, walking to the rhythm of their own lungs as the incline increased. Eventually they reached a granite wall, and as Ella glanced around for a route alongside it, their guide, wordless, started to climb. She looked at Isaak, who shrugged and gestured for her to go ahead of him, and so she stepped up and grabbed onto the crevice just vacated by the young man's shabby boot. Ella's arms shook as she hoisted and climbed, forcing herself to think of nothing more than footholds and handholds, and within minutes she was at the top of the outcropping, reaching for the strong hand of the farmer's son. She bent to catch her breath while Isaak cleared the rock wall, his face flushed and his eyes alight in a way she hadn't seen for months. He reached for her palm, squeezing as if in triumph, and they continued on through a verdant swale of forest, sweat glistening on their brows.

Eventually, a new sound mingled with the thump of three sets of boots, the sweep of their breath, and the snap of twigs. Ella had to cock an ear to catch it at first, but the murmur of voices grew somewhere ahead, mingling with a breeze jostling the trees. Soon she smelled the smoke of a cooking fire, and her heart skipped up. Something seemed to strengthen in her chest with each step, like the beat of an internal drum. There were really people out here in the woods. *Resisting.* For the first time, she understood that she'd doubted it, even when she'd agreed with Isaak that they should join the Maquis. Or, if she'd allowed herself to imagine this hideout at all, she'd pictured the Maquis as somewhat uninspiring. Surely they'd be a bedraggled throng of young men, living off potatoes stolen from a village garden and dreaming of an unlikely fight against the occupiers when, really, they were simply hiding. But as Ella and Isaak stepped around a final curtain of bushes up in these wild woods, the drum of her soul beat out a rhythm of something new—the glint of excitement, and the relief of hope.

Because it appeared that the Maquis was real. Here they were, gathered before her, pausing to look up and scrutinize the newcomers with many sets of serious eyes.

The encampment spilling out from the owners of those eyes was larger than Ella had expected. It was strung along the base of another short, granite cliff girding the bulk of a hill, which offered some shelter from weather and an advantage over anyone who might approach from below. There were perhaps fifty boys and men here, ranging from teenagers to middle-aged veterans of other wars. They knelt around cooking fires, leaned against tree trunks to smoke the stubs of cigarettes, and even dozed in patches of sunshine. Many had darkened beards and dirty clothes, and a few wore Basque berets. When their gazes left Ella and Isaak, who stood hesitating on the fringes of the encampment, she felt sure she saw something recognizable in their eyes. Was it conviction, vibrating out from some inner earthquake? Or fury, like her own?

The farmer's son turned, grinning, his eyes dancing as he took in their surprise. "Welcome to the Maquis. Sorry to only now introduce myself." His hand shot out and Isaak took it, shaking firmly. "My father always spoke well of the kids at La Hille. I'm glad you're here. Call me Gerard. And you'll both want to choose new names for yourselves."

"New names?" Ella echoed, shaking his calloused hand.

"In case you're caught," Gerard said affably, his demeanor failing to match his words. "Code names wouldn't lead them back to wherever you came from, you see. Give it some thought—you'll want to choose something that feels natural."

Ella frowned, thinking, but no possible names came to her. Instead, seemingly from nowhere, Rösli fell into her mind. She saw her old *directrice*'s forthright stare, the steel of her eyes that had once struck Ella as cold but now seemed only trustworthy. Where was Rösli now? Ella followed Isaak, picking her way into the center of the encampment, meeting the eyes of men who looked at her quizzically, most likely unused to seeing females way up here. She wondered, with sudden intensity: What advice would Rösli give her right now?

That night, Ella sat around a campfire, nestled into Isaak's rib cage, and listened to the boys talk. She looked between the faces of these Maquisards, with orange firelight flickering over their scruffy jaws and features sharpened by too little food, too much fear and rage. Here among this group of strangers, Ella felt less alone than she had in a long time.

"We've been instructed to disrupt communication and railways," Gerard explained, his eyes bobbing from the assembled group to Isaak, all of his earlier tension from the long hike gone. Gerard tucked his hair, clearly uncut for months, behind his ears, where it promptly fell back into his face. He reminded Ella of a friendly bird, with his quick movements, sharp nose, and pointed chin.

Isaak frowned as he focused. "Instructed by who?"

"We answer to the Free French, led by de Gaulle." A reverent smile flitted across Gerard's face, and Ella wondered how often his parents listened to illegal broadcasts in their little farmhouse in the hills, fanning the flames of their own urge to resist the Germans. Again, the thought buoyed her.

"And when you disrupt communications and railways," Isaak persisted, the fervor only growing in his stare. "How do you do it? What do you use?"

"The Allies drop weapons with parachutes, and couriers bring them to us and others. We don't have lots of material, though. We have to be conservative."

Isaak sat unblinking, his elbows on his knees, his excitement like static. "And these other groups—how many are there?"

"Countless. We're all over France." Gerard shrugged slightly. "Here, we're strung across the Pyrénées in groups like this one. We have Spanish refugees, escapees from internment camps, and also regular French in our ranks. People who are either persecuted or just want to fight the Boches. You understand."

Ella found herself nodding. Everyone knew the Maquisards'

numbers grew every time the Germans posted compulsory service notices in various town squares, commanding young men to work in Germany for the war effort. Instead, many of them packed rucksacks and fled to the woods, refusing to ship out to a country that fathers, uncles, and brothers had died fighting against, now in two terrible wars.

Isaak seemed to barely breathe as he took this in, and an older man shifted from where he'd been dozing in the glow of the fire.

"That's enough for now, Gerard," the old man grumbled, his lidded eyes skating from Isaak to Ella. "What are we calling you two?"

Isaak didn't miss a beat. "Jean-Paul."

Everyone's gaze swung to Ella, and she hesitated. Somehow, choosing a false name made all of this seem real. Did she want it to be real? Or, did she want to return to the château—to Hanni? She released a breath. It didn't matter what she wanted. "Call me Helene," she managed.

It was her mother's name, but sounded as French as it did German. Her eyes blurred unexpectedly and she looked away, watching a man stir the fire. Her mother's unformed face blinked in her mind, vanishing before she could catch it like smoke through fingers. What if her parents were out there somewhere, waiting to claim their daughters? What if something happened to Hanni while Ella hid up here, trying to fight? Or what if Ella herself were killed or caught, and when the war ended, her parents and sister had to grieve even more? Doubt splintered her excitement as she lay down, staring up through the trees at the spread of stars.

Isaak's arm wrapped tighter around her shoulders, warding off the chill of descending night.

"How are you feeling about all of this?" he whispered into her ear.

She turned to look at his face, so close, shadowed by the dying firelight. He looked worried.

"I'm all right. I'm with you," she assured him, and his lips found hers.

The very next night, Ella understood why so many men dozed in patches of sunshine and the warmth of cooking fires during the day: they weren't sleeping at night. Again, she and Isaak passed through trees under cover of darkness. She reached to brush away the shape of a branch with shaking hands, images rolling through her mind. Despite herself, she recalled another night they'd walked in darkness. The beam of flashlights blinking through tree trunks. Shouts. The rush of water, pulling on her limbs. Ella stumbled and Isaak's steadying hand found her, instantly. She took it, moving up alongside him, wondering if he could feel her tremble. Night had fully fallen, and they, Maquisards now, had risen with the darkness.

The trail pitched down, and she gripped Isaak, placing each boot to the ground by faith alone because she could see little. Somewhere stars glittered overhead, fading near the slice of moonglow, but here the trees were too thick to see any of it. She'd been surprised to be summoned for a task so soon after their arrival. They'd spent the day learning how the camp worked, and about its missions, and even hiked down a gully for a weapons tutorial. To Isaak's great delight, he seemed to have natural aim, though Ella turned away from the guns in distaste. Now here they were, out on their first mission already. Was it so they could prove their loyalty, their willingness to take risks alongside the rest of the Maquis?

Nobody had said as much. They were simply instructed to join a group going out after nightfall, and here they were. On their way to derail a train.

There were only six of them in this band. Gerard, calling himself a scout, led the way. He was followed closely by the gnarled old man who'd slept by the fire their first night, Monsieur Champeau, who'd surprised Ella by being in charge of everything. Behind Ella and Isaak, two boys who looked as though they'd been raised as peasants, with broad shoulders and thick hands gripping an iron bar and a sledgehammer, trod silently.

They walked hours before the trees thinned, allowing the moon to peek through the overhang. The trail continued to slope, surely toward a valley. Train tracks wound through a series of valleys strung between Foix and Saint-Girons, snaking along as if seeking level ground. Tonight, their task was to pull up a section of the track before morning. The first train, they'd heard through a resistance spy who worked undercover at the railroad, would be a freighter carrying German supplies. Gerard had explained that they would dismantle the tracks at the base of a slope, hopefully derailing the train in spectacular fashion.

"We'll use explosives on the track?" Isaak had asked earlier that afternoon, his brows knit low.

"*Non*." Gerard shook his head, and his hair flopped with the movement. "We used to do it that way, but it's not necessary and makes too much noise. We save our dynamite for other things now— bridges and tunnels, *oui*? What we do for the trains is pull up a length of track." Gerard's gaze flicked to Ella. "It's heavy work, and we always need a lookout. Champeau says that'll be you tonight."

She'd nodded, saying nothing. The danger of it all felt distant somehow. Perhaps living under the weight of fear for so long had made her numb. Still, her hands shook as she walked.

Near dawn, they reached a place where the forest thinned on a hillside, and a valley stretched below. Champeau held up an arm, signaling them to stop. "Just there," he whispered as they assembled close to his side, his voice low and rough as bark. "Along that other line of trees."

A strip of field ran between the shoulders of two hills, creating a narrow valley that sloped before carving into a pass. Ella stared across it, straining her eyes to make out what might be the gleam of rails. She shivered slightly.

The men started down, moving with the effortless quiet of felines. They picked their way through the final stretch of the wooded hillside and out into the open. The valley between the forest and the tracks was long, a hayfield gone to seed. They waded through it, blades of silvery grass shushing and parting in their wake.

Ella glanced around the quiet field and the beautiful, waning night. Surely nobody would catch them way out here? Germans and French Militia patrolled the railways, but the Maquis had chosen this stretch because it was far from roads. Anyone patrolling would have to come on foot. Still, Gerard had emphasized the need for absolute silence. The Maquis had derailed so many trains in the Ariège that the Boches were irate, heckled, and determined to catch them. But the Maquis slipped in and out of the woods like spirits, impossible to track.

After a few minutes traversing through tall grass, rails appeared in the moonlight. Ella followed the men as they veered alongside the spine of tracks, their movements quickening with purpose. Gerard, who had scouted this location, led them down the gently sloping field, his strides long, until he held up his palm and stopped.

They gathered in a tight circle.

Champeau spoke, his voice so low Ella had to strain to hear it. "Helene, you'll walk up and down the tracks, watching and listening. As soon as we start to swing the hammer, there'll be noise enough to bring any close patrols, so pay attention."

She nodded once. They'd gone over this, but perhaps the man thought she'd be too nervous to remember her role. And she was nervous, but her mind was clear. Her thoughts assembled despite her pounding heart, her mind untangling as she walked slowly back up the tracks, swinging her gaze across the dark sweep of field. Behind her, the clang of metal hitting iron began. She turned briefly to see the sledgehammer, raised in the powerful arms of a peasant boy, arc down to hit a connector plate binding two rails together. The tracks were heavy and the bolts strong, and the sledgehammer rose in the moonlight again.

Ella glanced around the silvery field, seeking movement. *Nothing*. How long would it take? Before they left camp, Gerard explained the surprising amount of track that had to be removed to derail a train. In the beginning, the Maquis had created small gaps in the rails, and then watched from the forest, stunned, as trains slid over their handiwork, hopping a little but chugging away unharmed. If they wanted to ensure a crash, they'd have to work harder.

The clang of metal on metal continued as Ella hugged her arms against her chest, shivering in the chill of the aging night, scanning the field and forests for any sign of patrols. She crested the slope, pivoting to study every detail of her surroundings, straining for noises other than the jolt of the sledgehammer. *Nothing*. She glanced at the working men. Their shapes stood out in the waning darkness: two bending now, the grunt of effort, and the scrape of iron across rock as a chunk of rail dislodged.

Ella walked back down the slope, watching and listening, and Champeau's deep voice prodded the boys on. The sledgehammer lifted, arced, and clanged again. Every hit rang in Ella's mind like a cathedral bell alerting the world to the hour. It echoed through the woods, sending a shiver down her back, and she turned to study the valley and perimeter of trees. If there were patrols nearby, they would hear.

Still, nothing caught her eye. Overhead, the moon dipped behind the hump of hills, retreating from the threat of day. She glanced back in time with the sledgehammer's fall, and another noise pricked her ears. For a second, Ella held her breath. *Listened.* And then she was sure.

"A train!" she called as loudly as she dared, scrambling to run down the tracks as the silhouettes of her group straightened. She didn't have to shout it twice. Before she reached the men, they'd swept up their tools and started off across the field at a dead run. Isaak waited the second it took her to reach his side, and together they flew toward the forest, the uncut hay whipping their knees.

When they reached the trees, the rhythmic chug of the engine was no longer distant. They gathered in a loose circle, panting and swearing, and Isaak dropped the sledgehammer at their feet and pushed his hair off his forehead. Ella couldn't read the expression on his face in the thin light, but his voice was frantic.

"At least an hour early," he whispered, his words choked by ragged breath. The rumble of the train, winding through the quiet hills, grew. "Do you think our contact was lied to? Like the Germans suspected something?"

Champeau, bent over his knobby knees to fill his lungs, shrugged. "Maybe. At least the track's ready for 'em." He straightened, gazing through the screen of trees to the valley below. "We'll watch to see that it derails, but the second it's over, we run. *Comprenez-vous?*"

Everyone nodded. Ella listened to the expanding sound of an engine, her heart pounding alongside its steady beat. *They were hitting back at the Germans.* Taking out a train full of supplies not only hurt them materially, but also stripped their sense of security in using French roads, French towns, and French railways. It seemed incredible that they, a group of little more than kids wielding a sledgehammer, could do such a thing. And yet, dread infected her sense of triumph. She glanced toward the dip in the tracks, and Isaak's hand fell to her shoulder, tightening. She thought of all the times she'd boarded trains, never imagining their vulnerability. Who was inside this one, trundling toward a gap in the tracks? The engine appeared, winding from a cleft in the dark hills. It shone, dull silver, in the vaguely brightening sky.

Isaak squeezed her shoulder, hard, and she jolted. He gestured to the rest of the group, eyes wide in warning. Ella and the other Maquisards followed his pointing finger to the valley, where a group of men appeared. They ran toward the approaching train, waving their arms and shouting in German.

"They heard the hammer," Champeau hissed as the train snaked toward the dip in the tracks. The patrol hesitated for a split second, and then they pivoted and ran away from the squealing train, tearing through the hayfield in the half-light, coming straight toward the hiding Maquisards as the engine dipped down the slope in the valley. Then, everything happened at once.

The scream of metal scraping metal ripped through the air as the engine rocked abruptly, lurched, and plunged off the tracks. It was still chugging, like a plow through the hayfield, while the procession of freight cars crashed in an earsplitting cacophony, crumpling in the sickening angle of a leg breaking backward before buckling completely. The entire mess tipped and groaned as the final cars throttled forward, colliding one after another in an explosion of metal. Smoke and steam plumed into the lightening sky.

The German patrol and the Maquisards all froze for one long inhale, captivated by the sight, rooted to their positions in the trees and the field below. But as the roar dissolved into hissing steam and shouts, the patrol burst back to life. Two of the men sprinted toward the wreck, their boots pounding across the valley, and the other three turned to scan the trees.

Champeau reanimated as though he'd been stabbed. "*Come!*" As one, they broke into swift movement, ducking and weaving through the forest, trying to pair stealth with speed. Ella sprinted into the thickening woods, the canopy shading what light fell from the sky. Had they been seen? The shapes of the men moving ahead of her vanished and reappeared as they threaded through trees and brush, and then one of the boys lurched forward, tripping over something on the dark forest floor, and fell.

Branches cracked under his weight and he scrambled up, limping back into a run. Down the hill, someone shouted.

Merde, Ella cursed as she overtook the boy who'd fallen, her footsteps keeping time with Isaak's. A short, steep bank appeared, and they all scrambled up it, breaking twigs and sending rocks skittering downhill. Ella had just cleared the top when a shot fired. She glanced back as the last boy appeared over the bank, unhurt. Her heart hammered with her boots as she wove through trees, her breath shallowing as the forest thinned around them. They could run faster but were no longer hidden. How long until the underbrush thickened again? She stretched her stride, legs burning, and more gunfire ripped through the forest. She glanced back in time to see the boy in the back lurch forward, falling again. The sledgehammer flew from his grip, and Isaak skidded to a stop, doubling back before the boy's body hit the ground. Ella ran to them, and Gerard called from the lead, his voice frantic, a half whisper. "*Leave him!*"

Isaak's hand went to the boy's neck as Ella took in the dark stain spreading over his chest. His mouth opened and closed twice, expelling a bubble of blood.

"*Allez maintenant!*" Champeau hissed from somewhere ahead, and in half a second Isaak was up, yanking Ella forward before she understood. They were leaving the boy? She felt as if two opposing currents roared through her mind. Downhill, a figure vanished and reappeared in gaps between trees, followed by another. The one in the back dropped to his knee, leveling his rifle, and Ella gave in to Isaak's urging. She turned away. They ducked into a patch of underbrush, barely breaking stride.

Two more shots fired, but now they were traveling a trail of their own making, like deer veering through hollows. They didn't slacken as the noise faded behind them. The trail pitched up, and still they ran, struggling and panting, moving as quickly as possible over uneven terrain. Ella's lungs ached in her chest. They wove around trees, jumped logs and roots, and finally, when the adrenaline faded from their limbs and the German patrol and fallen boy were far in their wake, they slowed.

They walked as the dawn brightened, saying nothing and gasping for air. A leafy gully appeared, and they moved into it, half climbing up boulders and scree, gripping roots exposed from heavy rains and hoisting themselves up sharper inclines. They wound up the gully, like a seam in the hill, and still they didn't dare talk. When they reached camp, still hours away on foot, they would debrief.

But Isaak leaned close to Ella, his breath hot in her ear.

"He was dead. We had to leave him."

She met his gaze, staring into his storm-gray eyes for two steps, and nodded in resignation. The implication was clear. If they hadn't left the boy, they'd be dead, too.

Ella hiked on, the pounding in her heart unrelenting, and the first sunlight of the day spilled through the trees. She scrubbed a tear from the corner of her eye, because she'd learned long ago that there was no place for sorrow in this life. Still, she couldn't knock the image of the dead boy from her mind: the dark stain on his chest, the shock of death on his shadowed face, the bubble of blood replacing his breath. She hadn't even known his name.

~~~~~

TWENTY-SEVEN

ANNE-MARIE

CHÂTEAU DE LA HILLE, SOUTHERN FRANCE

AUGUST 1943

*A*ugust trudged in hot and languid, and Anne-Marie and the other adults at Château de la Hille worked from sunrise to sunset to keep their children stable and occupied. It was no small feat. Many of *les Grands* were gone now, hiring out on farms without reporting it to the *préfecture*, hoping their whereabouts wouldn't be traced. The remaining teenagers were preoccupied with hiding, unable to help with the younger children as they once did. They were restless, fearful, and unsure of their options. Anne-Marie was frustrated as well. Since her return from her foray into Switzerland, she'd been waiting for forged documents to arrive from Toulouse so she could offer up her escape route. Tiring of the wait, several boys whispered about joining Ella and Isaak in the woods, trying their luck with guerilla fighters instead. She didn't blame them. The wait for false identity cards, claiming that they were younger, not Jewish, and, whenever possible, French—it felt interminable.

"Maybe Madame Tempi wasn't able to get them," Directrice

Tännler whispered one sweltering morning as they hung laundry between trees outside the courtyard's walls. Margrit Tännler, a devoutly religious, frail-looking woman who took over when Rösli left, had proven herself to be the best sort of person, in Anne-Marie's opinion. When she'd risked telling the new *directrice* about her escape route, Margrit Tännler had nodded eagerly, lowering her voice and blinking her watery, pale eyes.

"One can do anything so long as one doesn't get caught," she'd whispered, a conspiratorial glint in her gaze. "I'll help however I can."

So Anne-Marie had gone directly to Toulouse and enlisted the woman Maurice recommended, Madame Tempi, to secure false documents. She paused over the sheet she was pinning up now, thinking of Madame Tempi's shrewd smile and mysterious connections, and shook her head. "No, I think Madame Tempi can get whatever we need. The question is whether she can do it before we lose anyone else."

That afternoon Anne-Marie joined a dozen of *les Moyens* on a hike with their new teacher. Sebastian, an affable young man whose buoyant nature drifted into nervousness, waved the group forward over rocky hills. They picked their way down trails and when the path leveled into leafy greenery the youngest boys ran ahead, their lengthening legs brown from the sun and their voices cracking as they whooped and laughed. Anne-Marie swapped a smile with Sebastian.

"All that energy," he marveled, pushing sweat-dark hair from his forehead. "I've finally realized that I can't do anything with them until we burn it off. Know how we spent yesterday? I hiked them up to the old quarry, and they found a cart they could push around. Imagine—pushing a mining cart in this heat! But they came home content, listened to me read before bed, and slept well." He shrugged.

Anne-Marie chuckled. Sebastian, wiry and emanating an energy much like the young boys', was perfect for his role at La Hille. "Well, this should tire them out again," she laughed. "The castle at Foix is quite a hike."

He shrugged once more, and they followed their unruly crew on down the trail.

When *les Moyens* finally reached the castle, they settled into the shade of its old, stone ramparts overlooking Foix, and Anne-Marie squinted downhill toward town. "Sebastian," she ventured, still studying the jumbled red roofs of the pretty town, "I'm going to hike down to the *préfecture*. I've needed to ask about some of the food we're procuring for the winter, and I may as well do it now that I'm here."

"Food?" Sebastian glanced up, biting into an apple. He was still learning how things worked in occupied France, but he seemed a quick study.

She rolled her eyes. "Everything must be documented, you know."

He nodded, requiring no more explanation regarding the exhaustive occupation rules.

"I'll catch up with you all on the trail," she called over her shoulder, already picking her way downhill. Fifteen minutes later, Anne-Marie walked into the *préfecture*, wiping the sweat from her forehead and trying to straighten her rumpled dress, aware of how feral she appeared within this orderly, mahogany office. She patted her unruly hair, nodding at bored employees who glanced up before quietly resuming whatever it was they did all day. Anne-Marie walked straight to Madame Authié's desk in the back of the building. She slipped through a doorway and stood before the middle-aged woman, who looked up with a severe expression.

"Sorry to interrupt your day," Anne-Marie began, a bit breathless, feeling young and out of order standing before this woman with her lined-up pens and perfect, bunned hair. Madame Authié pushed her glasses firmly on her nose. She was a known collaborator with the Germans, and Rösli had said she was widely hated. Anne-Marie had visited her several times about official matters, and understood: with her prim, imperious manner, the secretary was easy to hate. But, Rösli had also whispered, Madame Authié wasn't what she seemed.

"I'm a caretaker at Château de la Hille, and, well, I was here in Foix on an outing. I need to check about supplies for the children this fall—"

"It's good you've come," Madame Authié said in a rush, surprising Anne-Marie. The woman stood and silently shut the office door. "I've been trying to figure out how to get word to La Hille without giving myself away. This morning I learned of a planned raid on the château. Today. There's new pressure from the Germans, and the gendarmes mean to come away with foreign Jews, mademoiselle. I apologize—I don't recall your name."

Anne-Marie's mouth hung open for a stunned second. "Today?" she stammered.

But Madame Authié was already moving to reopen the door. "I promised Rösli I would help when I could, you see. You need to go. Hurry back. You can borrow my bicycle, which you'll find parked in front of the building. Now go—you might get there in time."

Without another thought, Anne-Marie hurried back through the office of the *préfecture*, trying to appear unsuspicious, suddenly unable to catch her breath. She found the bicycle parked in the shade of the building, under a pair of posters; in one Marshal Pétain stared out, a look of mild challenge in his gaze, his image fading in the sun. The second, unfaded poster showcased a glossy mother, a child, and a loaf of bread. *Feed your children!* the poster exclaimed. *Work in Germany!* Anne-Marie yanked the bicycle away from the wall, climbed aboard with shaking legs, and kicked it up to speed.

Minutes later she was racing toward La Hille, pumping hard, her mind a blur. She rode through sun-speckled shade and the relentless heat of midday, up and down hills, and only one clear thought revolved with each passing second: *Pedal faster.* She stood on the pedals to force the bicycle up a long slope, her heart pounding against her chest wall. What if she didn't arrive in time? The police had done little more than stake out the château for weeks. *Mon Dieu,* she whispered, pouring sweat. Would they be taken by surprise?

When she finally swung onto the dirt driveway to La Hille, she rode the bicycle up its slope so hard her legs ached. She stared at the building emerging behind trees, pale in the sun, its familiar towers baking under a bright blue sky. Were there police cars in the shadows of those walls? She squinted through thinning trees, studying the grounds as she bounced toward them, but saw nothing out of place.

She exhaled, finally swinging off the bicycle before it even stopped, jogging it into the courtyard. Cupping her hands around her mouth, she shouted as loud as she could.

"Police!"

The heads of a few teenagers, lounging in the shade, snapped up. Without discussion they stood, closing books and looking toward the road as they hurried inside, moving as one to the stuffy confines of the *Zwiebelkeller*. A pair of small children, eyes wide where they played by a row of beans, started to sniffle quietly, slinging their arms around each other for courage. Frau Schlesinger appeared in the doorway to the building, a question in her eyes and a dishtowel in her hands, and Anne-Marie nodded.

"Get Pauli and go upstairs," she managed, still out of breath, moving to follow the château's beloved cook. "I'll run through the rest of the building to make sure everyone's hidden."

Not ten minutes later, a police car and a truck, big enough to cart away a dozen people, rumbled up the dirt road, dust swirling in their wake. Five gendarmes jumped from the vehicles and jogged into the courtyard walls, clearly hoping to surprise people likely to be outside on such a hot day.

Anne-Marie and Directrice Tännler met them in the courtyard with their arms folded tightly across their chests. Herr Lyrer, wearing suspenders and a frown, tried to block the door, but four of the gendarmes shoved around him, storming inside.

As always, the police chief gave the *directrice* his list of names, glancing about the empty courtyard, clearly furious.

"Where are they?" he said finally as Margrit looked over the list.

"Oh goodness. *Not* here." Margrit blinked up innocently. "The kids on this list left without our knowing, you see. They're probably in Spain by now."

"Lies." He shook his head slowly, his mouth puckered with disgust. "I'm so tired of you people and your flagrant disrespect. You're guests in France, *oui*? Yet you break our laws." He spit into the dust, and the glob of mucous-tinged saliva landed near Anne-Marie's shoe. "We'll search every inch of this building, and when we find where you've hidden the people on this list, we'll send you all packing to Switzerland. You can't hide them forever."

Anne-Marie glared at him, with his brocade cap and narrowed eyes, and anger boiled in her chest. She kicked dirt over his spit, purposely propelling dust onto his polished boots. When he looked down on her, she held his stare, speaking quietly. "I'd tell you to go to hell, monsieur, but clearly you're already headed there."

Margrit inhaled sharply, and for a long moment the chief of the gendarmerie stared at Anne-Marie as if calculating how to respond. Eventually he turned without saying anything, striding into the building with new purpose.

Margrit leaned over to whisper. "You shouldn't have said that."

Anne-Marie sighed, regret already smarting. "I know." Why

couldn't she hold her tongue? Her impulsive words could make things even worse.

Half an hour later, she hardly dared to breathe as the gendarmes filed out of the building with nobody in custody. Had they failed, yet again, to find the *Zwiebelkeller*? A small man with a caterpillar mustache swore under his breath as he passed, and the chief would meet neither Anne-Marie's nor Margrit's eyes. It wasn't until they left the courtyard, their vehicles roaring to life, that Anne-Marie allowed herself to believe it. *They'd given up.* This time, anyway. She and Margrit walked beyond the courtyard walls, the long, dead grass brushing their knees. Together, they watched dust rise through the trees as the empty truck turned onto the main road.

"*Les Grands* should stay in hiding tonight." Margrit's voice was thin with tension.

Anne-Marie nodded, saying nothing. No wonder the teenagers wanted to join the Maquis. Right now, nobody could offer them a better alternative. She kicked at a rock, watching it skitter. When would her documents arrive? Would they? Because, without them, the kids hiding in this ancient château couldn't board a train. And, like the chief of the gendarmerie had so stridently told her, it was only a matter of time.

One of these days, their luck would run out.

TWENTY-EIGHT

~~~~~

RÖSLI

GENEVA, SWITZERLAND

SEPTEMBER 1943

*R*ösli walked between beds in the sick wing on a sunny afternoon. Light the color of autumn fell over the linens covering little arms and legs, and she pulled a loose sheet over an exposed foot and squeezed the toe playfully, glancing up at its owner. The little girl, Louise, giggled, her russet hair catching the light.

"Mademoiselle Näf?" a boy ventured from the next bed, his voice hoarse. "Are you going to tell us a story about Africa today?"

"Would you like me to?"

"*Oui!*" he exclaimed, rubbing a hand over his dripping nose and adding, "s'il vous plaît," as an afterthought.

Rösli found that her smiles came more naturally in the sick wing, where she was surrounded by children who needed her. It was the only place she found any measure of peace, anymore. Here she could do something worthwhile. And here she was busy enough that there wasn't time to think. It was her free hours that had become a thing of dread. Without brisk work, she was ever more consumed by sorrow and anger, emotions she battled every night but couldn't seem to vanquish. She straightened, pushing her thoughts away and glancing around the assembled beds.

"I don't suppose any of you want to hear a story about crocodiles," she said, and with that she had the attention of the dozen children who were well enough to be awake and listening.

"Did you ever see one?" a blond boy with shaggy hair asked, lisping because he'd recently lost his front teeth.

"Certainly." Rösli looked around to catch everyone's eyes, and was considering all the animals they might like to hear about, and concocting the train of her story, when the door at the end of the room creaked open. Emilie strode in, adjusting her veil a little as she walked, her face bright with its usual flush against her white uniform, as though she'd been hurrying. She probably had, Rösli reasoned. Emilie, smiling now as she strode past beds, was one of the hardest workers she knew, likely for the same reasons as Rösli.

"I'll take over for you here," Emilie said, breathless. "You're wanted downstairs."

Rösli frowned. What could she be wanted for? She'd rather spend the afternoon right here, where she was most needed. "Can you take care of whatever's going on downstairs, Emilie?" She glanced around the beds full of ill and malnourished children, keeping her voice low. "I was just about to begin a story. Can't it wait?"

The children started to chat among themselves, though their eyes flicked to Rösli expectantly while they coughed, sniffed, and whispered. She wasn't good at telling stories, but it had become clear that this afternoon ritual was important. Her most ardent listeners clung to each word, as if her tales of African adventures were ropes, lifting them out of this quiet hospital room and into another world.

Emilie smiled through pursed lips. "I'll take care of it, Rösli— you really are needed downstairs, and I think you'll be happy you went." She hesitated. "You have visitors, you see."

Visitors? Rösli frowned, aware that the eyes of her little patients were still on her, appraising, waiting for crocodiles. Who could have come *here* to visit her? When she'd slipped back into Switzerland, she told as few people as possible that she'd returned. Some of her colleagues knew, of course, but nobody beyond those she couldn't avoid. Because she'd come back unwillingly, and disgraced. So now she left Emilie and descended the stairs, battling dread. Whoever had come was likely someone she didn't want to see, because she didn't want to see anyone.

When she stepped from the building into the sunny courtyard she'd been directed to, her mind abruptly changed. There, sitting on a bench, was a pair of visitors she hadn't expected.

"Regina?" Rösli's breath left her for a moment, and then she laughed. "Margot! Girls, I'm stunned!"

The last time she'd seen these girls, she'd been walking with them over the star-strewn hills surrounding Château de la Hille, escorting them on the first leg of their long journey to Switzerland. They'd been her first escapees, venturing out on a frozen December night, clutching false documents that nobody was sure would hold up to scrutiny, the address of Germaine Hommel and Renée Farny in Saint-Cergues hanging in their minds after rehearsing it in the *Zwiebelkeller*.

And now here they were. Safe.

"Mademoiselle Näf!" Margot exclaimed, rising from a bench. The young woman was as Rösli remembered, slender and tall, with buoyant dark hair and a sweet smile. "Your friend in Zurich told us you'd come back to Switzerland—the one you had us go to when we first arrived?"

"Yes, of course," Rösli managed, and suddenly she was laughing again. "Come here, please!" She beckoned and the girls fell into her arms, hugging her, grinning with a joy that mirrored her own.

"But how long have you been back in Switzerland?" Regina asked, pulling slightly away. "I'm surprised you didn't look for us."

"Not long," Rösli managed. She couldn't tell them that she'd been back for months. While she'd avoided family and friends, the thought had crossed her mind that she could track down those of her children who had successfully crossed the border. Yet, in the end, she'd subdued the temptation and gone about her lonely business, certain that finding her La Hille escapees would be unforgivably self-indulgent. She'd be doing it for no other reason than to assuage her battered heart at their expense. Because she'd inevitably have to tell them about the unknown fate of their friends who'd been captured, and about those who still hid in France, in danger, their futures uncertain. How would such admissions make them feel? No, she wouldn't add to the heartbreak they already suffered.

Now she looked into Margot's and Regina's hopeful faces, and her happiness crumbled. They would begin to ask the painful questions soon. But Regina slipped her hand into Rösli's, squeezing.

"We're just so happy to see you, Mademoiselle Näf. Please don't worry." She smiled slightly, cocking her head. "It's written all over your face, you know."

Rösli tried to return the smile. "I'm sorry. I just spend a lot of time thinking about everyone in France, as I'm sure you do, too. Tell me," she managed. "Have you connected with other La Hille kids in Switzerland?"

"Yes," Margot said. "The youngest are living with host families, from what we've heard. They contacted the people you told us to call on when we arrived, and many took in one or two kids. Some of the older ones are in refugee internment camps—that's where we ended up, but we just got out. Madame Goldschmidt-Brodsky intervened."

"And where will you go now?"

Regina glanced at her hands in her lap. "We're not sure, but hopefully—"

"Work here," Rösli interrupted.

Both girls glanced up, momentarily taken aback, but Rösli was already two steps ahead. It was one last thing she could do for these girls—for the La Hille children—here and now. She'd go into the director's office and stay there until he agreed to hire them as caretakers. They could work for their room and board. Heavens knew this refugee center needed more caretakers.

"If you want a job here, working for the Red Cross, I'll get you one. I'm sure they won't offer pay, but it would provide you both a place to stay. You'd be taking care of refugee children, mostly French, all of them here because on arrival they were too ill to move in with host families." She smiled, a bit sadly. "All something you know a thing or two about. I'll tell them how, as two of *les Grandes* at La Hille, you've already helped with younger children for years."

"Would you really?" Regina sputtered, glancing hopefully at Margot.

"It would be such a relief," Margot said. She clasped her knuckles in her lap, tightening them, and a little flame of energy sparked in Rösli's chest.

"Wait here," she commanded, rising, feeling something like her old self for the first time in a long time. "I'll go and speak with the director right now."

TWENTY-NINE

ANNE-MARIE

CHÂTEAU DE LA HILLE, SOUTHERN FRANCE

SEPTEMBER 1943

*A*nne-Marie stood in La Hille's courtyard alone, barely daring to breathe. She held a package in her hand, addressed to her from Toulouse. It could only be one thing. The light faded from the sky as she pulled the document carefully from its envelope. *Only one.* She exhaled, battling disappointment. It was a false identity card for Addi, the gifted mathematician with wavy dark hair and a perpetually serious expression. He'd been in the group who'd been caught attempting to cross the Spanish border, and when he'd returned to La Hille, it was with a vacant look in his eyes and lost friends. Anne-Marie nodded to herself as someone appeared in the courtyard. Addi would be her first escapee, and perhaps starting with only one was safer.

Margrit Tännler strode across the courtyard, her eyes wide and a glimmer of hope testing her lips.

"Did they arrive?"

"Just one." Anne-Marie met her stare. "Addi's."

Margrit glanced around, checking that the courtyard was empty, and nodded. "Addi goes first, then. We'd better do something with his real identity card, don't you think? In case we're ever searched?"

An hour later, Anne-Marie bent next to Margrit, watching as she dug a hole in the garden with a rusted old shovel. She dug far deeper than the roots of the nearby beans, scraping out dirt until she hit hardpan. Margrit glanced up at Anne-Marie, puffing air through her lips and wiping her brow with a dirty hand. The sun had dipped well beyond the hills, pulling the daylight with it but leaving the heat.

"That should do it," Margrit said, gesturing, and Anne-Marie dropped fully to her knees and bent, reaching into the cool earth with Addi's true identity card wrapped in oilskin cloth. They would bury all the real identity cards of escaped teenagers, just in case they had to come back. She helped Margrit push dirt over the hole, and nerves pricked her stomach as she stood. Bats swirled over their heads like fragments of night.

This was it. The commencement of her plan.

*A*nne-Marie had timed everything carefully, but as always, life proved capricious. On the date they were to leave, rising in the small hours of the night, she woke with a fever. She sat up in bed, pressing a hand to her forehead and swaying a little. Addi, who apparently hadn't slept at all, hovered in the hallway outside of her room like a nervous phantom.

"*Mademoiselle Piguet?*" he whispered. "Are you ready?"

She'd slept for only a handful of hours herself, and as she hoisted her fully clothed limbs onto the flagstone floors, it was all she could do to stifle a groan. Of all the days to come down with a fever! She pressed a palm to her forehead, trying to measure her own temperature. There was nothing to be done about it. She retrieved her rucksack, forcing herself into motion. It was too late to reorganize the venture. She'd telephoned Victoria Cordier from the village to arrange their plan. Victoria wore many hats, most of them mysterious, and her schedule was tight. Who knew when she'd be able to help them again? No, Anne-Marie wouldn't let Addi miss his chance. She joined the anxious boy, who hovered in the hall with a lifetime of fear on his shoulders, deciding on the spot that she'd pretend to be well.

After studying the silent bulk of haystacks and the frothy shadows of trees, they left La Hille, hurrying into the quiet hills. The first leg of the journey was long. The trail brightened with each passing hour, and Anne-Marie tried to ignore her throbbing head as she hiked. What was this? Hopefully no more than a cold? Perhaps it was simply exhaustion from long days and relentless worry. Addi whispered questions at regular intervals, his eyes on the trail, his movements furtive. He hadn't asked much until this moment, and she wondered if he'd been so determined to leave and find his sister in Switzerland that he'd forced the risks from his mind. Until now. Anne-Marie attempted to muster satisfactory answers, but he was quiet for a long time after each exchange, likely working through the probability of his own survival.

"What if the stations are heavily guarded?" he whispered, scanning the crest of a hill capped in morning sunlight. "I look like the kind of person they'd question."

She glanced at him, with his wavy hair, heavily lashed eyes, and long face. He looked as young as his false *carte d'identité* claimed, which worked in his favor. But he was also a young man, dark featured, with a German accent, and of course this combination did not bode in his favor. Her back trickled sweat, and a wave of dizziness washed over her. "If they're heavily guarded, you'll try to look inconspicuous. Pretend to sleep if we have to wait. Hurry to the train as soon as it arrives."

Addi frowned, increasing his pace as they started uphill. "What will I do if they check my documents and force me to speak? On the train?"

"You'll say as little as possible." This was her primary fear, as well. "Cough, as though you have a terrible cold, when you hand them your identity card."

"I wish I had a better accent. No accent."

She nodded, pressing a hand to her hot forehead. "Mademoiselle Tännler scouted out the trains for us, and we're taking one likely to be crowded. This should help."

A long interval passed before his next query. "After the train, we'll sleep at another Secours Suisse home? You're sure we'll be safe there?"

"I'm sure. They know me well."

"Perhaps I should have gone to the Maquis," he murmured solemnly, and Anne-Marie struggled to pull in enough air even though they now descended the slope. Perhaps he should have. Could she do this, really? Deliver him safely to Switzerland?

"I'm sorry," he said quickly, seeming to sense her sudden turmoil. He slowed to walk alongside her, his gaze fearful and sorrowful all at once. "I'm grateful to you for taking me. I'd do anything to rejoin my sister in Switzerland. I understand the risk you're taking, too—really, I do."

She nodded, forcing her thoughts to skim over this. There was grave risk to her own life in this venture, but this wasn't something she allowed herself to dwell on. She pulled in breath, feeling that the morning was too hot already. "It's okay to be afraid, Addi." He met her stare and she held it. "We'll both do our best, and I believe we'll see Switzerland this weekend."

Hours later, they arrived, exhausted, on the outskirts of Saint-Jean-de-Verges, and there they waited in the shade of a quiet forest until late in the evening. When they finally trudged down to the tiny station, it was just in time to catch a train running through the night. Addi hung in the periphery as Anne-Marie bought tickets, ignoring the shake in her hands as she animated her face for anyone who might be watching, appearing laughing and carefree, and then they climbed aboard the train, still hissing and steaming on its iron tracks.

It was all she could do not to smile. She turned to catch Addi's eye, and he, too, looked relieved. The train was packed. It would only become more crowded after snaking up through Pamiers and Toulouse. With people overfilling the seats and spilling into the aisles, it would be nearly impossible to do a thorough inspection of every passenger's papers.

They settled without discussion in an overcrowded corridor since the seats were all taken, and the train rocked on through the night, chugging past moonlit vineyards and fields of crops destined for German requisition. The long hike had drained whatever reserve of energy Anne-Marie could drum up, and she sat with her legs folded like a bow and her head rattling against the wall. Addi fell asleep with his chin on his chest, like a person praying, too exhausted for fear. Anne-Marie tried to stay somewhat alert, just skimming the surface of sleep, but eventually sleep won. She floated off on a current of dreams, streaming into oblivion like the train coursing north toward an unknown fate.

"*Papiers!*"

Anne-Marie and Addi jolted awake at the same time. The gendarme stood before them, pinned in the corridor lining full compartments, his boots straddling a series of legs and suitcases. Outside, light pricked the sky.

Anne-Marie's mind was fuzzy, and her throat felt full and scratchy, but panic kicked up nonetheless. She rummaged in her bag, producing her *carte d'identité*, and Addi readied his. The gendarme studied Anne-Marie's card, squinting slightly.

"Swiss?"

She cleared her throat. "I'm here on Red Cross work, sir."

He dropped it back into her hands and plucked up Addi's card. He frowned.

"You're traveling together?"

Anne-Marie was suddenly fully awake. What had she been thinking? She and Addi should have sat apart. "No, sir. I don't know him."

Addi blinked up at the gendarme without looking at Anne-Marie, as if she were of little consequence to him. She couldn't understand her foolishness. It was known among authorities that Swiss Red Cross workers had been responsible for escaping teenagers, and here was Addi, with his German accent and forged identity card, traveling north alongside a Swiss Red Cross worker. She cursed herself as the gendarme's frown deepened. Then, without planning it, she began to cough.

The spasm was genuine, deep and full, as if whatever had hold of her was dredging the pits of her lungs. She had to bend over the documents still on her lap as she hacked and gasped. Tears sprang to her eyes and streamed down her face as she struggled for a clean breath, sparking more coughing. She glanced up at the gendarme, trying to apologize, but her words were strangled. Disgust soured the gendarme's frown. She sounded like a tuberculosis patient.

"You shouldn't travel in such condition," he spat, dropping Addi's card and taking a quick step back. He stumbled over someone's legs, and though Anne-Marie's lungs had finally stopped seizing, she pulled up another cough, long and loud. The gendarme turned and struggled back down the corridor, one hand over his own mouth, clearly unwilling to risk illness to assuage his suspicions.

She heaved a clear breath as he disappeared, glancing at Addi.

He smiled faintly, whispering, "I thought I was the one to cough."

She suppressed a relieved grin. They'd been lucky. Even better, within an hour, they'd arrive at Gare de Lyon.

*T*hat evening, they settled in at Montluel, and Addi disappeared promptly for bed, exhausted. Yet Anne-Marie, her head pounding with fever and her lungs tight, had much to do before she could sleep. She had to say hello to the children, her children, who'd lodged in her soul like little wisps of light and stayed there no matter where she went.

"No, David," she said, laughing as the little boy, so much bigger already, tried to climb into her lap. She set him on the floor next to her and couldn't help fingering his hair, newly grown in and soft and golden as spring. "I can't hold you, darling—I have a cold and don't want to pass it along. Please sit beside me." She gestured to the rest of the children, encouraging them to find a space on the floor and settle around her, and with jumbled voices and lots of bumping and giggling, they did.

"Where have you been?" Rafaela demanded over the chatter, her black eyes glittering up. Yseult, the Swiss nurse whom Anne-Marie considered a friend, stood with her hip propped against the doorjamb, arms folded, smiling at this reunion.

"I've been in southern France, children. Helping at a colony somewhat like this one here."

"But why didn't you stay with us?" Sabine blinked up with her grave, blue stare. She scratched at her curly head, and Anne-Marie wondered absently about lice, the scourge of children's colonies. "I wanted to stay with you, Sabine. Sweetheart, it was very hard for me to leave all of you. But sometimes life makes us leave, *oui*? And we can't always know why."

"We can *never* know why." It was Joseph, with his lovely dark curls. He was the little philosopher, logical and serious, perhaps like a young Addi.

"That's true," she managed after a moment of thought. "We can't know why things happen." All the children were staring at her now, attentive as though she were telling them one of the stories she'd so often spun before bedtime. "We can't know why things happen, and we can't always change things. But do you know what we can do?"

Nobody called out an answer. Even Rafaela was quiet.

"We can keep going." She thought of Addi, who'd been thwarted so many times, who'd lost his family, his country, his friends. Yet here he was, traveling on. "We can keep hope in our hearts, children. Do you remember the little bird I told you about? In the snowy forest?"

It was David who answered, blinking under his crown of hair as fine as a newborn baby's. "Birds can be the people who love us. Watching."

"That's right. We have to notice them, wherever life takes us." She tried to smile. "Because love makes us brave."

That night, after the children were asleep and the big house was quiet, Yseult whispered with Anne-Marie over a cup of hot tea that was mostly water.

"Your arrival surprised me, Anne-Marie, but only for a moment." The Swiss nurse blinked her blue eyes. "Of course you're smuggling teenagers into Switzerland. I'd expect nothing less."

Anne-Marie warmed her palm on her mug, unsure of what to say.

"You were lucky to make it this far, though," Yseult continued. "The entire area surrounding Lyon is extremely dangerous now. Have you heard about the Gestapo here? They're relentless. I don't know if you should take that boy any farther."

Anne-Marie's gaze sharpened through the fog of her exhaustion. Her fever seemed to have abated, but her lungs were tight and her muscles ached. She had to muster concentration to consider what Yseult was saying. "What do you mean I shouldn't take him farther? You're saying I should leave him here?"

Yseult shook her head. "I'm saying you should take him back

south. Away from Lyon, and definitely not toward the border. I haven't been in a long time, but I've heard the train stations are full of Germans. What if he's questioned in the presence of a Swiss Red Cross worker? He looks the part of an escapee, Anne-Marie, and he sounds like one, too. And there you are, even sitting several seats away, a Swiss woman who works for the same organization known for organizing escapes . . ." She trailed off, shaking her head again.

Anne-Marie's heart started to beat up in her chest, sickeningly. Take him back to La Hille? Addi wasn't safe there, either. But Yseult's words made her think of the gendarme on the train, and how close they'd been to unthinkable danger. What if this was all a grave mistake? Would it be better for Addi to continue to take his chances in the *Zwiebelkeller*? Was she signing her own death sentence? She sighed, her thoughts stumbling. Surely, she couldn't force Addi to travel back to La Hille, yet again defeated. Just as surely, he couldn't remain in Montluel, so close to Lyon and its notorious Gestapo.

She held her mug tightly with both hands, wavering. Victoria's face rose in her mind, practical and confident. The feel of the Risoud forest, draping the mountains and concealing the border, swept through her. *No.* Somehow she knew that she had to take Addi on, that it was the next best choice.

"Yseult, what if I take the first train out in the morning, alone? I'll scout the route to the border, checking the stations between here and there. I'll discuss it with my contacts, too, and see what they think. Then, if it's safe, I'll telephone in the afternoon. You can send Addi on to meet me if it appears doable, and we wouldn't have to worry about being questioned on the same train." She glanced up, holding her friend's gaze. "What do you think?"

For a long moment, Yseult said nothing, clearly caught in thought. Then she nodded. "*Oui.* I'll wait for your call."

*A*nne-Marie left first thing the next morning. Her chest was ever pricklier with the urge to cough, and she broke down hacking several times on the trip from Lyon to Lons-le-Saunier. What if she had a coughing fit in the Risoud, alerting patrols to their presence? She sniffed, gathering herself when the train rocked into tiny Lons, and studied the station through a smudged window. A few bored-looking guards watched the platform, but not the swarm of Gestapo Yseult feared. She departed the train and walked through the station, aiming for the adjacent bus that would take her to Champagnole, and nobody gave her a second look. With every step she felt more confident. Nowhere was safe, but this route didn't appear any more dangerous than other places they'd been.

When she boarded the bus, drawing in a tight breath, it was with satisfaction. As soon as she arrived in Champagnole, she would call Montluel and tell Addi to come. He could take the same early train tomorrow, and they'd be on track to hike into Switzerland the following day.

In Champagnole, with little difficulty, Anne-Marie located the address she'd been given. Inside a modest, top-floor apartment, she found Victoria and her sisters, Madeleine and Marie-Aimée, who lived and worked nearby.

An hour later, having made her phone call to Montluel, Anne-Marie sat at the kitchen table, sipping at a mug of hot water and watching as Victoria kneaded dough to make brioche. All three sisters resembled one another, with their strong, angular bodies and observant, kind eyes.

"I'm not often in this apartment," Victoria was explaining as Madeleine blew on her mug. "Between work and my other activities, I'm fairly busy these days."

"Fairly," Marie-Aimeé laughed, putting on her coat, readying

for an obligation elsewhere. "There's an understatement. I'm off—
bonne chance, girls." She smiled her goodbye, kissing her sisters on
their cheeks before doing the same with Anne-Marie.

When the door closed in her wake, Anne-Marie turned back
to Victoria, still kneading the dough. "How often do you cross the
border?" she ventured, unsure how much they'd tell her. The sisters
clearly worked for the resistance, and though Anne-Marie was in-
tensely interested, she knew they could reveal little.

"Often," Victoria said, flashing a reassuring smile. "We mostly
go on Friday evenings, because it provides a good cover. We have
passes to visit our mother in the Forbidden Zone, since she lives
alone. We use the excuse of bringing her groceries and going to Mass
in Chapelle-des-Bois. Even if we have to sneak folks in who don't
have passes, the patrols are somewhat used to activity at our mother's
house. We try to keep it that way by visiting legally as much as possible."

"But we don't visit during the week," Madeleine interjected,
pulling her loose, dark hair off her neck. "Any variation from what
they're used to seeing brings questions."

Anne-Marie found herself nodding. "How closely do they mon-
itor your mother's house?"

Victoria continued kneading, her rhythm unchanging. "Pretty
closely. We hide people in the hayloft and upstairs, and our mother's
very good at playing her part. But patrols come to the door more
than we'd like, sniffing around. And they pass by the house at regular intervals along the road. The border is so close that they try to
watch it constantly. Our mother acts as a lookout." She stopped
kneading for a moment. "It's dangerous, but our system has worked
well so far, Anne-Marie. We just don't deviate from it."

"Your mother," Anne-Marie ventured after some thought. "She's
as committed as you are?"

"Maybe more." Victoria stopped kneading for a moment. "She seems like a simple farm widow to the Germans, and it's a huge advantage. She knows it. She believes in doing whatever can be done, no matter the risk." Victoria shrugged, wiping beaded sweat from her forehead and leaving a streak of flour. "We couldn't live with ourselves if we didn't act. That's the only way I can explain it."

Madeleine's eyes took on a shine, and Anne-Marie nodded. The risk, they all knew, was death. But she pictured Addi, with his broken heart and mathematician's mind, and she agreed with the Cordiers.

The next morning, Madeleine went to the train station at the appointed time to fetch Addi. She wore a blue hat, which he was to look for, and then he'd follow her from the Champagnole bus stop back to the apartment at a distance. Anne-Marie waited, anxious, her head pounding once again. Victoria was packing a meager bag of groceries to take to her mother. She was already dressed in trousers and boots, ready to go. Anne-Marie bent to tighten her laces. The journey to the Cordiers' childhood home was long. They would start with bicycles, and eventually stash them in a thicket to hike on. Hopefully, Addi had gotten some rest in Montluel. Anne-Marie felt worse than the day before, as if her fever was making a comeback, but she said nothing.

When footsteps finally sounded on the stairs, Anne-Marie and Victoria swapped glances. Anne-Marie held her breath to listen. Only one person seemed to be coming up. Was Addi that far behind Madeleine? Would he find the right staircase and the right door?

When the hinges creaked open, Madeleine was indeed alone, her face pale.

"He wasn't there."

"What?" Anne-Marie rose from the table, her pulse bounding up to keep time with her headache.

Madeleine shook her head, kneading her hands. "He wasn't there. I watched the bus unload and waited for ages, just in case I'd somehow missed him. There was no young man on that bus, Anne-Marie." Madeleine turned to Victoria, who stood with her hands on the shopping bag, eyebrows crimped in thought.

"We should go on as planned," she said after a moment.

"What?" Anne-Marie was incredulous. "Without him?" She pressed a hand to her forehead, feeling heat, and cast about as if she could do something. Where was Addi? Had he been questioned? Detained?

"Listen." Victoria stepped around the table, her posture straight and confident, and she took Anne-Marie by the shoulders. "We'll call Montluel in a moment to make sure he went to the station. If he did, you and I will go on to my mother's house, and Madeleine will meet the next bus and bring him along. He probably missed his connection."

Anne-Marie shook her head. There were so many other possibilities than a missed connection.

"Either way I have to go," Victoria said firmly, drawing Anne-Marie's attention back. "I'm making a critical delivery tomorrow. I think you should come with me and wait for him in Chapelle-des-Bois, where you can rest for the final climb into Switzerland. If Addi arrives, you'll need to be rested—you don't look well, Anne-Marie. Come and let my mother care for you while Madeleine waits for Addi."

Madeleine cleared her throat to speak. "We don't like people to be here long, Anne-Marie. I'm sorry to ask you to leave, but because we're involved in the resistance, we don't want our neighbors wondering who's up here. You should go."

Anne-Marie nodded, unconvinced, trying to breathe around a chest tightening both from illness and overwhelming dread. Had she made a terrible mistake by encouraging Addi to test this route? Had she erred in going on ahead of him to ensure the path was safe? She bent over, withholding the urge to be sick.

Madeleine, ever kind and steady, reached out and rubbed Anne-Marie's back. "I'll meet every incoming bus and bring him as soon as he arrives. I promise."

*H*ours later, they walked along the rural road leading to Chapelle-des-Bois and bordered with barbed wire fencing. Anne-Marie panted, more light-headed with each step, and she could feel the concern in Victoria's frequent glances. They would have to slip under the fencing to the Forbidden Zone, as Anne-Marie had on her first scouting mission, because she didn't have the pass necessary to enter through a checkpoint. But walking with Victoria conferred some confidence now. This was where Victoria had grown up, and she knew how it worked.

As they approached a dense thicket, Victoria turned and nodded once. The signal: this was the place. Anne-Marie was so tired she could barely think, but as they dropped to their bellies in the cover of brambles, sliding under the wire, her heart started to pound.

They were in the Forbidden Zone, and she had no pass. They couldn't be caught.

When they stood on the other side, Victoria picked up her bag of groceries, scanned the woods with shrewd eyes, and wordlessly motioned Anne-Marie forward. They threaded through trees, silent. They were on the French side of the Grand Risoud, weaving their way to Victoria's childhood home, and the thought buoyed Anne-Marie. Like her, Victoria had grown up in the forest, claiming its paths and gullies and trees as her own childhood palace. Surely the Risoud would protect them now.

Eventually, a farmhouse appeared in a field through the woods, and Victoria stopped and raised a hand. She scanned a dirt road across the field, searching for movement, and then signaled. Together, they ran noiselessly toward the house, and fear liquefied Anne-Marie's final reserves. If Germans caught her, what would they do? Arrest her? Shoot her? Ducks burst up from the meadow ahead, flapping into the afternoon sky, and Anne-Marie's heart nearly stopped.

Yet, moments later they slipped through the front door of the house, gasping, and a tiny woman with a lined face met them in the foyer. Madame Cordier grasped Victoria by the wrists, laughing, and they exchanged kisses. Then Madame Cordier took Anne-Marie by the elbow, frowning slightly.

"Heavens! You don't look good at all. Let's get you up to bed, dear, and I'll make some broth." She turned. "Victoria, where's the young man?"

Anne-Marie collapsed in the bed she was led to, her head pounding along with her heart, awash with regret. She closed her eyes and felt unable to move. *Where was Addi?* Would Madeleine find him? What had she done?

She fell asleep in a swirl of doubt, sick with worry and whatever plague still gripped her.

When Anne-Marie woke, the morning sun was high, and voices murmured downstairs. She sat up, blinking, and then swung her feet from the bed. She'd slept all night? What time was it? She hurried downstairs, bleary and still in yesterday's clothes, listening hard and daring to hope.

There, sitting at the kitchen table, was Addi. Madeleine and Victoria stood at separate windows, gazing out at the dirt road traveled by German patrols, and Madame Cordier whisked something in a bowl and fussed over the sheepish boy.

Anne-Marie was so undone by relief she released a laugh before she could even ask her questions.

"What happened? I was terrified you'd been caught. Addi, I'm so sorry to have gone on without you—I should have made sure—"

"It's not your fault at all," Addi interrupted, glancing up with his lovely eyes. His cheeks colored as he swapped a look with Madeleine. She gazed back toward the window and pursed her lips in anticipation of whatever story Addi was about to tell.

"I fell asleep."

Anne-Marie cocked her head, confused. "Fell asleep?"

His voice cracked a bit as he spoke again, the color in his cheeks deepening. "In the Gare de Lyon. I got there a bit early for my train and sat down, thinking I'd be less noticeable. I can't understand how it even happened—I was so scared I could barely think, and I sat there watching the clock, avoiding everyone's eyes, and pretended to doze. Like we'd discussed. Next thing I knew I was waking up."

"You missed your train because you *fell asleep*?"

Addi nodded, dropping his gaze to the table, clearly humiliated, and Anne-Marie stared at him for one more incredulous moment. Then laughter bubbled up in her chest again, and she couldn't subdue it. She pressed a hand over her mouth, trying to regain a more proper response. "*Asleep* in the Gare de Lyon. I can't believe it." Laughter flapped up again and Victoria turned, amusement lighting her eyes, and little Madame Cordier placed a bowl of soup in front of Addi and patted his back.

"No more fuss, girls," she commanded. "Teenage boys are known for sleeping in."

With that, both Anne-Marie and Victoria burst into full laughter. Addi glanced up, chuckling a little at himself, his cheeks still burning as he slurped a spoonful of soup.

When Anne-Marie reclaimed her composure, she pushed her unruly hair behind her ears and sighed, shaking her head. "Eat up, young man." She grinned, despite the fear hanging over them all, or perhaps because of it. She looked out the window opposite of those guarded by the Cordier sisters, assessing the cliff behind the house. Somewhere, not far beyond it, was Switzerland.

"We've done the hard part, Addi. Now we just have to climb a mountain."

THIRTY

ELLA

*I*t was merely October, and already the forest was cold at night.

Ella poked the fire with a long stick, expertly turning a log, and Isaak picked his way into its ring of light with an armful of scavenged wood. She'd learned so many new skills out in the woods, some of which she never could have imagined, years ago. She knew how to build and nurture a fire. How to cook all manner of things over it, mostly from the forests or gardens willing to donate provisions to the Maquis. Her legs were strong from hiking all over these hills, and she could navigate them easily. She knew how to scan for patrols. How to cut telephone lines. How to derail trains. She met Isaak's stare in the firelight, and he grinned reflexively where he crouched, long arms propped on his knees, muscles moving as he reached to place a log on the fire. Sparks burst and swirled in the darkness. She knew how to love, and she knew how to hide.

"Did you hear the news?" Gerard asked, approaching the fire, his eyes catching the light. He'd been away all afternoon, likely gathering supplies from his parents' farm. He often returned with as much information as food, passed along from his father's illicit radio.

"What news?" Isaak's gaze flicked to Ella and then back to Gerard, who settled into a crouch.

"Italy's declared war on Germany."

"What?" Ella and Isaak asked in unison, their eyes widening. "You heard this on the BBC?" Ella asked quickly, wondering if it could possibly be true.

"My parents did," Gerard said, and Ella looked back to the fire, thinking. Of course, news of Mussolini's fall had filtered through the Maquis over the summer, and only a month earlier Italy had signed an armistice with the Allies. Still, it was difficult to grasp that Germany's former ally had switched sides. It was difficult to hope.

"Good news for the war," Gerard murmured. "But we know what it'll mean for us."

They sat quietly for a long moment, surely thinking the same thing: it meant that France would become even more dangerous. With the Soviets advancing on all fronts, the Allies gaining another ally, and the resistance fighting back in France, the occupying Germans would become increasingly vicious. The Milice, the French Militia, would lash out as well. Rumors circulated of the Gestapo and Milice in Toulouse, hunting down and torturing members of the Maquis before executing them.

Isaak broke the silence. "It's nearly time to go." He ran his fingers through hair so shaggy it tucked and curled behind his ears. Gerard nodded.

Ella pushed an errant coal back into the flames. "You need a lookout?"

"You're it," Gerard said, flashing a characteristic grin.

They picked their way through camp, where boys and men slept in makeshift shelters, a couple chatted against tree trunks, and others stared into the shadows, lost to thought. There were several cooking fires strung across the camp, some with rabbits turning over them, others with newly harvested chestnuts—a staple, these days.

Ella breathed deeply, trying to stretch the tension from her chest. She'd been pressing a feeling away, for weeks now, but the news from Italy sent it galloping back: she didn't want to stay with the Maquis. Ella knew the importance of the Maquis, so she tried not to indulge the feeling bending her heart, tugging her away from this band of fighters. She was aiding the war effort in these wild woods, and she was good at it. She'd participated in so much sabotage that it felt almost routine: the long walks, the sweat on her palms, the way night air made her eyes water as she studied dark trees and fields, searching for trouble. It was a role she could play in an upside-down world. A valuable one. The Maquis bands were a constant problem for the Germans and the Milice. They chipped away at the resources and unfettered confidence the occupiers claimed in southern France. So why did she yearn to leave?

The answer came, as it always did when she allowed it to: *Hanni.* Ella missed her sister, and worried for her so constantly it was suffocating. Questions piled up whenever she closed her eyes to sleep. What if the Germans, frustrated by their losses, finally came for *les Petits*? What if Hanni *wasn't* safe at La Hille until the end of the war? When her mother and father propelled them out of Germany, entrusting Ella with her four-year-old sister, what had they envisioned?

Not this.

Well, she amended, they certainly hadn't envisioned any of her current options. Would it be better if she'd remained at the château, ever on alert for raids? Hiding in the *Zwiebelkeller*, holding her breath, listening for the men on the other side of the secret door to realize what they'd been missing all along?

At least in the forest, she could run if she had to. At least she could be useful.

They paused on the edge of camp, and Ella bent to tighten her boots. Isaak fetched the pistol Champeau had him carry, and they left camp alongside him and Gerard. It was time to go and cut some telephone lines.

With little formal discussion, they'd become something of a team. Champeau went out with other bands and directed the actions of even more, but he always seemed to join the escapades she and Isaak were assigned to.

They swung wordlessly from the woods onto a dirt road. In an hour it would lead them to a vulnerable line Gerard had scouted earlier in the week, isolated and accessible. Clouds skated across the sky, obscuring the moon before the wind pushed them away again. How many kilometers had Ella traveled in the dark? She glanced at Isaak, his features brightening and dimming in the fickle light. Their first, ill-fated attempt to escape into Spain rose in her mind, as it often did. Now she smothered the terror of that journey, instead conjuring moments she'd cherish, always. There was the morning on a mountaintop, on the day they were meant to earn their freedom. She'd leaned into Isaak's chest, her back warming against his heartbeat, and they'd stared out at a pink sky promising day. Isaak had spoken of marriage and, for a moment, they'd believed it was possible. That a future together, with a regular life—a house with apple trees and easels and children—was possible. That the war would someday end.

It was a dream that seemed so far away now.

Isaak held up a hand at her side, and Gerard, several paces in the lead, did the same. Ella felt herself frowning before anything became clear. In one swift movement, Isaak grabbed her by the elbow and pulled her off the road, while Gerard and Champeau dove into the black underbrush ahead, branches shaking above them. Ella's heart pounded so hard she felt it in her throat as she backed into a roadside thicket beside Isaak, dropping to a crouch, staring out into the darkness. In a second, she heard it. *Boots crunching gravel. Murmurs.* Four figures materialized, moving slowly, rifles in hand. Their flashlights roved the brush. Had they been waiting, using the telephone line as bait? Ella's mind raced. But how could they have known the Maquis would come here? She swallowed a swell of fear. Perhaps someone had seen Gerard scout the lines, and instead of arresting him on the spot, they'd crafted an ambush.

"Over here!" one of the uniformed men shouted in French, beckoning to his team. *The Milice.* Ella swallowed a bloom of panic, yearning to move farther into the brush but terrified of the noise she'd make. The Milice, comprising bullies, were as bad as the Germans. Maybe worse, if you caught them out in the forest. Isaak tightened his grip on her hand. His other hand fumbled at his waistline, and Ella remembered: he was the only member of this expedition carrying a gun.

In another sweep of breath, the Milice gathered near the spot where Gerard and Champeau hid. They aimed their weapons. Clouds detached from the moon. "Hands up!" one of them shouted, gesturing with his gun, and Gerard and Champeau crawled onto the side of the road, flinging their hands in the air as soon as they rose to their feet. Isaak's breath was hot on Ella's neck as he leaned in, his long torso curving over her body, ready. He spoke so quietly, and so close to her ear, that she could barely make out the words.

"If I shoot, you run."

She turned, the slightest movement, pulling her eyes from Gerard and Champeau straightening in the road, a stone's throw away, to meet Isaak's eyes.

"For Hanni," he whispered, holding her stare in the moonlight, and blackness welled in her chest. Like a curtain falling, she understood that her world was about to change again. She started to shake her head, but the force of his stare was so strong she stopped. It was as if he held her, like north holds a compass arrow, pointing her onward. And he was right. If there was a way to survive this, she had to do it. Pain shot through her heart as hot and vivid as a bullet, but she nodded. Promising.

"Just the pair of you?" a voice was demanding out in the road, and two of the Milice turned to examine the underbrush. They seemed to stare right at Ella, and she could feel Isaak's ropy muscles tightening, but then their gazes roved away, still searching. Was it possible that only Gerard and Champeau had been seen? Ella thought hard about the recent past, only minutes ago, when she was unaware of the sharp turn their fate would take in mere steps. How far ahead had the other men been walking? A flashlight's beam bobbed over the yellowing leaves sheltering Ella and Isaak, again wandering away.

"It's just us," Champeau barked from the street, his gnarled hands in the air. "This is my son. We lost a cow—went to feed it before bed and it wasn't there. Been looking all night for it."

"A cow." One of the militiamen glanced at the other, and even in the darkness Ella could sense the sarcasm in that glance. "Does that cow like to cut telephone lines, by chance?"

"I don't know what you're talking about," Champeau barked back. "I'm just a farmer—"

"Where is your farm?"

"Over these hills. Near Allières."

"Ah." Another militiaman spoke. "And that's why you dove into the ditch when you saw us coming?"

"It's past curfew," Champeau said, not missing a beat. "Just last month, you shot a local shepherd boy out with his sheep. Nobody's safe from you people past curfew."

A chuckle. "You people?" Two of the uniformed men swapped glances, and one of them peeled off to go rummage in the bushes Gerard and Champeau had vacated. The old man didn't even look in his direction, but Gerard's hands began to visibly shake in the beam of the flashlight. Isaak shifted slightly beside Ella, readying.

"*Voilà!*" A sarcastic voice called, and the militiaman emerged from the underbrush. "Wire cutters. For farming, I suppose."

The head Milice glanced at the tool in his young comrade's hand, shrugged once, and fired his outstretched gun.

Champeau's head jolted backward before his body toppled, and blood spurted in the flashlight's glare. Isaak's free hand found Ella, and he shoved her, hard, into the brush while simultaneously lifting his gun. Before she could turn to run, the man aiming at Gerard fell in time with a tremendous bang, and the remaining three militiamen lurched around, startled, swinging their weapons to the roadside. Gerard took off running, tearing back into the bushes, and all at once the road erupted into a crescendo of gunfire. Ella shrank low and scurried under branches and leaves, breaking out into the clearer forest beyond the brush bank, and sprinted several strides uphill. But then, without thought, she skidded to a stop. She turned, heart in her throat, cold sweat on her forehead, and glanced toward the ongoing fight.

She couldn't leave him. Hanni hung in her mind, but she couldn't make her legs move onward. She pressed herself against a tree, listening to the gunfire sputter out, questions and dread boiling up in her mind. Was Isaak hurt? Her mind led her to the next inevitable question. *Is he dead?* The thought made her gasp, choking against the tree, and she pushed it away. And Gerard? She stared down at the bushes hemming the road, trying to see through them as the last gun popped and the area was again quiet. Smoke wafted through the splintered beam of the fallen flashlight. She listened hard, desperate to decode the groans and shouting echoing up through the trees.

Still, nobody stumbled through the hedge of bushes.

Ella pressed a hand over her lips, willing herself to stay quiet though she wanted to scream. What had happened to Isaak? Champeau rose in her mind, his head jolting backward, and she pressed her own forehead into the tree trunk.

She had to go back down there.

Inhaling, she peeled herself from the trunk and stumbled a little, finding her stride. She crept down the hill, and then another gunshot sounded, echoing through the leafy wilderness. Ella froze. She held her breath, shaking, and listened.

When the bushes started to rustle, she crouched, not daring to move. Footsteps shuffled up the slope, and a figure emerged, dark and obscured by the underbrush. Questions skated through her mind like clouds racing over the night sky. Was it the Milice, or whatever remained of them, searching the forest? Who would take care of Hanni if they saw her, crouching among the leaves? If her parents survived the war, would they ever learn what had happened?

Grief expanded in her chest, far stronger than her fear of the figure creeping from the brush. Because this could be the moment that had come to so many others—the moment she vanished. Or, worse—perhaps she was about to learn that the boy she loved most in the world, Isaak, with his storm-cloud eyes and natural smile, was gone. The man emerged from the underbrush, straightening, and she braced herself for whatever was to come.

"Ella?"

She gasped, her held breath escaping.

"Ella, are you still here?"

She rose and there was Isaak, whole and unhurt, stumbling up the incline. She ran, falling into his arms. He buried his face in her hair. Every part of him shook.

"Are they gone?" she managed, her ear pressed to his heartbeat. She breathed in time with it, trying to understand that he was still alive. That they were both alive, shivering together in a forest, a gun hanging from Isaak's hand.

"They're dead." His voice was rough. "They couldn't see me, and—" A sob broke his voice.

Clarity fell over her like the chill of night. Isaak had shot the Milice. All of them. She turned from him, blinking as her thoughts scrambled. They deserved it, she told herself, trying to make her mind and heart align. Isaak had done the only possible thing. Yet the feeling she'd been ignoring reverberated inside of her like a struck bell.

She wanted to leave these woods. She wanted to find her sister and escape from this blasted country, with all its terror and death, for good. She wanted—*needed*—Hanni to survive this war, and she needed to survive for Hanni, as well.

"We have to get out of here," she managed after a second. He nodded faintly. Those gunshots would have been heard far and wide. Ella inhaled, forcing her final question. "Where is Gerard?"

Isaak shook his head, and Gerard blinked in Ella's mind like a pulse of light. His quick movements, his swift smile. *Gone.*

"We have to go," she said again, tugging on Isaak's palm, and his legs swung into dazed submission. She pulled him up the hill, urging him into rhythm, and without further thought, she knew she meant far more than the words she'd just uttered.

It was time to go. Away from the Maquis, away from these wild borderlands, away from France. If nothing else, they had to try. Because her parents had given Hanni to her, cupping her cheek before waving goodbye, sacrificing everything so their daughters might live. In a flash, Ella recalled Mutti and Papa on the train platform, their smiles fragile, their eyes full of hope. For the first time in years, she really saw them. And, for the first time in years, Ella felt sure of what her mother and father would want her to do.

They would want her to find a way out.

THIRTY-ONE

ANNE-MARIE

CHÂTEAU DE LA HILLE, SOUTHERN FRANCE

OCTOBER 1943

*I*t was a disaster." Ella's gaze flipped up from the tabletop to meet Anne-Marie's. Ella was eighteen years old, yet somehow she appeared both older and younger all at once. She hunched her narrow shoulders and wiped at the tears escaping over her freckled cheeks as if she could hide them, and Anne-Marie's heart ached. This girl who'd fled to the Maquis, whom Anne-Marie had barely had the chance to know, who braced herself at noises and stared up with earnest eyes— she was living an unimaginable life. She'd just described witnessing the death of both friends and enemies, all while severing communications lines and derailing trains. It was a story lived against the backdrop of lost parents, a lost country, a lost home. Lost childhood.

An image of Anne-Marie's own existence at age eighteen passed through her mind. She'd sunned by the lake that summer, dreaming of an upcoming adventure in Vienna. It wasn't so long ago, really, but to everyone living in this château, including herself, the memory would seem like something from another world. Her life had been laid out for her like pretty beads on a string. Until, of course, she came to France.

Anne-Marie cleared her throat. "Ella, listen. I'm arranging escapes for anyone who wants to leave France. A few weeks ago, I took a boy to Switzerland. Addi—isn't he Isaak's friend?"

Ella nodded. Her gaze was intent, shining with the tears she'd unwillingly shed.

"We have a route over the border, with people all along the way to provide refuge. I already have plans to take or send several other *Grands* to Switzerland—"

"Who?" Ella spoke the word quietly, but firmly.

"To start, Inge Joseph and Edith both want to go. We're waiting for papers for them. Inge has been hiding with a family. Mademoiselle Tännler is returning to Switzerland, and is planning to take her along my route in just a few days."

Ella nodded and looked down, clearly weighing this information. Margrit had just announced her intention to resign from her post, and Anne-Marie fervently wished she wouldn't. But Margrit, slight and sickly, didn't have the stamina to continue, and indeed the position was arduous. If *only* Rösli could have stayed. Would the incoming director allow them to break both the law and the rules of the Swiss Red Cross?

Footsteps in the hall interrupted her thoughts, and Anne-Marie glanced at the doorway. It was late, and the château was quiet.

Isaak appeared in the jamb, his face washed and hands slung in his pockets. He looked the part of a Maquisard now, all ropy muscle and dirty clothes and a fierce, haunted glint in his eyes.

"Ella, Isaak," Anne-Marie continued, keeping her voice quiet as he settled in a chair by the dying fire. "Would you be interested in crossing the Swiss border with me?"

Isaak glanced up, instantly focused, and Ella didn't miss a beat. "Could I take Hanni?"

Anne-Marie sighed, despite herself, and hesitated. Hanni was only eight. The journey was perilous, even for strong, grown people. She thought of Addi's hands shaking as he reached to climb the rocky cliff rising over the Cordier house, the Gy de l'Echelle. She thought of the gendarme questioning Addi on the train. How would a child Hanni's age maintain a false identity? If necessary, could she withstand scrutiny?

"I don't think so," Anne-Marie answered finally, meeting Ella's stare. "It's safer for Hanni to remain here, where she's known and cared for, until the war ends. Then I could bring her to you in Switzerland."

"What if the war doesn't end?" Ella leaned forward, the intensity of her gaze unchanging. Her voice was measured. "What if the Germans win?"

"The Allies are in Italy. The Germans are losing ground—"

"That's another problem—everybody knows what they'll be like if they really do lose ground. Mademoiselle Piguet, you know what I mean. They'll seek revenge. You ask me to believe that my sister would be safe here, just because she is at this moment?"

"The Swiss Red Cross is still able to protect her—"

"We all know how fast circumstances can change." Ella shook her head, resolute. "What if that protection fails, like it did for *les Grands* last year?"

Anne-Marie tented her fingers over her mouth. Ella wasn't wrong. But what if taking Hanni over the border put her in even more danger? What if they lost her, when she could have remained at La Hille until the war's end, sleeping soundly at night, attending Herr Lyrer's classes during the day, and climbing trees and swimming in streams on warm afternoons? Could Anne-Marie yank her from all this and send her into the unknown?

"Ella." She hesitated, still caught in uncertainty. "It's going to snow very soon in the Risoud. I . . ." She struggled to harness her thoughts. "I believe you could make it to Switzerland, otherwise I wouldn't suggest it. I also believe it's less of a risk than living out in the forest with Maquisards all winter, fighting the Germans and the blasted Milice. But, when I weigh the same set of risks for your sister—with what we know right now, I couldn't justify jeopardizing her safety to take her to Switzerland."

"I won't go without her." Chair legs scraped the parquet floor, and Anne-Marie grasped at Ella's slim fingers before she could pull fully away.

"I'll think about it," Anne-Marie said, hearing the conviction in her own voice. "But stay here while I do. Please? Both of you—don't go back out into the forest."

Isaak, sitting by the fire, said nothing. He stared at the floor, twisting his hands as if lost in concentration. Ella held Anne-Marie's gaze for a long moment, her bottom lip shaking a little as she nodded once, and then she pulled away and went to Isaak. Anne-Marie watched for a moment as Ella wedged in beside him on the bench, and another corner of anxiety stabbed her throat. Isaak, technically a man at eighteen, looked it. Many of the boys were small and slim, but Isaak had broad shoulders, long legs, and a firm jaw. There was no way she could pass him off as a child on a journey north, as she'd done with Addi. Could she transport a young man, clearly of age to fight or labor, seven hundred kilometers? He'd be questioned at every juncture.

Anne-Marie left the room, the hall darkening around her, and walked on by instinct. She would find a way—there was no other choice. Yet the question of what to do with Hanni echoed in her mind. Could Anne-Marie allow such a young child to leave the safety of La Hille? Ella's words rose in her mind. *We all know how fast circumstances can change.* She was right, of course. What if Anne-Marie kept Hanni from leaving with Ella, and the sisters never saw each other again? The most unthinkable possibility flitted through her mind, the one they all feared: What if the Swiss Red Cross lost its ability to protect the youngest children from the Germans? So far, *les Petits* and *les Moyens* were spared from raids because they were in Swiss custody, rather than the custody of foreign parents. It was a delicate shield, she knew, and Maurice Dubois had tried to reinforce it by adding French and Spanish children to the château. They would take the beds left by so many of *les Grands*, blending in with the Jewish children. France needed the goodwill of the Swiss Red Cross, her colleagues insisted. The shield would hold.

Anne-Marie could barely consider the ramifications if it didn't.

She paused in the hallway, next to a window, cracking the shutter to look out. An expanse of stars pricked the blackness over La Hille.

What was the best decision for Hanni Rosenthal?

THIRTY-TWO

ELLA

CHÂTEAU DE LA HILLE, SOUTHERN FRANCE

NOVEMBER 1943

*Y*ou have to go without me," Isaak said.

It was nearly dark in the courtyard, and Ella leaned into Isaak's chest, breathing his familiar scent while panic circled up in her soul like a tidal wave. *She couldn't do it.* This couldn't be. She closed her eyes, trying to find a rudder to steady her pitching heart.

An hour before, Anne-Marie had crawled into the *Zwiebelkeller* where Ella and Isaak hid with the other remaining *Grands*, all of them cold and restless at the end of another long day. She'd beckoned them out and stood before them in Herr Lyrer's room. Ella couldn't read the expression on Anne-Marie's face, which usually shone with whatever emotion passed through her. Laughter was never far from this young counselor, even in the worst circumstances, but today there was no sign of it.

"My news for you is difficult," Anne-Marie had said in a quiet voice, and for a second Ella felt weak. Isaak was very still, bracing himself, but his hand drifted to hers. Could it be news of her parents? Isaak's father? No—it was foolish to hope.

Anne-Marie seemed to sense the impact of her words, because she reached out and squeezed Ella's shoulder, interrupting her spinning thoughts. "It's nothing so awful—take a deep breath," she'd said, mustering a fleeting smile. "It's just that I organized papers for you, weeks ago, so you could escape along my route to Switzerland. Today, false identity cards came for you, Ella, and for Hanni. But not for Isaak."

Ella exhaled, perplexed. "Can't you get him one? I don't understand."

Anne-Marie nodded slightly. "We can, of course, but it will take more time. And meanwhile, the weather is worsening in the mountains, and I'm afraid you'll miss your chance to go if you want to. If you're going to take Hanni—"

"You have a card for her?" Ella spoke quickly, breathless. "You'll let her go?"

"I do, and I will. I've thought hard about it, Ella, and I think it best that you stay together." Anne-Marie nodded. She looked at Isaak for a moment, speaking quietly. "I brought you out here because I think Ella should go. I want you both to think about it, hard. It would require you to separate for now, and I know that's difficult. But everything is ready. I've arranged passage this week, hopefully before the weather turns. We're at the edge of winter in the mountains, but I've inquired and my contacts think you could make it if you go now. Isaak, you can follow later, when your papers come through."

For a long moment nobody spoke, but everything in Ella rebelled. She looked at Isaak, whose eyebrows lowered in thought, and her interior crumbled. It was too much. She shook her head like a reflex. Losing one of the last people she loved—she couldn't withstand it.

"Come," he'd said, catching her eye. "Let's go talk it over outside."

Now they stood close together in the darkening courtyard, and

Isaak was saying other things, trying to tell her to go without him, but she couldn't seem to breathe in the cold air. The sound of her own rushing blood filled her ears, and she couldn't think around the feelings whirling up, powerful and dizzying and incoherent. She couldn't listen.

She *wouldn't*. Pain wedged in her throat. How could she leave him? Isaak had become like a part of her, his shape fitting into hers as though their souls had been crafted to find each other, joining without seams. She'd learned to read his eyes. He'd learned to understand the grief waterlogging her heart, and to share his. He made her laugh, despite the wretched world. He was her life. Her future.

His wide palms lifted to her cheeks, and only then did she realize she'd continued to shake her head while her thoughts bucked. He held her, but she felt as if the ground were giving way, crumbling into a crevice so deep she could only hear echoes of falling rocks.

"Ella." He said her name so quietly she stilled. She sucked in breath. She met his stare.

"Ella," he said again, and tears, barely visible in the quickening dark, shone in his eyes. She started to sob uncontrollably, clinging to him while he pressed her face into his warm chest.

"We were going to have a house," she sputtered. "An orchard. Your apple trees, Isaak." It wasn't the right thing to say, but still she felt that her words meant everything. They represented the hope she'd carried, all this way. The coming darkness was heavy with fog, starless.

Ella would be alone again.

He rubbed her back while she cried, breathing into her hair. When she slowed, her sobs jagged and short, he spoke quietly into her ear.

"I can't go with you, love. And if you don't take this chance, you may not get another."

She pulled back a little, blinking the tears from her eyes, meeting his gaze. It was pained and fierce, all at once.

"I won't let you stay here because of me. Ella, if you go with Anne-Marie, you'll make it to Switzerland. You'll have a guide you can trust this time. You could dress the part and claim to be fifteen—you and Hanni together could pass as French schoolchildren, going north to visit relatives." He cleared his throat, struggling to push the words out. "You'll make it."

"But what about you?" She reached to touch his face now, cupping his rough cheek, running her thumb over the angle of his jaw.

"I'll stay here and fight."

"No—"

"Listen, Ella. I haven't wanted to say it, but I've been worried about my chances of making it all the way to Switzerland. It doesn't matter what papers I carry—they're going to question me at every opportunity. Look at me. A young man, clearly of the age they've conscripted to Germany. All they have to do is question me, which they will, to learn I'm not French. And then what?"

He sighed, looking from her to the stone walls surrounding them. "For weeks now, I've worried that I'd be your downfall on the journey north. That I would cause you to get caught. And now, my papers didn't come in time. It's a sign."

"It's *not* a sign. There's no such things as signs, or things that are meant to happen—"

He looked her directly in the eyes, severing her words. "I was meant to be with you." He smiled a little, shrugging, his gaze sad. "Maybe my mother, looking down on me from wherever she is, nudged us together. Moved me to stand by you, to take your hand on the day the gendarmes took us to Camp du Vernet. Maybe a small moment of grace brought you to my side." He tipped his head very close, his gaze boring into her own. "Ella, I've told you that I'll love you always, and I mean it. But what if the best way for me to stand with you, to love you, is to let you go? To fight while you travel on?"

"And if you're killed?" It emerged as a whisper. She feared even saying it out loud, as if the night sky and dark forest and tendrils of fog seeping around their feet could hear the words and make them true. Panic beat up in her chest again. If Isaak were dead, she wouldn't be able to continue on with this long walk that had become her life.

"I won't let anyone kill me. I'll find you, after the war."

She almost released a bitter laugh, but caught it. Still, the feeling laced her words. "How can you say that? Gerard didn't intend to die. Champeau. You can't make this promise."

Isaak stood immobile for a long moment. Ella shivered in his arms as the night seeped into her clothes, chilling her to the quick of her soul.

"I can't be sure," he relented. "But if you stay here with me, I can't be sure of your life, either. Or your sister's. Please, Ella. Take Hanni and leave with Anne-Marie. I'm desperate for you to live. If I survive, I'll come for you."

She saw the pain in his eyes, even in the deepening darkness. His pain held her for a long moment, the feeling so familiar it was like stiff old shoes, cold beds, old memories. She realized there was nothing she could do to change his mind. And that if the situation were reversed and she could send Isaak away to Switzerland, she would do it. She would make him go.

Now, on this frigid fall night, all she had the power to do was ease his pain. She harnessed the anguish spinning in her soul, forcing it quiet. The sorrow would stay with her, lodging into her heart like a trapped current, but she'd learned to live with sorrow long ago.

She pressed her forehead to his chest, listening to the beat of his heart, savoring the warmth of his arms and knowing this might be one of the last times she felt them around her.

"All right, Isaak," she whispered. She would live her life alone, unmatched by anyone ever again. But Hanni would live, too. She inhaled, calming the pace of her pulse, forcing her mind into cold rationality. She would keep her promise to her parents. If Isaak died, Hanni's life would be enough to make Ella's own existence worthwhile until she finally left this earth, too. Maybe in whatever afterlife awaited, which now seemed as dark and swirling as the fog surrounding Château de la Hille—maybe there she could find this boy she loved so much.

"I'll go," she promised.

He nodded, his head bobbing against hers.

She cleared the ache in her throat. "Wherever I go, I will love you. Always."

For a long moment, he said nothing. It wasn't until his body shook against hers that she understood, and she held him tighter.

It was Isaak's turn to weep.

THIRTY-THREE

RÖSLI

GENEVA, SWITZERLAND

NOVEMBER 1943

*R*ösli couldn't stop thinking of her children at La Hille.

She'd never stopped thinking of them, of course, but the way she remembered them, and the way she imagined them now, was shrouded in a terror that only seemed to grow the longer she was in Switzerland. The pain, the grief, the fear—every passing week was worse. She knew, from her long-ago studies in psychology at nursing school, that her mental state was deteriorating. What she didn't know was how to stop it.

Rösli often found herself freezing in whatever she was doing—folding linens, checking temperatures, administering medication in the sick wing—and gazing instinctively west. She yearned to go back. If she were allowed, she'd drop her work here in Geneva and travel straight to the old castle in the South of France. She'd walk all the way there, if she had to. By God, she'd *run*. If there were any way to return to her children and get them out of France, she would do it without thought.

It's what kept her awake during the night, the cool air from the windows stinging her wide-open eyes. There was no way to return. Worst of all, there was nothing she could do for the children of La Hille anymore.

Mein Gott, she breathed now and again, remembering episodes from her time in France as if seeing them afresh. She closed her eyes and recalled the prisoners at Camp du Vernet as they were loaded into cattle cars. She saw the heartbroken faces of her own children when they returned from the internment camp to La Hille, stalked by fear and grief, utterly trapped. *Hunted.*

It made her sick. Every day Rösli had moments when she suddenly couldn't move, gripped by a nausea so fierce it seemed to encompass her entire body. She'd clutch the laundered sheet she was folding, or turn from the child she'd been tending, or jolt upright in bed, abruptly unable to cope with her memories of France.

But why now? It made no sense. Shouldn't she have felt traumatized back when it was all happening, rather than now, here in the safety of Geneva?

"That's just it," Emilie whispered one day over lunch. "It's the same for me, Rösli. I think we simply didn't have time to feel it all then. We didn't have the luxury of contemplating things, not when so many people needed our constant, immediate attention."

Rösli nodded, turning that over in her mind, and blew on her soup. After she'd swallowed, she leaned toward Emilie's rosy, astute face, speaking quietly.

"But also, I think it's because we know it's still going on. And here we are, doing good work, yes, but we're powerless to save anyone else." Rösli glanced toward the far end of the quiet cafeteria where they sat, eating before the children tumbled in for lunch. Margot and Regina strode in and out of a kitchen door, carrying heavy tureens and stacks of plates. They looked healthy, and exchanged words and laughter as they brushed past each other, hurrying to prepare the tables. Regina noticed Rösli's gaze, and she smiled, raising a hand. Rösli nodded in reply. She turned back to Emilie, hesitating, trying to find the right words, and her voice cracked. "I'm haunted by those I couldn't save. Haunted by those who are still in danger. I don't think I'll ever recover from the regret I feel now, at having to leave them."

"Regret?" Emilie's voice sharpened. "Without you, would those young women be here, safe? And what about all the children who nearly boarded the trains in Le Vernet? You know the answer as well as I do."

"But I couldn't save them all."

"Rösli—"

Rösli shook her head, resolute, and after a long moment Emilie sighed, relenting. "I know," she murmured. Encouraging words, while tempting, were hollow.

"And I feel an urgency, like there's something I need to do, desperately, and can't." Rösli's thoughts came quickly now. "If only I knew what was happening at La Hille in my absence. If only I knew that my children would survive." An image of *les Grands* sleeping in the *Zwiebelkeller* rose in her mind. She saw them lined up in their bedding, stiff with fear, listening for gendarmes circling the château like wolves. *Mein Gott.* She shook her head, clutching her soup spoon and meeting her friend's stare.

"How will we go on with our lives, Emilie? The memories will never leave."

Emilie was quiet for a long time, her dark eyes distant as she thought. "There was a little boy who I came to love at Gurs," she said finally, her voice quiet. "He'd crawl up into my lap and ask me to sing. He was the sweetest child—when he smiled, he had a way of pursing his lips as though holding back laughter. He was only four years old. Jakob. It was like he sought joy, even though he cried for his parents and woke with nightmares every night. There was something in his spirit they couldn't crush. I would have taken him out of there, if there was a way. In a heartbeat."

Rösli listened, quiet. She already guessed the ending of this story, because it would be the same as all of Emilie's stories. She also understood the need to say it out loud.

"I ask myself what I could have done. Was there a way to conceal him in the laundry? To hide him under my skirt? I know that's ridiculous." Emilie paused, struggling to propel her words. "When Jakob was loaded onto the train, he needed help getting up. His legs weren't long enough, and his parents had already been sent away before I ever met him. He asked if he was going to Mutti, and then when they closed and bolted the door shut, he pushed his little hand through one of the slats. Reaching for me." Emilie looked at her clasped hands. "I tell myself that the Red Cross made a difference at that camp, and I suppose we did. We offered some comfort. But for the rest of my life, I will see that little hand when I close my eyes."

"*Mein Gott,*" Rösli whispered.

Emilie, the only person in Geneva who understood anything, simply nodded.

≪≪≪≪≫

THIRTY-FOUR

ELLA

JOURNEY TO THE FORBIDDEN ZONE, FRANCE

NOVEMBER 1943

*E*lla watched Isaak run toward the woods, his coat flapping behind him, his boots pounding the sparkling grass. She had just said goodbye to him, holding him in the courtyard in the clean, cold air, savoring the feel of his arms around her one last time. Anne-Marie had patrolled the grounds, as if out for a walk, and looked for any sign of gendarmes watching. But it was as they thought: the morning was frigid, and nobody had staked out the château. Isaak was safe to go.

Ella stood very still, forcing herself not to cry so the image of Isaak, running for his life back to the Maquis, wouldn't blur. It might be the last time she saw him on this earth.

Hanni, holding her hand, looked up, but Ella couldn't tear her eyes away from the forest for several minutes. She pulled in a shaky breath and glanced at Anne-Marie, who stood watching her with a pained expression.

"That's it, then," Ella managed. "Let's go."

*T*hat evening, after an arduous but uneventful hike to Saint-Jean-de-Verges, Ella and Hanni settled into a crowded train. Hanni held her rucksack tightly on her lap, and, despite the day's exertion, she sat as if frozen. Only her gaze moved around the train car, landing on each person, examining them before traveling on. Ella saw her pause, extra long, on a pair of German officers several seats away. They looked stiff in their gray uniforms and peaked caps. She reached for Hanni's hand, unclamping it from the rucksack and squeezing.

Please remember everything we told you, she thought, hard, as if she could make Hanni hear her. Anne-Marie was in another car altogether because, as she was a Swiss Red Cross worker, they were likely to scrutinize any children riding near her. Ella wished it were otherwise suddenly—that Anne-Marie could be near them on this part of the journey, with her confident warmth and reassuring smile.

She forced herself to draw a deep breath. *We will make it to Switzerland*. Ella had repeated this to herself ever since leaving La Hille, like a prayer. She and Hanni appeared unsuspicious, both of them dressed as French schoolgirls in simple skirts and sweaters Anne-Marie had found somewhere. Ella, thinner than ever lately, knew she passed as much younger.

She just needed Hanni to stay quiet.

At eight years old, Hanni had lived half her life in France, but still her accent would give them away in a second. Most of the La Hille children spoke German around the château, thus very few had lost their accents. Ella was lucky in this regard. She had a good ear for language, and was quite sure of her French.

The train rocked through barren vineyards, skeletal in the dusky evening, and Hanni shifted her attention from the German soldiers to the scenery. Her eyes were still huge, though perhaps with wonder as much as fear. Ella smiled faintly. Her sister had barely left Château de la Hille since they'd arrived there, nearly three years ago. What did she make of riding in a train now, whisking through France? Memory surfaced, and Ella's smile faded as quickly as it had come. Could Hanni be recalling other train rides? The first, when they'd rubbed at fogged windows to glimpse their parents one last time, waving on the platform? Or the last, when they'd rumbled into southern France in a cattle car, fleeing the advancing German army?

She tightened her squeeze on Hanni's hand, but didn't dare whisper anything into her sister's ear.

Hanni might forget herself and whisper back.

*N*obody spoke to them as the train wove through the deepening night, and eventually Ella fell asleep with Hanni snuggled in her lap. Ella jerked awake several times as they slowed, rumbling into barren stations and pausing for what seemed to be interminable, fuzzy lapses in the rhythm and rock of the car. When morning eventually brightened the sky, the train maintained its momentum. They couldn't be far from Lyon now. Hanni stretched and lifted her head, digging her sharp little elbow into Ella's lap and blinking her heavy lashes.

"Wo sind—"

Ella squeezed her hand so hard it must have hurt, and Hanni jerked fully awake, meeting Ella's frantic stare. She had nearly asked a question in *German*. Heart pounding, Ella glanced around the car to see if anyone had noticed.

A grandfatherly man, seated across the aisle, gazed at them through thick glasses, moving his mouth in a bovine manner. He frowned as Ella met his stare, and she shivered inside, looking away. Had he heard? Would he tell someone that Hanni had spoken in German, like a reflex?

Before she could tame her panic, one of the German officers caught her eye. He smiled, crow's-feet creasing around his eyes, and she glanced down. Her heart beat so hard she was certain Hanni could hear it, leaning against her still, her little body wooden with fear. The Nazi was much older than the usual soldier. Was he of high rank? Why had he smiled at her? Was it a jeer, to let her know that he'd heard her sister speak?

The Nazi officer was getting up. Ella could feel Hanni's eyes darting from him to her, but she simply tightened her grip on her sister's little hand, willing her to understand and stay quiet as the man ambled down the train toward them.

"Bonjour," the Nazi said, coming close. He knelt in the aisle in his stiff coat and gleaming boots, grinning, his stare startlingly blue. "I need to stretch my legs, and thought I might say hello. I have daughters about your age, back home."

Ella forced herself to return his smile, easing the fear from her face while her heart lurched with every word. "You must miss them," she said, her French perfect.

"*Oui*, very much. Very much." His German accent was heavy, his French halting. His grin fell a little and he seemed to study them. She could feel his eyes travel her worn sweater, just a little too small. Then they flitted to Hanni, who was visibly petrified, her mouth pinched into a thin line and her eyes unblinking.

"Where are you going?" the Nazi said after a moment, cocking his head. "So strange to see young children traveling through the night."

"We're visiting our aunt. She lives north of Lyon," Ella lied. Were her words cracking with the fear that held her, tightening around her like knuckles? "Our mother thought my little sister might sleep during the long journey. She doesn't like to sit still, you see."

"Ah. And you, little one. What is your name?"

Hanni didn't move a muscle. She didn't even blink her big eyes.

"She's very shy," Ella said quickly. "I apologize. Her name is Yvette."

"Yvette, how old are you?"

"She's eight."

The Nazi looked between them. "Can she not speak?" He straightened a little in his crouch. "Would you produce your documents please, mademoiselles?"

He said it nicely, but Ella sensed the sudden ice in his words. Her hand shook as she bent and rifled through her bag, pulling out the two false identity cards. Still, Hanni didn't move a muscle, but Ella felt her tightening like a strung bow.

"Here you are," she managed, handing over the cards, and as he scanned the photos, Hanni opened her mouth, her eyes wide, and lisped around her missing front teeth. Her voice emerged as a whisper.

"My *maman* tells me I talk too much, in fact." She smiled faintly, blinking her thick lashes and adding, "I'm sorry I didn't answer before. I only wish I wasn't so shy, monsieur."

Ella couldn't breathe.

The Nazi's eyes flicked up under his peaked cap, and Hanni hunched her shoulders winningly, smiling as though bashful, all gapped teeth and freckles. One would never guess at her fierce heart.

Across the aisle, the elderly French man watched, his gaze going cold. He slid his eyes from the Nazi to the girls, opening his puckered mouth.

"Such lovely children, *non*?"

Ella's hand moved back to Hanni's.

The Nazi pivoted, and the elderly man cleared his throat. The sound was wet, and his eyes clouded with the effort, but when he spoke the words were clear. "I'm proud of French children such as these. So beautiful, well mannered, and independent—children for a strong, collaborative future between our countries, *oui*? They do a heart good."

The Nazi officer seemed a bit off-balance. "Indeed," he murmured, nodding to the elderly man, and then he turned back to Hanni. "No need to apologize, little mademoiselle." He gave the identity cards to Ella, and reached out to cup Hanni's cheek with his big hand. "My Frieda is quite shy, too. Don't worry, I won't antagonize you further." Ella shivered inside, but then he smiled and stood, glancing out at a landscape that had changed from trees and fields to houses, increasingly close together. They were on the outskirts of a city. The Nazi turned, walking down the swaying car back to his seat.

The old man caught Ella's eye, nodding once. She returned the gesture, hoping her message came through. *Merci, monsieur.*

Hanni leaned very close as the train began to slow, her breath hot in Ella's ear as she whispered in French. "That soldier's accent was worse than mine."

Soon after, they wove into a crowded train station smelling of tar, hot iron, and musty bodies. Ella took in the red flags emblazoned with swastikas hanging at intervals, more numerous than in any station yet. They'd just come to the entrance, spotting Anne-Marie hovering outside, when Ella saw the guards flanking the doors. They were checking documents.

She bent slightly, whispering directly into the thick, bobbed hair covering Hanni's ear.

"I'll do all the talking this time. No matter what. Understand?"

Hanni nodded, and her hair bounced. Ella inhaled, her heart accelerating again, and they strode toward the guards.

"*Papiers*," one barked after they'd waited in line, shuffling forward in silent terror.

Ella produced both of their identity cards, working hard to tame the shake in her hand. The guard stared at her picture for what seemed like a very long time, then lifted his lidded gaze to her face. He studied her, scowling, and then flicked to Hanni's card.

Again, he stared at the *carte d'identité* for a very long time. His scowl deepened, and Ella found herself looking past him to Anne-Marie, waiting across the street now, tension clear on her face. Was there some kind of mistake on the forged cards? What would happen if he detained them? She imagined a gendarme marching Hanni away, separating her from Ella, and panic sliced her composure, sudden and sharp. *Don't let them take her.* She looked at Hanni, her face utterly emotionless this time, with no trace of the fear she'd shown on the train. Hanni was a quick learner.

Please, let us go.

A few more seconds ticked by, and the man handed their documents back. Ella didn't pause to put them away. Taking Hanni by the hand, she tugged her out of the station, walking far too fast for her sister's short stride.

But they'd made it. This leg of the journey was over, at least.

*T*he next morning, they left the colony at Montluel, which was strangely similar and simultaneously very different from La Hille, as it housed Spanish refugees and just a handful of young Jewish children. They boarded another train before light had fully reached the sky. Once more, Anne-Marie sat apart from them, and they rocked away from Lyon with its tall buildings and omnipresent swastikas. Outside the world became green again, and Ella found she could breathe easier.

It was an uneventful trip all the way to Champagnole, despite switching from the train to a bus. The guards looked right past them as they moved through stations and crowds, and Ella felt slightly more confident with each transition. She and Hanni were lucky, with their matching freckles, wide eyes, and buoyant hair. When she caught their reflection in a window, she understood why they slid through; they appeared to be French schoolgirls, entirely innocuous. Isaak rose in her mind, and her heart smarted. He'd been right, after all. Two girls could slip through train stations raising little suspicion, but a lanky, grown man would attract scrutiny. For a second, despite the hollow pain of his absence, she was glad he hadn't come.

That night they slept in an upstairs apartment in Champagnole, having been fed brioche and broth by Victoria and Madeleine Cordier. Like Ella and Hanni, the two women were clearly sisters, with their bright, shrewd eyes, brisk movements, and upright postures. They were tall and officious, but as Ella watched them conferring with petite, bubbly Anne-Marie in the kitchen, she began to see what they all had in common. Ella set down her spoon, thanking them profusely for their help, and Victoria waved a hand as if to bat the words away.

"It's our privilege to do what we can," she said simply. Anne-Marie smiled, and Ella understood that the same undercurrent of conviction ran through all three of these young women. They saw what needed to be done, and they did it.

The next day found them hiking, yet again. Madeleine stayed behind in Champagnole, and Victoria led the way through a cold forest, crunching over frosty spruce needles and dead beech leaves into a dense stand of trees, moving quickly and quietly. Hanni walked alongside the women without fuss or question, her little hand cold in Ella's grip and her nose pink. Again, her eyes were large and her mouth tiny as she took in the forest, darkening already in the late afternoon. Ella, too, was light-headed with fear. Every step brought them closer to the Forbidden Zone. There, their girlish looks couldn't save them. If they were seen, they'd be detained at best. At worst, they'd be shot.

A barbed wire fence divided the forest, and Victoria bent without ceremony and held up a loosened strand. When she looked back, she widened her eyes and dipped her chin toward the gap made by her fingers, hooked over a smooth patch of wire. The message in her gesture was clear: *Hurry*. One by one, they dropped to their bellies, scooting through a gap just big enough not to scrape their backs, the freezing earth smudging their cheeks as they emerged on the other side. When Victoria slipped through and scrambled up next to them, plucking a few brown leaves from her hair, she gestured again with urgency.

Hurry.

As quietly as possible, they moved through the forest. Hanni's cold fingers now shook in Ella's hand, and Ella squeezed them as they went, hoping to settle her. Each woman scanned the shadows of trees, stretching their strides to move yet more quickly, not daring to say a word. Ella's heart pounded and her mouth went dry as she sucked in cold air, trying to fill her tightening chest, shivering.

Eventually they came to the edge of the forest, and Victoria signaled for them to stop, still cloaked in the relative safety of shadows. Across a long rise of winter grass stood a farmhouse, silent in the muted light of late afternoon, waiting. Behind it, a hill rose sharply from another stretch of field, and its peak was crowned by a lengthy band of jagged, limestone cliff face.

Ella's breath left her. That was the route they'd take? Anne-Marie had warned her, but seeing the ascent of the Gy de l'Echelle rendered those warnings clear: the route into Switzerland was arduous. Maybe impossible. Yet, if that really was the way over the border, it was no wonder people made it through unscathed by patrols. The Germans couldn't patrol a cliff. She released a shaky sigh and glanced at Hanni, still holding her hand, her breath hanging in the air before her precious, terrified face. Could Hanni ascend the Gy de l'Echelle tomorrow? Had Anne-Marie been right when she'd tried to persuade Ella to leave Hanni at La Hille? Doubt overwhelmed her as Victoria continued to study the field and a thin ribbon of road beyond it, her eyes narrowed in concentration.

"*Now*," she whispered, fracturing Ella's thoughts, and in an instant they were all running, flat out, toward the house. Dead grass whipped at their legs, and Ella's heart pounded so hard the world blurred. The sky brightened overhead, absent of trees, and cold air stung her eyes. If anyone watched this field from the forest, they'd shoot. In a scramble of arms and legs, Hanni stumbled, yanking from Ella's grip and pitching headlong into the grass. The impact was so hard Ella heard the air thump from her sister's lungs. Hanni lay there for half a second, and Ella, without thought, strung her sister's arms around her neck, hoisting her onto her back, and went on running. Hanni clung on like a baby, bouncing with each step, and then they were on the threshold of the house and Anne-Marie, Victoria, and an older woman pulled them in.

The door shut tight in their wake.

"Oh, sweetheart." The tiny older woman, who could only be Madame Cordier, instantly knelt in front of Hanni. "That was quite a tumble. Are you all right?"

Hanni nodded silently, her hair bobbing. She reached up to touch her cheek, which was scraped and dirty, and Madame Cordier stood and bustled off, still talking.

"I'll get something to clean that cheek, *chérie*. And you all must be famished! I have lamb stew bubbling on the stove to warm you up—come, my dears."

Ella tugged on Hanni's hand, coaxing her into the warmth of a cozy farm kitchen. Her sister was still stiff with fear. Madame Cordier seemed to sense this, and she hummed softly as she returned, kneeling and pressing a warm cloth to Hanni's cheek. Anne-Marie drifted to a window, and Victoria sat to remove her boots.

A knock at the door made every one of them jolt in surprise.

Victoria froze, hands on her bootlaces, and met her mother's stare. Then she looked to Anne-Marie and whispered harshly, "Go upstairs and hide. *Quick*."

But Anne-Marie hesitated as someone again pounded the door, her startled eyes flitting between Victoria, Ella, and Hanni.

"Go," Victoria whispered. "I'll take them to the barn." She stood in her unlaced boots and waved Ella and Hanni forward, maneuvering them down a long hallway as Anne-Marie vanished upstairs. At the back door of the house she held up a hand, mouthing, *wait*, and stepped out cautiously by herself. She looked back and forth, studying the narrow strip of yard between the house and a barn, and as the front door creaked open behind them Victoria pulled them outside. Ella heard Madame Cordier welcoming men into the house, as if she had nothing to fear, and someone with a German accent began to speak. But then she was outside, darting with Hanni into the musty shadows of a barn, and for the second time in a year she was urged up into a hayloft to hide.

"Wait there. Don't make a sound," Victoria whispered from the darkness below, and while Ella pulled Hanni onto her lap and burrowed into a musty heap of hay, the barn door creaked shut.

It was very cold. Ella smoothed hair from her sister's cheek in the darkness, wiping the tears she found there. Somewhere below, animals crunched on feed, shuffling around in box stalls. She pressed Hanni's head to her shoulder, and her little sister, exhausted and shivering and terrified, rested in her arms. A horse murmured, and Ella staved off her own tears.

Thin light slid through a small, cobwebbed window across from the hayloft. Ella watched the day wane, and a memory of Isaak found her. She saw his smile, fleetingly, in another hayloft, months ago. The light had been golden that day. She remembered how he'd held her, making her feel safe. Ella shifted Hanni a little, continuing to pet her hair. There was nothing more she could do for her sister now. There'd been so little she could do for anyone she loved. Darkness fell like a shroud over this cold, wintery entrance to the mountains. Ella wiped silent tears from Hanni's cheeks, and she prayed.

Please don't let them find us. Her usual refrain, overused. It could only be a German patrol inside the house, searching. Would Anne-Marie be all right upstairs? Victoria had probably told her to go there because, with her Swiss passport, she possessed a layer of protection that Ella and Hanni didn't. If they were caught now, it would be clear that they were trying to escape into Switzerland, and it would also be clear why. But if only Anne-Marie were found, perhaps their suspicion would be satisfied.

Would Anne-Marie's Swiss passport protect her? Ella tipped her head back in the scratchy hay, closing her eyes. *No.* If they thought she was part of the resistance, or a *passeur*, nothing could protect her. She swallowed over the wedge blocking her throat. Her hands, wrapped around Hanni, trembled from fear and cold. What if Anne-Marie were caught working on their behalf? The thought made Ella's stomach drop, because she knew the answer. The fact that Anne-Marie was risking her life had never been more clear. And so was Victoria, and Madame Cordier.

Without planning it, a new prayer swam into her mind. *May it be Your will, Lord, our God and the God of our ancestors, that You lead us toward peace, guide our footsteps toward peace, and make us reach our desired destination for life, gladness, and peace.*

The Tefilat Haderech, the Traveler's Prayer, stayed with her.

Somewhere outside, a door creaked open. Boots moved on the barren winter earth. Ella pressed her hand over Hanni's head, holding her still and trying to give her strength. She listened. The boots scuffed, ambling. Perhaps turning while their owner looked around.

Searching.

The prayer continued on in her mind.

May You rescue us from the hand of every foe, ambush along the way, and from all manner of punishments that assemble to come to earth.

Hanni wept silently in her arms, and Ella, hardly daring to breathe, continued to pray.

THIRTY-FIVE

ANNE-MARIE

THE FORBIDDEN ZONE, FRANCE

NOVEMBER 1943

*A*nne-Marie watched the German soldier leave the house. She stared down through lacy curtains in an upstairs window, a hand clamped over her mouth as the back door swung shut behind him. He strolled out into the strip of yard between the house and the barn, looking up toward the Gy de l'Echelle one way, then down at the field Anne-Marie, Victoria, and the girls had run through not half an hour earlier. Had the patrol seen them sprint from the forest? *Mon Dieu.* This could be it.

This could be the time they were caught.

She swallowed, watching the German. He stood very still, but what was he doing? Listening? Without meaning to, Anne-Marie began to shake her head. *No.* He couldn't find those sweet girls. In what kind of world could an eight-year-old child, gap-toothed and stubborn hearted, be arrested? In what kind of world could an eighteen-year-old girl, lithe and brave and in love with a good boy, be deported? Anger bubbled up in Anne-Marie's chest, dislodging the edge of her fear.

Nothing was as it should be.

Below, the German pivoted, staring at the house, and then he began to move. He walked over to the shaded side of the barn, and Anne-Marie, verging on panic, tried to remember if there was a door there. A second later an arc of urine steamed where it hit the barn wall.

She exhaled slightly. She didn't yet dare to hope. The steam dissipated, and he buttoned up. Could that be all—he had to relieve himself? He pivoted, striding with his polished boots back toward the house.

When the door directly below her window opened and creaked shut, she let the rest of her breath go. Still, they were in the house. She crept as silently as possible to an armoire, climbed inside, and let the door fall softly shut behind her. It wasn't much of a hiding place. What would they do if they found her? She could claim that she was going to see her parents, that this was nothing more than an ill-conceived adventure, but she knew in the pit of her stomach that they would take her nonetheless. Without the girls, they wouldn't realize she was smuggling Jews over the border, but they'd probably suspect she was in the resistance. She held her breath, listening through the coats and dresses hanging around her.

She would be imprisoned. Maybe worse.

After an interminable wait, muffled footsteps sounded on the stairs. Anne-Marie pinned her eyes shut, unable to discern through the armoire whether the weight of the person was male or female. A moment later the door to the bedroom swung open, and a voice prodded her out.

"Anne-Marie," Victoria whispered.

She pushed open the armoire, hesitating.

"They've gone," Victoria said, still whispering. "We need to stay quiet in case they're lingering outside. My mother will go out to feed the animals soon, and she can have a look around to see if we're safe. When it's fully dark, we'll get those poor girls. They must be freezing."

Anne-Marie nodded, trembling. "What did they want?"

Victoria sighed, shaking her head a little. "My mother killed a lamb yesterday, which is illegal. All meat goes to the Germans, you know. Somehow they caught wind of it, which worries us immensely—it could be that we're under closer surveillance than we thought. So they came and sniffed around and basically tried to make her fearful. I don't think they were at all aware of people hiding here." She smiled a little. "My mother's so good at pretending to be simple and provincial, Anne-Marie—you should have seen her. She fusses around those soldiers as if they're boys in need of a mother, making whatever suspicions bring them here seem ridiculous in her kitchen. Acting was her second calling, apparently."

That night Madame Cordier fussed over all of them, chatting to the girls and serving the lamb she'd butchered, hidden, and cooked into a stew under the nose of a German patrol. Hanni and Ella ate silently, unable to smile but unfailingly polite, their large dark eyes traveling, over and over, to the door holding out the weather and the menacing world. When they went up to bed, snuggling together under a homemade quilt, Anne-Marie hoped exhaustion would win out over fear and allow them to sleep.

Because beyond this house there was yet a mountain to climb.

Before turning toward sleep herself, she peeked through a slit in a curtain to the Gy de l'Echelle, and what she saw nearly made her heart stop.

Merde, she breathed, opening the curtain a little more, letting her eyes adjust to the darkness.

It was starting to snow.

*T*hey were up before dawn, gathered around the kitchen table with only a large fire in the grate for light. If patrols were already out on the road, they wouldn't see that the house was awake.

"What should we do?" Anne-Marie said, hearing the strain in

her own voice. Ella went to the window, peeking out, and Hanni sat at the table with her cheek resting against the rough wood. Her eyes closed, despite the tension in the adults all around her, and Anne-Marie's heart clutched. The little girl was exhausted. She couldn't hike out into the storm whirling beyond the farmhouse windows. There was at least six inches of snow already. Anne-Marie's thoughts wandered to the other *Grands*, waiting anxiously for their turn to leave La Hille. She'd hoped, so fervently, that winter would come late this year, holding off long enough for a few more trips into the mountains.

Ella spoke without turning around, her gaze locked on the dark window. "We'll go anyway." Her voice was as cold as the frost fracturing the glass.

"But, *ma chérie*, it's a storm." Madame Cordier clasped her tiny, strong hands, glancing between the younger women. She frowned, and the spray of wrinkles around her eyes deepened in the firelight. "Perhaps the girls could stay here until the weather clears."

"No, Maman." Victoria dislodged herself from her spot next to the fire, moving to stand by Ella. "It's too risky for everyone. If that patrol had decided to search at all last night . . ." She glanced at Hanni, dozing on the table, and left the obvious unsaid. "Perhaps we can take the girls back to Champagnole and hide them in the apartment."

Anne-Marie cleared her tight throat, her stomach a nest of nerves. "There's always the colony at Montluel."

"No." Ella turned from the window, leveling her liquid eyes on every person in the room. "Not one of those options is safer than hiking over that mountain. We can't hide anymore." Her voice cracked, and for a moment it looked like she might cry, but when her words emerged, they were bold. "I can't spend another second living in the shadows, hoping beyond hope that those shadows will conceal us long enough to get us through. We want a life. I'm stronger than I look. I'll carry my sister if I have to."

The room was silent for a long moment. The fire, alive and dancing, popped in the grate.

Victoria finally nodded. She caught the eye of her mother, and then Anne-Marie. "All right. I'll go find enough mittens for everyone. Go get your boots, ladies—we need to leave before it's light. We must cross the field while it's still snowing hard, so our footprints will be covered over before morning patrols."

When they were gathered by the back door, bundled in borrowed mittens and hats, rucksacks with lunch packed on their backs, Madame Cordier ventured outside. They heard her crunching away in the snow, and for a long while it was silent. She went out at the same time every morning, an hour before the sun came up, and fed her animals. What a passing patrol wouldn't realize about this routine is that she was also looking for them. When she scattered feed for the chickens and threw hay to the sheep, cow, and horse, she turned with her shrewd gaze and scanned the road and surrounding forests. When all was clear, whether she had guests or not, she'd crow like a rooster. It was the signal to go, and it never varied. If any Germans watched or listened, they would simply think Madame was an early riser, unwavering in her routine, like every farmer they'd ever known.

Several tense minutes passed, and then a rooster crowed. If Anne-Marie didn't know better, she'd think it was a real rooster. And if times were different, she'd giggle at this little woman, out crowing so convincingly in the snow.

"*Now*," Victoria hissed, and one by one they slipped through the back door, hurrying outside.

The cold was breathtaking. Anne-Marie filed in behind Ella, who gripped tightly to Hanni's mittened hand. They walked as quickly as they could toward the cliff rising beyond Madame Cordier's snug house, stepping in each other's boot prints, trying to minimize their trail. Would their footprints disappear before anyone might see them? She glanced back, comforted by the snow already blowing over their wake. Soon, there would be drifts. She faced forward, her cheeks stinging. If only they could run. It was still dark, but she felt frighteningly conspicuous moving through this field, four figures in a sheet of white.

Before she knew it, they were at the forest rising toward the Gy de l'Echelle. Anne-Marie looked up at the cliff they were to climb, and her heart shrank a little. She'd done it before, of course, but never in winter. Now the path Victoria had carved up the granite cliff face was crusted in snow and ice. The footholds and handholds, precarious even in perfect weather, would be slippery. How would they grip the rock when the real climbing began?

Without discussion, they started up. The path was easy at first, winding through the trees, ascending gently. Snow fell lighter under the spruce branches, and the quiet was broken only by their soft footfalls and the whip of wind, high in the treetops. Eventually the trail switchbacked up the treed slope, steeper with each turn. Anne-Marie's breath quickened, warm against the scarf wrapped around her neck and pulled up over her face. She tugged it down, letting her breath plume into the cold air. The girls, walking ahead of her, wore snow on their shoulders and backs like knit shawls. They were both so thin, they would soon be freezing. Anne-Marie shivered at the thought, though she was warm enough through exertion. Certainly, they all were—it was after the work that one had to fear cooling sweat, and cooling limbs.

As they climbed, the hill broke off the narrowing trail, slick and steep, until eventually it angled into a vertical drop. They turned, one after another, trudging up another length of switchback. Everyone's boots began to slip a little with each step, unable to gain traction on the new snow. The trees thinned around them as they ascended, and light seeped through the heavy sky. It was morning. When the face of the cliff finally loomed, it was laced in white.

They stopped at the base of the rocky seam that served as a way up.

"Take off your mittens," Anne-Marie said, urging Ella and Hanni to strip down to their bare fingers. "It'll be easier to grip ledges." She pulled hers off and tucked them securely in a pocket. Her hands instantly ached. The snowflakes, falling heavily through the lightening sky, came faster. She grimaced, catching Victoria's eye.

Victoria nodded, all business, and spoke quietly. "*C'est bien*— make sure those mittens can't fall out. Now, the good news is that with this heavy snow, we are much harder to spot, and they're far less likely to be looking in the first place. I don't think German patrols will be able to see us at all, even if they're out on the road, so take your time. Hanni?"

The little girl looked up, her expression grave.

"You'll climb ahead of your sister. I'll go first, then you, then Ella, and finally Anne-Marie."

"I'm good at climbing," Hanni said solemnly. She sniffed, wiping at her nose with a pale, shivering hand. Her gaze tipped from Victoria to the cliff rising over them.

Anne-Marie forced a smile. "I know what a good climber you are. Off we go, then." She waved them on as if this were a youth scouting expedition rather than a flight for life. She watched Hanni turn and pick her way up after Victoria, her cheeks pink and her tiny hands gripping the first holds, so very brave. Ella went next, moving carefully, and Anne-Marie's heart rang with only one thought, like a plea to the universe.

We have to make it. Please, let us make it home.

For a moment she watched them pick their way up the crease in the cliff, strewn with loose boulders and vertical pitches, but offering places to cling on and climb. Victoria moved mechanically, gripping shelves of rock and carefully testing snowy footholds before giving them her weight. Hanni followed her movements, not even hesitating. She wore a tiny pair of wool trousers Anne-Marie had taken from the boys' dormitory, and real shoes that laced up, instead of the clogs all *les Petits* had worn at La Hille. Still, these were not mountain-climbing clothes. Anne-Marie hesitated a second longer, watching Hanni ascend, holding her breath while the child's feet kicked into the boulders and snow, finding purchase. An image of her, months ago at La Hille, flitted through her mind. She smiled despite her bounding pulse, remembering Hanni, high in a tree. The adults had continually coaxed and scolded the child, trying to get her to come down from various leafy perches. None of them could have predicted that Hanni's climbing would one day serve her so well.

Ella was already halfway up, moving cautiously in her sister's shadow, and Anne-Marie followed. Her hands ached as they brushed snow from boulders and cracks, finding places to grip. With each hoist her muscles strained, burning with effort, and for several minutes she thought of only one thing: climbing. The snow whirled and drifted down from the sky and her boot slipped, but just a little. She slowed even more, concentrating on the task. Trees whispered at their backs, swaying in the wind as Anne-Marie ascended past their restless tops.

Then Ella slipped above her. She skidded down several feet before lurching to a stop, inches from Anne-Marie, her slender arms shaking as she clutched a jag of rock. Victoria, already at the top, looked down with a pained expression on her face. But it was Hanni who cried out.

"Ella!" she screamed, forgetting herself as she thought her sister was falling, looking down from the rock she clung to like a marmot. Her little voice echoed through the trees and boulders, swirling with snow, and everything in Anne-Marie froze.

"Keep coming!" Victoria whispered at the same time a shot fired in the valley below.

Mon Dieu, Anne-Marie whispered under her breath, moving quickly. Holding fast to the rock, she pushed at Ella's backside so the girl could get a better grip, and another shot rang out.

Had they been heard?

"Quickly!" Anne-Marie whispered just as Ella regained her momentum. Hanni continued up, disappearing over the cliff's crest, and Ella and Anne-Marie scrambled after her. The snow fell thicker by the second, and the treetops rising around them tossed in the wind. Anne-Marie forced herself to focus. *Climb.* Surely they weren't visible from below—they would make it. Ella neared the top, and Victoria reached for her hand, heaving her over the cliff's edge. How far could a gun shoot? Anne-Marie shook the question away, ascending the final stretch and flinching as another shot banged. And then, she was over the top.

The second she reached flat ground, they were off. The girls sprinted in front of her, feet pounding, hair flying in the stiff wind whisking over the mountaintop. *They would make it.*

As one, they ran.

~≪≪≪~

THIRTY-SIX

ELLA

THE RISOUD FOREST, SWITZERLAND

NOVEMBER 1943

*T*he border wove like a seam through the Risoud forest. It was no more than a low, dry-stacked stone wall, and yet Ella gasped when she spotted it. Hanni glanced back at her, suddenly buoyant, and they both started to run again.

With no more than a hoist and a hop, their boots landed on Swiss ground.

Ella looked from Hanni to Anne-Marie and finally Victoria, who remained on the other side of the rock wall. Without expecting it, she began to laugh.

"We're in Switzerland?" Hanni said, her voice full of wonder as she reached out a mittened hand and touched the Swiss side of the wall, brushing off a patch of snow. Her arm shook slightly in the cold.

Ella shivered, too. Still grinning, she met Anne-Marie's smiling eyes and pulled Hanni close, trying to hold her tight enough to slow her shivers. Her sister's teeth chattered against her embrace, and Ella's smile faded a little. "How much farther now?"

Anne-Marie's smile relaxed, too, and she hesitated. "Several kilometers," she said, her gaze dropping to Hanni. "We have to be just as quiet and careful as before."

Ella rubbed Hanni's little arms and brushed the snow from her shoulders and hat. She knew they weren't safe yet, and she couldn't let the relief of scaling the wall, officially leaving France, disrupt her focus. If a Swiss patrol caught them, they'd be sent directly back. She thought of her friend Inge, who had been so close to Geneva that she could see its lights—nearly free. Yet the Swiss officer who found her hurrying along the road followed his orders, marching her right back into France. Ella shivered harder. They had to travel twelve kilometers into Switzerland to avoid the rigid immigration policy Inge had fallen victim to.

"Bonne chance," Victoria said, reaching across the wall and gripping her by the elbow. "These woods are Anne-Marie's territory now, so I'm going to head back to check on my mother."

Ella nodded. Madame Cordier would have heard the gunshots, and was probably worried sick. The German patrol could be searching her house again, their suspicions reignited by the shouts they'd heard bouncing off the cliff. Victoria had been quiet with worry ever since.

"Tell them it was you that they heard," Anne-Marie said, her arms wrapped around her torso, fending off the cold. "I'm quite sure they couldn't see us. Those were likely warning shots, attempting to flush us out."

Victoria nodded. "I'll say I was after a loose sheep in the forest." She smiled briskly. "Ella, Hanni, I'm so glad to see you on your way. Go on and lead good lives."

Ella swallowed. "Thank you so much," she managed.

"No need to thank me." Victoria leaned over the wall and kissed both of her cheeks, and a strange feeling swept through Ella; it was her last French goodbye. Victoria motioned to Hanni, who stepped forward so her cheeks could be kissed as well. Then Victoria turned, striding away from the long stone wall. They watched her tall, dark silhouette disappear in the tumbling snow and encroaching forest, and then, without further discussion, they went on.

Anne-Marie walked ahead confidently. She held her mittened hands up to her mouth periodically, blowing on them, and Ella and Hanni did the same. Several times Ella stopped, bent before her sister, and rubbed her arms vigorously in an attempt to warm her. But Hanni shivered more violently with each minute. Her eyes became glassy as she walked, almost dreamlike, and her freckles brightened against pale cheeks. Ella's fear moved away from Swiss patrols, settling instead on her sister, like the snow drifting heavily from the slate-gray sky.

"Anne-Marie," she whispered eventually, trudging up to walk alongside her. "Is there somewhere we can warm up? I'm worried about Hanni."

Anne-Marie glanced back at the little girl, walking dutifully behind them, her eyes on the pillowy forest floor. "I know—me, too. There's a forester's hut not far from here. It's near the wall, a bit south, in the direction we need to go before heading east. We'll warm up there for an hour or so before continuing on. Let's hurry— I brought matches to build a fire."

"Should we worry about getting caught?"

Unease lit Anne-Marie's eyes, and she pinched her lips together for a second of thought while Ella moved her toes, currently numb in her damp leather boots.

"Yes," Anne-Marie admitted. "But right now, I'm more concerned about hypothermia. Anyway, if the Swiss patrols have even a bit of good sense, they won't be out in this snow."

Ella nodded and paused, bending and gesturing to her sister. Without a word, Hanni climbed onto Ella's back, her thin arms slung about her neck and head resting on her snowy shoulder. Hanni's whole body seemed to chatter as they walked. When a small, wooden hut appeared in the woods, Ella weakened with relief. She set her sister down, and Anne-Marie hurried inside ahead of them, unpocketing matches she'd had the foresight to bring.

"Come, settle around the fire," she said, wiping spots on the dusty floor with her damp, mittened hand. In a daze, Ella and Hanni sat while Anne-Marie pulled out kindling and small logs someone had stacked in a corner, piling them expertly into an old woodstove. "We used to come here all the time when I was little." Her voice shook with cold as she peeled off her mittens and struck a match. For a second she focused only on the fire, but when it caught, Anne-Marie leaned back and grinned. "Know what we call it?"

Ella shrugged, her interest glazed over.

"L'Hôtel de l'Italie."

"Why?" Hanni managed, and the word trembled so much Ella scooted over, taking her sister in her arms and again rubbing her limbs.

Anne-Marie laughed, clearly trying to boost their spirits. "I have no idea why we called it that. Rather a grand name for a woodsman's hut, *non?*"

"This is where you lived, when you were a little girl?" Hanni asked. She leaned heavily into Ella.

"*Oui.* I grew up in these woods. I know it's cold and wintry out there, but these trees rising over us are like old friends, Hanni. We'll be out of danger in no time, snug in my parents' house. We just need to warm you up first."

"What's your parents' house like?" Hanni scooted a bit from Ella's arms, drawn to the fire as it began to pop in the grate.

"Oh, it's not fancy, but it's cozy. My mother will have made soup for us to eat, and fresh bread."

Hanni's voice still shook. "What's she like, your mother?"

Ella's heart hurt as if poked. She rarely spoke to Hanni of their mother and father, but she couldn't be sure why. Was she afraid it would make Hanni sad? Make her ask questions Ella couldn't answer? Or was she afraid of feeling even more sorrow herself? She glanced at Hanni, whose face glowed in the growing firelight, and realized it was very much like their mother's. The face she'd tried to remember for so long? That flitted through her memory, just out of reach? Its echo knelt before her, warming in a Swiss woodsman's hut.

"Oh, my mother is much like me, I suppose." Anne-Marie leaned forward to stir the kindling, blowing gently. "A bit like Madame Cordier, too. She'll love to welcome you girls tonight. She'll have a warm bed waiting for you after supper. And, when I've gone back to France, she'll help you get settled in Switzerland."

The fire leapt, and Anne-Marie fetched the food from their rucksacks, packed by Madame Cordier. They sat in the warmth and ate cold bread, a bit of cheese, and apples, which tasted divine in the dark little hut. As she chewed, Ella let her mind drift to the home Anne-Marie described. It was hard to imagine that they would be there, really be there, in mere hours. The idea of a snug house, a hot supper, and beds you could sleep in without fear? It seemed like a fiction. A fairy tale from another world.

A knock made her jolt.

Anne-Marie's gaze darted from the fire to the crude wooden door, and her face drained of color. Hanni clutched her bread, freezing mid-chew, still faintly shivering. Ella held her breath, looking frantically around as though there was still time to hide.

"*Merde*," Anne-Marie breathed, scrambling up to her feet. She turned to the girls, her face drawn tight, and shook her head. "Stay right here," she whispered, and she pulled her mittens back on.

When the door creaked open, spilling daylight into the dark, warm hut, Ella flinched. A man stood in its gap, craning his neck to see in. His eyes latched on to hers for a second before Anne-Marie could bustle out, shutting the door tightly.

Ella gave her bread to Hanni and held a finger to her lips. *Shhhh.*

She stood on weak legs, her heart in her throat, and crept to the door. Placing her ear near the jamb, she listened. There was no mistaking their visitor. He was uniformed, his expression stern as he'd peered inside. *Police.* For a moment Ella heard nothing, her cheek scraping on the rough wooden wall as she pressed closer, and she felt as if everything in her was teetering. When his voice broke the silence, booming in the quiet forest despite the wall between them, she knew.

It was over.

Like shattering ice, everything inside of her—her fear, her grief, her love, her wild hope—it all tumbled down in a glittery cascade, settling sharp and irreparable in the pit of her soul.

"It's my duty to return them," the man's voice declared.

He was cut off by Anne-Marie's quieter response, indiscernible through the door.

Tears stung Ella's eyes, and she didn't bother to wipe them away. The fairy-tale house on the other side of the Risoud was just that. It had all been a fairy tale, this belief that they could crawl up out of a grim reality that wanted only to claw them back. She closed her eyes, and there was Isaak, months ago, his gaze alight as he tried to subdue a smile, hazy mountains galloping into the distance behind him. She sighed, imagining his arms around her as they'd been on that morning, when everything in her had tilted toward hope.

When we get somewhere safe—Spain, or maybe Portugal—he'd whispered, the warmth of his body beating in rhythm with her own. *Will you marry me?*

Everything ached in Ella's beaten soul, and she opened her eyes to the dark of the woodsman's hut. Hanni still sat by the fire, clutching her bread, not daring to utter a sound.

Ella crept back to her sister, kneeling and wrapping Hanni in her arms. Perhaps Anne-Marie would be able to save Hanni and send her back to La Hille. She was only eight. Ella swallowed the heat of her tears, imagining Hanni surviving, growing up. *Living.*

Ella would be deported to the camps in the east. She knew it now, with certainty. The cold gripping her, and hunger—it would be her future until she passed out of this wretched, beautiful world. Perhaps Isaak, out fighting in the forest with the Maquis, would live. Hanni and Isaak would have to go on alone, separately, forging some kind of life.

Hanni clutched her, and she kissed her sister's forehead. But what kind of life could Hanni forge? And Isaak? In this dark woodsman's hut guarded by a Swiss police officer, she suddenly found no solace in the future of those she loved so dearly. Because no matter where they went, hate would follow. There would never be an escape in this world that seemed to hate them so much.

Ella closed her eyes, pressing her lips to the crown of Hanni's shivering head, and wept.

~~~~~~

THIRTY-SEVEN

ANNE-MARIE

THE RISOUD FOREST, SWITZERLAND

NOVEMBER 1943

*A*nne-Marie folded her arms tightly across her chest and lifted her chin, as though she could stare down this tall, uniformed officer of the Swiss border patrol. He gazed at her with dark, calculating eyes. Thoughts thrashed in her mind, and her heart pounded, but she didn't let fear shake her voice.

What could she say to him, to change his mind?

"Really, it's your duty to return them? What about your *moral* duty, Officer? Do you not answer to anything higher than your position?"

"I answer to God and country, mademoiselle. I have my orders."

There it was.

"And would God want you to send two young girls back into France, where they will most certainly be interned and deported? Sir, I've been in French camps. There isn't enough food, clothing, or bedding. The children are ill and covered in sores and lice. They watch as their parents are loaded onto trains and deported—those who still have parents. They deport children, too—did you know that?"

He shifted uncomfortably, and she held his gaze. Her voice was as quiet and cold as the snow drifting around them. "And those are French camps. I cannot begin to imagine the horrors they would face in Poland or Germany. If you send these young girls back into France, their blood is on your hands, monsieur."

He glanced around, adjusting his cap, agitated. "What would you have me do? If I lose my job, how will I feed my own children?"

"You won't lose your job. How would anyone ever know that you let us go?"

"They'll interview the girls when they arrive wherever you're taking them. You must know that. If one of them slips and says she saw a Swiss officer, I'll be investigated. That little one, especially, could let it slip." He straightened a bit.

Anne-Marie sharpened her glare, but her confidence faltered. She saw in the way he looked from her to the hut, squaring his shoulders and hardening his expression, that she'd said nothing to convince him. For a moment, it was as though everything paused around her, and all the ramifications of this blunder rose up in her mind, looming. Ella and Hanni would be lost, which made her dizzy with grief. But also, this route, which had promised salvation to the rest of the endangered kids stuck in the *Zwiebelkeller*, would be compromised. If he marched them back over the border, he'd tell the German patrols where they'd sneaked through. The Cordier sisters and their mother would be compromised. No, she corrected herself—they'd be arrested. Their entire operation, including the hazy tasks Victoria performed for the resistance, would collapse.

And what would become of La Hille? Would the authorities finally have an excuse to shut down the Swiss Red Cross colony and take all the children, as they'd long wanted to? Had she erred, beyond her own comprehension, when she'd set out to save what lives she could?

Anne-Marie stood there in the snow, breathless with over-whelming despair, when something caught her eye above the Swiss officer's head. She squinted a little, trying to get a clearer glimpse of it high in the snowy trees, flitting from branch to branch.

A bird.

She nearly gasped. It was a yellowhammer, strangely deep in the winter forest for a bird that preferred open spaces. What was it doing up here? Her own voice murmured in her mind with the echo of a story she'd invented over a year ago. *Did I ever tell you about the time I got lost in the snowy wilderness, children?*

Her little audience had stared at her, blinking up in the fire-light, their attention rapt.

. . . just as I was about to lose hope, something happened. A little bird dove down from the trees, and do you know what color it was?

Yellow. The bird in her story had been yellow.

She dropped her gaze from the tree branches, which tossed high overhead in the capricious wind, to the officer standing before her. His frown deepened.

"Those girls are counting on you," she said, with new strength in her voice. "*You.* You have the power to save their lives. What choice will you make?"

He faltered. She saw it in his face.

"All of this will fall away, sir. The war, your orders, the ever-changing laws along the border. When you lie on your deathbed someday, will you be proud of the life you lived? Or ashamed?"

The man scratched under his cap, again glancing back and forth, assessing their surroundings, his expression tense.

"What will you tell your children, when they ask what you did during the war? Will you say that you sent two little girls to their death?"

For a long moment, the Swiss officer stared at the door of the hut, frowning, his eyes dark as the tree trunks against the snow. When he finally whispered a reply, he rushed his words.

"Promise me: You will tell nobody that I saw you. Those girls can tell nobody. Do you understand?"

"I give you my word."

For a long, tense moment Anne-Marie and the Swiss officer held each other's stares. He broke off first, shaking his head.

"Go now—get out of here. I'll put out the fire in the cabin."

Anne-Marie didn't hesitate. She nearly ran the few strides to the Hôtel de l'Italie. When the door flung open, she found the girls wrapped together before the fire, their faces wet with tears.

"Quick!" She gathered their rucksacks, flinging them on her own back. "He's letting us go."

Ella scrambled up, her face pale and drawn. "Letting us go?"

"There's no time to discuss it. Get out of here before he changes his mind."

In a blur of urgency, the girls hurried from the cabin, not even daring to look toward the waiting Swiss officer. But Anne-Marie did glance his way, and when she caught his eye, her words cracked with emotion.

"Thank you."

*T*hey shivered again as they walked through the forest, and Ella carried Hanni on her back. The little girl looked exhausted, but her eyes stretched wide and solemn.

"I can take her," Anne-Marie said gently, for probably the fifth time in an hour. Again, Ella shook her head, her damp hair swinging.

"I'm fine."

Anne-Marie hoisted the rucksacks, which were mostly empty now, and glanced up at the trees. She found herself scanning the green boughs crowned in drifts of heavy white, looking for the bird. There was nothing. Had she imagined it?

She moved to walk up alongside the girls. "Can I tell you something? A story?"

Ella glanced over, her expression devoid of emotion. It was as if whatever feeling remained in the girl had drained out in the foresters' hut, like water in a sieve. Hanni, limp on her back, nodded eagerly.

"Well, I used to tell the children at Montluel about a time I was lost in the woods when I was a little girl. I had gone out walking, and it began to snow. In the story I walked for a long time, admiring the wilderness around me, before realizing I was lost. And shortly after admitting I was lost, a storm blew in."

"Did you really?" Hanni asked, her interest piqued.

Anne-Marie smiled. "I confess that I made up parts of the story, *chérie*. So, in this imaginary tale, it began to get dark, and I was truly lost. Imagine me, as a child, lost in these woods, on a day much like this one."

Hanni glanced around, and Anne-Marie remained quiet for a moment, letting the child take in the glittery woods. The snow had ceased falling, perhaps an hour ago, and intermittent sunlight dropped in brilliant shafts through the trees. It was cold, but glorious.

"Well, as the story goes, I became very frightened. I thought I might never find my way. And then, a little yellow bird appeared in the branches above me. I followed it, and it led me home."

"Is that true?" Hanni asked, shifting her gaze back to Anne-Marie.

"I made that part up, too." She winked. "But here is something I didn't make up—something that just happened. Are you listening closely?"

Hanni nodded, earnest. Ella's gaze slid over for a second, belying her interest.

"Well, when I was speaking with that Swiss officer, for a moment

I lost all hope. It seemed that he had already decided to take us back to France, and that nothing I said would sway him. Then I glanced up, and I saw a little yellow bird in the trees."

"That can't be true," Ella said quickly, her voice stony.

Anne-Marie shook her head, nervous all of a sudden. Was it right to share this with the girls? Ella was not a child, but rather a young woman who had lost nearly everything. Anne-Marie could scarcely imagine how she felt. How would she react to what Anne-Marie's intuition, impulsive as always, prodded her to say?

"I promise you," she said, speaking quietly, "I'm not making it up. It was there in the trees, above the officer. I've been asking myself ever since if I imagined it, but I really don't think so."

For a long moment, the only sound was their crunching boots. The forest sparkled around them, the fallen snow catching sunlight like a million scattered prisms.

"This is the part I want you to hear. It's the reason I'm telling you this story, and risking that you'll think I'm half-mad." Anne-Marie caught Hanni's eye, smiling. "I used to tell my children at Montluel that birds carry a certain magic. That I believe they fly about and look down on us with the eyes of all the people who have loved us, and all the people we've loved, whether they are still alive or gone. So, when I saw that bird, I thought it might mean something. To both of you."

For a long moment, nobody spoke. They moved through the breathtaking wilderness, lost in their own streams of thought. And then, abruptly, Ella knelt and let Hanni slide off her back. The little girl pivoted, and Ella kissed the crown of her head, tears silently rolling down her cheeks. Her dark eyes shone as she smiled at Hanni, whose brows raised in puzzlement.

"Do you understand, Hanni?"

Hanni's voice emerged in a whisper. "Mutti and Papa? You think it's true?"

Ella reached to tuck Hanni's hair, chunky with melting snow, behind her ears. "I think so," she whispered back, wiping a tear from Hanni's freckles with her thumb. "We can never know for sure what things mean, Hanni, my love. But yes. I believe they found a way to help us."

~~~~

THIRTY-EIGHT

ELLA

LE SENTIER, SWITZERLAND

NOVEMBER 1943

Ella couldn't understand all that had happened to her and Hanni, or to any of the people they loved, or really to all of Europe. She was quite certain that she never would.

But as she ate soup in Madame Piguet's warm house, safe in Switzerland, she understood one thing for certain, finally: She and Hanni would fulfill Mutti and Papa's fervent wish, for which they'd sacrificed in a way she couldn't begin to fathom. They would go on and live.

As Monsieur Piguet began to coax out a song on his violin, and Madame plied them with yet more food, joy and sorrow dueled in her heart. This snug little house, with its bustle and music, reminded her of her own home from long ago. Perhaps that was how Ella's life would always be—a blend of light and dark, loss and hope.

That evening, Ella waited for Hanni to fall asleep in her arms, and she thought of Isaak, as she did every night before sleep. She turned over in bed to stare at the stars shining down on the crisp, cold forests, poised at the edge of winter.

If Isaak lived, she would never again leave his side. If he didn't live, she would never forget him. She would not allow her heart to let him go.

*T*wo mornings later, Ella woke while the sky was still dark. She sat up, shaken by a reflex of terror, waiting for her pulse to slow and reality to assemble before her. She wasn't in the woods, hunted by patrols. She wasn't in the *Zwiebelkeller*. She inhaled, glancing at Hanni softly breathing under a hand-stitched quilt beside her. They were safe, in Switzerland.

But what had woken her?

Voices murmured downstairs, and she remembered. Anne-Marie was leaving this morning, attempting to make the trek back to the border before daylight. Glancing at Hanni again, she swung her stockinged feet to the floor. She tiptoed to the staircase, her borrowed nightgown flowing around her, and crept down.

Anne-Marie was in the kitchen with her mother, finishing a bowl of porridge by the light of a fire already leaping in its grate. Her father hovered in the doorway, pulling on an old pair of leather boots. He glanced to the staircase, his kind eyes the same blue as his daughter's.

"You're up early." He smiled under his mustache. "Came down to say goodbye?"

Ella nodded, looking from Monsieur Piguet to Anne-Marie, who scraped the last of her breakfast from her bowl. Her parents were very much like her, with the same optimistic outlook and steadfast warmth. Monsieur Piguet expressed his kindness in a quiet way, and Madame was as buoyant as her daughter.

"I'm glad you came down, Ella." Anne-Marie looked from her to her father. "We're just about to leave. He's walking me to the border."

"Would you like some porridge, dear?" Madame Piguet asked,

tightening her robe a bit. "Or perhaps you'll go back to sleep when they've gone?"

Ella smiled. "Back to sleep, but thank you."

Madame Piguet drifted to the foyer to confer with her husband, leaving Ella and Anne-Marie in the kitchen.

"I don't know how to thank you," Ella managed.

Anne-Marie grinned, batting her hand a bit. "It's like Victoria always says—there's no need to thank anyone."

Ella shrugged, unsure of what to say. "You'll remain at La Hille, then?"

"*Oui*. But I'll be back here soon enough. I plan to bring anyone seeking escape over this same route."

Ella frowned slightly. "Will it still work, after the Swiss patrolman caught us?"

"Bien sûr. The Risoud is an enormous forest. We'll vary our route on the Swiss side so they'll never know quite where to search." Anne-Marie took Ella's hand and squeezed reassuringly. "I'd love to hear how you and Hanni are getting along, so my mother will keep up with you, if that's all right."

Ella smiled. "Of course. I'd welcome it. So, which of *les Grands* are next?"

"Edith and Inge, I hope." Anne-Marie stood, smoothing her slept-on hair. "They've been waiting, but the weather may interfere over the next months. I'll ask Victoria if we might use skis—" She paused, thoughtful for a second, calculating, and then she shrugged and drained the last of her coffee. "I'd like to convince Frau Schlesinger and her little boy to come, too. Perhaps Walter Kamlet. And anyone else still hiding, really."

Ella nodded, knitting her hands together. Clearly Anne-Marie planned to continue on as long as she was needed, doing what she could. Perhaps she might bring Isaak over, eventually? Or was it safer for him to hide in the forest, unseen by official eyes until the

winds of war shifted? With the Allies in Italy, battling up the peninsula, rumors circulated about an imminent invasion in southern
France. Some people whispered that Italy would be won in mere
weeks, while others pointed out all the other predictions that failed
during this war, starting with the stunning collapse of France itself.
There was no way to guess at the future. Ella crossed her arms over
her nightgown as though to subdue her worry, pressing it back so
she could carry on.

Anne-Marie picked a coat up off the chair where she'd been
sitting, shrugging it on over a thick sweater, her expression grave.
Her mind was no doubt on the journey ahead.

"You're very brave," Ella said finally, stepping closer.

Anne-Marie smiled. She reached for Ella's hand, gave it a squeeze,
and then held on, as if to make sure her words seeped in.

"So are you, Ella. So are you."

When Anne-Marie and her father trudged out into the snow,
Ella hovered in the doorway alongside Madame Piguet, watching
them go. Anne-Marie, petite and courageous, walked out into the
vast Risoud forest without hesitation. She glanced back once to wave
cheerfully, and then Ella watched her vanish under the darkness of
the murmuring boughs. Madame Piguet, sighing heavily, wandered
into the kitchen, but Ella watched that darkness, empty and full all
at once, for a long time.

Anne-Marie was gone. Her walk through Ella's life was over.

She inhaled shakily, contemplating the phenomenon of a young
woman sneaking *back* into occupied France, willingly facing the
dangers waiting there. Indeed, tempting them.

Yet Ella found herself nodding. It was as it should be. The war
was over for her and Hanni, but it roared on through the rest of
Europe.

The children of La Hille still needed Anne-Marie Piguet.

❦

THIRTY-NINE

RÖSLI

The days marched on with little variance. Rösli woke after sleepless nights, unrefreshed. Over breakfast she sat alongside Emilie and sometimes the girls, Regina and Margot. They whispered about news and rumors of the war, endlessly speculating.

"Surely the Allies will advance in Italy soon," Margot insisted, morning after morning, hope clear in her furtive smiles. Nobody wanted to admit that they seemed frozen on the Italian peninsula, locked on one side of a line while the Germans held the other. Their yearning for the Allied troops to reach southern France was likewise frozen.

"They'll have to enter France on a different coast, I'm afraid," Emilie said often, her dark gaze flitting around the room. Like Rösli, she didn't dwell on news of battles and suspended advances, allowing her hopes to engage. Like Rösli, she was simply eager to immerse herself in work.

Each day after breakfast, Rösli went up to the sick wing, finding the only purpose there was for her in Switzerland. She worked relentlessly, the daylight hours vanishing in a blur of fevers, dysentery, lice, and scabies. She gave baths, coaxed weak children to swallow medications, and rubbed ointment on thin, rashy little limbs, all the while telling stories about Africa. Her tales pulled the children from their worries the same way they themselves pulled Rösli from hers. She'd gotten better at recounting and embellishing memories of her life abroad, a life that seemed so long ago now.

One cold afternoon, the snow outside transformed abruptly into sleet. Rösli went to the window, watching as the heavy flakes narrowed before her eyes, hitting the glass with a ping. Geneva would soon be glazed in ice.

At the far end of the sick wing, the door creaked on its hinges. She turned, expecting to see Emilie's rosy face, and then she gasped.

A different pair of brown eyes sought her, and for a moment she couldn't move. Ella Rosenthal stood in the doorway with her little sister, Hanni, at her side.

"Mademoiselle Näf!" Hanni called, pulling away from Ella and running down the aisle between cots. Several of the children turned to look at her, a girl near their age moving on sure, swift legs. When Hanni thumped into Rösli's waist, it was with the intensity the little girl had always possessed, her feelings oversized and fierce. Rösli instinctively reached her hand up to smooth Hanni's thick, untamed hair.

"*Mein Gott!*" she managed, recovering from the shock. She knelt before Hanni and touched her freckled cheek, laughing as she took in the child's grin. "How did you get here?"

"Took a train from Zurich."

Ella came up behind her, smiling faintly, and Rösli stood and pulled the young woman into her embrace, stammering, "Zurich?"

"We've been there since November," Ella said, straightening. "We hiked over the border with Anne-Marie Piguet, and since then we've been living with a host family in Zurich."

Rösli shook her head while the pieces fell into place in her mind. Anne-Marie, with her infectious laugh and noble impulses, was doing what Rösli had hoped she would. For months, she'd wondered what became of those furtive conversations that had taken place amid her own dismissal from La Hille. Had Anne-Marie acted, or were her impulses just that? There had been no way to find out.

Until now.

"Is she sending others over the border?"

Ella nodded. "Addi was the first, and Edith and Inge Joseph came over recently. I'm sure they would all love to connect with you, Mademoiselle Näf. You made yourself hard to find, you know."

Hanni drifted away toward the windows, resting her elbows on the cold panes and staring out at the pinging sleet. Rösli watched her for a moment, pinning her lips.

"I'd love to hear from them," she said finally, and relief seeped into her heart. The most threatened of *les Grands* had found a way out, and it seemed to work if five of them had already crossed the border safely. But the sense of relief was fleeting, waning before the weight of her next question. "What about the others? And where is Isaak?"

Ella's face fell, ready worry sliding into her eyes. "Anne-Marie said she'd offer her route to anyone who needs it. But Isaak joined the Maquis over the summer. He's fighting with them still."

Rösli hesitated. Fighting? She knit her hands together, tightening them. "How many have joined the Maquis?"

Ella shook her head. "I'm not sure. Several of the boys were talking about it when we left."

They held each other's stares, and in the background sleet quickened against the windowpanes, the sound filling the silence between them like a gentle percussion. Hanni wandered between the beds, chatting with the patients, still never shy. Rösli shook herself from her thoughts, turning to Hanni. She shouldn't be in here—some of these children were certainly contagious.

"Ella," she said quickly, linking her by the elbow and maneuvering her toward the door. "Months ago, Regina and Margot found me here. They needed work, and I was able to secure them positions. We may also find work here for Regina's sister, Else, soon."

"I know," Ella nodded. "I saw them downstairs."

Rösli turned at the door, beckoning to Hanni, who didn't come. "Do you get along with your host family in Zurich?"

Ella hesitated. "Not particularly. They would like to send me on to an internment center and keep only Hanni, because of my age. I worry we'll be split up."

Rösli paused, digesting that. "Well, how would you like to work here? Not in this wing—I'm concerned about Hanni catching something from my patients, to be honest. But perhaps you can be a caretaker with the other girls, and Hanni can stay on as a refugee child with all the rest?"

Ella bit her lip and glanced around, hesitating as she thought it over. "Yes," she said after a moment, nodding slowly. "I'd like to stay here with you, Mademoiselle Näf. But do you think we can stay here together for however long it takes? For the war to end? I won't be separated from Hanni, you understand. And, if we can stay, I'll send word to Anne-Marie's mother to tell Isaak where I am."

"To wait for him." Sorrow pinched Rösli's joy. She hoped, fervently, that Isaak would be safe in the Maquis, and that someday he would find his way to Geneva. That Ella wouldn't wait in vain. "I'm sure there will be work here as long as you need it. We're always shorthanded."

Ella nodded again, her expression clearing as her decision solidified. "Thank you."

"*Gut.* It's settled, then. Now, let's get you out of this ward, and I'll go see the director."

But Ella shook her head. "There's one last thing I wanted to say. I've been thinking about it ever since you left La Hille. Do you remember the day you reprimanded Hanni for playing instead of doing her chores, and I got so angry with you?"

Rösli fished that memory up easily. She could still see the heat in Ella's cheeks and her dark, searching gaze as she spat words, voice shaking. *Don't you see that our hearts are breaking? You know nothing about what kids actually need.* Only days later, the gendarmes had come for Ella and the rest of *les Grands.*

Rösli cleared her voice. "I remember that day well."

Ella smiled ruefully. "I never told you that I was sorry for shouting at you. It's bothered me, ever since."

"Oh, for heaven's sake—"

Ella interrupted. "It's important for me to say it, because I don't know if you understand what you've meant to all of us. That's why Hanni and I came here today, actually. We wanted to thank you, and yet here you are helping us again."

Rösli shook her head as if by reflex. "Don't thank me. I did what anyone would do. I only wish I'd done more—"

"Anyone would not have done what you did." Ella spoke with conviction. "And anyone else wouldn't have been you."

"No, I was too harsh, Ella, too regimented." The words Rösli told herself, night after night when she couldn't sleep, spilled forth. "I made so many mistakes—"

"Mademoiselle Näf, you're the only person I know of, on this whole wretched earth, who could have gotten us through those years."

For a suspended moment, Rösli stared at Ella, and something caught within her chest, burning like a small fire in the wind. Yet even as it flickered, she knew the feeling would fade. The beds behind her were full of children, sick and malnourished amid a terrible, unending war. Tonight, she would struggle with memories of France, and tomorrow she would again worry about the fate of her kids. Those still in danger, and those she had lost. There was no way to make sense out of the senseless.

Nevertheless, here stood a young woman, wise beyond her age and relentlessly brave, whose name undoubtedly still circulated on the gendarmes' lists in southern France. Over by the window, watching sleet with her nose pressed to the cold glass, was an eight-year-old child who had climbed mountains in the dead of winter, saving her own life.

Perhaps there was reason to hope, against all odds.

"Mademoiselle Näf?"

Rösli turned back to Ella.

"I once claimed that you didn't know what kids need, but as it turns out, you were it." A faint smile warmed Ella's dark eyes. "Rösli, you were the person we needed in France."

~~~~~

ELLA

DENMARK, 1956

Ella leaned her forehead against the glass, watching the landscape slide by. It was remarkably flat, yet it had the cold, wind-whipped look of a mountaintop. The train rocked gently, winding through a copse of naked trees, and then an expanse of gray opened beyond a field of silvery grass. There it was. The sea.

They must be getting close.

A wave of nausea swept through her, and she closed her eyes, placing her palm on her stomach. Would it never end? She felt the firm rise of her own abdomen, breathing heavily, and a hand landed on her own.

"Sick?"

She nodded, inhaling, and opened her eyes. "Do you know some women don't get sick at all? And here I am, months in and still undone."

Isaak smiled gently. He leaned forward, kissing her temple. "I've been told that it means we're having a girl."

Ella laughed. "You can't always believe Hanni, you know. I don't know where she gets her ideas."

He patted her knee good-naturedly and shrugged. "Oh, I don't know. Maybe her studies."

Ella looked back to the window, watching as they approached the wild, wind-chopped sea. Isaak was fervently proud of Hanni. He told people as often as he could wedge it into conversation that she was nearly finished with nursing school, with plans to find work abroad. Hanni had boundless ideas of the places she would travel and the people she would serve. Ella imagined she'd live her life like a skipping stone, working her way across the world. Hanni was the kind of girl who could do anything.

Sometimes, watching her sister thrive as she studied and found her way, Ella wondered if she, too, should have sought higher education. After Switzerland, she and Isaak had taken Hanni and gone to Paris, where several La Hille kids landed temporarily, stateless and adrift in the wake of the war. But for Ella and Isaak, Paris became home. Over the years they'd settled in a house on the city's outskirts, and Isaak planted apple trees in its tiny yard. Ella worked and Isaak pursued teaching credentials, and slowly, carefully, they had built a modest life.

Yet, Ella did study, in her own way. True to his long-ago promise, Isaak had built her an easel as soon as they had a room to set it in. Now she sat before it for entire days sometimes, drawing and painting. Their walls were covered in her work, the mediums ranging from charcoal to watercolor and oils. She remained fascinated by the dance of darkness and light, the harmony of color, and visual chaos contrasted with absence. Drawing and painting seemed, to Ella, an endless seeking of balance, and when she finished a canvas, it was as though a part of her had become more whole.

She closed her eyes again, waiting for another swell of nausea to subside, and thought of the day Isaak had returned to her. She'd been in the cafeteria at the refugee center in Geneva, setting tables. Southern France had fallen, and she waited, ever more anxious, to hear from him. Somehow, she hoped, he would send word.

And then he was there. She'd looked up past the table she was setting and nearly dropped the stack of plates. Isaak appeared on the staircase, taking the steps two at a time, quickly approaching. She'd relinquished the plates with a clatter and run toward him, and he ran, too. When she thumped into his chest, he picked her up, twirling her, and her shabby dress whipped around her legs, and she was laughing and crying, overwhelmed with happiness.

"How?" was all she could manage, and he set her down, kissing her for a long time.

"I kept the address Anne-Marie gave me, months ago. When the Germans fled before the Allies, I wasn't far behind them. I came over the border using the same route you did, just last night, and caught the first train—"

She felt his face, her hands on his cheeks and jaw, unable to believe he was real. He was really standing with her, alive and whole.

And she would never let him go.

She opened her eyes as the train slowed. Up ahead a small station appeared, and Isaak caught her eye. "Here we are. We'll be there within the hour. You okay, Ella?"

She nodded, using his offered arm to rise, and together they found their way to the platform, gazing at the incomprehensible signs, figuring out which way to go.

There was one taxi in the little town, and they managed to hire it for the drive up the coast. They sat together in the back, a suitcase between them, looking at the addresses on intermittent farmhouses, searching for the one they'd been given. When the taxi finally slowed, turning up a long, thin driveway, Ella caught her breath.

Up ahead, a scatter of small houses, almost like huts, stood out against the roaring sea. Beyond them fields unspooled. Some were strung with fences and sheep, and in others a few cows grazed. Chickens pecked alongside the gravel drive, flapping out of the way as the car edged toward them. When the taxi neared the string of houses, Ella spotted a field all in furrows and nearly laughed. It was a huge garden, spreading toward the sea, buffered by a fence made of driftwood. Standing in the freshly plowed earth, soil-stained hands on her hips while she squinted at the approaching car, was Rösli.

They met her at the edge of the garden, watching as she picked her way through the rows to greet them.

"I wasn't sure when to expect you," she called, her voice carrying with the wind. "Let's go in and I'll wash up. It's potato-planting time, so I've been busy. Effort brings reward, you know."

Ella and Isaak swapped glances, amused, and they followed her into a cottage.

When they were seated in a small, austere living room, listening to a kettle sizzle over a burner, Rösli settled across from them. She wore simple trousers and a faded shirt, and though she'd washed her hands, they were still dark around the fingernails.

"Ella, look at you," she said, grinning. "Do you think it's a boy or girl?"

"Girl," Isaak said quickly, and Ella laughed.

"Mademoiselle Näf, it's so good to see you." Ella glanced around, taking in the window facing the sea. "This place is beautiful. Now, you wrote that it's a collective farm?"

Rösli chuckled. "I'm not mademoiselle anyone anymore, Ella. Call me Rösli. And yes, it's a collective. We all work together, much like we did at La Hille. Though there are obvious differences."

Isaak sat with his elbows on his knees, a look of faint amusement still on his face. "I have to say, it was no surprise to catch you out planting potatoes, even after all these years. You haven't changed a bit."

Rösli pursed the smile from her lips. "I haven't—that's true.

Now, I understand from Ella's letters that you're a teacher? And, Ella, I know you downplay it, but I'm well aware that you're an accomplished artist."

"She really is," Isaak said quickly. "You'll see."

"I'll see?" Rösli glanced between them, but Ella let the question hang, changing the subject.

"I've heard recently from several La Hille kids, Rösli. Did you know that Peter joined Ruth on her kibbutz a few years ago? He married a girl there. And I hear that those who went to America are doing well also."

Rösli smiled. "My children are all over the world, it seems."

Ella nodded. "Hanni will join them soon, I'm sure. She's nearly finished with nursing school, and she talks about serving in Africa. I can only think she was inspired by you."

"Oh, surely not." Rösli waved away the praise. "With her adventurous heart, I'm not at all surprised she's finding her way out in the world. Now, did you also manage to see Anne-Marie on this grand trip you're taking?"

Ella laughed. "It's not a grand trip. We just wanted to see a few places from our past before the baby comes—I don't expect to travel much after that. And yes, we did see Anne-Marie. You know she's married now, and with children of her own? She still has the same warm, passionate heart."

Rösli nodded. "I hear the news through letters." She grinned. "It's such a treat to see you two in person, though. I don't get many visitors all the way out here."

Isaak cocked his head. "I've always wondered about that, actually. What brought you to Denmark?"

Rösli glanced down. The kettle began to whistle, so she stood and walked the few steps to the kitchen, frowning a little as she hushed the noise. Ella, sensing a change in her manner, swapped glances with Isaak.

Rösli poured three cups of tea, the steam rising around her face, still frowning in thought. She looked exactly as Ella remembered her, though perhaps a bit more weathered. Her bunned hair frayed around her head, messy from the wind, and there were faint lines at her temples, darkened by the sun.

She set the kettle down and began to speak as she delivered the teacups. "After the war, I couldn't stomach living in Switzerland anymore. Not after what had happened with the Red Cross, and the way they sealed their borders to refugees. So I looked for a country with one main priority." Rösli took a sip and lifted her gaze. "I wanted to live somewhere that had done right by its Jewish population during the war. Here, in Denmark, the majority of Jews survived. It happened because ordinary Danes, hearing rumors of roundups and deportations, hid their neighbors." She shrugged, unsmiling. "I decided I wanted to live among such people, so here I am."

For a moment, Ella couldn't breathe. In its old, familiar way, her heart stung in her chest. It was a feeling of anger, and longing, and it rose up whenever she thought of all she'd lost.

If only such neighbors had hidden her parents.

She managed to sip her tea, nodding. "I understand that completely, Rösli. It almost makes me want to live in Denmark, too."

Nobody spoke for a moment, and Ella thought of her parents, as she had for so many years. She'd searched after the war, scouring for any news of her family and finding nothing but heartbreak. Isaak and Ella had been left with only each other, and Hanni, in the end. On both sides, their entire families had perished.

She felt Isaak's gaze on her, concerned, and his hand found hers.

"Oh heavens, I'm so sorry," Rösli said quickly, her stare darting between them. "You know I've never been good at saying the right thing—"

"That was the right thing." Ella cleared her throat a little. "It's just that I will always miss my family. I've thought about my parents even more lately, with the baby coming. I wish she—or he—could know them."

Rösli nodded slowly, her face grave. "I do, too."

Silence dropped over them for a moment before Isaak broke it. "You know, Rösli, that La Hille was a bit like Denmark?"

She blew on her tea. "How so?"

Isaak shrugged. "Most of us survived. And ordinary people, like you, and Herr Lyrer, and Anne-Marie, and the Cordiers—you saved us."

But Rösli looked past Isaak to the window, gazing out at the wide, gray sea. It took her a long moment to speak, and when the words emerged, they were firm. "Your gratitude means the world to me. And seeing you, healthy and thriving—I can't explain the good it does my heart." She smiled and looked back to them, but her gaze was sorrowful. "I'm so proud of you both. And don't worry about me, please. I'm content. I live in the garden, and when I'm out there in the wind and sun, I feel that I've found my place. But when I think of France—" Rösli sighed, and the words she spoke were raw and well-worn, like Ella's own familiar sorrow. "I will always wish I could have done more."

Again, nobody spoke for a moment, and then Isaak tapped on Ella's knee, gesturing to their suitcase. She rose, shifting her dress over her abdomen, and made her way to the luggage, unzipping it and rifling for a canvas tube she'd tucked along its edge. When she turned, Rösli's head was cocked in question, and Ella couldn't subdue her sudden nerves.

"I'm not sure how you'll feel about it, but I brought you something."

"Oh, you didn't need to bring anything," Rösli chided as Ella tapped the end of the tube and pulled the canvas carefully out. She went to the coffee table and spread her painting open, and for a long, hushed moment, they all stared down at it.

In the colors of southern France in the summertime, she'd re-created La Hille. The château rose among hills, familiar, rich, and textured in oil paint. Forests seemed to dance around the pale building, alive and shadowed, spreading all the way to the distant Pyrénées. Ella could almost hear it: the whisper of branches in the wind, the scuff of boots on trails, the voices of people she'd known. She'd added children playing in the surrounding fields, barefoot. In one of the trees overhanging the courtyard, a mischievous girl balanced on a thick limb.

Rösli wiped a tear from her cheek, covering her mouth, unable to look away. For a moment, Ella's doubt swelled, but then Rösli laughed.

"I see Hanni there. Always in a tree, the little devil. And those boys are playing tug-of-war? How they used to love tug-of-war. There's a troupe of *les Moyens* heading off into the forest." She shook her head, grinning. "It's just how I remember it."

"It was a tragedy," Ella managed, "but there was beauty there, too."

Rösli nodded, wiping her tears, and the three of them sat together in silence for a long time, studying Ella's painting. It all rose up before them, forever preserved in their memories: the story of Château de la Hille.

Author's Note

~~~~~

The Winter Orphans springs from the stories of real people who, during the unthinkable events of World War II, responded with astonishing courage to save lives. Château de la Hille was indeed a Swiss Red Cross children's colony in the Ariège region of southern France, operating from 1941 through the end of the war. The old castle sheltered a fluctuating population of approximately one hundred Jewish refugee children who had escaped from Austria and Germany. Despite continual danger and persecution, all but twelve survived, and this was due to the collective efforts of numerous heroes.

In researching this novel, I came to understand what some of the children of La Hille asserted in their memoirs: the first heroes of their story were their parents. As the Nazis rose to power in Germany, and then annexed Austria in 1938, many Jewish parents began to comprehend the growing threat looming over their families. They thus sought emigration through increasingly narrowing channels, ultimately placing their beloved children into the custody of foreign strangers to save their lives. Unable to leave the country themselves, these parents chose a route of breathtaking bravery and sacrifice, and propelled their children onward.

Approximately one thousand of these refugees ended up in the care of the Comité d'Assistance aux Enfants Juifs Réfugiés in Belgium. Later, when Belgium was invaded and occupied by Germany, ninety-three of them escaped on a cargo train to southern France, washing up in an old granary barn. This is where Rösli Näf first met them.

As in the novel, Rösli was a Swiss nurse who had worked in Africa before volunteering to serve as director of the children's colony of La Hille. Though by all accounts she was a somewhat stern, difficult personality, under her management the colony became an organized, nearly self-sufficient harbor in an increasingly chaotic world. More importantly, when crisis struck on August 26, 1942 in the form of a raid on the château, Rösli responded with exceptional fortitude and ultimately freed her children from Camp du Vernet. She then organized and facilitated illegal escapes from France, until five of her teenagers were caught along the Swiss border, as occurs in the novel. For valuing the lives of her charges over the principle of Swiss neutrality, the Red Cross castigated Rösli, firing her from her post at La Hille.

As recounted in the epilogue, Rösli spent most of her postwar life in Denmark, choosing to settle in that country because she admired the way it saved the majority of its Jewish population. In 1989, when she was named Righteous Among the Nations by Yad Vashem, she initially declined the honor, saying that she only wished she could have done more. Later, at a ceremony honoring Germaine Hommel in 1992, Rösli finally accepted her medal. She passed away in Glarus, Switzerland, in 1996.

Anne-Marie Im Hof-Piguet (her married name) was also recognized as Righteous Among the Nations by Yad Vashem in 1990, alongside two of the Cordier sisters, Victoria and Madeleine. Anne-

Marie was a passionate young woman who followed her conscience over the law, and thereby forged an illegal escape route through the Risoud forest of her childhood. She partnered with Victoria Cordier, an active member of the French Resistance, to save the lives of twelve people by smuggling them over the border and connecting them with support in Switzerland. After the war, she went on to champion human rights causes for the rest of her life.

Again echoing sentiments of La Hille survivors, in particular those expressed in Walter W. Reed's *The Children of La Hille*, the children themselves deserve great recognition. In creating Ella, Isaak, and Hanni, I endeavored to reflect the firsthand accounts of La Hille survivors, which tell stories of young people who played tremendous roles in saving their own lives. After lengthy reflection, I decided to make my point-of-view character Ella Rosenthal, her sister, Hanni, and boyfriend, Isaak, entirely fictional. I chose this route because for many of the real La Hille children, there is simply not enough information about their lives to construct an accurate retelling of their experiences during the war. For those who left memoirs, it seemed clear that they had already written their stories. Therefore, I placed fictional characters, heavily inspired by the legacies of real people, among the group of one hundred refugees. The names of their friends and peers, however, spring from actual young people of La Hille.

Tragically, twelve of the original group of refugees did not survive the war. Several were caught attempting to cross borders; one group fell victim to an underhanded guide on the Spanish border, which informed the fate of Ella and Isaak in their attempt to scale the Pyrénées. Others were unfortunately caught in a raid at the château, much like the one recounted in the novel. Those who were arrested by the Germans and French gendarmes were murdered in Majdanek and Auschwitz. One young man, Werner Epstein, survived Auschwitz.

Like Ella and Isaak, several La Hille teenagers joined the French Resistance and the Maquis. Those in the Maquis lived out in the woods, engaging in acts of sabotage and resistance. One of them, a young boy named Egon Berlin, was killed in a 1944 battle between Maquisards and the French Milice.

There are many other secondary characters in this story who acted with extraordinary heroism. Maurice Dubois was a tireless advocate not only for La Hille, but for all the children's colonies he managed in France. He was also directly responsible for saving the lives of the forty teenagers and four staff members interned in Camp du Vernet. As in the story, he traveled to Vichy in the wake of their arrest, ultimately threatening Vichy officials with authority he did not possess. He claimed that if the La Hille group was not released, he would sever all Swiss Red Cross aid to France; in the chaos of the moment, his threats were believed and Rösli Näf was authorized to take "her children," as she called them, back to the château.

In the wake of the ordeal at Camp du Vernet, Germaine Hommel and Renée Farny collaborated with Rösli to create an escape route for La Hille's teenagers. At their children's colony at Saint-Cergues, only three kilometers from the border, they supported clandestine escapes at great personal risk. They also enlisted the help of Léon Balland, a young French farmer, to escort groups through the woods and over the border. When the group of five La Hille refugees became lost and were caught near Saint-Cergues, Germaine and Renée lost their positions, alongside Rösli. After their dismissal, both Germaine and Renée continued resistance work, until Germaine was caught and sent to Ravensbrück concentration camp. She managed to survive, but never recovered from her experiences and spent the rest of her life in care. In 1992, she was posthumously honored by Yad Vashem as Righteous Among the Nations.

Numerous details in the story spring from memories and firsthand accounts of survivors. The *Zwiebelkeller*, for example, was an actual hiding spot in the château, constructed and used as described. There was indeed a woman at the *préfecture* named Madame Authié whom Rösli created an alliance with, though the exact nature of it is unclear. It seems that she was sometimes able to warn the château when raids were expected. Rösli also secured a quarantine order from a local doctor, who claimed that scarlet fever was rampant at the château, thus providing respite and privacy while illegal escapes ensued. The heartbreaking story told by Rösli's colleague in Geneva, of the little boy deported without his parents, was inspired by the memories of social worker Annette Monod Leiris. Horrifically, thousands of children were separated from their parents in French internment camps to be deported east without them, certainly in terror, agony, and confusion.

The memorandum from Bern, which was issued to all Swiss Red Cross workers, is also real. It began, "The laws and decrees of the government of France must be executed exactly, and you do not have to consider whether or not they are opposed to your own beliefs." Of course, Rösli, Anne-Marie, and many other teachers and caretakers involved with the Swiss Red Cross ignored this order and went on saving lives.

It is important to note that there were numerous other people, instrumental in saving the children of La Hille, who do not appear in the timeline of this novel. For example, several members of the Belgian committees, who cared for the children after their initial escape from Germany and Austria, continued to advocate for the group even after they fled to southern France. There were also other caretakers, teachers, and counselors who came and went from La Hille in its years of operation, playing important roles in the lives of the children there. Interestingly, some of these employees were Spanish refugees. Prior to partnering with the Swiss Red Cross in 1941, the Secours Suisse began its work in France with relief efforts for Spanish refugees fleeing civil war. Therefore, Spaniards, too, found safe haven in the Swiss children's colonies in Vichy France.

Whenever possible, I used firsthand accounts to construct the personalities, actions, and personal lives of my main characters. However, as the historical record doesn't always provide the depth needed to write a novel, their interior landscapes often had to be imagined. Similarly, there were places where I had to adjust timelines or minor details for the sake of the plot. For example, Anne-Marie worked for a period at the Toulouse office of the Secours Suisse, dividing her tenure at the children's colonies. This clerical work wasn't well explained, nor was it crucial to the heart of her story, so I chose to omit it. Also unclear was the extent to which Anne-Marie and Rösli might have met and collaborated, though they certainly shared a mission. When details such as these weren't to be found, I used my imagination to fill in the gaps and write what very well *could* have happened. Therefore, this novel, while heavily inspired by true events, is foremost a work of fiction.

As I was writing this book, I sometimes had occasion to tell friends and acquaintances what it was about. My brief descriptions were usually met with exclamations about the sadness of the subject, and I would pause. Much of this story, it's true, is devastatingly sad. There were countless moments when, as I researched and wrote, my heart shattered for my characters and for the real victims of these events. And yet, in the end, I think this is a tale not only of tragedy, but also of great hope. It's a saga woven with threads of both cruelty and humanity, of both loss and the will to survive. The heroes of Château de la Hille displayed unwavering morality, selflessness, and courage despite tremendous odds, and ultimately prevailed. In their story, we see how even amid great darkness, goodness can shine through.

Acknowledgments

The Winter Orphans was largely written during the pandemic, amid a world turned upside down. There are numerous people who are integral supporters of my work, and I'm especially grateful for their encouragement during such unusual and challenging times.

So many thanks to my extraordinary agent, Kevan Lyon, for her unwavering advocacy, guidance, and warmth. I'm also deeply grateful for the wisdom, insight, and enthusiasm of my amazing editor, Kate Seaver. I am beyond fortunate to work with you both!

Thank you to the hardworking team at Berkley, including Ivan Held, Christine Ball, Claire Zion, Jeanne-Marie Hudson, Craig Burke, Fareeda Bullert, Chelsea Pascoe, and Jennifer Myers. Special thanks to my cover designer, Rita Frangie.

My work benefits immeasurably from patient and discerning early readers, to whom I owe much gratitude. Among them are my parents, Hugh and Lois Judd, whom I can always count on to swiftly read and critique anything I write. You are both outstanding readers, and I can't thank you enough for your unflagging willingness to listen, problem solve, and cheer me on! I'm a lucky daughter indeed.

I wouldn't know what to do without my dear friend and critique partner, Carrie Kwiatkowski. Thank you for the ongoing brainstorming, feedback, and discussion—may it continue for many years, and many books, to come!

I am indebted to Stephanie Thornton, Eliza Knight, and Bryn Turnbull for reading and critiquing early drafts and chapters of this novel—thank you for your invaluable feedback. Lyonesses, I am grateful daily for our virtual conversations and camaraderie. Thank you for always being there both to celebrate and commiserate. I'm awed and inspired by every one of you!

Julia Hofmann, I thank you again for reading and fixing my German phrases. I'm also grateful for Rachel Feinmark's and Dill Werner's insight and advice regarding my portrayal of Jewish experiences in this novel.

Finally, I am profoundly thankful for my family's unfailing support of my rather unconventional path. Finn and Lily, you bring meaning and joy to everything I do, and I am so grateful for you both every day. Jeremey, I would be lost without you—thank you for being my person.

THE
WINTER ORPHANS

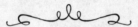

KRISTIN BECK

Discussion Questions

1. In the beginning of the story, Rösli views herself as an outsider who has trouble connecting with other people. She frequently doubts herself, and yet by the end of the novel, Ella tells her, "Rösli, you were the person we needed in France." In what ways is Rösli an unlikely hero? How is her personality, which has always caused her difficulty, just right for the challenges she faces?

2. From the outset, Ella believes that it is dangerous to maintain hope. In her experience, "the second hope swam in, the world's hatred crashed down like a wave and washed it all away." Yet, as the story progresses, Ella slowly changes. What gives Ella hope amid the darkness? What helps her carry on?

3. At the first meeting between Rösli and Anne-Marie, Rösli gives some crucial advice. "In France," she says, "your conscience may require much of you, but it's the only guide you can trust." How does this become true for both Anne-Marie and Rösli? How is this true for Ella and Isaak?

4. Anne-Marie gathers much of her strength from nature. How does she use her connection with the natural world to bring the children under her care not only safety, but also hope?

5. There are numerous heroes in this story, all from varied walks of life and backgrounds. What qualities do they have in common? What do you think gives them the courage to act despite consequent danger?

6. Were you surprised to learn that Rösli, Renée Farny, and Germaine Hommel were dismissed by the Swiss Red Cross for their actions? Can you think of other examples of people incurring condemnation for doing what is clearly morally right?

7. What do you think about the yellow bird that appears toward the end of the story? Do you think its presence is mere coincidence or, as Anne-Marie suggests, something more?

8. At its heart, *The Winter Orphans* is a story of refugee children trying to find safe haven in a hostile world. In what ways is their plight similar to stories we see in the news today? What can we learn from the tale of the children of Château de la Hille?

9. The Author's Note explains that when Rösli was named Righteous Among the Nations by Yad Vashem, she initially declined the honor. Were you surprised to learn this? Why do you think she shrank from recognition?

10. In her final line of the novel, Ella says of Château de la Hille, "It was a tragedy, but there was beauty there, too." Many of the real children of La Hille communicated similar feelings in their memories and memoirs. What do you think they meant? In what ways did beauty exist at La Hille?

Kristin Beck has been captivated by the often unsung roles of women in history ever since growing up hearing her grandmother's stories about her time as a World War II army nurse. A former teacher, she holds a BA in English from the University of Washington and a master's in teaching from Western Washington University. Kristin lives in the Pacific Northwest with her husband and two children.

Ready to find
your next great read?

Let us help.

Visit prh.com/nextread